D1531783

FROM THE LIBRARY OF:

Anne

I hope you enjoy it!

Praise for the novels of Patricia Rice

Carolina Girl

"Full of the warmth, humor and poignancy that make Rice's books very special."
—*Romantic Times*

McCloud's Woman

"Intriguing and passionate."
—*Booklist*

Almost Perfect

"Brilliant and riveting, edgy and funny."
—MARY JO PUTNEY

Impossible Dreams

"Patricia Rice shows her diverse talent as a writer in *Impossible Dreams*. . . . [It] will leave readers with a smile on their faces."
—Kentucky *Murray Ledger & Times*

Blue Clouds

"Totally engrossing! Fast-moving, great characters, suspense, and love—a must-read!"
—*The Literary Times*

Also by Patricia Rice
(published by Ivy Books)

GARDEN OF DREAMS
BLUE CLOUDS
VOLCANO
IMPOSSIBLE DREAMS
NOBODY'S ANGEL
ALMOST PERFECT
McCLOUD'S WOMAN
CAROLINA GIRL
CALIFORNIA GIRL
SMALL TOWN GIRL

Books published by The Random House Publishing Group
are available at quantity discounts on bulk purchases for
premium, educational, fund-raising, and special sales use.
For details, please call 1-800-733-3000.

SWEET HOME CAROLINA

A Novel

PATRICIA RICE

BALLANTINE BOOKS • NEW YORK

Sweet Home Carolina is a work of fiction. Names, characters, places, and incidents are the products of the author's imagination or are used fictitiously. Any resemblance to actual events, locales, or persons, living or dead, is entirely coincidental.

Copyright © 2007 by Patricia Rice

All rights reserved.

Published in the United States by Ballantine Books, an imprint of The Random House Publishing Group, a division of Random House, Inc., New York.

IVY BOOKS and colophon are registered trademarks of Random House, Inc.

ISBN-13: 978-0-7394-7896-7

Cover illustration: Ben Perini

Printed in the United States

For single mothers everywhere:
Enjoy the moment, and keep hope
in your heart and your eyes on the
impossible . . .

❧ ONE ❧

"Take that, Dr. Evil!" Amy Warren pointed a wooden spoon at the currently offending appliance—her toaster oven. A small gray cloud of smoke swirled upward from its frying innards, filling her stainless-steel kitchen with the acrid stench of burnt bread.

The microwave was already erratically blinking error messages, and the clock on the stove had permanently hovered on twelve since the day Evan had driven off with his tall, slender, and gorgeous boss. But she didn't need either appliance to bake her special croutons.

"That's right. I'll zap your sorry behind into the ether and back again," she muttered, referring to her uncanny ability to royally screw up electrical appliances.

But it was really Evan she'd like to zap into infinity. How predictable—the machine didn't respond to her dire warnings any better than the man. The toaster oven still smoked.

"If I could fix anything, I'd fix my damned life." With disgust, Amy used the wooden spoon to yank the oven's cord out of the socket.

The wall phone rang and Amy grabbed it, praying it was her Dr. Evil-Ex telling her he would be early and had time to pick up a new toaster oven on the way up the mountain.

"Ames, sorry, but I—"

No wonder she couldn't fix anything. She lived in la-la land if she still thought *Evan* would come through. She crossed her eyes and looked down her nose at the overflowing sink, hunting for a frying pan amid the clutter. "I trust you're calling to say you're picking up ice cream, and you'll be here on time. Josh has been waiting for you all week."

"I'm still at the office." Losing his apologetic tone, Evan quickly went on the defensive. "It's a new job. I've got to show them that I'm willing to do what it takes."

"Evan, I have to be at the café in an *hour*. It's Labor Day weekend, our last big moneymaker. There has to be *food* available for tourists to fling their plastic at."

"My job is far more important than your sister's little café. Leave the kids with your mother if you have to."

"The kids can see Mom any day. They need to see *you*." Using a pot holder, Amy yanked the charred croutons from the dead toaster oven. "How soon can you get here?" Propping the phone on her shoulder and waving a towel, she attempted to clear the air, literally if not metaphorically.

"I've got a dinner meeting this evening with some bigwigs who want me to attend a charity golf tournament in the morning. Tell the kids I'm sorry, and I'll try again next weekend."

Amy knew enough by now to recognize the lie in his voice. There had been a time when she'd meekly told herself she must be imagining his shallow selfishness. She no longer had to pretend that was true. "Tell me another, Big Boy. Hot Mama have tickets for a theater opening tonight?"

"Dammit, Ames, I have a life down here! Just because

you want to hole up in the boondocks doesn't mean I have to anymore."

"Oh, and it's my fault you had two kids and got stuck with this monster McMansion and had a job that paid well and meant something to the community when all you really wanted was to be a drone in the city, uh-huh."

They'd had this argument so many times she could probably recite it backward. Come to think of it, it probably *was* her fault that Evan had made something of himself. On his own, he would still be droning his way up the corporate ladder, instead of sitting in an executive office. She dumped the ruined croutons in the trash.

"You're getting bitchy, Ames," he warned. "You're letting yourself go and reverting to your half-baked hippie days. Learn to play golf, fix yourself up, and you'll find another man to pay your rent. Don't take your frustration out on me." He hung up.

Amy shoved an overlong lock of ash brown hair out of her eyes and scowled. A year ago, Evan's comment would have cut her to the quick. She would have run to the mirror and stared at her flour-studded hair with dismay and wept her heart out.

Today, she saw her ex's mean streak for the ego trip that it was. So, hooray for her side. She'd finally learned she'd spent too damned much of her life caring what Evan thought. Why bother explaining that perms, highlighting, and salon cuts cost more than two weeks' groceries?

She despised perms and highlighting anyway, and she no longer had to care what he wanted.

She glanced around for a working timepiece and heard the grandfather clock in the foyer strike four. *Sugar, shoot, dirty word.*

Refraining from cursing for the kids' sake hadn't broadened her vocabulary, just made it more creative.

The phone rang again. She almost ignored the insistent clamor, but years of worrying about her mother's health had her grabbing the receiver.

"Good news!" Marcy, the real estate agent, chirped. "I have a terrific prospect who loves your location. I'm bringing them out tonight."

Amy slumped against the counter. She had all but forgotten the For Sale sign that had been in the front yard all summer. It had been weeks since anyone had even looked at the house. She'd given up chewing her fingernails at the thought of losing her beautiful home and started chewing her thumb in fear of bankruptcy. She ought to be jumping for joy, but panic took first place as she glanced around the chaos of the kitchen.

"What time are you coming?" she asked, turning on the hot water in the sink and searching for the scrubbing pad.

"I'll wait until you've left for the Stardust. Probably around six. Make sure you leave all the interior lights on. I have a good feeling about this one."

Amy tried not to wince as she hung up the receiver, but her stomach had just attempted a triple axel and plummeted to the ice. In an effort to de-stress, she punched the under-cabinet CD player to pop in her sister's latest recording. The player opened, then immediately slammed shut before she could insert the disc.

"Dammit, my next house will run on kerosene!"

She already had her next house picked out, a wonderful cottage with character, not like this shiny mausoleum dedicated to a dead marriage. She simply needed to persuade the mill's bankruptcy judge to take nada for it, and find a job that paid enough for her to fix it up.

Rolling her eyes at the fantasy, she resisted pounding her head against the polished cherry cabinet and dialed her mother to make arrangements for the children.

"Mommy, Josh is coloring on the walls!" Three-year-old Louisa bounced in from the family room, where she was supposed to be watching a video with her six-year-old brother.

Chunky and golden-haired like her father, Louisa reached up for a hug, and Amy's heart nearly split in two. Frustrated, she wanted to stomp her feet and throw a tantrum. Instead, she reached down to give her girl a hug.

"Are we being a telltale?" she scolded gently, carrying her baby into the family room, where, sure enough, newly rebellious Josh had drawn stick figures in indelible red crayon on the apricot walls.

Reining in a cry of dismay, Amy closed her eyes and tried to put herself into his child-size nines. He was smart enough to know his father was skipping their visit—again. There was a For Sale sign on the front lawn of the only home he'd ever known. And his mother was losing her mind. She was certain that Josh, somewhere in his very bright brain, had a reason for personalizing the walls.

When she opened her eyes again, he was scowling at her mutinously.

"Is that your daddy?" she asked.

"No, it's Tommy, and I'm going to punch him." Which he proceeded to do, intelligently wearing the boxing gloves Evan had given him.

"Tommy's sad and acting out, just like you are." She needed to pick up toys, clear smoke out of the kitchen, and boil cinnamon to add a welcoming scent to fool visitors into thinking this was a happy home. Maybe she should light a cinnamon candle, burn the house down, and save herself the effort of moving all these *things* that would never fit anywhere she could afford.

Of course, if not fitting in was the criterion, she'd have to go up in flames as well.

Amy stuck her tongue out at the oil painting over the mantel, where Evan's golden image taunted her with its confident smirk. Perhaps the painting ought to be the first thing to go up in smoke. That woman sitting beside him, with the carefully highlighted, styled hair, the glossy lipstick, matching manicure, and pearls, wasn't her any longer. She didn't know who that woman was.

But the portrait of bright-eyed Josh and giggling baby Louisa was too precious to destroy. She was such a sap for babies.

"You'll have to clean off that wall before we go," she said with a sigh, giving up images of leaping flames.

She set Louisa down and patted her on her bottom, pushing her toward the sticker dolls scattered across the handloomed rug. "Pick up your toys so you can take them to Nana's."

Finding the strongest cleaning spray she dared let Josh use, she handed the bottle and a scrubbing sponge to her son. It wouldn't clean crayon, but he had to be taught a lesson. She'd have to push the chair in front of the wall until she could fix it. Miserably, he took the bottle, refusing to look at her.

Drawing on her experience as the kids' short-order

cook, she returned to the kitchen and threw bread cubes into the frying pan, dousing them with butter and basil.

So, what did it matter if she'd spent years of her life carefully choosing paints and sewing draperies for this bloody McMansion, locating the perfect antique pieces that she'd damned well refinished herself so she could stay within her budget. They were just *things*.

Evan and the house weren't the real problems here. *She* was the one she blamed. She'd wasted a third of her life being the perfect wife and mother and housekeeper and had nothing practical to show potential employers. She could point at her two beautiful children and her lovely home, but how did that look on a résumé?

Losing her fight with tears, she wiped her eyes with the back of her arm. She knew her anger had nothing to do with the loss of a house, and everything to do with the loss of the self she'd thought she was.

Amy tossed the croutons, turned off the burner, and pulled the chickens from the oven. The smoke alarm screeched in panic.

Stomach still churning over an hour later at the café, Amy yanked the stuffed mushroom caps from the dead microwave and shoved the pan in the oven with the warming chickens. "Fine, tough toadstools it will be."

"Tough toadstools is the story of our life," Amy's sister, Joella, half owner of the Stardust, said philosophically, tying on her *Star of the Stardust Café* apron over her flashy red hostess gown. "You'd think someday, one of those toadstools would have a pot of gold under it."

As tall, blond, and flamboyant as Amy was petite,

brown, and wholesome, Joella studied the pots and pans simmering on the stove, and clucked in disapproval. "No wonder you're frying appliances. I know it's Saturday, but how many customers do you realistically think we'll have?"

Amy spun a pot lid on her finger before dropping it on the pot of creamed peas. "Not as many as you need to make a profit. Even I can see the writing on the wall."

Jo tsked sympathetically. "Evan didn't send the support payments yet?"

"Evan deserted the kids again this weekend." Amy reached for an onion and whacked it with her butcher knife. "I hate being a cliché." Onions gave her an excuse for tears, but she'd had her cry. Now she just wanted to whack things.

"He was never there when you were married. The kids won't notice. It's you I'm worried about. You walk around with a big black cloud over your head. I don't suppose you've talked to a therapist." Jo slipped a flask from her apron pocket, glanced furtively over her shoulder at their few early-bird customers, and twirled the cap.

"No, I have not." Amy checked the rolls browning in the bottom oven. "I can't afford a therapist. Evan's job doesn't supply medical insurance for ex-wives. Besides, I don't need a therapist to tell me I'm stressed out and so angry I could spit."

"Do what Jo does when she gets mad, throw dishes." Jo's husband and the other co-owner of the Stardust, Flint Clinton, emerged from his office to sniff the mouth-watering aromas. Taller than Jo, his craggy face more striking than handsome, Flint examined the roasted chickens. "What is this, Thanksgiving?"

"Can you fix microwaves, O Great Wise One?" Setting

aside the flask, Jo steered her husband toward the broken appliance and out of Amy's line of fire.

Not that Flint was in any danger from her, Amy thought. Jo was the plate-throwing diva in the family. As appealing as throwing things sounded, Amy was too practical to waste the energy of throwing crockery she'd only have to clean up afterward.

Amy had always been the responsible member of their irresponsible family. The sensible one who'd slaved hard to earn a scholarship and put herself through school. She'd been rewarded for her efforts by marrying an ambitious man who worked as hard as she did—and she worked harder still helping him up the ladder to success. All she'd accomplished was to make Evan look good to the kind of wealthy socialite he should have married in the first place.

Jo filled three glasses from her flask and shoved one into Amy's hand, hiding it from their customers. "Until Flint persuades the town to go wet, this will have to do. It's just lemonade with a little extra," she said when Amy hesitated. "Call it an intervention. You need a break. Your pot is about to boil over."

Grabbing the pot of peas from the stove, Amy set it to one side, then sipped Jo's weird cocktail. She was perfectly aware Joella wasn't referring to the peas. She grimaced as the sour punch hit her tongue.

Jo dipped the spoon in the dressing and offered a sample to Flint, who moaned appreciatively while investigating the insides of the microwave. "Mom and her quilting friends just took a big order. If they finish before Christmas, there will be money to spare and carols sung throughout the hills."

Christmas. A hollow opened in Amy's middle that

would never be filled. She took another sip of the spiked lemonade, but she might as well have thrown alcohol on a fire. How would she pay for Christmas? She didn't even know where they'd be living then.

"If we could get the mill back in production by Christmas, there would be reason for caroling," Amy declared fervently. A real job would solve half her problems, anyway.

"Other than the Music Barn, those old mill buildings are useless if the bankruptcy court decides to sell off the machinery instead of letting the town buy it," Flint commented, completing his repairs now that the coffee was simmering. "We can't put people to work in empty buildings."

"And the tourist business is dead after this weekend." Amy slid the browned mushrooms from the oven, trying not to think of the stack of bills on her desk. "There go your biggest-spending customers."

Flint leaned against the counter, crossing his arms while brandishing a screwdriver. "We can pay you to stay on, but we may have to go back to being a coffee shop instead of a restaurant."

"Only if you want to hand out free soup," Amy predicted.

Returning his screwdriver to a drawer, Flint grabbed a hot mushroom. Throwing it from hand to hand, he retreated toward his office. "We'll do what we have to do," he called over his shoulder before he disappeared back into his world.

"We know you've been handing out free meals," Jo said with a shrug, taking a bite of a mushroom and humming with pleasure. "It's okay by us. Flint's so tickled with the Music Barn you helped him get that he'd knock heads for you."

"And endanger his guitar-playing hand?" Amy joked. Fighting wasn't a solution to this problem. Besides, his hand had just recovered from surgery.

"The Barn brought in tourists all summer," Jo reminded her. "The whole town knows you talk sense. The judge ought to just let you have the mill so you can set people to working again."

"Oh, that's *so* going to happen." Amy whacked a bell pepper. "If I were Queen of the World, I'd make a lot of changes around here, starting with ordering all men to line up for common sense tests."

"If you don't watch out, you're going to cut off a finger. Have another drink." Jo grabbed the knife and nudged Amy back to the stove with her hip. "Is this about losing the house?"

Flipping off a burner, Amy lifted the heavy frying pan and poured the gravy into a waiting gravy boat. "I can't look for a new house until I know where I'll be working."

"You're working here," Jo said firmly. "We can't replace you."

Amy slapped the pan back on the burner, put her hands on her hips, and glared at her younger—taller—sister. "That's what I'm trying to tell you. You cannot pay me on what this restaurant is making. *I'm* facing facts. You and Flint are the ones with your heads in the clouds."

As if on cue, the cordless phone Flint had installed by the counter rang. Amy snatched the receiver before Jo could. "Stardust."

"Amy, this is Mayor Blodgett."

Amy took another swig of Jo's spiked lemonade to calm her suddenly shaky nerves. "Is there a problem?"

"That depends on how you look at it," the mayor enunciated slowly. "Another interested party has asked to look at the mill. As I understand it, the company is European and cash heavy. It could be just the investment we're hoping for."

"A foreign company won't want to hire our workers," Amy warned the mayor. "The whole point of our buying the mill is to keep Northfork residents employed."

"You don't think they'd bring in illegal immigrants, do you?" the mayor asked in alarm.

Amy rolled her eyes, handed the receiver to Jo, and opened the bottom oven to check on the rolls. If she were Queen of the World, men would be relegated to hard labor. They were obviously not meant to think. Parallel parking maybe, they could do that. Make them chauffeurs. Hole diggers. Brick layers. But not politicians responsible for the lives and welfare of entire communities of women and children.

While Jo chitchatted and applied her charm to the mayor, Amy removed the rolls and began buttering their tops. She glanced at the clock. She never wore watches. She was tired of replacing them. But the clock wasn't working either, so she checked the mullioned windows to see if the sunlight had faded. After the first of September, the sun dipped behind the mountain around five. It should be almost time for the early dinner arrivals.

As she watched, a sexy, dark maroon sports car rolled to a stop, parking half on and half off the sidewalk in front of the café. The low-slung front end halted inches from the snout of the concrete purple pig adorning the café's corner. The narrow mountain highway had no shoulder room for parking. The shiny car would end up as a hood ornament on the next semi coming around the curve too fast.

No one in town owned a car like that. Had ever *seen* a car like that. Which meant it was European. After the mayor's call, Amy had a very, very bad feeling about that car.

She turned from the window and tossed back the glass of spiked lemonade, superstitiously deciding if she didn't look, the car might disappear.

Jo hung up and turned to see what had Amy tossing back alcohol. "Oh, my. That's one of the new Porsches," she said with reverence.

"That will soon be a flattened Porsche," Amy replied.

The low rumble of another powerful vehicle forced her to glance out the window again. A shiny black Hummer sporting satellite antennas drew up behind the sports car. Amy mused, how far would a Porsche travel after being slammed into by a Hummer propelled by a semi?

Deciding bad news could wait, she checked the various pots on the stove and missed seeing how the Porsche owner squeezed out of the low front seat into traffic. Jo's chuckles as she exchanged observations with the locals sipping coffee at the counter were sufficient commentary for amusement.

The café's red door swung open. Amy unconsciously waited for a biting *What a dump!* from the owner of a car that cost more than her house.

"Catarina, look!" a smoky baritone with a sexy accent Amy couldn't quite place called to someone outside. "Did you see the *brilliant* pig on the corner?"

She couldn't resist. Just like everyone else, she checked out the new arrivals.

The speaker was a lean, elegantly dressed gentleman propping open the door to let in an entourage of characters as out of place as their vehicles. Given the amount of animal-skin fabrics, feathered collars, and leather worn by the gentleman's exotic entourage, they looked like escapees from a zoo in this land of denim and polyester. But the gentleman holding the door looked as if he'd been born to wear a top hat and tux.

"Do you think he's the ringmaster?" Jo murmured in amusement, echoing Amy's thought.

At that instant, the object of their fascination whipped off his designer shades and winked in their direction. Amy almost dropped the mushrooms. The stranger's scorching gaze paused on her and triggered her hormones like neglected hand grenades. She could have sworn he actually *saw* her, except no man who looked like that ever noticed her when she stood next to Jo.

He could have just walked off the pages of a fashion ad, one of those where the male models had six-pack abs and deliberately mussed hairstyles that cost a fortune to achieve. Straight-cut brown hair brushed his nape and fell Hugh Grant–style across his wide brow. A black ribbed polo shirt pulled taut over his admirable chest, and the camel sports jacket topping it was probably Armani and tailored to emphasize his square shoulders.

The likes of Hugh Grant didn't appear around here without reason, and after the mayor's call, she had a sinking feeling that she knew the reason.

The visitors milled about the nearly empty café, gazing at the unconventional décor as if hoping a real restaurant would pop out from under the eccentric tablecloths.

"Are we too early for dinner, my fair lady?" the stranger asked playfully.

It took Jo's elbow in her ribs before Amy realized he was talking to her and not to her beautiful, blond baby sister. Jo was already peeling off her apron in preparation for acting as hostess. The foreign gentleman watched Amy expectantly, making her nervous.

"Dinner's on," she agreed with assumed nonchalance. "Take seats anywhere."

"You are a lifesaver," he purred in a wickedly sexy voice that had every woman in the café panting. "We've just driven up from the airport in Charlotte, and there wasn't a decent eatery in sight."

"There's a Cracker Barrel on the interstate," Jo said with amusement, gathering napkins and silverware.

"What's a Cracker Barrel? It sounds *appalling*." The gentleman sauntered—Amy swore that was the only word that could describe the way he caught his hand in his pants pocket and gracefully dodged tables and chairs without looking at them—to the counter.

He smelled even better than he looked. The subtle scents of musk and pinewoods intertwined with the aroma of her cooking, and her mouth nearly watered as he took one of the seats at the counter, putting his boyishly tousled hair within reach. Dark eyes watched her with impish laughter. She poured another swallow of Jo's lemonade.

Not wishing to see shiny cars smashed into grease slicks, Amy nodded toward the door. "There's no parking allowed on the street. The police don't tow cars because they're usually scrap metal before tow trucks can reach them. There are parking lots coming into and on the way out of town."

Before the European hunk could respond, a lithe, towering beauty swayed up to brush her breasts against his shoulder, drape her tousled mane of tawny-streaked hair down his front, and whisper in his ear. Amy recognized the Italian accent. Although she couldn't translate the words, she maliciously translated body language to *What are we doing in this hole, sweetikins; let's go somewhere fabulously expensive and sip champagne and make beautiful love.*

James Bond turned on his stool to wrap an understanding arm around the lioness. He patted her hip and responded reassuringly in Italian; then to Amy's amazement, he gently nudged Blondie away and turned the intensity of his focus back to her.

Amy's wariness shield shot into full alert.

"You will pardon my friends? I was so eager to arrive, I did not think of their needs. They deserve a lovely resort, do they not? Can you recommend such a thing?"

"An hour back down the road in Asheville. Would you like coffee, tea?" Amy lifted the coffee carafe in an age-old gesture of hospitality that she couldn't neglect despite all suspicion.

"Tea, if you would be so kind." He smiled in delight, and his eyes crinkled in the corners. He turned and spoke more unfamiliar words to his audience.

The blonde in the slinky leopard-print skirt sulked, and a tall man with an Asian cast to his eyes replied in a bored French drawl.

Not knowing whether to provide sweet or unsweetened iced tea, Amy poured unsweetened and pushed the sugar packets in the gentleman's direction, then took another sip of her spiked lemonade.

She began filling cups and glasses to Jo's hand signals and sighed in relief when Janey, their teenage waitress, shoved open the door, followed by the first of the local curiosity seekers. The Porsche was better than a neon sign. Word spread fast in a town like this, and the visitors were better than any entertainment they'd had since the last country music show at the Barn. Well-heeled foreigners didn't often find the less-traveled paths through these mountains.

At least the café would have one last profitable evening.

After a brief exchange, the tall Asian-looking man and a lanky, ponytailed twenty-something went outside to move the cars.

With his lackeys doing their jobs, the gentleman turned back to Amy and stared at the sweating glass of ice and tea with raised eyebrows. "What is this?"

"Tea. I have sweet tea if you prefer." She slid him a small plate of the mushroom appetizers thinking it wouldn't hurt to butter up the man paying the bill.

"Tea." He studied the glass with curiosity. "My mother warned me about this country, but I didn't listen." He lifted the glass and sipped cautiously. "Strong. Not bad."

He looked up at Amy with a thousand-watt smile and extended his hand. "Hello, I am Jacques Saint-Etienne . . . and I have come to look at your antique mill."

❧ TWO ❧

"No, no, it is not like that," Jacques Saint-Etienne protested into the phone his assistant handed him. He scraped the last of the scalloped oysters from his plate.

Amy wiped a spill on the stove and blatantly eavesdropped.

"Sahn Eshan?" Jo attempted to repeat his name as she refilled tea glasses.

" 'Saint Stephen,' " Amy translated, warily following the conversation. His accent became more clipped when he argued, almost British despite the fancy French he spewed to his entourage.

"Yes, yes." He barked irritably into the phone. "A suite, yes. Coffee in every room. And tea. *Hot* tea," he amended. "Reserve the Jacuzzi room, if you will."

"Uh-oh, I better go stand by my man." Carrying a tray of espresso for the newcomers and peach cobbler for one of the locals, Jo aimed for the back booth where the sultry blonde had cornered Flint, who had emerged from his office to help with the unusual rush of customers.

Riding high on spiked lemonade and oddly revived by the exotic company, Amy hummed under her breath and poured boiling water over the leaves of her favorite Keemun in her special china teapot. She'd heard that comment about *hot* tea. And she was feeling just spiteful enough to get even for this invasion of demanding, temperamental customers—ones she suspected would steal her livelihood from under her nose if they could.

She helped Janey load the dishwasher while the tea steeped. Only one of their new guests had eaten her delicious roast chicken. None of them had touched the whipped potatoes or creamed peas. She'd had to send Flint down to the grocery for arugula, spinach, and fresh mushrooms, or whatever facsimile he could find, plus *oysters*. The local store seldom carried more than iceberg and canned mushrooms. Seafood of any sort in the mountains was suspect.

She had created an entire new menu of salads and appetizers to suit their vegetarian, noncarbohydrate diets out of the barest scraps at last-minute notice, and not one of them had expressed appreciation. Not even Saint Stephen, who'd adroitly switched between flirting with every woman in the room, barking at his cell phone, and ordering his lackeys about, all at a dizzying pace. Amy wasn't certain how he managed to eat a bite.

A little too aware of her own padded figure in comparison to all these anorexic creatures, Amy poured her perfectly steeped Keemun into a china cup with malice aforethought.

She sliced a fresh lemon and added just a touch of sugar. The fragrance of Chinese tea leaves wafted upward from her delicate teacup as she leaned back against the stove and took a restorative sip.

Saint Stephen snapped his cell phone shut and dropped it into his jacket pocket. He eyed Jo's flask with interest.

"The oysters and vegetable couscous were admirable," he murmured. "But I do not share my friends' affinity for espresso. I don't suppose I could prevail upon you for a martini?"

Amy would have smiled at the compliment, except if he really was the infamous idiot who meant to take the mill away from the town, she wanted him nailed to the floor with sharp steel, not good liquor.

"This is a dry town, no alcohol," she replied. Dry towns tended to discourage most business types interested in the area. She could hope.

His aristocratically thin nose twitched as his formidable gaze settled on Amy's cup. "Perhaps you have something that would appeal to my more British tastes, then?" he suggested.

"British?" Amy raised her eyebrows and sipped her tea with the bravado of half a flask of whiskey. "I may not be a world traveler, but I recognize French and Italian when I hear it." Still, *British* would explain the posher edge to his English.

He flashed a wide smile. "My mother is from West Virginia, my father is from Paris. I have a villa in Italy, but I was raised in London. I eat *British*."

"You ate oysters instead of the steak I offered," Amy argued. "Even I know Brits like their beef."

Saint Stevie was probably in charge of tips. She should be waiting on him hand and foot. But she'd done that all evening, and he hadn't bothered to express his appreciation—until she'd deliberately taunted him. *Now* she had his attention. Men, European or not, were all alike. She was learning to play this game.

"I like oysters. That does not change my nationality. Is that hot tea I detect?"

"Yes," she said with a smile. "Keemun. Would you like to know the province?"

"I would like the tea, please," he said decisively, shoving the icy glass away. "Hot."

Hmmm, Mr. Pretty Boy wasn't averse to giving orders instead of flattery. Orders, she hadn't learned to ignore, especially when they involved food and hospitality.

Now that she had his attention, she counted this round won, and reverted to her true nature, sort of. She shuffled through the café's cluttered cabinet until she located Jo's prized Fiestaware cups, in orange, and poured tea from her delicate, hand-painted Staffordshire pot into one. Let the rich man see how the other half lived.

"Lemon?" she asked sweetly.

He studied the obnoxious color and design of the chunky Depression-era American cup that she pushed toward him. "Please."

Someone had taught him manners, too. Amy rewarded him with a saucer of lemon wedges. "Our mill isn't an antique." She saw no reason to delay the confrontation longer.

"According to my research, the first mill was built here in 1855 by Ezekial Jekel, who married a local southern belle and applied his Yankee ingenuity to harnessing the river." The facts reeled off his tongue without hesitation. He sipped the tea with a nod of approval. "Delicious, thank you."

She admired his research, but his knowledge made her stomach hurt. His interest wasn't that of a tourist.

At Jo's signal for two espressos, Amy returned to work. Tourist revenue had paid for the espresso machine. Most of the locals preferred their caffeine fix with the cheap bottomless-cup special. Sliding the slender mugs onto a doily-decorated tray, she handed the order across the counter to her sister.

Oddly, the gentleman didn't turn to admire Jo's best red hostess gown with the plunging neckline. His smoldering gaze remained fixed on Amy, and she hid a shiver of reaction. She definitely didn't need bored, irresponsible playboys in her dysfunctional life, especially ones who wanted something she was much too wise to give.

"Impressive research," she acknowledged once Jo departed. "But the current buildings were designed in 1955 and the machinery updated in 1999. The plant was in operation until last year. The fabrics you see in here were all created on those looms by our local employees."

Sipping his tea, the newcomer half turned to study the rich purple-and-rust tapestried upholstery and wine-colored damask tablecloth. "Foolishly expansive for so small an operation, but well done. Your mill has a reputation for sound design and expensive products."

From this angle, Amy could see the beard stubble on his angular jaw and the tired lines at the corners of his eyes. If there hadn't been some danger that he was her worst enemy, she would have urged him to go home and get some rest.

"Foolishly expansive?" she asked, smothering her instinctive need to nurture.

"The mill went bankrupt because it couldn't afford those employees," he pointed out. "You cannot sell fabric higher than the market rate, and that doesn't cover your labor cost."

In the same way his drawl became more clipped as he spoke, his carved features sharpened, his dark gaze smoldered, and Amy would have to quit calling him Saint Stevie if he got any hotter. She was starting to suspect a hungry wolf lurked beneath the designer sheep's wool.

"The rich will pay whatever it takes to get what they

want," she replied, then snapped her mouth shut. No sense in giving away her market plans.

"Don't be naïve. The wealthy like a good bargain as much as any, and they can find them in the Asian bazaars. Your only hope is computerized looms and designs, and that takes expensive technology you don't possess."

"Computerization doesn't put cash into the local economy," she argued. "Any plant, anywhere in the world can produce computerized designs."

"Exactly," he said with satisfaction, setting down his empty cup and rising to offer his hand. "It's been a pleasure speaking with someone who so thoroughly understands the business. I don't believe I caught your name?"

"Amaranth Jane Sanderson Warren," she replied with every name she could legally claim, "textile designer and former wife of Northfork Mills' CEO." Not offering her hand in return, she smiled pleasantly over her teacup.

Wearily, Jacques drove the Porsche down the narrow winding mountain highway. He couldn't remember when he'd slept last. There had been the bon voyage party in London that had gone into the wee hours, the early overseas flight where he'd spent his time reading research material, the long tedious customs lines at the airport, delays in obtaining their vehicles, all compounded by the long drive up here. And now he had to drive right back down again to the hotel, with his trick knee growing stiffer for lack of exercise.

He'd have to find a place to stay in Northfork. He needed to be in the thick of things while he worked. It kept his mind occupied.

But tonight, his mind was too tired to think of anything except the intriguing woman he'd encountered.

When he'd first entered the café, he'd thought he'd found a charming haven of mouthwatering aromas presided over by a curvaceous angel. Her eyes had widened in surprise at their arrival, her lush lips had parted in invitation, and for a very brief moment, he'd felt the welcome of home.

Until the lovely angel had revealed her decidedly sharp mind and tongue. He appreciated her subtle digs and couldn't resist his curiosity about what else hid behind her calm demeanor. A kitten with claws might be an apt description.

He chuckled at her *coup de grâce* over the tea. He appreciated her stubborn refusal to be walked over. He was wary of the soft, malleable types who wrapped themselves around him. Usually, they wanted something, and became intractable when he would not give it.

Gabrielle had been like that—soft, sweet, intelligent, and very young. But then, so had he. He'd given her everything she'd wanted, so she had no reason to be stubborn. Until the day he *hadn't* given her what she wanted.

Which was why he tried to stay busy and not think. If he hadn't been so young and stupid, maybe things would have been different. Even after all these years, the guilt and the pain ate at him.

In some ways, staying busy acted as a tonic. He could party all night, harass his employees all day, and still live quite comfortably with himself. If he could just erase all memory of Gabrielle and his beautiful Danielle . . .

It had been ten years of working and partying, and he still hadn't succeeded in that one simple task. New tactics were needed, which was why he was in this outpost of nowhere. He was getting too old for regrets. He needed a different challenge.

After parking outside the elegant resort his assistant had located and handing his keys to the valet without noticing his surroundings, Jacques limped into the majestically rustic lobby of the Grove Park Inn.

Brigitte, his assistant, was already inside handling the reception desk. He assumed Luigi, his driver and bodyguard, was overseeing the luggage and checking out the accommodations. Jacques cornered Pascal and forced him to pace the spacious lobby while he worked out the kinks. Everyone else scattered looking for bars and entertainment. He'd been assured the resort had a spa. The women would be happy, and he could ease his aching ligaments in the hot waters. Perhaps an American masseuse would have a new trick to force his muscles to behave.

"I think we'll have some local resistance," Jacques informed his financial adviser. Pascal dressed in black like a Parisian, carried his Nikon like a Japanese tourist, and had the razor-sharp mind of an international financier. "We need to keep the staff contained and as unobtrusive as possible until I've formed a solid foundation with the locals."

"What about Catarina? We have no control over her. I don't know why you brought her, other than the obvious." Pascal jingled the change in his pocket and scanned the lobby as if searching for industrial spies.

"I did not invite her." In truth, he would have preferred she'd stayed where she belonged. He was aware she was using him as a ticket to enhance her fading fame and boost her design business. Mixing sex with work was too messy for his preferences, so he was avoiding her. "I cannot keep her from buying a ticket. She has a good eye for color and design, so maybe we can use her and her friends. Maybe they'll get bored and go home shortly."

Jacques doubted she would, but eventually she might get the message that he wasn't interested in a relationship. He wasn't on the lookout for permanence anymore. He'd once thought a stable home and family was everything he desired, but his parents had the right idea—you can't lose what you don't have.

"We have less than two weeks to find the cards and determine if they're worth bidding on," Pascal said. "Perhaps we could give a party and let Catarina talk to former management, see if they are aware of the historic patterns, and where the cards might be stored."

"They'll want to talk about how many employees we'll hire." Jacques shoved his hand through his hair and grimaced. "It is not a good thing that we befriend these people."

"It's no big deal," Pascal assured him. "We buy the mill, get what we want from it, and we can give the town the old buildings when we're done. They can turn them into antiques stores and tourist craft shops."

Jacques had a decided notion that was not what the sharp-clawed kitten had in mind.

The thought made him shift uncomfortably inside his skin, but they'd be gone in two weeks. And he'd have a fascinating new project to keep his mind occupied.

≪ THREE ≫

"I could start an antiques store in Asheville," Amy mused, cleaning the stove at the café after the Sunday lunch crowd departed.

The prospective buyers who had looked at her house last night had made an offer first thing this morning. If she accepted it, she had to start house hunting immediately. And job hunting.

Her one prayer of staying here rode on the town acquiring the mill property. Not only could the mill provide her with a decent job, but its assets included the vacant, run-down Craftsman cottage that she coveted. She had high hopes of persuading the mill committee to sell her the cottage for a price she could afford.

But she couldn't restore a single floor tile without money.

"Just what the world needs, another antiques store." Jo held open the door so her friend Dot, the artist, could carry in a three-foot plaster goose. "And who would take care of the kids if you moved down there?"

"Back in a minute." Dot set the goose on the nearest table and rushed back out.

Amy eyed the sculpture skeptically. "We're selling statues now?"

"Dot has a customer coming in tomorrow to pick it up, but she has to go out of town. I told her we'd handle it."

"Better have her sit it on the floor. That thing looks like it will topple any minute." Amy started unloading the dishwasher, her mind covering so wide a field of must-dos and should-dos and what-ifs that she might as well have been spinning inside a tornado.

No matter how much she disliked the bland McMansion, the thought of selling her children's home terrified her. Where would they live? If the foreigners really made a legitimate bid on the mill, what would happen to the cottage? In her head, she'd already remodeled every inch of it. Losing her home, the cottage, and a chance at a real job all at the same time—her imagination simply couldn't leap that many hurdles. She had enough difficulty trying to think of a mill anywhere in the state that was still open and might accept her ten-year-old degree as experience.

Awakened to her surroundings by the bustle of activity, Louisa piped, "I'm hungry, Mommy," from her place on the floor, where she'd been engrossed in energetic coloring.

Jo lifted her three-year-old niece to the counter and fed her a slice of apple.

"Besides, if you move, you'd have to sell all those gorgeous pieces of furniture you refinished. You don't want to do that, do you?" Jo asked, continuing their interrupted conversation.

"What else will I do with them? I'll be lucky if any house I can afford has room for a few beds and a table." She was trying to be practical about this, but her heart protested hysterically. The old cottage would have been an ideal fit for her antiques.

Dot walked in carrying a plaster Humpty Dumpty and

set it beside the goose. "Thanks, Jo, Amy! I really appreciate this."

"Put them on the—" Amy started to call, but Dot had already rushed out, her long green braid flying. With a sigh, Amy shoved the still-hot-from-the-dishwasher plates on the shelf.

"Flint and the boys can store your furniture upstairs, if you like," Jo suggested, ignoring her friend's weird artwork. "We've not found any renters for the apartment. Are you certain you have to sell the house? If the mill bid goes through, surely you'll be hired at a decent salary. You're the only one around here with a textile degree."

A ten-year-old degree with no evidence that she had ever used it, since Evan had taken all the credit and never put her on the payroll. She knew she was good. She simply had no proof.

"I've drained my bank account making the house payments, praying for a rainbow to save it. I've got to be realistic about this and find a place within my income."

Amy could mouth the words pragmatically, but the sentimental mother inside her wept at the idea of leaving behind all the childhood markers the house represented. On their birthdays, Josh and Louisa had drawn pencil lines on the bathroom door frame marking how much they'd grown. Josh would have to leave behind his playground designed for his fascination with trains. She'd stenciled pink ribbons around Louisa's nursery before her daughter was born and embroidered pillows to match for the rocking chair. She knew she could do it all again—eventually—but she needed the security of a home to go to before she could consider this move with anything other than a sinking feeling in her stomach.

"Well, with real estate soaring like it is, you ought to

make a tidy profit. It's a good thing your lawyer wrung the house out of Evan." Done wiping tables, Jo unfastened her apron from her church dress and sent her sister a sympathetic look.

"I borrowed against that profit and have been living off it this past year," Amy reminded her. "Selling the house will pay off the mortgages and leave me a few thousand for starting elsewhere. If I just knew for certain I'd be staying here, life would be simple."

"Well, you know Flint and I will back you, whatever you choose to do," Jo said. "All these years you've put up with me, it's my turn to be the sensible one. Without you paying for Mama's medicines, we'd be up a creek by now."

"There you go—I'll buy a trailer up the creek." Amy managed a smile, although the idea of eccentric Joella being the responsible sister threatened to give her hives. She was used to doing the caretaking, not the other way around.

"I'm going to bake some cupcakes." For distraction, Amy kissed her docile youngest's curls. She always baked when she was worried, which explained her extra pounds lately. "Are you going to decorate them, sweetheart?"

"Pig cakes," Louisa agreed serenely. "With snoses."

"Are you sure I shouldn't take her with me? It's no problem, really," Jo offered.

"Josh needs some male bonding time with your guys. He doesn't need his kid sister crowding him. The lunch rush is over. I'll just get the baking done and take her home."

"All right then, give Aunt Jo sugar." Jo hugged her niece and accepted a ripe kiss. "You be good now. I'll pick you up with Josh and the boys after school tomorrow, and we'll all go to my house and *parta-aay.*"

"Dora the Explorer," Louisa demanded.

"Cartoons instead of partying," Jo agreed blithely. "Are you sure you can handle the café next week without me?" She directed this last at Amy.

"It's a kitchen, Jo. I can handle it," Amy assured her.

She was less sure of herself after Jo departed and Saint Stevie sauntered in without his retinue. The tiny piece of her that still believed in dreams had been hoping he was an illusion that would disappear with the sunrise.

Instead, he looked more solid and gorgeous in daylight. Sporting a movie actor's groomed stubble, a small gold stud in one ear, a fabulous black-and-tan silk shirt rippling over a chest-hugging black knit, and a pair of tan slacks that had to have been tailored for him, he defied any category of man with which she was familiar.

His lanky, tailored elegance gave the appearance of height, but he didn't loom like a formidable gorilla over her five-foot-two frame as so many men did.

"Ah, my fair lady!" he exclaimed, limping to the counter with a brilliant smile and a wolfish gleam in his eye, as he unexpectedly swept Louisa into his arms, tickling her until the room chimed with childish delight.

It had been a long time since Louisa had opened up and laughed like that—since Evan had left, to be precise. It was hard saying anything nasty to a man willing to take time to make a child laugh.

Unable to resist any man who liked children, Amy added Keemun leaves to the teapot and filled it with boiling water while Saint Stevie admired her daughter's coloring efforts and asked questions about the pictures portrayed in the book.

"Your daughter?" he asked, taking a seat at the counter and bouncing the beaming little girl on his knee.

"Louisa," Amy agreed. "Do you have children?"

A shadow crossed his face, but he tugged his ear and smiled again. "I don't really lead a life that suits family."

Well, at least the man was honest. She poured the tea—into a persimmon Fiestaware cup this time—and pushed it toward him. "What would you like?"

He looked momentarily perplexed at the question, and then apparently realized he was sitting at a counter where food was served. "The tea is perfect, thank you." He glanced around. "Where is everyone?"

"It's two on Sunday afternoon and we only serve brunch on Sundays. The rest of the world is eating dinner, napping, or watching football. Where's your entourage?"

"My entourage?" Sculpted lips turned up temptingly at the corner, and Amy resisted drooling at the image they invoked of sultry kisses. "My *staff*," he corrected. Pascal is my adviser, Brigitte is my assistant . . ."

Amy held up her hand. "More than I need to know if you will be here only a few days."

She definitely did not need to drool over a man who had just admitted he was commitment-phobic. Just because he gave her a glimpse of a fascinating world outside her own did not make him drool material.

He lowered his long lashes and watched her from beneath them until her lost hormones ignited all over again. He probably knew exactly how that look affected her, damn his sexy eyes.

"Ah, that is a pity," he lamented, sipping his tea, pretending he wasn't turning her into a puddle of melted butter. "I had such hopes of taking a little dove for ice cream on this beautiful day." He murmured French endearments and tickled Louisa again.

Amy's heart cracked when Louisa lit up with delight at the attention and attempted to repeat his phrases. Had she been neglecting her children that much?

Of course she had. Until Evan had left, she'd never worked away from home. Since then, she had done everything possible to juggle the café and her commitments and make up for their father's absence, but the day simply wasn't long enough.

"Can I have ice cream, Mommy?" Louisa piped, just as the rotten scoundrel had to have known she would. Amy refused to fall for that shallow charm and good looks ever again.

"If you are very good while I clean up here, you can have a chocolate-raspberry-vanilla with sprinkles on top," Amy assured her.

"Can he have some, too?" she asked politely, not knowing Saint Stevie's name.

"You must call me Jacques, mademoiselle," he assured the child, carefully enunciating the French *Zhock* for her. "And I would be very pleased to have chocolate-raspberry-vanilla with sprinkles on top."

"Zock," she replied with satisfaction. "I wanna go play Dora now."

Louisa squirmed from his knee and dashed off to Flint's office and the DVD Jo had given her last Christmas.

Christmas. There was that dirty word again.

"More tea?" Amy lifted the teapot questioningly, as any good waitress might.

The timer on the oven started shrieking. It hadn't worked since the clock stopped.

He lifted his smooth eyebrows questioningly at the racket while nodding for the refill. "You are cooking something?"

"Just myself," Amy muttered. She filled his cup, then slammed her hand against the clock. The buzzer stopped. She had just been admiring a man who would destroy the future of her children. Jo was right. She needed to have her head examined.

"I have come here for a reason," he said when she didn't explain the shrieking timer or her comment. Sipping his tea, he turned the stool to study the plaster goose and Humpty Dumpty.

"Tell me something I don't know." Resisting giving him the scone she'd saved for her break, Amy took down the mixing utensils.

"I am sorry if we got off on the wrong foot," he said in a tone of regret, turning his full attention back to Amy. "My staff was rude and demanding last evening, and they did not express proper gratitude for your outstanding efforts."

Amy couldn't resist his contrite expression—it looked good on his Hugh Grant face. "Your tip said all that needed to be said," she admitted, reaching for the scone in the warming oven. "But if they plan on eating here again, you'd best warn me in advance. I can still get fresh greens, but not at an instant's notice."

"When in Rome, they must eat as Romans do." He gestured dismissively, then eyed the fat, currant-filled scone she placed in front of him with surprise. "What is this?"

"A scone," she said, annoyed with herself for giving in

to his charming apology. "I can't provide clotted cream, though. What's your preference? Butter, jam, honey? Scones are British, aren't they?"

His smile brightened like a harvest moon as he sniffed the still warm biscuit. "My mother used to cover them in strawberries. Jam is fine, thank you."

"It's too late in the season for fresh strawberries, but I have some of Mama's homemade jam." Amy was quite certain she had lost her mind when she offered this stranger the delicacy reserved for her family. Did she think buttering him up would persuade him to go away? That was quite a head trip, if so. "I have whipped cream if you want the whole shebang," she added, because that's how she would have fixed it.

"Whipped cream, yes," he agreed, his carved jaw set with hungry satisfaction.

When she showed him the can of pressurized whipped cream, he still nodded. Shrugging, Amy covered the jam scone with the instant cream.

Just as she was returning the can to the refrigerator, the café door bounced open and Dave, the owner of the hardware store, barged in. "Two Coke floats to go, would you, Ames? Inventory is filthy work." He stopped short at the sight of the stranger in tourist clothes at the counter. "Sorry, didn't mean to interrupt."

"Dave, this is Jacques Saint-Etienne, our competitor for the mill. Mr. Saint-Etienne, Dave Boggs, head of the Chamber of Commerce's mill committee."

Sighing in regret at this interruption to their delightful tête-à-tête, Jacques rose and offered his hand, adding his best disarming smile while studying his competition. Mr. Boggs was an older gentleman of sturdy build, wearing

Dockers and an off-the-rack short-sleeved shirt. Not an international financier by a long shot. "Mr. Boggs, it's good to meet you."

"Same, I'm sure." Dave slapped Jacques's hand but didn't try the usual competitive crushing handshake. "Anyone who gets the mill back in production is a friend of mine."

Jacques preferred not to get into that. He'd much rather romance the lovely cook and find out if the mill still had the pattern cards he wanted, but he supposed it never hurt to be friendly.

"A man of business, I like that. I was hoping to find someone to drive me out to the plant and show me around, but Ms. . . . . Ames?" She'd introduced herself as *Amaranth,* but Jacques couldn't bear to call an attractive woman by such an unwieldy name. He had already noted she still wore her wedding band, although he'd heard, with definite interest, when she'd told him she was a *former* wife. "Ms. Ames has distracted me with her delicious cuisine."

"Isn't she a great little cook? The food has gone upscale since Amy took over the kitchen." Dave fished a bill out of his wallet and shoved it across the counter in exchange for two large drink cups. "I'd be happy to take you out later, but I'm in the middle of inventory right now." He glanced at Amy. "What about Jo? Isn't she in town?"

"I'll call and ask, but I think she had plans. I can give Mr. Saint-Etienne—"

"Jacques, please," he insisted.

She nodded curtly, transformed from an understanding hostess dispensing delicious delicacies to hard-eyed businesswoman at the mention of the mill, although her soft

curls and unmanicured fingers lacked the necessary lac-
quered finish to successfully carry off the attitude.

"I can provide directions and a map," she said.
"Doesn't Hank's real estate company have the key?
Someone over there might show you around."

That wasn't what Jacques wanted. He wanted time to
go through files and pattern books. He didn't intend to
steal anything. He simply wanted to know he was getting
what he was willing to pay for. "I would prefer the guid-
ance of someone familiar with operations. Did I not understand that Ms. . . . Amy has some familiarity with the
mill?"

"Amy knows the place inside and out," Dave agreed
cheerfully. "You will be in good hands with her. Why not
today, Amy? The café closes at three, doesn't it?" With
the problem settled to his satisfaction, Dave rushed for
the exit with a "Good to meet you, Jock," farewell.

Jacques winced at the mispronunciation.

He didn't have to pretend a smile as he returned to his
seat to finish his scone. Judging from the sour look on the
lady's face, *she* could use a little sweetening, though.

"You will take me, yes?" he asked in the accent he'd
earned from his father. He could reproduce his American
mother's West Virginia twang if necessary, but women
always smiled so delightfully at a foreign inflection. He
would like to make Ms. Amy smile more.

Gathering from his hostess's quirked eyebrows that she
knew she'd been outmaneuvered, Jacques shrugged and
insouciantly devoted himself to consuming the scone
while she called her sister.

"Mama, I gotta go potty!" the child cried from the
other room.

She was an exquisite fairy child, chubbier and more

golden than his Danielle at that age. It warmed what was left of his heart to see mother and daughter together. For a long time after the accident, the knifing pain of loss had caused Jacques to turn his head away from the sight of children, but he enjoyed their innocent exuberance too much to ignore them forever.

He turned the stool in expectation at the sound of small shoes rushing across the old wooden floor. She ran into the room, pale curls bouncing, carrying a ragged doll, and disregarding all in her path as children did. His eyes widened as he took in the precarious juxtaposition of top-heavy goose and plaster egg.

"Watch the table," he called. He slid from the stool in order to catch the table and prevent the statues from toppling.

Her little shoe tripped on a chair leg before he could reach the artwork.

The chair slammed into the table and the heavy pieces rocked precariously, tilting on their flimsy perch. Trapped behind the counter, Amy screamed.

With the swift coordination of the athlete he'd once been, Jacques lunged between the child and the toppling statues, twisting his already twisted knee in the process. He heard the telltale snap, but he caught the child under him before the heavy goose slammed into his back and rolled harmlessly off him. Amy's cry covered the shattering crack of the egg hitting the floor.

The child shrieked in startlement, but he was fairly certain he hadn't crushed her. Wincing at the bruise to his spine, Jacques propped up on one arm and reassuringly brushed blond curls from her forehead.

With his motion, a sharp pain cut through his knee. Biting his tongue against the agony, Jacques wished he could shriek as loudly as the toddler. Instead, he merely grimaced while the lady rescued her weeping daughter, cuddling and cooing over the child, drenching him in the intoxicating scents of vanilla and jasmine, while he lay there, helpless.

Maybe he'd just pretend he was a carpet.

❦ FOUR ❧

"Thanks for coming, Elise." Amy rubbed the sinus ache above her nose and tried to shut out the excruciating odor of Lysol in the hospital emergency room. "He'll probably sue me, the café, and the entire town, and right now, I can't blame him. We've probably lamed the poor man for life."

"I've talked to one of the interns," Elise said reassuringly. "Your macho dude is back there now telling the nurses that he just needs a brace and ice."

Originally from Knoxville, on the western side of the mountain, her lawyer and friend possessed a city-bred aggressiveness that made Elise successful in everything from negotiating contracts to suing the biggest music publisher in the country. She had taught Amy how to stand on her own and fight her ex with steel instead of mushy sentimentality.

"Apparently, he had an old knee injury that was already inflamed when he came to visit. If he's injured it again, it's his own fault; so quit fretting," Elise insisted.

Amy combed the hair out of her eyes. She needed a haircut as much as Saint Stevie did, only the unruliness looked better on him. "I don't know what we'd do without you, Elise. I think God must have sent you."

Caught by surprise, Elise began laughing as if Amy had

just performed the best stand-up routine since Bill Cosby's. Every head in the room turned to see what was so funny.

With jet black hair, startlingly blue eyes beneath long lashes, a tall, slender build more elegant than Jo's country buxom, and garbed in a striking red suit, Elise held the attention of every male with eyes in his head.

"If you listen to my ex, my partners, or a few of the people I've tangled with in court, I'm the product of the devil," Elise explained when she caught her breath. "Never confuse me with a nice person."

"I want to be you when I grow up," Amy insisted, anxiously watching the doors where they had taken Jacques. "I want to be able to fix things."

Jacques might be the competition, but she couldn't wish him the agonizing pain she knew he was suffering. He had saved Louisa from what could have been a tragic accident, and she owed him everything for that. Torn by conflicting emotions, she had wanted to weep at his stoicism while she drove him down the mountain to the hospital.

Dave had come from the hardware store to help her carry Jacques into her SUV, which she'd driven up to the front door. Jacques had been so calm throughout the process. He merely swallowed anti-inflammatories as if they were candy. But his face had twisted in agony with every bump, especially when she'd had to take Jo's gravel drive to drop off Louisa.

"I can't cook, and my daughter thinks I'm the meanest mother on the planet," Elise said as the glass emergency room entrance slid open. "Be careful what you wish for."

"Where is he? Where is my Jacques?" a weeping voice wailed over the chatter of foreign languages bursting into the room. Jacques's entourage—*staff*—had arrived.

He must have found his cell phone and called for reinforcements, Amy decided, watching the elegant creatures spreading out in all directions. The tall, Asian-looking cameraman had his arm around the shoulders of the weeping lioness, while a bobbed, bespectacled woman approached the desk. The lanky boy turned toward the coffee machine. A well-built man wearing a billed cap and gray jacket lingered at the door.

"I don't think he needs us anymore," Amy whispered. "But it seems awful to desert him." She really wanted to see for herself that he was all right, but she thought that would be dreadfully presumptuous now that he had his staff to look after him.

Elise assessed the situation with narrowed eyes. "I'll handle this."

Amy watched her friend march up to the bespectacled woman, who was probably the assistant Jacques had mentioned. The two women exchanged a few words, shook hands, and that was that. Not a single member of his cosmopolitan staff acknowledged Amy's existence.

"His knee is sprained. He'll have to walk on crutches for a while. They're taking him back to the resort. Let's go." Elise nearly dragged Amy from the waiting room.

Throwing one last glance over her shoulder, Amy gave up the fight. She might never have a chance to see Jacques and thank him for saving Louisa.

But if he left town, the mill bid was left wide open again. . . . She hated herself for wanting to do a happy dance at someone else's expense.

"If you start breaking people the way you do machines when you stress out, we ought to patent you," Elise said with a laugh as they traversed the parking lot.

Amy managed a smile at the warped humor. "Jo has

you convinced I'm death to machines, too? I thought lawyers were too logical to be superstitious."

"I've heard of human magnetic fields. I know people who can't wear watches because they destroy them." She glanced knowingly at Amy's bare wrist as they stopped at the SUV. "Do you fry computers, too?"

"I avoid computers," Amy admitted. "Guess it's a good thing I won't be around Saint Stevie if he buys the mill and installs computerized machinery. If I believed you and Jo, I'd blow his looms sky high."

"'Saint Stevie'?" Elise asked, her ruby lips quirking upward. "I really need to meet this man when he isn't under the influence of narcotics."

"I'm crossing my fingers that he'll take the next plane home, so you'd better hurry over to the resort if you want to meet him." Amy opened her door and leaned on it a minute, letting the mountain breeze blow her hair off her face and cool her overheated forehead. "Thanks again, Elise. I appreciate it."

Elise waved dismissively. "Between the kids and your mother, you and Jo have spent enough of your time in that emergency room. Give the kids hugs for me."

Amy waved, climbed in, and started the engine, letting the AC take out the sun's heat while she leaned her head against the headrest.

The goose could have crushed Louisa. Instead of fretting over cottages and furniture, she needed to think about kids and safe workplaces and doctors and deductibles she couldn't afford. She had to have a job.

She would have to accept the offer the buyers had made on the house. If nothing else, Saint Stevie had scared her back to reality.

*   *   *

"No, I do not want another pain pill." Two days after the accident, Jacques was already tired of being treated like a baby. He waved away the bottle Catarina held out.

She'd been shoving medication at him all weekend—probably because he'd spent the nights in a recliner with his knee elevated instead of in the bed she'd hoped they'd finally share. His parents' outrageous performances had taught him all he needed to know about manipulation.

Give him honest Amy's pragmatic hauling of his injured carcass to an emergency room any day. She'd done what needed to be done and hadn't hovered.

Thoughts of Amy automatically raised the image of her beautiful daughter charging headlong into harm's way. As it always did at the image of an injured child, his stomach lurched, and deeply rooted fear washed over him. In trained response, he breathed slowly and forced his mind back to the moment.

"Those pills will rot out my stomach faster than they mend my knee," he complained, shifting his position in the Jacuzzi so the water jets worked on the aching ligaments. "What are all of you doing in here anyway? We have less than two weeks to make this bid."

Catarina pouted and tossed her mane of hair. "Buy the damned mill and let us go home to civilization. You cannot be climbing up and down that mountain like thees."

"Are you saying I'm old and decrepit?" he asked in a stinging tone that made her glare at him. "Go away and find a younger man." He was thirty-five to her thirty-four, but there were days he calculated a twenty-year maturity gap between them.

"I do not know why I put up with you." She flounced out, her commendable backside swaying with indignation.

She put up with him because she liked being surrounded with beautiful people and beautiful things, just as he did. Only, he did it because the image of wealth and success fed the gossip columns and promoted his business. Unlike Cat, he wasn't foolish enough to believe the attention was anything more than glitter.

That was unfair to Cat. She had a clever head on her shoulders, and she could be useful once he had the designs in hand. Her production crews would know the best places to reproduce them, and she would know the best places to sell them. It would have been less of a headache, however, if she'd waited to come over here until he'd actually *found* them.

"Pascal, have you called the bankruptcy judge for permission to visit the mill?" Now that he was rid of Cat, Jacques reached for a towel, scowling when Brigitte handed it to him. His illusion of a public life meant he had no privacy. "*You* are supposed to be arranging a tour with Ms. Warren."

"She isn't at the café today. Tuesday is her day off." His assistant checked her BlackBerry. "The home number for Ms. Warren is unlisted. I have left a message at the hardware store, as you asked, but their answering machine says they are closed for inventory."

"Find Ms. Warren's address. Google under her husband's name and see if that helps. Or call the post office and pretend you're UPS. Rural houses are hard to find." Over the years, he'd absorbed his eccentric mother's knowledge on all things American. It was occasionally helpful.

Holding the towel around him, taking Luigi's arm for support, Jacques climbed out of the tub. He shot a pointed look at Pascal, who wisely got the message and steered Brigitte back to the suite.

"Damned knee," he muttered, lowering himself to the chair so Luigi could attach the elastic brace.

"Knee surgery isn't that big a deal," Luigi reminded him. "It's either surgery or have the ligaments rip the bone off."

"Why don't I just find a nice wheelchair and a retirement home?" Jacques asked sarcastically. "The operation isn't always successful, and when it is, it doesn't mean I won't need it again in another few years. I'd rather let it mend on its own."

"Then quit hopping off bar stools."

Despite his name, Luigi was all American. He'd been Jacques's coach, personal trainer, masseur, and bodyguard since his teenage years. Luigi had been there for him more than his own father. More than two decades of sage advice gave him privileges the rest of the staff hadn't earned. That didn't mean Jacques had to listen to him.

"Just get me back up the mountain and help Brigitte find me a place to stay while I'm up there. I can't shift the Porsche like this." He winced as Luigi yanked the brace tighter.

"She told you there's just a Motel 6, and unless you want the ground-floor handicapped room with the noise of other guests pounding overhead, that means hobbling on crutches up and down stairs."

"And how is that worse than hobbling across acres of lobby here?" Jacques asked crossly. He knew he tended to be surly when he was in pain, but anti-inflammatories didn't help. "If you can't find anything more appealing, book the room closest to the stairs. The rest of you can stay here in luxury. I'll manage."

Luigi snorted. "Yeah, I see how well you manage. I'll look for wheelchair rentals."

Using one crutch to stand, Jacques swung the other at Luigi, who dodged it without effort. "I am not a cripple."

"Yeah, you are, but it ain't in the way you think." With that parting remark, Luigi trundled off.

He wasn't a cripple, physical or emotional, Jacques swore, finishing dressing on his own. He'd had a lot of experience with athletic injuries. They healed. He didn't have to run marathons anymore. When he wanted to release frustration, he had gyms and stables and swimming pools.

Just because he'd chosen not to pursue home and family again after the accident that had taken his wife and child didn't mean he was an emotional cripple. He was healed. He was living. He had the body of a man ten years younger, but in all other ways, he was older and more mature and didn't need the emotional calisthenics of youth. He preferred intellectual challenges these days.

Expertly balancing on one crutch, Jacques tugged up his trousers, and decisively snapped the fly closed. He had despised Amy's looking on him with pity on the drive to the hospital. He didn't know what it was about her sad eyes and infrequent smiles that crawled under his skin, but now that he was back on his feet, he could return to business. If business included making the CEO's ex-wife smile, it just added spice to the deal.

That he wanted to banish the sadness and protect her from any recurrence was a purely primal instinct any male would feel for a pretty, girl-next-door like Amy. He had lots of instincts. That didn't mean he had to follow them.

"To Northfork, my comrades," he called, swinging his crutches into the suite. "It is time to get down to business."

⫷ FIVE ⫸

"The quilt is beautiful, Mama." Amy stood back to admire the complex design of blues, yellows, and greens of the abstract flower garden her mother had created.

Marie Sanderson was a tough mountain woman, a hard-living single mother who'd worked in the mill most of her life—until Evan had laid her off. Amy and her mother had old issues, but they had spent these last years since Amy's marriage and return to the mountains resolving them.

Mature enough now to recognize the difficulties her mother had faced raising two young daughters on no education after their father had abandoned them, Amy had forgiven Marie for their neglected childhood. It was a precarious basis for a relationship, but better than the combative one they'd had before she'd left for college.

Telling her mother of her decision to accept the offer on the house, especially when she couldn't promise to keep the kids in Northfork, could tilt their relationship back to rocky.

She dreaded giving up the dream of someday remodeling the cottage and earning an income from a B and B so they could stay here.

Riding on a high of unjustified optimism, she'd asked her real estate agent to write up an offer on the cottage,

separate from the town's mill bid. She didn't know if the
Saint-Etienne bid was still a possibility or if Jacques had
left town. She was betting on hope—against all odds.

"That quilt didn't turn out too bad," Marie Sanderson
acknowledged, settling carefully into her recliner.
"Reckon it will pay for a turkey come Thanksgiving."

"You ought to charge twice as much for an original design. Jo's music friends can afford it."

"Nobody would pay that much for a bunch of scraps."
Marie brushed off the suggestion. "Most were pieces left
from those bolts Evan threw out."

Amy recognized some of the quilt pieces as from the
tapestries the mill had been experimenting with before it
went bankrupt. After redecorating the Stardust, her
mother and friends had begun recycling the remainders
as quilts for extra income. "You deserve a decent hourly
wage plus the value of your creativity," Amy argued.

Marie lifted a weary hand. "I don't want to scare off
the customers. I gave them a price, and I'll stick with it.
That's how I was raised."

If her mother's old four-room mill house had any electronics, Amy would have short-circuited them with the
steam building inside her. Exasperated and unable to yell
at her mother, she began folding up the quilt. "Next
time, ask more," she said quietly, knowing full well her
suggestion fell on deaf ears.

At the sound of car tires on the gravel road, Amy wandered to the window. The phone rang, and she heard her
mother's side of the conversation.

"She's still here. You want to talk with her?"

Amy sent a questioning look, and her mother mouthed,
"Jo."

The black Hummer cruising past the overgrown azal-

eas on the drive said it all without further need of expla-
nation. Amy groaned aloud. There went all her hopes
that Jacques had given up and gone back to Paris.

He hadn't left. She ought to be annoyed. Frustrated.
Instead, her pulse suddenly raced like a schoolgirl's. Did
she never learn? Good-looking men who used people
weren't good for her.

"You were supposed to show some city slicker the
mill?" her mother asked, hanging up the phone.

The driver stepping out of the Hummer was six feet tall
and bulky. Not Jacques. Amy couldn't control a little
quiver of disappointment. She blamed it on her admiration for a man who could act so swiftly and competently
to save a child not his own. He'd been a real-life superhero.

"I didn't think he would be back," she admitted.
"Louisa nearly crippled him the other day, or Dot's goose
did, depending on how you look at it. I guess he's sent his
staff."

"Jo told them how to find you, then forgot to warn us.
Some days, that girl's head is on backward."

"Jo is all heart and can't say no. I'd better go. I'll bring
you up some pork roast and fried apples later." She
kissed her mother's weathered brow, knowing she
wouldn't receive the same affection in return. Her
mother wasn't much good at expressing the softer emotions.

Amy stepped out on the porch before the driver could
knock.

"Ms. Warren?" the older man asked, touching a hand
to his billed cap.

"I am. Mr. Saint-Etienne sent you?"

"He's waiting to see the mill, madame."

"Is he in the car?"

"He is. I'll be happy to give you a ride."

The tone of the driver's voice held more interest than she expected from hired help. She cast him a quick look but could discern nothing from his blank expression. He had a bodybuilder's stockiness and a nose that had been broken and not reset. She decided he was the same man who had stood guard at the hospital.

"I'll take my car. You can follow," she told him.

He looked pained, and considering the shine on his expensive vehicle and the dust of the drive, Amy could understand that. But he didn't know how to locate the mill, and she did. And she was damned well keeping her distance from seductive eyes.

She climbed into her driver's seat without stopping at the Hummer. She was torn between wanting to hug Jacques's neck for saving her daughter or kick his shins for wanting to steal the mill. She would maintain a businesslike distance. She couldn't repay him in a thousand lifetimes for saving Louisa. So, she'd show her gratitude by being polite, and hope he went away. Soon.

She tried not to stir up too much dust as she drove down her mother's drive and the side streets through town, but the gravel entrance into the mill complex hadn't been maintained. She winced at the potholes and hoped a Hummer had good springs to shield its injured passenger.

Driving over a small metal bridge surrounded by pines and cedars, she then took the turn up to the main building. The complex of two-story, fifty-year-old brick buildings towered tall against the scenery of trees and mountain. Once upon a time, the mill had been the reason for Northfork's existence. The spot had originally been chosen for the river as power for the mill wheel. Small cabins like the one her mother owned had been built by the mill company and rented to their workers. A number of them, like the mill manager's cottage that she coveted, were still standing on the road up the mountain behind the complex.

The newer mill buildings, built in the days of electricity, were built farther from the river, making them less prone to flooding, but they were no less haunted by the town's—and her family's—history. Amy remembered company picnics and turkeys at Christmas in the good years, union walkouts and living on grits in the bad years.

She watched the Hummer's driver hurry to help the occupant out. A pair of crutches appeared first, and she flinched, feeling responsible.

Using the crutches instead of taking his driver's hand, Jacques effortlessly swung out of the car. His assistant and the Asian cameraman climbed out on the other side.

His injury hadn't harmed his square jaw and flashing smile. When he turned provocative dark eyes her way, Amy nearly melted into a puddle of lust.

She watched his powerful muscles bulge beneath his knit shirt when he used his arms to manipulate the crutches. He was so coordinated she didn't think he even noticed that he wasn't walking with his legs, but with the strength of his arms. Instead, his dancing gaze pounced on her as if she were a delicious sex goddess presented for his satisfaction.

The look sizzled any cold corner of her heart she might have left. The men around here had known her since childhood and treated her as part of the scenery. Jacques looked at her the way a man looked at a woman. She'd forgotten the power of it, and it rather alarmed her now. She didn't want to be attracted to the enemy, even if for a brief moment he'd been a superhero.

Waiting in front of the entrance, she stepped forward to greet him, trying to pretend he hadn't tingled her in all the right places. Even with crutches, he was a head taller than she. "I had no idea your injury was so serious," she said with concern. "Should you be out here? These old floors are worn and uneven."

His gaze immediately lost its predatory gleam, and he scowled at her insinuation that he was incapacitated in any way. "It is nothing, an old injury from my foolish youth. How is your daughter? Unharmed by the incident?"

Just the low rumble of his voice was sufficient to shoot adrenaline straight to her racing heart. And his scowl only made him more human, damn him.

"She's learning how to walk in the house instead of running." Trying to act as if she didn't have the world's most eligible bachelor at her back, Amy unlocked the steel doors to the office and pushed them open. A cold gust of musty air greeted them. "Humpty Dumpty will never be the same, though."

The driver chuckled and again offered his hand to help Jacques. "Humpty Dumpty had a great fall?"

Jacques glowered and ignored the offered hand. "The king's soldiers are notoriously lousy surgeons." He swung into the tiled reception area to survey his surroundings.

Did employees normally poke fun at employers? Amy wondered if she'd mistaken the driver's relationship as she followed them in. The cameraman stayed outside to take pictures of the buildings.

"Dot has plaster molds. Humpty will rise again," she said, just to smooth over any riled waters. "It's a pity surgeons can't make new knees. Aren't you supposed to keep knee injuries elevated?"

"Always the little mother." He sent her what might have been a look of approval, except it drifted past her to regard the unfurnished room with dismay. "Has the court already sold off the contents?" Without waiting for an answer, he swung through the empty reception area toward the office corridor.

Just like Evan, business first. Amy shook off the instant's warmth of his appreciation. She did not need anyone's approval for being who she was—a mother, first and foremost. "The court sold off most of the inventory and office furniture to appease creditors." Shivering in the unheated emptiness of tall ceilings and empty rooms, she hastened after him.

"The original pattern cards?" he inquired, poking a crutch to open a door, checking an empty office, and moving on to the next.

"Pattern cards? You mean the modules for the looms?"

"No, no, the Early American pattern cards Ezekial Jekel brought with him from New England."

"You're talking a hundred and fifty years ago! The originals were probably hauled to the dump with the old buildings." Amy frantically sought her memory of textile history class. She couldn't imagine why anyone would want what were essentially the punch cards of the eighteenth and nineteenth centuries.

"I have fabrics produced by these mills during the 1960s' craze for Early American design. They compare extraordinarily well with the original eighteenth-century fabrics in museums. So the patterns must still have been around fifty years ago."

"If they haven't been used in fifty years, I doubt anyone has seen them since."

Amy didn't know if the muscles of his jaw tightened because he was in pain as he started up the stairs, or because of her reply. She wanted to yell at him for risking his neck climbing narrow stairs with crutches, but Jacques was an adult and not a child. His driver stoically followed behind him, hanging on to both banisters and bracing himself for a fall—although given Jacques's solid muscle, she didn't think anyone could stop him if he tumbled backward. "Why would you want those old cards anyway?"

"Because the designs are historic and unavailable in any of today's software." He spoke each word with a swing of his crutches.

She was exhausted just watching him, but he wasn't even breathing heavily by the time they reached the second floor. "There's a reason for that," she pointed out.

Jacques frowned at her from beneath a tumble of dark hair. So much for his charming façade. Here was the real man behind the rakish image. And he was still gorgeous.

"The designs are complex and expensive," he insisted stiffly. "That does not mean they should be forgotten."

"But Early American designs are *ugly*," she retorted.

"No, they aren't. They are part of a revered tradition dating back to France and England in the 1600s. The varieties are as infinite as the tapestries that were being made in this plant just last year." He spoke with pleasure on a subject of interest to him.

Fabric design was an art form, and his knowledge and appreciation of that made him even more appealing. She liked a man who knew what he was doing. Not that she was interested, or anything.

"You intend to produce historical reproductions?" Amy asked warily, working her mind around the possibility. That could work. She simply couldn't figure out a market for the fabric.

"Yes," he said without explaining, before diving into a file cabinet, to root through it ruthlessly and efficiently.

A germ of inspiration wiggled into Amy's brain.

If she found the patterns he wanted, patterns that were of no interest to her or the town, would he buy them and go away?

Trying not to hope out loud, she spoke to the muscular expanse of his back. "We could spend weeks looking through all these buildings for those cards. I think we need to call some of the former employees and ask for their help."

Jacques stopped his search and looked at her with interest. "We can do that?"

"If you pay them," she replied with suppressed glee at the thought of the competition paying her unemployed friends to find some means of getting rid of him.

⋘ SIX ⋙

"Give Pascal your keys. He can drive your car back to town. We must make lists of people who might help," Jacques ordered, wishing he had a free hand to steer Amy into the Hummer before she fled. "Do you know which employees will be available to search?"

Instead of looking satisfied, his tour guide had a deer-in-the-headlights look at his instant agreement to her suggestion, as if she were afraid he was about to run over her.

Which he was, admittedly. But something about Amy made him want to reassure her. Stupid of him, he knew. She was a smart woman who could obviously take care of herself and everyone around her. Just because she was soft and curvy with big green heartbreaking eyes and a mouth so tender it demanded kissing didn't mean she needed his help. He just had a need to smooth her path a little, sprinkle a few rose petals . . .

See what she was like in bed. It had been a long time since the thrill of the chase had caught up with him. He had given up foxhunting as unfair to the poor animals, but a woman as intelligent as he was . . . that was quite another story.

Switching a crutch to his other arm, he took Amy's elbow and used her for a brace before she could escape.

"We will just go back to the café. I promise not to eat you." Yet. That pouty underlip of hers was a tempting morsel he had to quit watching.

"Where is the rest of your . . . staff?" she asked, giving her SUV a wistful look before reluctantly following him toward the Hummer.

She was humoring him so he didn't lose his balance, Jacques realized in amusement. He'd had so much experience with crutches he could run a marathon on them, but if her nurturing soul needed to be useful, he could humor her in return. Only a macho jerk would reject an opportunity to wrap an arm around soft shoulders and draw them closer so he could inhale her arousing scent. Jasmine?

"This is my staff." He gestured to Brigitte, Pascal, and Luigi. "The rest are Catarina's *entourage,* as you call them. They have decided to spend the day at the spa."

She looked nervous as he pried her car keys from her and passed them to Pascal. Luigi closed the door of the Hummer once she was inside, and she clung to the armrest, apparently prepared to leap out if Jacques looked at her wrong. He didn't want her to be nervous with him.

Once the car started, she released the door handle and knit her fingers together. The day was warm, and she was wearing a sleeveless woven silk shell of an almost olive hue to enhance her lovely eyes. He knew a little something about women's clothing, and recognized the fabric of her ivory slacks as good quality, draping her admirable curves in a way that had him watching from the corner of his eye and imagining what she wore under them.

He loved her scrap of shoe that barely caressed the top of her foot, exposing perfect toes with clear polish. She crossed her legs and bounced the sandal up and down, swinging the dangling heel and exposing shapely ankles. He wondered if she knew he was watching.

"Brigitte, take notes," he told his assistant in the front seat. "Now, Ms. Amy, who is most likely to know the location of the old pattern cards?"

"Evan," she muttered in response to his question.

"Evan?" he asked, encouraging her.

"My ex. It used to be his job to know the plant inside and out." Her sandal bobbed faster. "He never mentioned any historic patterns."

"Add his name to the list," he ordered Brigitte. "It won't hurt to call him and ask." He had second thoughts about that and consulted Amy. "Will it?"

She shook her head. "It will make him feel important to be consulted, and he'll brush you off if he doesn't know the answer. We might have better luck getting an answer from his last secretary. Emily's parents and grandparents all worked the mill at different times."

"Excellent. Secretaries know everything. Designers? Did you have a design department?"

He watched in delight as she bobbed her sandal and tugged her sweater, unknowingly giving him a better view of the curve of her breasts swelling above the draped shawl neckline.

Then his gaze drifted back to her vulnerable eyes. He was supposed to be immune to eyes that revealed much more than she would like. Lust was easier. He dragged his observations back to the safer territory of luscious curves.

"No," she answered curtly. "I suggested colors and yarns. Evan located the patterns from his contacts in the industry. They had jacquard equipment, but mostly, our designs came down to colors and materials."

"And you chose those?" he said in delight. "Like the ones in the café? You have an excellent eye."

"For expensive yarns and fibers," she said wryly. "I'm the reason they overextended."

"Nonsense." He brushed aside the suggestion. "With the labor costs here, a wealthy market was your only option. Management did not manage cash flow correctly."

She looked at him with curiosity. "You know mill management?"

Jacques shrugged. "I know money. I know textile markets. And I know history."

"Saint-Etienne Fabrications is the finest historical reconstruction firm in Europe," Brigitte said without inflection. "They reproduce historical fabrics and wall coverings for museums and palaces."

"I am just the whiz kid," Jacques said deprecatingly. "I find the appropriate historical designs and create the programs to replicate them. A little knowledge goes a long way."

"Virginia Adams is his mother," Brigitte added, as if that explained all.

Apparently, it did. Jacques almost squirmed under Amy's astonished regard. He didn't want to be known for his damned *mother*. She had no part in his company. His family had a civilized relationship. His mother traveled the world hawking her art and her knowledge. His father traveled collecting art and knowledge. Jacques had spent his growing-up years in boarding schools. It worked out well as long as none of them required any emotional commitment.

"Virginia Adams, the art historian who helped restorations from the White House to Buckingham Palace?" she whispered. "*That* Virginia Adams? Her knowledge of British and American art and design are *famous*."

"Infamous, more like." It was his turn to mutter.

"Infamous? She's highly respected," Amy argued, finally stopping her nervous bouncing and turning to look at him fully.

"It is nothing." Jacques waved off the subject. "Let us go back to our list."

"His father, her husband, is an international art collector and historian. The two cannot live in the same country without starting a small war," Brigitte said matter-of-factly.

"Whatever could they fight over?" Amy was now talking to Brigitte and ignoring him. "I would think they'd have a lot in common."

"They disagree on the color red," Brigitte said with a shrug. "One is French, the other British-American, each with their own prejudices."

"It is a match made in hell," Jacques finished curtly as the Hummer stopped in front of the café. "And now we have wasted our meeting on old news. Let us try to be more productive over lunch."

"It's two in the afternoon," Amy protested. "I have to pick Josh up at school. I'll make a list of employees who might help and give you a call later."

"Nonsense." He waved his hand dismissively. "Brigitte, you will get out here. You and Pascal can reserve us a table. Luigi will take us to the school. Give him the directions." He sat back and crossed his arms expectantly.

Amy studied him through narrowed eyes, but he had her number. She had little practice in defying direct orders.

"Reservations are hardly necessary," she said quietly.

"It's well past the lunch hour. There is no reason for Brigitte to get out."

Jacques grinned. "There is if she knows what's good for her."

And Brigitte did. He hired only bright assistants. She was already out of the obnoxious tank of a car Luigi had insisted on renting.

"Now, where is this school? Josh? Is he your little boy? He will like a ride in this car, no?"

Amy rewarded him with a suspicious glance—obviously she was very bright—gave the directions to the elementary school, and returned to nervously slapping her sandal up and down. "Yes, of course. He's a first grader. Listen, I've already had lunch, and the café closes at three. We really should save this for the phone."

"The café closes? How can that be? Where will we eat?"

"In Asheville, I assume, since you don't like red meat or iceberg lettuce. That's about all the steak house down the road serves. The Stardust only serves dinner on weekends, and now that the tourist season is over, we may quit doing that."

Amy watched as he mulled that over. Despite his nonchalance, Jacques was obviously a man who took control and kept it. It should be interesting to see how he dealt with this minor hitch in his plans. She was beginning to understand that, despite his tailored elegance, he wasn't the kind of man who would walk away from an obstacle, as she'd expected.

It was hard to ignore the sense of anticipation that seemed to crackle in the air when he was around. If she'd let herself think about it at all, she'd know it was because his flamboyant charm covered a deep pool and not shallow waters, and she wanted to see what he did next.

His slacks outlined the brace on his knee, but the man exuded male energy that negated any minor handicap. Amy wore heels so she didn't feel short next to everyone else, but sitting down, he still towered over her. She wouldn't call herself fragile, but she'd seen the strength of Jacques's upper arms when he wielded the crutches. This was not a man she'd want to tangle with physically or intellectually.

His mother was Virginia *Adams*. Amy couldn't decide whether to weep or knock her head against a wall. A man with those kind of high-powered connections would not want to run their tiny little country mill. He moved on a scale so far beyond that of her world that she could scarcely imagine it. His smiles were meaningless. He was simply using her to get whatever it was he wanted, and that seemed to be the pattern cards.

Sinking deeper into the leather seat and glaring out the window, Amy decided that when her ship came in, she'd hire a therapist to find out why the only men who interested her were men who wanted to use her.

"You are open for breakfast and lunch, no?" he asked, tapping his fingers against his knee and studying the more immediate problem of food.

"We are open for breakfast and lunch, yes," she agreed, trying to be polite, as one would, to a guest, but fearing the sarcasm bled through. Or her fear. "But the lunch menu is hamburgers and not sun-dried-tomato panini. This is a blue-collar town where people work hard and eat large. French fries are as close to European dining as you'll get."

She felt him turn that sizzling blue-black gaze on her

and wished the driver would turn up the air-conditioning before she roasted beneath the blaze of Jacques's regard.

"You can prepare tomato panini?" he inquired.

Assertive, she told herself. Be assertive. "It requires equipment the restaurant does not own." Well, that wasn't exactly assertive, but it was better than admitting that she could prepare them, yes.

"Ah, if that is all . . ." He snapped open his cell phone, pushed a few numbers, and as the Hummer skirted the line of parents waiting to pick up their children at the elementary school, he began a rapid spate of French to his assistant.

Amy was ready to crawl under the front seat as people stared at the flat-topped monstrosity bypassing the line.

While Jacques talked, Amy leaned forward to talk to the driver. "You'll block the school buses," she explained quietly. "Pull around back where the teachers park. I can go in and find Josh."

Instead, the driver halted the Hummer directly in front of the school, next to the line of buses and cars, climbed out, and held open the door for her.

Amy thought she would shrivel up and die of embarrassment as she took his hand and climbed down. As Evan's wife, she'd been one of the wealthiest women in town, but she had never, ever flaunted the fact. She'd grown up here. These people had known her as a snot-nosed kid. Pretension would only get her snubbed at church on Sunday.

Chin high, she marched up the walk as if she arrived in a chauffeured Hummer every day. One day out of a lifetime was no big deal.

Josh ran out to meet her, and with relief Amy kneeled

down to hug his sturdy little body. She didn't mind if he got chocolate stains on her silk shell—it was washable, and she reveled in the nondemanding love and acceptance of his hug. She blew a raspberry on the back of his neck just for the reassuring familiarity of his giggle.

Holding his hand, she hurried back to the drive, praying a dozen buses weren't blowing their horns in fury.

The Hummer wasn't there.

She almost had a panic attack until she realized Luigi had merely circled the drive and was pulling back around again. She was used to being abandoned. She wasn't used to intelligent drivers.

Luigi parked, and Amy hurriedly opened the latch before he could get out and perform the whole door-opening ceremony again. Josh was wide-eyed and openmouthed as she lifted him into the back and scrambled up after him. She buckled him into the middle seat and slammed the door after her, under Luigi's disapproving gaze.

Off the cell phone now, Jacques held out his hand. "Good to meet you, Master Josh. Did you have an entertaining day at school?"

So eager for male attention that he would have spilled his guts to any hobo wandering through town, Josh bounced excitedly and began reciting his day in detail, punctuated with a barrage of questions about the masculine vehicle they were riding in.

Amy gave up any hope of fighting her competition when—instead of impatiently brushing off Josh's questions—Jacques answered them all in a manner a small boy could comprehend. She wondered if he knew pain shadowed his eyes when he looked at Josh. It could be his knee, of course, but somehow, she didn't think so.

If she didn't drive the man out of town soon, she could learn to adore him just for taking time to listen to her children. Obviously, Josh wasn't the only one starved for male attention.

❧ SEVEN ❧

Jacques thought he deserved an Academy Award by the time Luigi pulled up in front of the café. He'd done a superior job of keeping up an amusing conversation with the towheaded charmer while a knifing pain of regret minced his gut into pâté. He'd thought he'd gone beyond grief years ago, but the interaction with the child was too close and personal without a shield of activity and people to protect him.

He could have had a son of his own by now. He hoped any son of his would have been as bright and eager as this child, with his mother's shy smile and inquisitive mind. Danielle had been a mama's girl, loving frilly dresses and shiny shoes, and he'd worshipped her, but he'd never had a son to wrestle about the floor and romp in the grass with. And now he was too set in his ways—and too busy—for wrestling and romping.

An auto accident on a snow-laden highway had stolen that dream ten years ago, and it was too late to regret his decision not to pursue another. He couldn't let a child's smile and a woman's winsome nature make him question his choices or distract him from his goals—not for more than a day or two, anyway.

You can't lose what you don't have, he reminded himself. He'd lost quite enough for one lifetime and doubted he'd survive losing more. He'd learned to endure physical pain as an athlete. He'd just have to learn to endure a little emotional discomfort for as long as it took to get those designs.

Under the interested stares of an audience of locals, Jacques swung his crutches into the café. He glanced at his Rolex. It was two-thirty on a Monday afternoon. Shouldn't the place be nearly empty if it closed at three?

"Hey, Hoss, what are you doing here?" Amy asked, confirming Jacques's suspicion that the number of customers at this hour was unusual.

While Amy helped Josh onto a counter stool, Jacques took a seat at the booth occupied by Pascal and Brigitte. Both were sipping espressos and pushing french fries around their plates with distaste.

"You found a grill for the panini?" he asked Brigitte.

"I will have to order it," Brigitte said. "I could not locate a local shop."

"Bed, Bath and Beyond in Asheville," Amy suggested, returning to their table. "But if you're staying in Asheville, you don't need a grill. I'm sure the resort can fix panini if you ask."

Jacques gestured for her to sit across from him, next to Brigitte. She hesitated, but he would not speak until she finally surrendered and joined them. It was obvious Amy did not quite grasp the intensity of his determination once he'd made up his mind, but she would.

"I am staying here in Northfork," he enunciated carefully, looking straight at her. "I need to spend more time at the mill and speak with these people whose names you will give me."

He smiled hopefully to get his point across, while erasing her concerns. An interesting blush stained her cheeks, and she tightened her lips and looked away rather than flirt with him. It was a challenge wooing a woman who didn't wish to be won.

Did he wish to woo her? He would be here only briefly, but he had a feeling they could warm the cockles of each other's hearts very nicely, and still part friends.

She had recently come out of a broken marriage. Perhaps temporary was exactly what she wanted.

"Hey, Amy, you gonna introduce us to your friends?" The man she'd called Hoss earlier propped a possessive hand on the back of the booth behind her. Tall, forty-something, muscular and stocky, with gray in his close-clipped beard, the stranger eyed Jacques as if he were another species besides human.

Not wishing to drag out the crutches to stand, Jacques merely extended his hand. "Jacques Saint-Etienne. My assistant, Brigitte. My adviser, Pascal. How do you do?"

Hoss gripped his hand and squeezed. Jacques squeezed harder.

He didn't have the pleasure of seeing the other man wince. Interestingly, Amy tugged Hoss's work shirt to force him to release his grip in an apparent attempt to protect her guest. Jacques grinned at the idea of his needing a woman's protection.

"Cut it out, Hoss. Jacques is here about the mill. Hoss owns the white-water rafting company on the river."

"Jack, is it?" Hoss asked. "I thought *you* was buying the mill, Amy."

"You know perfectly well that the town is trying to buy the mill, so quit your country-bumpkin act. Everyone profits if the plant is returned to production, no matter who buys it. Now play nice," she scolded mildly.

She wanted the town to acquire the mill. That explained a great deal. Jacques suffered a twinge of guilt at her words. He wasn't in the business of operating mills and had no intention of putting the outdated plant into production. The logistics were far more than his small company could manage. He could not see how it mattered to a woman like Amy, who had family all around her and no need of a filthy mill.

"Hey, Hoss, you got the turkey shoot lined up yet?" a blue-jeaned farmer-type called from the counter.

Hoss turned toward the speaker. "Ain't got enough entries yet to make it worth my time, Jimbo."

"Now that Jo isn't the prize, you're not offering anything worth ours," George Bob, the man introduced as the local insurance agent, complained.

The young waitress arrived with glasses of water—with lemon slices, Jacques noticed with approval. "Can I bring you anything?"

"Heat up some of the soup I have in the freezer," Amy told her before Jacques could say a word. "There are some seven-grain rolls left in the bread drawer, and chicken salad in the blue container on the second shelf. I'll be there in a minute to help, and I'll clean up so you can leave on time."

The waitress looked relieved and rushed away. With increased interest at this bossy side of the lady, Jacques raised a questioning eyebrow.

Amy pushed up from the booth and shrugged. "It's that, or french fries. At least the minestrone is vegetarian. Back in a minute."

Across from him, Brigitte snickered into her espresso.

"When in Rome," Pascal quoted back at him, "you take orders from Romans."

Not only had the woman chosen his meal, she'd

walked off and left him! Obstinate. And bossy. Intriguing. Jacques surreptitiously watched Amy behind the counter. There was something ultimately sexy about a woman preparing a nurturing meal.

"Laugh, if you will," he said gallantly, "but see, she is taking care of the boy, and her hired help, and us, all at once." He nodded toward the counter, where Amy was kissing her son's head and handing him a plate of peeled fruit, while helping the young waitress prepare a plate for their late customers. "She is kind even to strangers who are her adversaries."

He'd not intended to get involved when he'd come here. He had just been looking for new mountains to climb. It looked as if he'd found more challenge than he'd anticipated.

"Hey, Ames, reckon Flint would want to join the turkey shoot if he's in this weekend?" Hoss had returned to the counter when Amy did, as if he were standing guard over her.

Jacques narrowed his eyes and considered the beefy older man following her around. Surely this was not his competition?

"Ever shot a turkey?" Pascal murmured, following his thoughts.

"There are some turkeys I would not mind shooting," Jacques replied noncommittally, sipping his water.

"Flint might if the boys are allowed to enter," Amy replied while arranging the chicken salad on a bed of lettuce. "You'd snare him even faster if you let Jo shoot."

Male laughter erupted throughout the café. A lifetime of competition had enhanced Jacques's ability to size up the opposition. He observed the byplay with interest.

"Girls can't shoot!" Jimbo protested from the counter. "It takes a man to handle a shotgun."

"Maybe we could set up some targets for the kids and women and their little popguns," some other wit in a John Deere cap suggested.

Target shooting was for women and children? Jacques heard Pascal snort derisively, but he held his tongue. This wasn't their world. He was just an observer. For now.

He smiled with pleasure as Amy returned to the table with an overflowing tray of deliciously arranged food.

"It's not much," she apologized, distributing the plates. "The minestrone is made with vegetable stock, but if you're not vegetarian, you might try the chicken salad on the rolls. I think you'll like it."

She looked more delectable than the food with her cheeks pink and her eyes shining, and the shimmery thickness of her hair brushing the delicate curve of her nape. He knew she was as aware of him as he was of her.

"This is extremely generous of you," he said with genuine delight, hoping to distract her from her nervousness. He couldn't remember the last time anyone had prepared food with their own hands just for him, and now she'd done it twice. "We certainly didn't mean to make you work on your day off."

He shot a severe look to Brigitte, who immediately removed her Gallic nose from the air and murmured her gratitude. Pascal expressed his thanks in French, to which Amy responded in a halting high-school accent, before she retreated to the counter.

"Hey, Amy, I betcha if both you and Jo would offer kisses as prizes, we could get more entries!" Hoss called, still in pursuit of his own agenda.

"You want Flint to aim for your head?" Amy shooed

the young waitress toward the door and began loading the dishwasher. "It's three o'clock, you clowns. You don't have to entertain the company any longer." Although Amy had to admit that she appreciated having them here to shield her from Jacques's searing gaze. She really didn't want to know what was going on behind those long lashes and knowing eyes as he observed everything around him.

"We're just looking after you, Ames," George Bob replied, rising and pulling out his wallet.

She was almost two years older than George. As much as she might welcome his presence, Amy disregarded his paternal attitude. She handed him his change.

"Reckon Amy's reputation is safe here with the girls," Jimbo drawled for everyone to hear.

Amy threw his coins in the register and attempted a glare. "Watch your mouth, Jim, or I'll have to wash it out with soap."

"He didn't say a dirty word, did he, Mommy?" Josh asked, following the adult conversation with interest.

"I took French class with your mom," Jimbo explained, sliding his billfold into his back pocket. "She knows how to say dirty words in three languages." Tugging on his cap, Jimbo waved at Jacques's table. "See y'all later, Jackie."

Amy sent Jacques an anxious glance, but he was watching with amusement. No matter what his intentions, she hated having a customer insulted. Just because Jacques dressed fancy didn't make him a wimp, but the men around here didn't understand anyone different from them. Any female with operating hormones could tell the newcomer was hot enough to scorch.

"Well, if Flint won't let Jo be the prize, how about you, Ames? It's for a good cause." Hoss leaned against the counter, not ready to leave until she threw him out.

The annual turkey shoot was a haphazard event designed to raise money for Fourth of July fireworks and Christmas decorations. Winning a kiss from Jo had been a popular contest these last few years, but Jo was a married woman now. And Amy wasn't any longer.

"What about Sally?" she argued. "Have you asked her?"

"Aw, c'mon, Amy, give us real men a chance for a change. You don't need to go lookin' for furriners. We'll raise enough to buy a new star for the tree if you'll say yes."

She hadn't thought Hoss looked at any woman except Jo. A blush crept up her neck even though she knew he was all bluster and few brains. She hadn't kissed any man except Evan in ten years.

"When is this event?" Jacques asked in a quiet manner that still made him heard above the ringing register.

Hoss turned. "This weekend, if Amy will agree. Why, you interested in rifle shooting?"

Turkey shoots were all about heavy shotguns and manly men. Hoss had asked about the ladies' rifle competition with a smirk that said he'd set this up intentionally.

Before she could intervene in a contest of twisted machismo, Jacques tugged his ear and smiled that boyish smile that made her knees melt and sent warning signals singing through her blood. Why the devil did he have that effect on her?

"I'll even sponsor an event, if you like," Jacques suggested. "Do you know skeet shooting?"

"Skeet? Ain't no critters called skeet around here." Hoss crossed his arms, leaned his hip against the counter, and regarded the table of strangers as if this were a spaghetti western, and he were Clint Eastwood.

Amy smacked him against the back of his head with a plasticized menu. "They shoot skeet all the time. Don't let the local yokel fool you."

Hoss belatedly dodged her blow and shot her a mournful look. "Aw, Ames, you're gonna take all the fun out of it. Jackie here's gonna think we're easy marks."

"Can I shoot skeet, too?" Josh asked eagerly.

"If your mother agrees, Master Josh. I will sponsor an event for children, as well. Ms. Amy, would you be so good as to tell me the appropriate prize for children?"

"What event you gonna enter?" Hoss demanded, pushing his luck.

"Any event in which Ms. Amy is the prize, of course." Jacques held out his hand to Pascal, and a money clip stuffed with green appeared in his palm. "What is the entry fee?"

Amy thought she might just sink through the floor. She had no desire at all to be the *prize* in this masculine tug-of-war. She had no idea why a man like Jacques would allow himself to be drawn into Hoss's little joke, but she had to end this *now*.

"Jacques, you don't have to do this. Hoss got his name because he's always horsing around." And because he could be a horse's ass, she should have added. He just wanted to best the rich stranger in a sport he excelled at—and suck as much money from him as he could.

Jacques winked at her admonition, making it clear that she was the reason he was doing this. "I assure you, Amy, this will be my pleasure."

Amy contemplated what might be under the café floor

if she sank through it. Spiders, mice, cobwebs, all would be more acceptable than this insane contest. Were they really betting on a kiss from her? Her, Amy Warren, Miss Invisible USA? What the *hell* did they hope to gain from this?

But as Jacques laid his money on the table and Hoss scooped it up, Amy couldn't prevent her neglected hormones from boiling over at the thought of Macho Man claiming his *prize*. Just watching Jacques's confident laughter had her way past overstimulated without imagining kissing him. She was *so* not going there.

The café phone rang, distracting her from that embarrassing leap of imagination. Relieved to be removed from the action, she grabbed the receiver as the rest of her customers, except for Playboy and Company, filed out.

"Stardust, Amy here," she said curtly.

"Amy, they accepted the counter offer!" her real estate agent crowed. "You've sold your house."

Shocked, Amy grabbed the stove to keep her knees from crumbling out from under her. *She'd sold her house?*

It was real, then. Instead of cheering, panic grabbed her. They had nowhere to go.

She scarcely heard the agent's litany of explanations of what would happen next while her mind leaped like a frog from one terror to the next. She couldn't find a new home without knowing if she had a job.

If the town lost the mill bid . . . Her gaze widened in horror as the agent rattled on, and Amy watched the man who threatened her future complacently plot with his partners across the room.

By the time she hung up the phone, Jacques was looking at her with lifted eyebrow, and his staff had hurriedly finished their meal and departed. She didn't even feel guilty for deserting her hostess duties and driving them away.

She needed to write up his bill and get him out of here so she could think, even if what she really wanted to do was reach across the counter and shake him until he spilled his plans for the town's future. Her hand trembled as she scribbled on the café's green order form and tried not to look at him again.

"Is everything all right?" Jacques asked, setting down his cup and reaching for his wallet.

No, everything wasn't all right, especially when the sympathy in his voice made her want to fall into his arms and weep. Better for all concerned that she saw him as the fly in her ointment, the bad guy she was supposed to chase out of town as quickly as she could say "vintage patterns." She summoned her courage and slapped the meal ticket on the table. "Just exactly what are your intentions?" she demanded, unable to phrase her desperation more precisely.

Jacques's look of mischief warned that not only had she garbled the question, but he hadn't taken it seriously.

"Purely dishonorable, I assure you," he replied, rising from the booth—putting him entirely too close to her flushed embarrassment. If he touched her, she'd probably faint.

The villain practically exuded *sexy*. And the heated look he bestowed on her left no possibility of mistaking his meaning, which flustered her even more. She was a mother. She didn't do dishonorable.

Shaken in too many ways to comprehend, Amy let her anxiety run away from her common sense. "I mean about the mill." She backed up a step, but didn't retreat entirely, determined to have facts to base her decision on.

"The town is bidding on the mill to put families back to work. If you win the bid, will you find the patterns and abandon us?"

How pitiful was that? Amy bit her tongue to keep from spilling her guts and her tears. She tried to look away, but she couldn't. She needed the answer too much.

Jacques's grin disappeared. He removed a large bill from his wallet and laid it on the counter. "I never make promises. We shall just see what happens next, shall we?"

If there was concern or regret in his reply, she refused to acknowledge it. Nor did she acknowledge his hesitation as he continued to watch her, waiting for . . . what? Acceptance? Anger? She shook her head, saying nothing.

He walked out without waiting for change, leaving her hot and bothered and wondering if she was her own worst enemy.

With her stomach sinking to her aching feet, Amy almost wished he'd lied, so she could despise him for being the same calculating fraud as Evan.

But he hadn't lied. He wasn't Evan, and she couldn't despise him for stating the cold, hard facts, just as she'd asked him to do. This was purely business to him.

If only she could let her heart freeze over in anger.

But she'd never learned to hate, and she couldn't start now. Not with the first man who'd caught her interest in a dozen years—even if he had the power to destroy her and her home in the name of all-mighty business.

❧ EIGHT ❧

"I've sold our house," Amy repeated in shock, staring at the walls of her bedroom at seven that evening.

The electric clock next to her bed began to buzz . . . alarmingly. With an absentminded smack, she turned it off. Her gaze drifted to the family photos centered on the wall over the antique walnut dresser. From there, it fell on her grandmother's hand-stitched quilt draped over a century-old stand Amy had lovingly restored. She'd had a designer create the draperies on the big bay window to match the beautiful old roses in the quilt. The draperies were attached to the house, the Realtor had said. She couldn't take them with her.

She started to shake as the reality sank in. She might have despised this bland house when Evan bought it, but she'd made it into a *home* designed with love especially for her family. And now strangers would inhabit it.

Her agent had said the buyers had cash and wanted to close early. She'd made homelessness sound like a *good* thing.

Fighting tears, Amy focused on the big painting of Josh as a toddler that centered her photo display. How did she go about packing paintings?

How on earth would she rip out her roots and transplant her entire life?

Better yet, where would she transplant them?

Feeling as if her entire world were rocking precariously, Amy drew a deep breath and put her foot down. She refused to sit here and weep over what was done. She'd sold her home. She could start moving things to Jo's old apartment over the café. But she'd be damned if she'd live in that cramped space for long.

She needed a positive goal to work toward. She needed a home.

Wiping her eyes and biting her trembling lip, she marched down the hall to the kids' bedrooms—rooms she'd decorated specifically to their interests. She could do it again—eventually—if she had a home. The judge hadn't accepted her offer on the cottage yet, but now that she had the money, she would fight tooth and nail for it.

"Want to go look at a house?" she asked, lifting Louisa rather than putting on her shoes, shooing Josh toward the stairs.

"What house, Mommy?" he sensibly inquired.

"Our house," she informed him. "Our new house, right down in town where you can walk home from school when you're a big kid."

He looked at her as if she were crazed. "We already have a house, Mommy."

No, they didn't. It would belong to someone else in another month. *Don't look back.* "Remember how I told you that this house is way too big and we're moving somewhere nearer to your aunt Jo?"

"Oh, yeah. And Johnnie and Adam can come play with me!"

Burying her face in Louisa's golden hair, Amy swallowed a sob at her child's easy acceptance of such an earthshaking move, and determinedly marched down to the car. She would never let her children see her heart-break. They were going to love their new home. The cottage had a million times more character and more kid-friendly space than this boring old monument to Evan's ego. It would be perfect for them when she got it fixed up, much closer to their aunt and grandmother.

If she could buy it. If she could get a job. If the mill opened again.

An entire nightmare of childhood insecurities stalked her.

"Man, that is the best lookin' thing that ever happened to this town," Jo said admiringly, watching the entertainment around the Hummer the Saturday afternoon of the turkey shoot.

Settling Josh and Louisa on the blanket with their popcorn, Amy tried not to watch. Jacques had come into the café for breakfast and lunch every day this past week, bringing with him whoever had tagged along to search for the pattern cards or write up his bid. Despite his best efforts to sweet-talk her, she'd avoided being sucked into his world as much as possible.

Her mangled ego longed to lap up his flattery, bask in his smoldering looks, and succumb to his seductive voice. When was the last time Evan had ever said anything complimentary? How about half past never? When had any man actually *looked* at her, seen her as she was, and smiled in delight? Jacques did all that and more, and it was getting harder not to notice on a visceral level.

Staying up to midnight every night packing all her belongings made her too weary—physically and emotionally—to manage more than a thin layer of detachment in his presence.

"I mean, Flint is a hunk, but that there is pure eye candy."

Amy didn't have to look to know whom Jo was talking about. And from the wolf whistles of the testosterone-pumped crowd, she could tell Jacques had brought Catarina and friends.

"If you've brought your camera, you can take pictures. Pictures will be all that's left of the eye candy by next week," Amy said dismissively, plumping up a cushion for her mother's lawn chair. "He's had Emily and everyone else digging through the mill vaults all week looking for those design patterns. At least he's paying them well. He only has until Tuesday to submit a bid, and I assume if he doesn't find what he wants, we'll never see him again."

That was what she wanted, wasn't it? Rush the boy out of town and let her life return to normal. Or what passed for normal these days. Yet the idea of Jacques leaving was shockingly distressing.

"Shame, that," Jo concurred with Amy's reflection. "This town could use a little elegant decoration. Don't suppose that lioness draped over his shoulder can shoot, do you? I'd like to take her on in a contest."

"If she's wearing Pradas and a thigh-high skirt, it would be amusing to watch her try." Amy couldn't resist. Now that the kids were occupied and her mother was gossiping with her cronies, she had no choice but to watch the entertainment. She had to look at it that way, and not with the pang in her insides at the sight of Catarina draped over Jacques like a Roman toga.

The instant she looked in his direction, Jacques waved for her to join him. He was sitting in a *director's* chair, of all things. Luigi was setting up a half-circle of them around a picnic basket the size of a small kitchen. At Jacques's right hand was an open stainless-steel cooler filled with what appeared to be champagne bottles. He must think they were at a steeplechase.

Every other family here had arrived in beat-up pickups and minivans packed with ratty blankets and plastic coolers filled with beer. She'd spent a lifetime blending in. He merrily flaunted his differences, and pulled it off with sex appeal to spare. She envied his confidence.

"Go join them, Ames. Persuade them to spend a couple of million bucks here. I'm happy to watch the kids. Grab your place in the sun while you can." Jo put a hand to Amy's back and gave her a shove. "Besides, it will juice up the competition and bring more entries if the home-boys get to feelin' competitive."

"Oh, right, I so crave a mangy dogfight." But judging from the overflowing parking lot, Jacques had stirred up real interest in this shoot, which had languished with the local economy. She'd grant him that.

She didn't know whether to be flattered or ticked when the lioness snarled unpleasantly at Amy's approach, then repositioned to the far side of the circle. Jacques's gaze didn't waver.

Walking toward him under that appreciative stare, she felt heat begin to form at the tip of her toes and work its way up to her head. His heavy-lidded gaze even had her noticing the way her hips swung as she walked on the un-even ground. She'd not worn anything fancy, just her khaki walking shorts and wedge-heeled sandals. Instead of her usual vanilla shirt, she'd pulled a rose sleeveless one out of the back of the closet and recklessly tied the tails, but Jacques's stare had her exposed midriff blush-ing as heatedly as her cheeks.

His brows rose and a slow smile curved his lips as his gaze caught on the swingy hoops in her ears that Jo had persuaded her to wear. Now, Amy felt like kicking herself for indulging in feminine vanity—she'd *wanted* his gaze to linger just like that, she realized.

"Ms. Amy!" Jacques called, rising from his seat. "We have saved you a chair so you may explain this amusement to us. Where are the turkeys?"

How many men these days actually stood up in a woman's presence? She couldn't resist relaxing under his genuine enthusiasm. In this sea of denim and logo-branded T-shirts, Jacques looked amazingly British and suave in his tweed sports jacket and designer ribbed-knit shirt. She hoped he wouldn't be too offended at Hoss's little game.

"Where are your crutches?" she asked, taking the chair beside him that he held for her.

"They are no good on this terrain." He gestured dismissively, returning to his seat. "I only need good eyes for this contest. I am in fine form," he added with the barest edge to his voice, as if he'd had to say it more than once today.

"Yes, I can see that," she said drily as he handed her champagne in a glass that appeared to be Baccarat crystal. This felt way too personal, too much like flirting. She'd watched Jacques's active mind dart from subject to subject all week, but when his attention was on her, she knew it with every female cell in her body.

She concentrated on steadying her foolishly racing pulse by reverting to her role as mother. She turned to Luigi and gestured at Jacques's leg. "He needs to elevate that knee. Do you have another chair?"

Luigi smiled triumphantly and snapped open a folding

stool, waiting for Jacques to lift his leg so he could position it.

Jacques glared at her from beneath heart-stopping dark lashes. "I will get even for this, Ms. Amy. He has been pestering me all day to do this."

"Then Luigi has more sense than you." She sipped the champagne to quell the tiny fires ignited by his smoky gaze and her wretched imagination. Cool and delicious, the wine tasted marvelously decadent. She could blame the pleasure bubbling through her on the champagne.

For just one moment, she let herself relax and take in the gorgeous September day. The heat and humidity of summer had disappeared almost overnight. The sky was a sparkling blue, pines scented the air, and goldenrod had just begun to bloom along the edge of the field. She caught a glimpse of her sister tussling with Josh and Louisa, and contentment washed over her. Whatever else happened, she still had family.

"You are so very beautiful when you look like that," he whispered almost wistfully. "Your love for your children glows in your eyes."

Embarrassed, she tugged at her shirttails. She knew rose looked good on her, but she hadn't dressed for success today. Jo was the tall and slender model type in the family, not her.

"Love is my reward for looking like a teapot, I guess," she admitted.

"A teapot?" he asked in startlement, then burst out laughing. "Porcelain angel, maybe, or a Lalique madonna, but *teapot?*"

Maybe it was the champagne. Maybe it was the sunny day, or this brief escape from the heartbreaking task of packing up her cherished belongings and deciding which to give away. But Jacques's blatant flattery soothed raw wounds like a healing balm. She'd been such a dunce to let Evan's indifference dictate how she felt about her appearance.

She hadn't flirted in ages, but Amy smiled and unwound under his silliness. "A Lalique, hmm? One of the crystal clear ones you can see right through? Or the mysterious opaque ones?"

"A mix," he said decisively. "A madonna with child, all sparkly and mysterious. Now, down to business. If I am to win your kiss, I must understand the rules of the game. Where are the turkeys? I do not have to walk through the woods and find them, I take it?"

He'd come prepared to walk through the woods on torn ligaments to win her kiss? He was pure male nuts. And she shivered a little at the possibility that Jacques could mean anything by the sweet talk. Considering their competition over the mill and his inevitable departure, she'd better keep her wits firmly about her.

She noticed Luigi and Pascal plainly waiting for her reply. Brigitte had applied suntan lotion and retired to the hood of the Hummer with a book. Catarina was sulking on the far side of the half-circle, adjusting her enormous sun hat.

"They don't shoot turkeys, unless Hoss got fancy and ordered turkey-shaped targets this year," she explained. " 'Turkey shooting' refers to the kind of gun they use—usually outlaw shotguns around here. Some turkey shoots limit the kind of weapon they use, but we're open. Everyone brings whatever they have."

"Shotguns! Ah, I see." Jacques studied the men setting up targets at the far end of the open field. "One shoots turkeys with shotguns. Excellent. At what distance, do you know?"

"We'll have several competitions, especially since you sponsored a shoot for the kids and women. But the men usually stand fifty-eight feet from trigger to target."

He looked at her with unfeigned interest. "Do you shoot?"

"I grew up here," she replied. "It's what we did for fun when I was a kid, although we used BB guns and air rifles. I haven't been to one of these in years." City-bred Evan hadn't approved of such unsophisticated rural activities.

"So your son will not compete?"

"This is his first shoot. I'll wait to see if he's interested. His father doesn't approve, and I hate to cause dissension." The story of her life—avoiding conflict.

"Target shooting is a man's sport dating back to the beginnings of weaponry. Why would he disapprove?"

She had assumed Jacques and his sophisticated friends had come here to laugh at their primitive entertainment, much as Evan and his city friends might have. She was surprised that he showed such interest. "Evan thinks hitting a ball around a golf course is a man's sport because it costs more."

Jacques laughed. "Golf was invented by poor Scots who had only sticks and stones to play with."

Amused, she sipped her champagne and enjoyed conversing with someone who could see more than one side of things. "I imagine shooting was invented by someone who was hungry and needed meat to fill a pot, so don't go all snobby on me."

"No pot-filling in Europe. Not for centuries." He

waved away her argument. "It is about equipment these days. But I see this is not so here. May I look at these out-law shotguns?"

"You've never used a shotgun?" Since he'd entered the competition, she'd assumed he had some knowledge of the sport. Well, that took care of one worry. She'd kissed Hoss before she'd left for college. She could plant a smacker on him and walk away untouched when he won.

But it was a shame . . .

"I am a connoisseur of guns." Jacques lowered his leg from the stool and pushed to a standing position with the strength of his arms. "I own a pair of Manton's finest, but they are kept in glass cases. Modern weapons can be exceedingly dangerous in comparison. Will you show me the field I am to compete on?"

Amy grabbed an ebony cane with a brass horse's head handle that was leaning against the cooler and shoved it at him as he limped across the weedy ground. "You don't have to do this. Just sit and watch. No one will think any-thing of it."

Jacques took the cane, but caught up in his new obses-sion, he ignored her suggestion. Accustomed to being ig-nored, Amy led him over to Flint and some of the judges, then left them to their man talk.

It seemed odd to watch an elegantly dressed Brit en-gaged in deep conversation with a bunch of truckers and farmers. Normally, such disparate company would not give one another the time of day, but Jacques slid right into the conversation as if he'd lived here all his life. She was just used to Evan setting himself apart from his workers with designer suits and attitude.

She had spent years believing his assurances that she needed to copy the board of directors' wives in their

Nordstrom ensembles. She'd given up gardening to keep her manicure neat and given up her weaving because Evan didn't like anything as plebian as a loom cluttering up the family room.

Where could she find another handloom? Maybe Flint and Jo could sell her handicrafts in Nashville with their mother's quilts, she thought, with a quiver of excitement. Once upon a time, she'd loved creating her own designs on her mother's loom. She adored working with fabric.

She didn't need Dr. Evil telling her she was a fool to dream. She had the freedom now to make her own life, a fun one this time.

If she could buy the mill manager's cottage—she could set up a handicrafts store in the front room in that bay window! She knew a B and B wasn't a highly profitable operation, but a small shop of her own goods . . .

She still needed a job with a salary and benefits. But this inspiration gave her hope. And determination. She would win the mill for the town and the cottage for herself, come hell or high water.

Amy returned to the kids and Jo. Hospitality had been assuaged. She'd stay with her own kind now, thank you very much. It was high time she realized who she really was—a country girl with a knack for homemaking and a determined drive to achieve her goals.

Scoping the modified twelve-gauge shotgun Flint had handed to him, Jacques still knew the moment Amy drifted away. It was as if the sunshine dimmed and the world grew a little colder without her gaze.

Not that she let him see that she watched him. Oh, no, not Ms. Amy. She hid behind modestly lowered lashes and pleasant smiles and small talk. But he knew when a woman was interested. And he was interested in return. The question was, should he pursue that interest for the short time he would be here? In these past days, he'd learned Amy was not one of the jaded females with whom he normally socialized. She could not be treated like one.

He could hope she expected no more than a moment out of a lifetime. He hoped she was ready for what little he had to offer, because his interest was hooked by her shy glances and brave words, and this shiver of excitement hadn't happened in too long a time to ignore it now.

He handed the weapon back to Flint. "It's a very large barrel for so small a target, more a contest of strength and equipment than speed and dexterity, true?"

Flint's bronzed face crinkled up in a smile. "A test of testosterone, yes."

Jacques grinned. "Don't judge a book by its cover. If there are wagers on this event, save your money."

"I'm a judge. I can't wager. But I got a feeling this is going to be more fun than the state fair. Hey, Amy packed our basket. Why don't you join us? I bet our fixin's are better than the hotel's."

"The company will make it so." Whistling, Jacques accepted Flint's invitation and sauntered back to the blanket where Amy and her sister sat, sipping from plastic glasses and watching the children wrestle in the grass.

"Lemonade?" Jo offered at his approach, holding up a plastic jug.

"Thank you, I think I will." He gestured at Amy, who was already looking for Luigi and his chair and preparing to get up to find both. "You need not wait on me." Using the cane as a brace, he swung down to the blanket beside her. He was close enough to smell the delicate scent of jasmine lotion that she wore. He leaned over and blew a wisp of silky hair from her ear. "I am not made of glass. I promise," he murmured in an insinuating tone.

To his delight, she blushed clear to her hair roots.

"Buckingham Palace?" she inquired softly, apparently to get even with him for disturbing her. "We looked you up on the computer. It's not just your mother who has worked with princes."

"Only princes can pay my prices," he said, in hopes of passing off his connections as a joke. He could tell by the fire in her eyes that he'd failed.

"You think we don't have a chance of winning that bid after the judge finds out who you are, don't you? With the investment money you can command, the town can't come close."

In this relaxed setting that had nothing to do with business, Jacques heard the pain and concern behind her anger, and understood far more than he liked.

Looking around, he could see the tiny world she knew, heard her awe at the distant planet he came from, and realized the lovely, confident woman beside him was overwhelmed. By *him*. By his world, his knowledge, his experience. That insight into her vulnerability threatened to rouse his ridiculous need to protect.

"This is no topic for a holiday," he scolded in self-defense. Generally, women did not get angry with him, and he was uncomfortable being the target of Amy's resentment.

"Do you shoot?" Jo asked, handing him a tall red glass, giving him an excuse to turn away from his irate companion.

"A little," he said modestly. "Not guns of that caliber, normally."

"Look, Mommy, Unca Flint is lining them up!" Josh dashed over to demand his share of the attention.

Jacques slid over so the boy could settle between him and Amy. Children still made him uneasy. Admittedly, *Amy* made him uneasy, but he assumed it was her open, honest nature that made him occasionally squirm with discomfort. The children touched him on so many levels of grief and yearning that he couldn't begin to sort out his emotions. He could no longer avoid children if he wished to be with Amy. He understood they were a package deal.

"Tell me which are your cousins," he said to the boy, seeking some topic that would keep him distracted.

"That's Johnnie, he's twelve," Josh said importantly, pointing out a gangly youngster with long dark hair and a skull-and-crossbones earring. "And that's Adam, he's thirteen. He's going to show me how to shoot." A slightly older youth with sharp cheekbones and chiseled jaw much like his father's sighted along the barrel of his air rifle beside his brother.

"They look like very competent young men." To hide his discomfort, Jacques took a swig of lemonade—and almost spat it out. The fiery concoction burned all the way down.

Jo hooted with laughter at his expression. Holding Louisa, she cackled and pounded the blanket trying to rein in her amusement, but she only succeeded in reducing Amy to giggles.

That, he didn't mind. Beneath her mop of loose curls, Amy looked like a mischievous little girl when she laughed, and he had to smile at her merriment at his expense. She covered her mouth to hold back her chuckles, but her eyes still danced.

"Sorry," she whispered, ever the concerned hostess. "It's Jo's latest idea of a cocktail."

"Not quite perfected yet, I assume?" he asked with as much ease as he could manage while his eyes watered and his gullet burned.

"It might be smoother if she used something besides cheap rotgut," Amy admitted, pulling a bottle of beer from the cooler. "I dilute mine."

He accepted the cold beer without comment.

The firing began after that, and all attention returned to the field. The shouts and yells of the audience and the blasts of the air rifles prevented further conversation.

Josh's little body squirmed between them, nearly upsetting his mother's drink. Watching the field with practiced eye, Jacques absentmindedly lifted the youngster onto his lap to hold him still. Leaning back against the tire of the truck behind him, his shoulder brushed Amy's.

She glanced from him to her son in surprise, but another volley of fire and rebel yells prevented any comment besides the brief flash of approval in her eyes.

He felt as if a benediction had been bestowed on him just for the simple act of holding her son. It felt so good he was almost reluctant to set the boy aside when the adult competition began.

But knowing the prize to be won, Jacques returned Josh to the blanket without compunction.

If the men of Northfork wanted a pissing contest, he wasn't so sophisticated that he couldn't beat them at their own game.

⋘ NINE ⋙

Amy watched Jacques stroll back to the Hummer and retrieve what appeared to be a shiny new twelve-gauge from the back of the vehicle. Most of the guns here were old, often inherited from fathers and grandfathers. The advantage of an old shotgun was that one knew its idiosyncrasies. New ones needed to be tried and tested.

"Ten to one, he brought an arsenal with him," Jo murmured.

"They'll have Homeland Security checking them out," Amy said with amusement, torn between following Jacques and staying here, pretending she wasn't interested.

Why should she pretend any longer? She was a free woman—about to be a homeless one. She might as well take advantage of this terrifying independence to practice her flirting.

Of course, somewhere in the back of her mind, she kept hoping she'd find a way of talking Jacques out of the mill. So she had to watch out for that fantasy world of hers.

"Watch the kids, will you?" she said to Jo. "I'm going to check out the duke and company."

Her sister laughed and waved her on.

Jacques could easily have passed for royalty in this casual crowd. Amy wondered if he even owned an ordinary cotton T-shirt or jeans. But despite his expensive attire, Jacques's easy manner and genuine interest in what was being said around him gained him ready acceptance. Catarina, in her halter dress, big hat, sunglasses, and haughty attitude, looked as out of place as a peacock among banty hens.

Amy figured she had the home-court advantage. She'd let her feminine attraction get pretty rusty lately, but she might just be ready to brush it off and test it out. Jacques's interest, his kindness to her children, and his many fascinating facets had finally pushed her out of her safe place.

Checking out his new shotgun, Jacques smiled absently at her approach, snapped the weapon closed, and immediately transferred his vibrant awareness to her by offering his arm. "My lady, would you be so kind as to give me your favor in this competition?"

"You mean, like medieval ladies gave their knights?" Deciding she could play to his charm, Amy took his arm and chuckled at the conceit. "I would have worn hair ribbons if I'd known you would ask."

"Take off the ring on your finger, and I would count that as a favor," he murmured smoothly.

Take off her wedding ring? Even in jest, she hesitated. The ring had been a part of her for a third of her life, yet it meant nothing to her anymore, right? Still, the idea of removing the symbol of ten years of her life was an even bigger step than she'd anticipated.

Frowning at her thoughts as Jacques steered her through the crowd, Amy realized after a moment that he wasn't carrying his cane. He had the shotgun on one arm and her on the other. He would cripple himself carrying manliness too far.

"Will you use your cane if I take off my ring?" she de-manded, figuring she ought to have a good reason to re-move it besides flattery.

"I need two hands to shoot, and I have you for support when I walk," he reminded her. "I do not want to kiss a woman wearing a wedding ring. It is bad luck."

"Who says you're going to win?" She hooted at his au-dacity, and he slanted her a dry look that jump-started her long-dead heart. She sent his ring finger a meaningful glance to balance herself. "Do I need to ask where you keep your ring?"

He held up his evenly tanned hand for her to inspect. "No ring. No impediment to my prize. I am free for the taking."

Amy had to laugh at that. "Free spirit, maybe, but there is nothing else free about you."

"And you?" He raised his eyebrows and nodded at her hand again.

His teasing attention fired way too many previously dormant hormones. Images of kissing this man who hid his toughness behind a coat of charm stirred them into a frenzy.

Not that she believed Jacques would be kissing her any-time soon. Hoss was a regional champion, after all.

Amy twisted the ring until it popped off. He was right. She shouldn't be offering kisses to *anyone* as a prize while wearing it.

Her finger felt strangely bereft. She looked for a place to put the plain gold band, but she'd left her purse back at the car.

With satisfaction, Jacques took the ring and slid it into the deep pockets of his tailored trousers. "I will return your boon after the contest. You have granted my fondest wish."

"And you will be fortunate if you can lift that gun much less aim it," she scoffed. "Hoss is a champion turkey shooter. You still have time to cry off."

"What? And forfeit the prize?" he said with a glorified posh accent and a mock bow.

Amy observed the predatory set of his square jaw, and understood he was deliberately steering her toward a goal all his own. She had wonder who the real man was behind the gallant exterior.

Once they reached the shooting line, his focus diverted entirely to the competition lining up at the targets. Some of the contestants were wearing camouflage and lying on the ground to sight their targets. Jacques had not come attired for rolling in the dirt. Some squatted or kneeled. Jacques could do neither with his bad knee. A few men, apparently handicapped by attire or arthritis or disposition, stood upright.

Two conflicting and equally strong emotions clawed at Amy's insides as she realized the deadly earnestness of this contest.

One was pure feminine excitement at being the object of Jacques's interest—enhanced by curiosity at how it might feel to be kissed by a man with muscles of steel.

The other was complete dismay at knowing a man of this determination could very likely rip the mill and her dreams to pieces.

Confused, she remained frozen where she was when Jacques released her arm to check in his gun with the judges. Flint winked at her as he examined the new shotgun. Hoss grinned and raised his gun in a gesture of confidence. Amy's mind was racing too fast to respond.

From this angle, she could see the stubborn jut of Jacques's jaw, the sharp ridge of his cheekbones, the shadowy hint of beard stubble. Despite torn ligaments and a knee brace, he stood solidly in a professional stance best suited to bearing the brunt of the gun's recoil. He'd discarded his jacket, and the short-sleeved polo shirt revealed carved biceps that could only have been developed by serious weight training. Amy gulped and tried to ignore the flames of interest licking at her neglected sex.

The first three rounds were test rounds. She winced at the loudness of the barrage, then strained to see the results. The judges didn't announce test-round winners, but it looked to her as if all Jacques's slugs had missed the center—but they'd hit the target in a pattern, one concentric ring at a time.

That could have been coincidence—or his deliberate attempt to find the gun's spray pattern by shifting precisely with each round fired. That was not the performance of an amateur.

She watched him joking with the other men, submitting to their friendly slaps and punches, but beneath Jacques's gregarious façade, she thought she noticed something she'd failed to treat seriously before—single-minded resolve for anything he did.

That ought to *really* scare the heck out of her.

She glanced behind her to Luigi and Pascal standing with arms crossed. They looked smug despite the whispers and wagers prevailing around them.

A shiver of anticipation warned that this contest was a setup, not by Hoss, but by Jacques.

Now she was scared to the point that her heart thumped against her rib cage and her palms were sweating.

A goldenrod brushed her leg when she backed toward the trees at the edge of the clearing. If she was smart, she'd turn and run right now.

Instead of running, she listened to the judge call the first round. Lump in throat, she followed Jacques's movements as he raised the shotgun with a practiced swing, fired without flinching at the powerful recoil, and lowered his weapon to study his shot.

The slug pattern was dead center.

The audience roared. It was impossible to tell whom they were cheering, since there were twenty contestants all shooting at once. Amy watched only Jacques.

The judges walked down the row of targets and eliminated the lowest scores. The remaining contestants reloaded and joked quietly among themselves. Hoss and Jacques were at opposite ends of the line.

The second round was called. Amy tore off the goldenrod and began to shred it between her fingers. The ten remaining contestants positioned their guns, some with cocky arrogance, some with nervousness. Jacques showed only professional detachment. He fired both rounds—and wiped out the paper target's bull's-eye.

The audience erupted in good-natured catcalls and rebel yells at the announcement of the three finalists. It was hard to resist a newcomer doing so well. The two men Jacques was matched against were big and burly and accustomed to winning all physical contests. Jacques in his lean elegance rested his shotgun over his shoulder and whistled without concern as the judges consulted. Noticing Amy's gaze, he raked a recalcitrant hank of hair off his forehead and winked.

While the targets were replaced, Flint stepped back to stand beside her. "He's a pro," he said quietly. "He's got a steady arm and the eye of an eagle, and I'd bet my bottom dollar he knows sharpshooting. You comfortable with Hoss losing? We can announce the turkey as a prize. Just say the word."

The town always offered a frozen turkey as an alternative prize, but Amy knew full well Hoss and Jacques weren't going head-to-head over a frozen turkey.

She didn't have a good answer. "Jacques is a gentleman," she said to reassure herself as well as Flint. "But Hoss won't take losing easy. You might suggest a runoff with different weapons."

"I like the way you think," Flint said with approval, before returning to the judge's box while the remaining three shooters returned to the line.

"Two rounds, four shots, and time is a factor," the mayor announced after a whispered consultation with Flint.

By calling for two rounds, they'd not only upped the stakes, but handicapped Jacques, who obviously wasn't familiar with reloading his brand-new weapon. Amy winced, but the judges made the rules. Capability was as important as accuracy.

Hoss looked confident firing his rounds, reloading, and firing again in rapid succession.

Slower at loading, Jacques fired his last shot a few seconds after Hoss. The third contestant came in last, in both time and accuracy.

Amy held her breath while the judges examined the cards.

"Zack Saint Ettyann in accuracy; Hoss Whitcomb in

capability," the mayor announced in his dreadful accent to a crowd screaming in excitement.

"Give me some money on that Zack," one of the voices behind her whispered to whoever was taking bets. "I think I gotta cover my losses."

Zack. Amy smiled and wished the betting proceeds were going to charity. From the noise and the odds, she'd say wagers were running high.

The judges consulted with the final two contestants. Hugging her elbows, stomach tensing, Amy didn't stand close enough to hear. She was beginning to feel conspicuous as it became apparent to everyone that turkeys weren't the goal of this shoot. A friendly buss on the cheek to a man she'd known all her life had seemed simple enough when she'd finally given in to popular demand. But a real contest with her as coveted prize was a way-out fantasy the practical part of her mind hadn't anticipated. She was a thirty-something divorcée with two kids, not a teenage beauty queen.

Jacques emerged from the consultation with a smirk of triumph. Hoss looked equally cocky. Jacques glanced in Amy's direction and tapped the pocket where he carried her ring. Hoss gave her a thumbs-up.

Amy wished for a sudden thunderstorm.

"The contestants have agreed to a shoot-off," the mayor announced in a voice that barely carried over the noise of the crowd.

Amy couldn't hear the specifics he was explaining, but she could see Hoss unloading his expensive new rifle from the cab of his pickup. She glanced around, and sure enough, Jo had been right. Luigi came running with a rifle for Jacques. He'd brought an arsenal. She was willing to bet that he could be challenged to pistols, swords, and AK-47s and stand ready. Jacques was evidently not a man to leave things to chance.

She shivered a little and blamed the breeze. She had always appreciated a man who knew what he wanted and went after it with competence, but she'd never had to go up against such a man before.

Jacques might be competent, but he wouldn't help the town. Or her. She had to keep thinking of him as the enemy, not the kind of man who could provide security.

Hoss had national sharpshooting awards. But Jacques was going over his weapon with the same cool professionalism he had displayed using an unfamiliar shotgun. The crowd grew quiet when the contestants stepped up to the line.

The contest was no longer a joke. A puffy white cloud dimmed the bright Carolina sunshine, reducing the glare so Amy couldn't miss a motion. Riveted, she dug her fingernails into her palms and watched Flint give the signal to shoot.

Both men unloaded their ammunition into the targets in a rapid succession of gunfire. Apparently reloading wasn't part of the contest, because they lowered the barrels once they emptied their magazines, waiting for a judge to collect the cards and examine them.

Amy thought she saw a trace of weariness in Jacques's eyes when he glanced toward her, and his crooked smile tugged at her tender heartstrings. She needed to stop that nonsense right now. She was such a softhearted sucker she let the kids drag home any wounded creature they found. Jacques was very definitely not a helpless creature in need of mothering.

"And it's Zack Saint-Ettyann by three shots," the

mayor screamed, grabbing Jacques's wrist and lifting his arm into the air.

Jacques almost staggered as his weight shifted to the wrong leg, but he caught himself and straightened using the rifle stock for a prop. Tugging his wrist free, he offered his hand to Hoss, who slapped it with goodwill and shook hard. Amy winced, but she noticed the bulkier man backed off from the hand-crushing contest first. And then the crowd was shoving her forward, and she quit thinking anything at all.

Caught up in the marksmanship, she had succeeded in briefly forgetting she was the prize.

The same manicured hand that had crushed Hoss's now caught her elbow with gentleness, drawing her so close that she could look up and not only see the whites of Jacques's eyes, but the blue sparkles in his dark irises and the hint of mustache bristles beneath the skin of his upper lip. A firm mouth turned upward in the corners while he studied her the same way he'd studied his competition. Long, strong fingers tapped the hoop in her ear, the gold warm and caressing as it brushed against her neck. Her knees almost buckled.

"Your favor brought me luck, *Aimée*," he murmured, lowering his mouth to hers.

Aimée. Emmy. Beloved.

She was out of her ever-lovin' mind and in way over her head. Jacques's mouth coming down on hers blew whatever working brain cells she had left. Amy closed her eyes and sank into his arms and his kiss as if she'd known them all her life—cradled in comfort, wrapped in strength, and blessed with passion.

≪ TEN ≫

Jacques had wanted this kiss . . . worked for it as single-mindedly as he did everything that mattered.

If he had known the jolt of electricity from Amy's plush lips would bring him to his knees, he would have used his cane.

Instead, he grabbed Amy's shoulders for support and deepened the contact, digging his fingers into her hair and refusing to release her once she responded to his insistent pressure with a hunger as strong as his own. His weariness abruptly fled. Only the noise of the crowd reminded him that this was not the private moment he desperately craved.

Shocked by the extent of his desire for this woman who thought him little more than an idle playboy, Jacques regretfully stepped back. Amy's wide-eyed look assuaged some of his own surprise. At least, he wasn't the only one reeling.

"Come, Amy. Let's give others the chance to win their turkeys." Keeping his arm across her shoulders, he tugged her next to him.

He enjoyed the caress of her hair against his jaw as the wind tossed it back at him. He wanted to catch the shining strands, turn her head to him, and continue that mind-blowing kiss—somewhere a good deal more private than this.

"I'm thinking I'm the turkey here," she muttered under her breath as he led her toward the picnic blanket. "I should have known better."

"Turkeys do not have lovely lush lips for kissing. Is there a barn we can hide behind?"

She laughed at his teasing, but there was wariness in her eyes. She needed to defend her heart—just as he did—so he supposed he shouldn't drive away her suspicion. But he saw no reason they could not enjoy one of the great pleasures in life for a while.

"Not on a bet, mister." She halted at the blanket to introduce him to a tall, older woman with the lines of an education in life's hard knocks etched into her face. "Mama, we've told you about Jacques, the man who's bidding on the mill. Jacques, this is our mother, Marie Sanderson. She worked at the mill for decades."

He could see the resemblance to Amy in Marie's wary eyes as he bent over her hand in a gesture meant to impress. The tough woman looked more suspicious than impressed, and he bit back a grin. Like mother, like daughter.

"My pleasure, Mrs. Sanderson." This time, Jacques allowed Amy to direct his chair to be placed next to Marie's. He had too much work ahead of him to be crippled by a bad knee.

He didn't let Amy go but squeezed her hand as he sat down. "Tell Luigi to carry our things here, please." He didn't want to let her go, but he had only a few days left to submit his bid, and his fine-honed instincts told him that Marie Sanderson was a resource he could not ignore.

Encouraging Marie with questions, Jacques followed Amy with his eyes, watching as she admirably dealt with their disparate guests. He pondered her willingness to leave the champagne with Catarina and her followers when they refused to join the family circle, and hid a smile when she carefully divided the food between the two parties so everyone could sample all the delicacies. He did not often encounter such unselfishness, or such natural hospitality.

After seeing that plates of fried chicken and side dishes were distributed from the two coolers, Amy finally— almost reluctantly—took the chair reserved for her beside Jacques.

"I don't want to hear about the mill today," she warned, cutting his intentions off at the pass while sipping her iced tea. "Tell us how you learned to shoot so well."

Jacques shrugged. "When I was a boy, I would visit my father's estate every summer. It was a wonderful place to grow up. I rode the horses in his stable, swam the ponds and river, took fencing lessons from a neighbor. My father had groundsmen who taught me how to shoot. Not so different from here."

Amy rolled her eyes in that droll manner of hers, and Jacques had the urge to kiss her button nose. Since he was hungrily devouring her delicious chicken, he resisted.

"I'm sure you shot the possums ransacking the chicken coop, just like here, too."

"Sarcasm does not become you, Amy," he chided. "My father inherited his land, yes, but we are land rich and cash poor. We must all work to pay for the expense of upkeep. I have used my skills to shoot vermin."

"He was on the Olympic pentathlon team," Pascal asserted, reaching for another piece of chicken. "Do not let his modesty trick you into any more wagers."

"Sore loser." Jacques laughed. "It is your own fault for thinking an unfamiliar weapon would deter me."

"Pentathlon?" Flint looked up with interest from his plate. "Fencing, riding, shooting . . . ?"

"Swimming, running, yes, but I do not do all these things so much anymore. The running ruined my knee and put a finish on the fencing. And then life became too busy."

"The *Olympics,*" Amy breathed with awe.

Jacques brushed aside his self-deprecation to bask in her admiration a little. He was no longer an athlete and people seldom cared if he had been, but he was prouder of the innocent accomplishments of his youth than of the mercenary prizes he'd accumulated since. "Only once," he reminded her. "Training for events kept me from terrorizing my parents." Or vice versa, but his dysfunctional home life was not a subject worth dwelling on.

"That's what I need—coaches to keep John and Adam busy every minute of the day. Put that on our wish list, Jo," Flint said through a mouthful of golden biscuit.

The others laughed and jested, but Jacques watched Amy's wistful expression as she gazed upon her own children. He remembered that feeling of pride in Danielle's accomplishments, wondering if he should hire coaches or teachers so she might be all that she promised to be. He'd thrilled at her first steps and words, her determination to ride a pony, her willingness to fall asleep in his arms rather than let him go anywhere without her.

The familiar knife of pain ripped through his heart as he once again remembered that life cut too short. He clenched his back teeth to prevent the pang of anguish and looked around brightly for a different subject.

"So, Mrs. Sanderson," he addressed Amy's mother. "You have worked many years in the mill, but you are too young to remember their Early American designs from the sixties. Are there others here I might ask?"

Sipping a soft drink, Marie studied him as if trying to decide if his flattery was worth answering. Her cropped graying blond hair framed a weathered face more angular than Amy's. But her eyes were sharp and watchful.

"I was a kid then," she answered slowly, "but I remember my mother covering all the living room furniture in that ugly brown and orange. The mills had bolts of that fabric left even after I started there. What do you want with it?"

"Mama, I asked you about those designs earlier," Amy protested.

"So, I forgot." Marie looked unrepentant.

Jacques took that to mean she purposefully forgot to mention the fabric. For what reason? Him? He could understand that. How could he persuade her to trust him?

"What goes around, comes around, madame," he said carelessly, hoping to hide his interest. "The *toile de Jouy* print has been back for some years. I prefer to work with original design rather than imitation."

"Oh, these were original, all right. Tiny colonial figures and clapboard farmhouses and sailing ships we never saw in these mountains. I always thought they ought to do dogwoods and rhododendrons and outhouses. Maybe some figures in overalls."

"Dogwoods aren't historical, Mama," Amy said in amusement.

"That's a matter of opinion," Marie answered gruffly; but apparently accepting Amy's comment as approval of Jacques's search, she continued. "Last I saw, all those old pattern cards and platens were in the wooden chest they used for a window seat over in Building Two, but don't be surprised if someone decided they'd make good kindling and scrap metal. That old barn was cold, and we were always poor."

Startled that she actually claimed to have seen and recognized the cards, Jacques almost didn't respond. "Building Two?" he finally regained the sense to ask.

"The Music Barn," Amy said with excitement. "The mill sold the equipment in there a decade ago. Flint, do you remember an old wooden chest in the barn?"

Dragged away from his conversation with Pascal, Flint had to stop and think before responding. "There's a window seat filled with junk. Does that count? Jo covered it in cushions."

"That must be it!" Jacques jumped up from the chair, winced, then gestured excitedly at Luigi. "We must see if they're still there. Come along, Amy; show us where to look."

Instead of leaping up in excitement, she lifted one lovely arched eyebrow, glanced around at all the people talking and eating, and remained where she was. "What's your hurry? The cards aren't going anywhere."

A smirking Luigi settled deeper in his chair while Pascal returned to his discussion of country music.

Jacques clenched his fists in frustration. "We could finish the bid tonight if I knew for a fact that the cards are there. It is what we've been looking for all week. Don't you want to see if they exist?"

Watching this interaction, Amy had to admit if she was honest about it, she didn't. She was enjoying this escape from reality. The flirting and attention reminded her that she was still female and apparently attractive. That kiss had stirred her sleeping hormones into a restless hive of bees. She didn't want to go back to attempting to outbid a man who had access to more money than Midas.

She didn't want the most excitement she'd seen in years to depart the moment they had what they were looking for. And if she really had to be truthful, that meant she didn't want to see Jacques leave—at least not until she got to know the woman Jacques saw in her.

Which meant she'd slipped into fantasy again, and she'd better kick his ass out of here as fast as she could, find the cards, and hope he went away. Soon. Reluctantly, she rose from her chair.

"Everyone is entitled to a day off," she reminded him, nodding at his entourage. If she was going to be reduced to begging to save the mill, she didn't want an audience. "Let your friends relax. If Jo will look after the kids, I'll drive you over. It won't take long to verify the cards are what you want, will it?"

"We came in your SUV, remember?" Jo shot down that suggestion. "If you linger too long, we'll be out here when the drunks take over."

"We will take my car," Jacques said with his usual arrogance. "Amy will drive, and I will rest my knee as promised. Luigi can drive the others when they are ready to return to Asheville. I have my room here. It will all work out, you see?"

Amy saw, all right. She saw Luigi grimace and Pascal look amused. Jacques's type A personality was no doubt running roughshod over all their plans.

But she wanted this over. She wanted Jacques out of her life before she did something stupid. She wanted to know if life as she knew it was about to end. The mill wasn't that far away. They could be back within the hour.

"Where's your car?" she asked in resignation. She

thought he'd arrived in the Hummer. That's what Luigi had been driving him around in all week, but he surely couldn't mean she should drive that. Catarina and friends would be stranded.

"Over there, on the far side of the Hummer." Jacques caught her arm in one hand and the walking stick in the other. Displaying more strength than Hoss on a good day, he proceeded to haul her toward his goal and away from the safety of family.

Amy dug in her heels, refusing to let the locomotive on his one-track mind run over her. She kissed the kids and reassured them that Aunt Jo would be right there until she got back. Since they worshipped Johnnie and Adam, Josh and Louisa accepted her reassurances without protest.

Amy was the one who protested when she saw where Jacques was leading her.

On the far side of the Hummer, a group of men surrounded a low-slung dark vehicle that looked as if it could reach outer space. She hadn't seen the Porsche since Jacques had hurt his knee. Apparently he'd had Luigi drive the sports car here rather than ride with the others today.

"I am not driving that car." She came to an abrupt halt, almost tripping Jacques in his hurry to cross the lot.

"Don't you know a stick shift?"

"My Ranger spits at me if I look at it cross-eyed. I'm not about to touch anything that runs on computers and costs more than a house."

"Don't be foolish. It is an engine with wheels. I will drive, if you wish. I suppose it's not so hard if I do not use the clutch too often."

Amy imagined careening down the mountain road to the mill without a clutch pedal and closed her eyes in denial. "You are going to regret this," she warned.

"Oh, I seriously doubt that," he murmured huskily against her ear, his breath dancing her earring against her neck as he opened the door and helped her in to the tune of admiring whispers. She stifled a shiver of pleasure. Who knew earrings could be so erotic?

She respected his tenacity in maintaining his playboy act until he had what he really wanted. All she had to do was pretend she was accustomed to it. Jacques seriously misunderstood the situation if he thought they were sallying off for an intimate rendezvous. She didn't do *intimate* or *rendezvous*. They were heading for a showdown.

Sinking into the driver's luxurious seat, she stared at the cockpit of gleaming dials set in the sumptuous leather of the dash and almost cried. Already, she was at a disadvantage.

"I garden with a hand hoe," she told Jacques when he lowered himself into the passenger seat with the judicious use of his cane. "I sew quilts by hand and weave on handlooms. I do not touch computers or DVDs or anything that goes buzz or bing."

He laughed, wrapped his arm over the back of her seat, and leaned over to indicate the ignition. Just his proximity caused alarms in Amy's head to buzz and bing.

"It practically drives itself," he assured her. "You will see. We will be there and back before anyone notices we are gone."

"You have no idea how very wrong you are." With a sigh, Amy pushed the ignition, and the powerful engine roared to life.

Men backed out of the way as she eased up on the clutch and down on the gas. The race-car tires scratched gravel and flew forward without a hitch, except for an insistent *bing, bing, bing* from one of the instruments.

≪ ELEVEN ≫

Jacques hunted for the source of the binging sound to hide his frustration. Amy cautiously eased the car's brutal engine down the road at the speed of a child's pony. He wanted his knee back so he could show her what the car could do. "There's no one out here. You can go faster," he remonstrated. "Enjoy a beautiful machine."

"You may as well tell me to enjoy a rocket launcher," she replied, her knuckles white on the steering wheel. "Next time, I'll let you ruin your knee on the damned clutch. What possessed you to drive this monster up here?"

"It takes curves like a dream. We'll take it up the mountain someday, and you will see. It is like a magic carpet ride." They could put the top down and let the wind blow her hair and color her cheeks and make her laugh like a girl. And then he would kiss her again until both their heads spun.

His head was still spinning from that last kiss. He wanted to see if they could do that again—if he could persuade her to throw caution to the wind and just let life happen.

"Give me real carpets any day," she argued. "They're at least useful."

"Magic is about beauty and dreams. These things are

useful in their own way. One needs to step back from grim reality occasionally to appreciate the wonders of the world."

"It's a trifle difficult for the rest of us to live on dreams. Right now, I don't want to imagine paying for this car the rest of my life if anything should happen to it."

"It's insured," he said with a careless gesture. "But nothing will happen. Maybe a few dings from the gravel. You fret too much."

"You fret too little. As Aesop points out, there's a reason grasshoppers who fiddle away the summer don't last to see spring, while ants who work to store food survive."

He kept his arm over her seat back, enjoying the familiarity of brushing her shoulder while leaning over to read the dials. The sun through the windshield formed a warm cocoon around their little nest of leather and chrome. "Aesop was a pessimist. People bring food to my door in return for my fiddling. A woman like you shouldn't have to worry over such things."

She tensed so tightly when he stroked her bare arm that he feared she would bite his ear off. He blew teasingly on a strand of warm brown hair curling on her forehead and watched the sunlight dance on her gold hoops. She hit the brake, and he laughed.

"What will you do if you find the pattern cards?" she demanded.

"Do you think to drive the thought of kisses out of my mind?" he teased, caressing her shoulder with his fingertips.

"There will be no more kisses," she said firmly, keeping her eyes on the road and her hands in a death grip on the wheel. "If I'm helping you to find those cards, I have a right to know what you mean to do with them."

She meant to force the issue she'd brought up the other day, one he did not want to discuss with a lady he wished to seduce.

"I will produce beautiful fabrics, of course. Or the company will, after I write the program." He knew this wasn't what she wanted to know, but he wasn't prepared for candor. "I am not a thief. I am willing to pay well for what I want, so do not worry so."

"If all you want is the cards, why don't you work with the mill committee? With your wealth, we could buy back the whole property and put it into production by Christmas. You could have your cards and designs, and we could have our jobs back."

Jacques sighed and sat back where he belonged. He truly didn't want to have this discussion now, but she left him little choice. "The wealth is not my own. I have a company and stockholders who expect a good return on their investment. I have seen your plan. It is a bad investment."

He waited for her angry argument. Instead, the *binging* noise became a more insistent clang. Frowning, Jacques checked the instrument panel again, then opened the dash for the manual while she summoned her forces. He had no expectation that even a woman smelling of jasmine would leave the subject alone.

"Investing in people, in your community, is never a bad investment," she argued. "The returns just aren't necessarily monetary, not at first. The money comes later, when the economy stabilizes. You have to plan for the future."

At least she had chosen an intriguing argument, if not one that would sway him. "But this is not my future," he said regretfully. "We have different purposes."

"Then why not leave us the mill and simply purchase the cards from us?" she asked, her tone so carefully steady he knew she fought desperation.

Following emotion was not a rational approach to business. A pleasant interlude with a charming woman, yes, but more than that could only end badly. Very badly.

He didn't want any part of knowing Amy to end badly.

He might possibly be in trouble here.

He unclenched his jaw and forced it to relax. "I can buy the mill and the patterns for the cost of the machinery, then sell the machinery and walk away with the patterns for nothing," he said, brutally bringing out in the open what had gone unsaid.

"Then I will simply have to win the bid," she retaliated with such firmness that he had to glance at her to be certain she hadn't transformed into a woman he did not know.

He admired the stubborn tilt of her round chin, and he chucked it lightly to get her to smile again. "May the best man win," he agreed. Competition, he understood.

The clang became a whining alarm, and she clenched the wheel tighter, slowing to a crawl to make the turn onto the gravel mill drive. A narrow metal bridge traversed the rocky river ahead. "I won't let you win," she yelled over the noise of the alarm.

As she turned the steering wheel, smoke seeped from the electronic panel, a wheel locked, and before Jacques could form any reply or take any action, the Porsche slid into a spin on the gravel, hit a soft spot on the side of the road, and flipped down the embankment.

"Amy, Amy! Are you all right?"

Black panic wiped out everything except for the sight

of the fragile, lovely woman slumped over the steering wheel. For years, Jacques had had full-blown nightmares of another woman, a child, and a car smashed against trees down a mountain hillside. His wife. His child. His world . . . all taken from him in the space of a breath. That time, the image had been only in his head, since he'd arrived much too late to see the actual scene.

The reality was far worse than a nightmare.

Mind screaming with sheer terror, he fought the air bag, beating it back so he could reach the woman not answering his cries.

Thanks to Amy's cautious driving, the car had flipped only once, landing on its no-doubt flattened tires, but every battered bone in Jacques's body ached from the crushing seat belt. He could see only Amy's cinnamon brown hair falling over her face as her bag deflated. He could not tell if she breathed. Panic crushed the breath from his own lungs.

Frantically, he wrestled the air bag aside and unfastened her seat belt without a glance out the windshield at the destruction of the gorgeous machine. He simply prayed he had not failed to save another woman from harm. "Amy!" he repeated.

Her hand raised shakily to push the hair back from her face, and he almost choked on relief that she lived and moved. Still leaning against the steering wheel as if it were a pillow, she opened her green eyes and glared at him. "I *told* you so" were the first words out of her mouth.

After a sharp intake of air, relief simply exploded from his chest, and Jacques laughed. He couldn't help it. He grabbed his sore ribs and roared until tears streaked down his cheeks.

"It's not funny!" She sat up straight, or as straight as

she could, since the car was at a forty-five degree angle with the rocky riverbed. The knuckles of her fingers gripping the wheel were white.

"No, I think I am hysterical," he blurted out between chuckles. "My heart stopped when you did not speak, and then your first words are not of relief or fear but recrimination." His ribs really did hurt when he laughed, but he couldn't hold it in. He hadn't laughed so hard in years. Eons of pain and fear ripped loose and exploded—he'd faced his worst nightmare and survived.

"It's not funny." She propped her arms straight against the wheel as if that would hold the car in place. She didn't sound anxious or in pain, just dazed. "I've killed a monster machine. Jo always told me I could."

In his relief, that seemed even funnier. Jacques tried to muffle his mirth, but chuckles kept bubbling up. "One cannot kill machines, and you haven't killed us, so all is well," he tried to say reassuringly, but another snigger escaped, earning him a glare.

"We're dangling over a riverbed in a hunk of broken metal. We could have been *killed*."

"We're *alive*," he crowed. "We're alive, and I very much want to kiss you. So let me help you climb out of here, and we will forget to call for assistance for a while."

He eased open his door until it lodged against a tree trunk. Using his cane, he wiggled free and studied their situation. He breathed deeply of the mountain air and admired the scenery, letting the adrenaline rush settle down. The river was no more than a babbling brook over a bed of boulders. They were in no danger of drowning.

The angle of the hillside and the uneven terrain made his ability to clamber about doubtful, but *perseverance* was his middle name. Deciding the front of the Porsche was firmly wedged between a massive boulder and a pine tree, he limped uphill around a shiny fender lying on the ground to help Amy from the driver's side.

She was shaking so badly when she stepped out, that his laughter dissipated.

"I am so sorry," he murmured, wrapping her soft curves in his arms. "I should not have laughed, but it is better than crying, is it not?"

She bunched his shirtfront in her fists and wept into his shoulder. This was not how he had wanted to persuade this woman into his arms.

But he had spent the past week watching from the distance she held him at, and he could not ignore her plump breasts now that they were crushed against his chest. Her jasmine scent filled his head, the tears wetting his shirt unmanned him, and the brush of her hair against his jaw electrified every nerve ending in his body. She spun him faster than the Porsche, so that he didn't know whether to lust or cherish.

A part of him that he'd long buried pressed reassuring kisses into her hair, letting her weep, blessing the stars that she trusted him enough to cry on his shoulder. It had been a long, long time since he had held a woman just to comfort her. He knew the sexual urges aroused by her closeness were inappropriate, but he could not command his body to disregard her welcoming softness. So he stroked her back, trailed his kisses from her hair to her ear, doing his utmost to remind her how thrilling it was that they were alive.

She was hiccupping by the time his mouth found her lips. Jacques thought she meant to protest, but he firmly shut out her words with his kiss. The shock of attraction was instantaneous, and after the first gasp of surprise, she accepted his invitation with the delightful passion he'd experienced earlier. With her mouth melded to his, she shuddered and pressed into him with a desire for life and living that equaled the one welling in him.

"Amy," he murmured when they came up for air. To stop kissing her would be akin to tossing away a delicious ice cream. He couldn't do it. He tasted the corners of her mouth, swept his tongue along her bottom lip, and claimed her mouth when she parted hers in welcome.

He'd meant to go slow, not frighten her, but he couldn't seem to stop. He'd enjoyed many women, but none had opened this rapidly filling well of desire for life and love that he had denied himself these past years.

The powerful surge of need frightened him far more than the crashing car. He could not *need* again.

Gasping, Jacques caught her upper arms and set her back from him just enough to save his senses, but not enough to let her go. Amy looked wonderfully tousled, aroused, and fascinated as she studied him the same way he studied her. Here was the sex kitten he'd sensed. Her lips were moist and swollen from his kisses, and he'd scraped her fair cheek with his beard. But her eyes—her eyes would be the end of him. They held such trust and wonder—and fear.

"I did not mean to take advantage," he said, totally uncertain for the first time. He wanted her, yes. But need? He was not prepared for that. "But there is this current, this electricity . . ." He gestured helplessly. "You're a magnet."

The sun returned to her eyes, and she giggled infectiously. At his puzzled look, she laughed louder.

"Jo says my magnetic personality destroys electronics," she explained between giggles. "You must be a robot."

He had to smile at that, if only because her smile was so catching. "Hmm . . . robotic. It's true, I have been accused of that. And now you have messed with my wiring, and I'm at a loss of what to do next."

"Climb out of here and call for help would be my suggestion." Eminently sensible now that he'd indicated a need for help, she lost her vulnerable look and studied the path of destruction created by the crashing sports car. "I recommend sliding up on your rear. You'll destroy your knee trying to climb."

He adored the way she metamorphosed from vulnerable sex kitten to sensible lioness when called upon. She had learned strength for her children, and she used it for everyone, even a grasshopper like him. And the entire town, he realized with regret.

"I am not sliding about like a cripple," he protested, releasing her to reach for the cell phone in his inside jacket pocket. "You must have bumped your head hard to think I would do such a thing." Hitting Luigi's programmed number with his thumb, he brushed her hair from her forehead with his free hand, checking for bruises.

By all rights, she ought to be forcing a wan smile and sitting down to wait for rescue. Instead, she shook off his caress, grabbed a tree trunk, and began hauling herself up the hillside, no doubt running from the vibrations still electrifying them.

Jacques's knee ached just watching her. It was obvious she was no stranger to mountain climbing. She found foot grips with grace and agility, braced herself on rocks and trees so as not to slide backward, and had reached the roadbed by the time he had finished talking to Luigi.

He liked watching the sway of her rounded buttocks and the way her firm calves curved enticingly with her climb. He wanted to slide his hand up the legs of her loose shorts and discover what dainty feminine garment she wore beneath the practical outerwear.

He was distracting himself with lust rather than think about the woman he was longing to know. He couldn't do that much longer. Amy was not a shallow beauty looking for fame and fortune, but a real woman with a life of her own that he must take into consideration.

She sat down on a rock at the side of the road and gazed down on him like a princess at a toad. "I dare you to slide up before Luigi arrives."

"I will make you pay for that when I get up there." After watching the effort it had taken for her to climb out of the small ravine, Jacques knew he'd be risking surgery to try it upright. But he'd never turned down a dare, and she knew it.

He didn't have time for surgery. Cursing the ignominy of crawling while the woman he wanted watched, he clenched his teeth and lowered himself to the ground torn up by the crashing car. He'd have to ease up backward, using his cane as a brace to reduce the strain on his bad knee.

"You realize I can never look you in the eyes again," he declared, inching upward, feeling his way with his hands. "I am an Olympic champion, and you have reduced me to a crawl."

"I won't look," she promised cheerfully. "Although I must say, I don't think many men have the biceps to do what you're doing now."

He couldn't help grinning. "You warm my heart. I am again master of all I survey."

"If that means you're again an arrogant cockroach," she said blithely, "I daresay that's innate and nothing I can take away. Watch the blackberry cane on your right."

"You are not supposed to be looking!" he chided, finding the thorny branch and working around it.

"I'm not. I've gone cross-eyed with pain, and I'll probably black out at any moment. You will have to hurry to rescue me before I fall."

She was poking fun at his need to take care of her, but he had to laugh at her accuracy. "You are wicked and much too perceptive. I like this side of you. You must say what you think more often."

"No one listens when I do. You're a captive audience. Besides, you have enough dignity for both of us. It doesn't hurt to dust it off occasionally."

"Dignity? Is that another way of saying arrogance?" Without warning, he reached behind him and grabbed her ankle. His hand easily wrapped around her slender bones so he could pull himself up the remainder of the way and pull her down to him at the same time.

She slid off her rock and into his arms as if she belonged there. And she did. This amazingly strong woman belonged in his arms, in his bed, and in his dreams. Another crashing car could have shattered him. Instead, this accident had opened another dimension of possibilities.

Covering Amy with his greater size, pressing her into the soft grass along the roadside, Jacques straddled her hips and claimed the prize of her mouth again. He could feel her curves along the length of him, arching against his chest and groin as she wrapped her arms around his neck. Desire, thick and warm, flooded through him. She drew on his tongue to show she felt the same, and he almost lost his senses enough to take her there, with the mosquitoes and poison ivy. All the blood rushed from his brain downward, and he ground desperately against her until she groaned with equal desire.

Perhaps he could not have all he wanted, but he wouldn't let this opportunity pass unrewarded. He slid his hands beneath her shirt, popping her buttons as he did so. He filled his palms to overflowing with the bounteous breasts she hid behind her tailored clothes. He unhooked her brassiere and teased her aroused nipples until she moaned for him and the zipper of his trousers cut into his swelling need to take her.

At the noise of a heavy vehicle roaring around the bend and throwing up gravel on the road, Jacques leaned over and gently suckled at sweet buds to ease both their needs, just a little. Then, with regret, he rehooked her garments and rolled onto his back.

He needed to slide back into the river to douse his throbbing erection. He hadn't been this uncontrolled since . . .

Since Gabrielle.

That dashed an icy bucket of water over his raging libido.

❧ TWELVE ❧

Amy retired to the Music Barn's restroom, ostensibly to clean up after the accident. In reality, she needed private time to fall apart.

Staring at her reflection in the fluorescent light of the renovated Music Barn, she gripped the porcelain sink and tried not to shatter into a thousand bits. Her breasts were on fire. Her panties were wet. Parts of her that even Evan had left unstirred ached with hunger. Men shouldn't have hard muscles like Jacques's. They made a woman weak.

That was half the problem. She was a woman now, not the child she'd been when she'd met Evan. She had a grown woman's desires for a mature adult male. A raging river of yearning scoured her insides—including her brain, obviously—leaving her hollow of everything but need.

Outside the restroom, she could hear Jacques ordering Luigi about as if nothing had happened. He could wield his charm like a sword to challenge people, or he could use it to purr and persuade. That he used honesty and logic—despite his obvious reluctance to admit the truth—was far more devastating.

With a character as strong as his, he could lead men into enemy fire. He'd said everything she hadn't wanted to hear, and still, she'd kissed him. The man was terrifying.

She was terrified. She wasn't the kind of woman who rolled in the grass half naked. But the grass stains on her Liz Claibornes said otherwise.

She'd forgotten how it felt to be held and loved. Her breasts had forgotten the wonderful arousal of a man's caress. She refused to heed the physical craving gripping her lower parts. She could not get involved with a man who would be here today and gone tomorrow, probably killing all her dreams while he was at it. Her mother had done that, and look how horribly that had turned out.

She ignored the niggling voice that said a hasty hot affair would burn out these desires quickly enough. She knew herself better than that. She would do emotional backflips and turn herself into a pretzel for any man she chose to go to bed with. *So* not going there again.

Then, what had just happened out there?

Jacques had happened. He was the salt that made the water boil over. She had no business driving exotic race cars or kissing a fancy stranger who could charm a cardinal from a cherry tree. She was the kind of girl who went to church on Sundays and baked cupcakes for school parties. She was *way* over her head trying to deal with this charismatic James Bond.

He charmed with words she wanted to hear, and she believed them—because he was honest with words she didn't want to hear.

Amy rolled her eyes at her reflection, pulled a wet wipe from her purse, and tried to wash the evidence of her stupidity from her face. Maybe the Sanderson women had some kind of malfunctioning gene when it came to smooth-talking men. Her mother had fallen for a good-looking musician who'd walked away one day and never returned. Jo had fallen for two slick bastards before getting smart and landing salt-of-the-earth Flint. Amy had been sensible in choosing stable, sturdy Evan, but even that hadn't worked.

Except Evan had consistently lied to her. And Jacques had been brutally honest.

Excited shouts in the plant warned that she was missing the action. She'd have to quit hiding.

Flint had brought Luigi in his pickup with a hitch, but once Luigi had seen the Porsche, he'd decided to call a tow truck rather than risk more damage. She shuddered at the image of that beautiful ruined car in the ravine.

From the exclamations in the other room, she gathered Jacques had now found what he wanted. She wouldn't be seeing him again. That was fine. That was more than fine. That was *safe*.

She scraped the dirt off her shirt and shorts where she could, tucked her shirttails into her waistband, ran a comb through her hair, and threw back her shoulders like a soldier marching off to war. After what they'd done, she just didn't think she could look Jacques in the eye once she went back out there.

The instant she walked into the cavernous building, Jacques waved enthusiastically, and she was hooked all over again. In one hand he held an ancient wooden pattern card, and in the other, the cardboard versions mechanically punched out in the sixties.

"It is a treasure trove!" he shouted, referring to the once-upholstered window seat the men had torn apart in their search.

He'd thrown off his muddied sports coat in the unair-conditioned heat. His trousers were filthier than hers. He had a bruise forming on his forehead, and twigs in the mink-brown hair brushing his nape. And he looked happier than a child with a brand-new bike.

"Museum pieces!" he called in ecstasy. "Some of these designs have not seen the light of day in decades, maybe centuries."

How was she supposed to resist a man who could be as thrilled with an old-fashioned fabric design as she could?

"At least the seventies," she said, tongue in cheek, taking the mechanized cards from his hand. Reading the design in the cards was as impossible as reading the data on a punch card. The wooden cards from before the turn of the twentieth century were even more fascinating and impractical. No wonder her mother had called them junk.

Luigi and Flint merely poked with disinterest through the window seat. Jacques sprawled on his injured leg to lay the flat wooden plates out on the floor in some futile attempt to determine their relationship with one another.

The town couldn't afford to keep museum pieces like that. With a lump in her throat, Amy kneeled on the other side of the cards. She didn't want to get caught up in his excitement. The town's future demanded that she remain businesslike.

It was damned hard to do while sitting near a man whose shoulders strained the seams of his expensive shirt. Just the dark hair on his forearms had her remembering how those muscled limbs had felt around her.

She wanted to return to their earlier argument, but she doubted if he'd even hear her, so intense was his concentration.

It was contagious. Fascinated in spite of herself, she skimmed the wooden plates with her fingers, wondering how many hands had touched them, what kind of mind had created this bit of brilliance so long ago. "Can you really determine the patterns without building a loom and running the design?" She used to do her own weaving, had created her own design cards, but even she couldn't see the whole without threads.

"Computers," he muttered, looking for markings on the plates. "We match the holes using my software program. Designs are done on CAD/CAM these days, but we can translate these once the computer matches the order."

"Wouldn't it be simpler to just copy the design from the material you already have?"

"I have a few pieces, a few patterns. I do not have them all. And it is better to have the actual weft pattern. My business depends on historical accuracy."

"How much do you think they're worth?" she asked, then kicked herself when Jacques's dark eyes sent her a laughing look. As if he would tell her. So much for businesslike.

"To me, they are priceless. To anyone else, they are junk."

Damn if her hormones didn't have her head spinning when he looked at her like that—with respect for her knowledge. Maybe she ought to go to bed with him—or somebody—so she could think straight again.

"Then let us have the mill, like I said earlier, and we'll sell the patterns to you at a price that won't make your board of directors flinch." She waved her hand grandly. "Everyone wins." Apparently some part of her head still worked. That was a realistic suggestion.

Jacques glanced up as if she'd startled him out of deep

thought, then shook his head. "Amy, you are an *amazingly* stubborn woman." His voice trailed off as he returned his concentration to the cards.

She had no idea what he meant by that. She'd always done what Evan had told her. That didn't sound like stubborn. Hiding hopes that they could still make a deal, she stuck with the tangible. "Is it safe to leave them here? Should we take them to the bankruptcy judge and ask that he lock them up?"

Jacques sent her an admiring look that almost had her melting between the wide cracks of the worn floor.

"They have been here a very long time. I would say they are safe, but—"

"The river floods, word gets out, things happen," Flint said gruffly, coming to stand over them. "I vote we lock up the junk."

"The river floods?" Jacques began hurriedly stacking the aging cardboard as if the river would steal it before he could escape.

"It doesn't flood often, and it hasn't rained in a month, so I think we're safe," Flint said gravely, the hard planes of his face effectively concealing his smile.

His movie star looks expressing relief, Jacques rose stiffly and dusted off his knees. Bent over like that, he exposed the grass and mud stains of his ruined trouser seat.

She bit back a snicker, but he seemed to hear her anyway. Straightening, he cast her a sideways glance, then turned and checked the back of his trousers. He made a wryly Gallic expression, brushed ineffectively at the stains, and then shrugged his broad shoulders.

"But a storm could come up anytime," Flint continued, ignoring their byplay. "The last hurricane through here wiped out a lot of houses and changed the river's path. Better to be safe than sorry."

"These are mountains," Jacques protested. "How can you have hurricanes in mountains?"

"It happens, usually when one comes up from the Gulf." Standing, Amy looked around for containers to carry the priceless cards. Anything but look at Jacques, who was dashing even when wearing muddy pants. Evan had carried a lot of fat around his middle. His back had never formed a V from broad shoulders to narrow hips like Jacques's did. And she shouldn't be noticing. Or aching to dust his butt. "It doesn't take much to make the river flood."

Together, they scavenged the buildings for file drawers and crates to carry the heavy old plates, rollers, and boxes of cards. When they ran out of room, Jacques used his expertise to choose the pieces to be left behind. Amy had the feeling that if he could stuff them in his pockets and down his shirt like valuable jewels, he would. He shut the lid on the window seat with obvious regret— more regret than he'd displayed for the smashed Porsche. The man was a fascinating contrast of ideals.

Now that Jacques had found his prize, no one seemed willing to talk of it. Had he said one word about putting the mill back in operation, questions would have flown. Amy filled the strained silence with small talk.

"I need a pickup like this to start hauling stuff down to the apartment," she mused aloud, climbing into the narrow backseat of Flint's extended cab. "I don't think I can get the mattresses into our SUV."

Flint slid in beside her, letting Luigi drive and leaving the larger front passenger seat for Jacques and his stiff knee. "You can use this truck if you want. We ought to trade. The boys are getting too big for backseats like this."

"Child seats would fit back here, wouldn't they?" She'd rather talk of anything than wonder what was behind Jacques's studious frown right now.

"Yup, and still have room for groceries. There's just no room for legs." Flint squeezed sideways to stretch his into her space.

Flint was a good-looking, muscular hunk, and Amy could see why her sister adored him. But their legs were touching, she was practically sitting in his lap, and she didn't feel an iota of excitement. Jacques, on the other hand, was as far from her as he could be, and his every move and gesture raised goose bumps of awareness.

"I've been thinking of trading in the SUV." She continued the desultory conversation rather than shout sense at Jacques. He wouldn't listen to her anyway.

"I'll make you a good deal," Flint offered, continuing the pretense that they hadn't just terminated the town's dream. Or maybe he was so oblivious he didn't understand what Jacques meant to do. "My pickup for your gas-guzzler, plus the difference in blue book value."

She nodded agreement. "Elise can draw up something if you talk Jo into it. Maybe we ought to work out rent on the apartment. I might have to move in for a while."

"You are moving?" Jacques swung around in the seat and pierced her with his sharpshooter gaze.

"I've sold my house," she said with as much dignity and composure as she could manage. "So if the insurance company intends to sue me over your car, they'll get nothing."

"The car is nothing but metal and plastic," he said dismissively. "It obviously had faulty wiring. My lawyers will threaten their lawyers. It's no matter. Why sell your house if you have no place to go?"

"Your *car* costs as much as my house," she said tightly. She wasn't relieved at his dismissiveness. "I blew up your car! We could have been killed. Don't tell me it's no matter."

Tight-lipped, Jacques turned to Flint. "She is avoiding the subject. Why is she selling her house?"

Flint bared his teeth in the grin that had won Jo's heart. "Jo says Amy blows up things when she's upset. We didn't want her blowing up a house."

Amy's first impulse was to protest, but then she realized that in his own foolishly male mind, Flint was protecting her. She wasn't too proud to admit that she couldn't afford her house, but she'd rather not show Jacques any sign of weakness.

Jacques narrowed his beautiful blue-black eyes at this reply. "You seriously believe you blew up my car?"

"That's Jo's theory. My theory is that machines are like dogs and sense my fear."

In the driver's seat, Luigi chuckled. "Keep her out of the Hummer, Boss."

Amen, Amy whispered fervently to herself. Keep her far, far away from a man whose lean, hungry look concealed a key to her heart. Or, at least, her libido.

"Are you sure you shouldn't have that knee looked at again?" Luigi demanded as he opened the door to the dinky motel room Jacques had taken in Northfork. "That woman is a walking disaster area. You should stay away from her."

No doubt very smart words, but not ones Jacques in-

tended to follow. "The knee is fine. A little ice and eleva-
tion. Rent something nice for Catarina."

"I'm not driving that lot of pretty pussies." Luigi
scanned the room. "If they're staying down there, they
don't need a car. Let Pascal rent something."

"We've found the cards. There is nothing for you to do
up here now." Jacques pushed the meager bed pillows up
and settled into them, then hauled his aching leg onto the
hard mattress for a rest. He'd sprained ligaments running,
had concussions from diving, broken his leg when thrown
from a horse. He'd learned how to work past physical pain.

He'd thought he'd learned to deal with emotional pain
these last years, but Amy was stripping off his shallow
bandages and revealing the raw wounds beneath. He
could follow Luigi's advice, slap the pretty bandage of
work back in place, and leave now. Or he could air the
wound Amy had opened and see what happened.

"The same can be said of you. Your job here is done,"
Luigi pointed out. "If you mean to chase after that female, I'll be here to tow you out of ravines."

Jacques laughed. "You are as superstitious as the locals. I think I'll attend church tomorrow. I want to find
out more about how this town works." He wanted to
know why Amy had to sell her house. A woman like that
loved her home and did not give it up without reason. Yet
she showed more passion about obtaining the mill than
about leaving her home.

It did not cost so much to live here. Surely her husband
paid for the children. She had a job. Why should she lose
her house?

Personal involvement. He was digging himself into it
up to his neck—and it was holding his interest as much as
his work.

"Pascal and his pals want you to work on that bid. They'll not be happy," Luigi warned.

"We have telephones. I'm not a number cruncher. If they want my approval, they can call. That's why I hire them. Did Amy say she was cooking at the café tonight?"

"You want her to blow up the stove? I'll go over and pick up something. You need to keep that leg raised."

"I can fetch my own supper," Jacques replied patiently. "I know my limits and will not exceed them. I am no longer twelve."

"And you're no longer twenty and able to bounce back from another attack of female-itis. That one's a heartbreaker. Do both of you a favor and leave her alone."

Luigi was most likely right, but Jacques was beyond reason. He'd tasted her kisses. Her moans of desire still sang in his ears. He had no place he needed to be once he won the bid. And lots of reasons to linger.

"Go guard the cards." Jacques waved him away.

Since bank vaults wouldn't open until Monday, they'd had to leave the valuable pattern cards with the bankruptcy judge handling the mill's business. The judge's wife had been less than enthusiastic with the dirty assortment of crates on her carpets.

"Anyone stealing those filthy old things would have to be crazy. Crazy people are easy to spot." Jerking his cap on again, Luigi stalked out.

He'd been called crazy before. Jacques shrugged and relaxed into his pillows until he realized he'd sent Luigi away before he'd carried in ice.

Maybe he would call Amy over here to nurse him. She would do it, he knew, although she might pour the ice on his head first. Or parts lower.

❧ THIRTEEN ❧

"Yes, Bill, calculate the income from the sale of the pattern cards into the plus side. We may as well make the bottom line look good."

Amy brushed a strand of hair from her perspiring forehead, balanced the cordless between shoulder and ear, and returned to rolling up her crystal wedding glasses in sheets of newspaper.

Saturday night, and she was wrapping up her life instead of enjoying it. She really needed that shrink Jo had told her to get.

"They are only valuable to one buyer that I know of," she replied to Bill's question. "If we don't get this bid, Jacques will walk off with the mill's most valuable asset and leave the place empty."

She wasn't ignorant. She knew what Jacques intended to do to the mill. She was too tired to cry over it. And too mad to go down without a fight. The town had to beat his bid.

She'd all but begged the man to listen to her. Instead, he'd told her she was *amazingly* stubborn. Fine, that's what she would be.

The mayor was huffing and puffing about it being preferable for a professional to run the mill rather than a lot of unemployed mill workers, and she considered driving to town and cramming the receiver down his throat. Learning to throw dishes would be just as useful.

"You have to pay professionals, Bill," she said calmly when he wound down. "Read the newspapers. Look around. CEOs are emptying corporate bank accounts with golden parachutes worth millions of dollars. We can't afford that. We *have* experienced people. It just means a few minor changes in the figures. We'll be ready by Tuesday."

She hoped for once in her life someone was listening as she clicked off the phone. Maybe she should have Jo speak for her. When Jo talked, the whole town listened. Amy really wished she could learn that trick.

Her back ached from kneeling on the floor, bending over boxes. Her ribs ached from the beating they'd taken from the air bags. She was lucky she didn't have a broken nose or collarbone. Enduring unquenchable lust for her competition added insult to torture.

She ought to take a long soak in the whirlpool. It might be the last time she'd have that luxury. She needed to be out of here by the last Friday of the month. That gave her barely three weeks to pack years of accumulated junk.

She rolled another delicate glass in inky newspaper and set it on the fancy guest-bathroom towel she was using as padding between layers. Glasses packed, box full, she sealed the carton with packing tape and used her Sharpie to mark the contents of a life she was leaving behind.

To save electricity, she had opened the windows instead of turning on the air conditioner, but the day's accumulated heat hadn't dissipated. She used a kitchen towel to wipe the grime and perspiration off her face and debated which of her cooking items she could spare for the next few weeks, and which she absolutely had to have at her fingertips until they moved.

An insistent buzz interrupted her reverie. The doorbell hadn't actually chimed since Evan had slammed out last year.

Who the devil would be at her door at nine at night? Running her fingers through her dusty hair in a vain attempt to straighten it, she crossed the living room and checked the side window.

Jacques?

Her heart did an excited little skip, then sank to her knees as reality set in.

He stood under the one working porch light looking as if he'd stepped straight from a magazine ad. Wearing a sporty European-cut jacket and clean trousers, he had one hand in his pocket, pushing back his jacket, while he rested the other on the brass handle of his ebony cane and studied the geranium hanging in her recessed entry.

Curiosity forced her to open the door. Or else she feared her racing heart was the first sign of a heart attack and she didn't want to die alone. Six of one, half dozen of the other.

His attention swerved instantly to focus on her, and he beamed with the charming delight that left her defenseless.

"It is Saturday night. You are supposed to be at the café!" He stepped inside before she could slam the door.

"We had no customers. I left early." She stepped back, feeling grubby in the face of his groomed sophistication.

"But the food doesn't taste the same unless you are serving it." He studied her weary face, glanced around at shelves devoid of ornament, and caught her elbow with the authority of a man accustomed to having his way. "We will sit and drink some of your delicious tea."

"I don't have time to sit and chat." She slid her elbow
from his grasp and led the way to the kitchen, trying to
put as much distance as possible between them. It didn't
help. She could feel his gaze through the shirt on her
back. Her arm still tingled from his touch.

She should get rid of him. Now.

But she couldn't ask a guest in and not offer refresh-
ment. He'd have to drink iced tea out of plastic glasses. "I
have to wait until the kids are asleep before I can get any
packing done."

"Where are you moving?" he asked casually, poking
with his cane at a box marked *tea set* and glancing
around instead of taking one of the matching golden oak
kitchen chairs she offered.

"To the apartment over the café for now. We close on
the house at the end of the month, so I've been moving
things down there every time I go in."

He didn't argue when she set a plastic glass of ice and
tea in front of him and poured more for herself. Hot tea
on a hot night was obscene. He was learning their ways.

"Sit." He gestured imperiously at a chair.

A few hours ago, he'd been swallowed up by his staff,
plotting the demise of the mill at the judge's house. She'd
gone to work as usual, feeling gut sick that she'd just
given him the excuse he needed to steal the mill, instead
of talking him out of it, as she'd hoped.

She was amazing all right. Amazingly stupid.

Figuring he wouldn't sit unless she did, Amy took a
chair, trying to relax. She'd needed a break anyway.
When he finally sat opposite her and, at her pointed look,
obediently propped his bad leg on another chair, she un-
leashed her curiosity. "I assume you're not here just to
tell me I'm not at the café."

Jacques flashed his devastating smile. "Direct and to the point. I like that. I could say I was bored sitting in the motel, pining for your company. We are very good together."

"Hmmm, *amazing*," she murmured, avoiding his wicked gaze. Just the image of Jacques on a motel bed was enough to raise her libido to full throttle, without putting herself into the picture. "And I could say," she said, mimicking him, "that you have Catarina to visit, and I'd rather climb in my whirlpool and pretend today never happened. I don't know why you're still in North-fork now that you've found what you want."

"But I want many things, and Catarina is not one of them. Your bath sounds tempting, though."

His boyish grin sent her hormones spinning even though she could swear she was too tired to even think of sex. If nothing else, she was comfortable handling little boys. "Stop that," she told him crossly, irritated with herself more than with him. "We had an overreaction to the accident this afternoon. That's all. So if you came up here looking for more of the same, you can go away now."

"While admittedly," he continued as if she hadn't said a word, "sharing a bath with you is one of my fondest desires, I would settle for just the whirlpool," he said with such fervency he almost sounded sincere. "My room does not have one. You have a marvelous house. I have never seen so many modern conveniences." He studied the flashing clock in the built-in microwave and the stainless fixtures that had been cutting-edge when she'd had them installed. "In Europe, all is old, old, old. This is as modern as my late Porsche."

"If you're trying to make me feel guilty, it's not working. You can afford the resort in Asheville. I'm sure if you ask, they'll let you admire their kitchen." She wouldn't ask what he wanted again. She didn't think she could face the humiliation. Mama had warned that men thought divorced women were easy, and Amy had certainly made it seem that way by her behavior earlier. She still cringed in embarrassment.

And burned with the desire for a human touch again. She refused to believe it was just Jacques's touch she craved. That would be too desperate. She studied her glass instead of the mouth that had driven her wild in one-point-two seconds, faster than his Porsche.

"I am trying to find a way to beg you to take me in," he said, forcing Amy to jerk her head up and stare at him in incredulity.

When she said nothing, he continued, the expression in his dark eyes intense, as if willing her to cooperate. "The motel is old and musty and has no whirlpool. My leg cannot bend so easily for the long drive down the mountain to the resort. It would be a kindness if you can find a place for me here until I find something else. I will pay generously."

Amy could only stare at the confident idiot. If she let herself fully comprehend his request, she would burst into tears. "Do I look that desperate?" she asked before she could bite her tongue.

"I am that desperate," he replied. "It would be a kindness, and I will try very hard not to impose upon you in any way."

If he'd tried to deny her question or answered with flattery, she wouldn't have taken him seriously. Instead, his look of discomfort seemed real, and her stomach hurt as if she'd been punched. He was sitting here like a very human man, not an object she could classify as Enemy or Fraud or Foreign or all those other classifications she'd used to keep a distance between them. She had never been able to deny someone in need.

He glanced at her packing boxes. "I could even help you pack. And haul furniture."

She wanted to laugh at the thought of the elegant Brit lugging her antiques up the stairs to Jo's tiny apartment with his bad knee, but tonight, she was too tired and embarrassed. "How did you get up here?" she asked, feeling her determination to keep him at a distance dissolve.

He shrugged in an attempt to look nonchalant. "In the Hummer."

"Did you drive it?"

He scraped his cane back and forth on the slate floor. "It's automatic."

"Does Luigi know?"

He scowled, and she knew she'd finally scored a point. "You couldn't stay here without Luigi," she insisted. "He'd have a stroke. I have two kids who will be up at sunrise."

"I like your children. I need a whirlpool. I will deal with Luigi. I wish to stay a mountain away from Cat and friends. Money is no object." He swung his cane dismissively.

"You realize your accent gets stronger when you want something?"

He widened his eyes in surprise, then grinned, destroying the intense seriousness he'd built earlier. "Does it work?"

"I hate you, and yes, it does. It turns women into putty, and you know it."

His smile would have done a Cheshire cat proud. "No

other woman has ever admired my accent, but it's only you I wish to turn to putty."

"Putty is messy. And then it gets brittle and cracks," she reminded him, before swallowing the rest of her tea and sitting back. To her amazement, she was actually weighing the argument. She seriously disliked being steamrollered by a man who didn't know how to take no for an answer, but she could use the cash. Babysitters for Louisa were expensive. She couldn't ask Jo to do it all the time. Josh needed more school clothes, they both would need new winter coats, and she couldn't count on Evan for anything extra.

Besides, a day of this madhouse, and Jacques would run for the door. Why deny herself a little extra money just because she couldn't control her responses to him?

She was being logical, reasonable, practical—and she'd defend to the death her right to believe her own lies. "Until Tuesday?" she asked.

"For as long as is feasible," he corrected. "I will pay daily, like the motel."

"I'm not offering maid service," she said decisively. "I have way too much to do as it is. If you want me to feed you, you have to eat when we do and eat what we have. Otherwise, you're on your own."

Instead of laughing in triumph, Jacques nodded seriously. "I can make my own bed. Boarding schools teach a few useful things. In the morning, I will have Luigi help you, and I will pay what I was paying the resort, plus extra for meals. Will that suit?"

No, it scared her absolutely to death. But then, so did moving and looking for a job. If she were really truthful, the entire world terrified her. She didn't know the entire world, but she was coming to know Jacques. She *liked* him, against all better judgment. They even had more in common than mutual lust, although she was reluctant to admit either, because it was dangerous to her emotional well-being. She knew she could trust him—to a point.

"You will be my first B and B customer," she stated, adding one more reason to agree to the absurd. "It will be a learning experience."

For a moment, Jacques looked as apprehensive as she felt, but then he wiped away the expression with a smile. "Excellent. I have a bag in the car."

The dirty rat fink. He'd *known* he could sway her. She could see it in his laughing dark eyes. But she wasn't backing down now that she'd made her decision. She'd spent ten damned years learning to be a proper hostess.

He held out his hand for her to shake.

Touching him would be a serious mistake. Amy did it anyway. Jacques's clasp was warm, hard, and reassuring, and his gentle squeeze was meant to convince her she was doing the right thing.

All she had to do was convince him that she made the rules.

For once, she intended to be in charge of her life.

Jacques turned on the water faucet in the enormous ivory tub surrounded by sumptuous limestone tile and decided he'd lost his mind. Gardenia candles and jasmine bath salts in delicate rose-crystal containers were grouped artistically next to luxurious rose-colored towels. If that wasn't feminine enough, Amy had added a bouquet of pink roses and ferns to an antique Waterford vase.

The bathroom was so very sensual, so very much the hidden side of his sensible Amy that he grew hard just looking at it. Or smelling it. Even her perfume lingered in the air. It wasn't often that he felt out of place, but he felt like a stallion in the mare's barn right now.

A light rap at his door confirmed he'd lost his famed elusiveness. He usually used crowds as a defense against intimacy, and now he'd opened the gates to a woman so vulnerable he couldn't ignore her.

Well, he supposed he could ignore her right now. She tapped so lightly he assumed she hoped he wouldn't hear. He shrugged on his robe over the slacks he hadn't removed yet.

He opened the door, catching her in mid-knock. "I was just thinking I should ask you to join me in your lovely tub."

She blushed and stared at the V of his robe rather than look up and meet his eyes. She'd brushed out the layered brown curls of her hair, letting it fall loose about her face, and pulled a pretty turquoise tunic over her tank top, effortlessly creating her own understated style. He admired a woman who didn't feel compelled to spend an hour in front of a mirror to be comfortable with her appearance.

"I just wanted to warn you to lock your door. The kids are used to running in and out without knocking," she said hurriedly, as if ready to run once the words were out of her mouth.

"Will they worry if they cannot find you? I will be happy to take another room if this is an inconvenience." Jacques refrained from smacking his forehead for his stupidity. Of course the whirlpool was in her room. He'd seen her things in there. But he'd been equating them with a candlelit bath for two and not thinking about the mundane—like children who jumped on their mother's bed every morning.

"No, I know how to distract them. Locking the door is simply a precaution. I put clean sheets on the bed this morning. I hope you'll be comfortable."

She backed away, and Jacques grabbed her wrist before she could escape. "Amy, wait, please."

He didn't know what he meant to say. He simply knew that he didn't want her to leave. She finally lifted her gaze to his face and waited patiently for him to speak.

"I want to talk to you but don't know how," he admitted, surprising even himself. *Talk* wasn't what he wanted, was it? "I look in your understanding eyes and want to say things I haven't said to anyone, but I cannot." He thought that might actually be true, but he would try not to dwell on it too much. "You back away like a frightened doe every time I try."

"That's because I *am* a frightened doe, with two fawns to protect," she said bluntly. "You will find someone understanding among your own crowd. Brigitte seems a very intelligent listener."

Brigitte was an astute cynic with a heart of ice. He did not want Brigitte. He was discovering he preferred a backbone of steel well padded by feminine curves and a loving nature.

"Perhaps I should go, after all," he said, surprising himself. "I did not think this through. I would not upset your children. Routine is very important to them."

"You say that as if you've had experience," she said with a shade of suspicion.

He had to work at flashing a grin. "I was once a child." He arched his eyebrows, challenging her to argue the point.

Amy tilted her head to study him, and it was all he could do not to avoid her too perceptive gaze.

"Take a look around, Jacques," she replied with a gesture at the stacked boxes in the hall. "Their lives are already in complete chaos, and they're handling it just fine. Stay. You've convinced me it will work." Amy pried his fingers loose from her wrist and escaped.

This time, Jacques let her go.

Shutting the door, he locked it, but no lock would shut out his raging libido.

Or the echoing loneliness of the empty room after Amy's departure.

⫸ FOURTEEN ⫷

Jacques heard the children whispering in the hall outside the bedroom door. He tucked in his shirt and zipped his trousers, wondering how to deal with Amy's children. It was not as if he'd seduced their mother, but he felt a vague sense of guilt anyway.

Both his parents had refrained from bringing home their lovers while he was there, but then, he was in their homes so seldom that it could hardly have imposed on their love lives much. The women he'd slept with these last years hadn't had children, or if they did, he didn't know about them. It was all very civilized.

He wasn't Amy's lover yet, but dealing with her children was far more intimate, and intimacy made him edgy. One couldn't easily have brief affairs with children around.

He buckled his belt and left his coat in the closet. The aroma of coffee drifting up from Amy's fabulous kitchen told him breakfast was nearly ready, and he knew from experience that children and breakfast were not good for suit coats. Amazing how quickly all the old instincts returned.

He'd always wanted brothers and sisters. He supposed, if he was inclined to examine his actions, he'd married Gabrielle not just because he was insanely in love and wanted his child to bear his name, but because he wanted a family of his own. He no longer lived a life that would be good for young ones, but the old longing apparently hadn't gone away with time.

He crouched down, eased open the bedroom door, and put a finger to his lips. Before the giggling children could escape, he scooped them up and carried them down the hall to their bedrooms. They shrieked in joy and tried to cling to him as he heaved them on separate bunk beds. "Where are your clothes, my friends?" he intoned in his best giant voice.

He heard Amy calling his name anxiously from the bottom of the stairs, and he stuck his head around the doorjamb to call back. "We're quite fine. Go back to what you are doing, and we'll be down in a minute."

He could almost swear her uncertainty sent a big question mark floating up the stairs. He smiled and proceeded to direct the process of dressing for church. It had been a very, very long time since he'd done this, but he remembered the basics. Charm and flimflammery worked very well on children.

After much tussling and giggles, he followed the children down the stairs sometime later, all three of them wearing crowns of underwear on their heads. Louisa's hair stuck out at all angles, and Josh seemed to have on mismatched socks, but all in all, he thought he'd done well.

Amy stared at their little parade with wide-eyed astonishment. He'd expected laughter, but the blaze of wonder and admiration in her gaze worked just as well. So, he was showing off, but if it made her happy, then where was the wrong?

He knew, but he wasn't prepared to admit it, not on this bright sunshiny morning with a beautiful woman wielding a spatula like a director's baton to produce a symphony of mouthwatering aromas and two engaging youngsters chattering at the cheerfully set table.

"We got dressed," Louisa chirruped.

"Yes, I can see that. And very pretty you all look, too." She sent Jacques an appreciative look that said his informal attire had not gone unappreciated either.

"We had to leave off our robes of office," he explained with a grin. "It seems Louisa's is just a little bit wet, so we came in casual dress today."

"Ah, that explains it," she nodded knowingly, doing her best to bite back a grin of her own. "And will we have oatmeal or eggs this morning, Your Majesties?"

"Oatmeal!" Louisa cried loudly.

Amy looked at Jacques apologetically. "I'll have to toast your bread in a skillet. The toaster oven expired a while back."

"Under the influence of your magnetic personality?" he asked, sweeping the crown off his head and reaching for the coffee mug she'd set on the table.

She shot him a glare that had no sharpness, and he laughed. "Where is the oven and your screwdrivers?"

"You can't put a screwdriver into an electrical appliance; you'll electrocute yourself!"

"Not if you pull the plug." He found the oven, carried it to a counter with a bar stool, and sat down to examine its innards.

"You fix appliances?" she asked with a note of awe, handing him the requested tool.

He flashed her a grin. "I have no idea, but I'm thinking if I stay here for long, I'd better learn."

Amy dropped her spatula into the pan and stared at him as if he'd spoken in an unknown tongue, and

Jacques realized what he'd said. It had just been a figure of speech, a silly remark. He couldn't stay. Surely she knew that.

Clearing her throat, Amy picked up the utensil again. "No danger there. The bid for the mill is this week. You'll be safely away before you have to resuscitate more appliances."

She returned to stirring her cooking pots, leaving Jacques cringing at the accusation hanging in the air.

"Amy Warren, have you lost your mind?" Elise whispered, pulling Amy aside before she could escape with the kids to the church's nursery later that morning. "Why are you arriving with the competition? You know what he is, don't you?"

Besides being Amy's lawyer, Elise DuBois was Amy's best friend and everything Amy wanted to be when she grew up. Model tall, and gorgeous, she was also extremely intelligent and a sharp lawyer, though her brains weren't what men noticed first when Elise swayed into a room.

A moment ago, Jacques had shaken Elise's hand without reacting to her blatant sexuality. Not offering Elise any of the flirtatious smiles or flattery he bestowed on Amy, he'd let the children drag him off to say hello to Jo and Flint.

The man confused her.

"He offered me three hundred dollars to use my *whirlpool*," Amy whispered. "He came downstairs this morning wearing Josh's underwear on his head and carrying Louisa's teddy bear. He put raisin smiley faces in their *oatmeal*. Kill me, would you, please?"

"He's *bribing* you," Elise hissed. "He's trying to distract you while he robs the town blind. Don't let those midnight eyes fool you."

Amy was afraid it was already too late for that. She could resist surface charm, but Jacques had somehow managed to convince her that he was far deeper than the eye could see. And what the eye could see was too tempting for her to be thinking about.

"That's what terrifies me. It's just so hard to believe anyone so wonderful with children could be so cruel," Amy answered gloomily, watching Jacques swing Louisa into his arms as naturally as if she belonged there. Hoss yelled "Zack" at him across the parking lot, and Jacques returned the greeting cheerily. "The kids adore him, and he's hauling boxes in his Hummer, and he's so damned good-natured! How do I say no?"

"Watch me."

Amy followed behind her friend as Elise marched across the lot to steal Louisa away from Jacques. Always obedient, Louisa wrapped her chubby arms around Elise's neck and kissed her sloppily on the cheek. Jacques grinned, pretended Josh was his cane, and leaned on his head, much to the boy's delight.

"My daughter is with me this weekend, and I've hired a nanny for her," Elise announced to an amused Jo and Flint. "The three of us can help Amy haul furniture. Mr. Saint-Etienne ought to spend the afternoon with the mayor, learning more about Northfork and the mill. Come along, sir, and I'll introduce you around."

Briskly, Elise handed Louisa back to Amy and appropriated Jacques's arm. In her heels, Elise was nearly the same height as Jacques. Both with sleek dark hair and designer clothes, they made an elegantly sophisticated couple.

Jacques resisted the lawyer's pull long enough to wink. "A Tartar, this one. I will see you later, yes?"

Amy didn't have time to reply before Elise signaled several councilmen and dragged him away.

"Two of a kind," Jo said, laughter edging her voice as they watched the couple stroll off. Elise gracefully maneuvered the gravel drive in spike heels, swaying her hips in a manner Amy could imitate only if she wished to endanger life and limb. Jacques sedately swung his cane in accompaniment, not appearing to limp at all as he tilted his ear closer to Elise to catch her words.

"Do sharks devour other sharks?" Amy asked, almost relieved that Elise had come to her rescue. She didn't relish being shark bait.

"I thought last I heard, he was a wolf," Flint commented. "Do we need to move you into the apartment tonight so he can have the house to himself?"

"That hunk is too slippery to be a wolf," Jo decided. "But why shouldn't Amy have a little fun? After stuffy Evan, a man who laughs could be nice to have around for a bit."

"Sharks aren't nice, and wolves aren't big fuzzy dogs," Amy retorted. "I do not need a man to have fun, thank you very much. Moving into the apartment sounds like an excellent idea. Then I can open the café in the morning."

It also sounded like a miserable, lonely idea after the laughter of this morning, but Jacques would be gone shortly, leaving two brokenhearted children if she wasn't careful.

She was a realist. Elise might be a shark in business, but she was also a saint crusading for lost causes. Jacques, on the other hand, rationally explained the reasons why a cause was lost and moved on. She couldn't fault him for it.

"Moving into an apartment and opening the café isn't fun." Jo squeezed Amy's shoulders. "Take a walk on the wild side, Sis."

"You sound just like Jacques, and here we are talking sin standing in front of a church. I'm telling Preacher Mark on you." Doing her best not to weaken, Amy shooed her children toward the church school. That was all she needed—her family approving of a fling.

She cast a glance at Elise, who was commandeering Jacques, the mayor, and two councilmen. For just a moment, she was jealous, but not of Elise and Jacques, she assured herself. They were handsome together, admittedly, but what she really wanted was to be self-assured and competent like her friend.

"I wuv you, Mommy." Louisa pecked her cheek as Amy set her down in a roomful of toddlers.

For kisses like that, she would forgo being businesslike.

"And I love you both." Kneeling, she hugged them. "How about we spend the night in Aunt Jo's apartment tonight? We'll have pizza and cupcakes."

They shouted in agreement—not really understanding how drastically their lives were about to change.

Jacques refrained from wincing when the mayor called him "Zack" for the third time. *Zack* was better than *Jack* or the *Saint Stevie* he knew the locals had been calling him. Apparently, sometime during the turkey shoot, he had been promoted to Zack, a graduate summa cum laude of the manly man school.

They could call him whatever they liked if they'd only

let him get back to Amy. He knew she'd scurried away as soon as his back was turned, but he wasn't a man to quit once his interest was aroused. No other woman had held his fascination as this one did. She was even more intriguing than the pattern cards. His pulse picked up just watching her.

He couldn't keep his mind from returning to Amy as she'd appeared this morning, flushed from the heat of the oven and humming while she decorated muffins with raisins and sugar crystals. She'd looked as delectable as the muffins in her ice-cream-white shorts and golf shirt, her hair curling in the humidity. But the best part had been when she'd looked up to see him standing there with underwear on his head and children hanging off his arms, and she'd flushed with as much pleasure as if he'd just made love to her.

Transforming her persistent worried frown to light-hearted laughter made him feel as though he'd just won the Olympics. He didn't know how else to describe the incredible joy her smile aroused. He would have stood on his head and sung "La Marseillaise" if she'd asked it of him.

Which meant he was probably losing all perspective, if not his entire mind, he reflected. Right now, he didn't care. He was on the prowl, and his prey lay ahead. Following the mayor into church, Jacques scanned the sanctuary, locating Amy's shiny hair as she sat in a pew beside her nephews.

He disengaged the claws of the woman on his arm. Cold women like Elise were wonderful business partners and very bad bed partners. He needed a woman who gave in the soft, generous ways that Amy displayed in every word and action.

Shaking hands with his companions, Jacques escaped and slid into the pew beside his hostess. Amy glanced up at him in surprise and with what he hoped was a little blush of pleasure. From the far end of the pew, her brother-in-law acknowledged him with a nod.

"Where is your sister?" Jacques whispered.

Amy nodded toward the choir. "Listen. You can't miss her."

Sure enough, when the congregation settled down, the piano struck a chord, the choir swung into the first note of a hymn, and a clear soprano carried the melody soaring to the vaulted ceiling, raising goose bumps up and down his arms. Jacques located Joella in the front row, garbed in somber choir robes instead of her usual spangled bright colors. The choir director very rightly singled her out to drag the rest of the lackluster voices triumphantly into song.

"She ought to be on CD," he marveled, whispering into Amy's ear.

"She is," Amy acknowledged proudly. "It came out a few months ago and did very well on the country music charts for a first album."

Jacques sat back and pondered that marvel. He had grown up in Europe and visited his mother's country only briefly, with quick hops to New York City or D.C. for business. His mother's parents had died when he was young, so he'd never seen the mountains where she'd been born. She'd spoken disparagingly of ignorance and poverty and prejudice, so he'd never had any urge to learn more.

Only a desperate need for distraction from the painful memories of Europe and his stale life had dragged him into rural America. He hadn't wanted anything more than unfamiliar faces and new sights. But here he was, in the presence of the American equivalent of royalty—an entertainment star and her family. He saw no evidence of ignorance, poverty, or prejudice, just people living their lives as they did everywhere else on the planet.

Jacques had lived all his life in cities with art and museums. He had never known a country music singer. Or a woman who put icing on muffins and pigs' faces on icing because her little girl loved pigs. He'd never known a woman who short-circuited machinery when she was upset—he didn't have any trouble believing it. She short-circuited him every time she came in view.

He grinned hugely. Losing the Porsche had been an expensive lesson, but he now knew never to upset Amy when near delicate equipment.

Her jasmine scent drifted around him, and he could sense all those lovely curves just an arm's breadth away. She tried not to touch him, but every time one of her nephews squirmed, she had to adjust her position. Jacques deliberately shifted closer when she did, until his arm brushed hers, and she had to sit up very straight so their hips didn't touch.

He crossed his leg over his knee and let his shoe tip nudge her stockinged calf. She had changed into a taupe suit with a short jacket that was very attractive on her shapely figure.

She shifted her leg out of his reach. He put his foot back down and slumped so his hip and leg pressed along hers. *Oo-la-la*. He liked that position.

She elbowed him—hard.

Yes! She was as aware of him as he was of her. Jacques nearly laughed out loud.

He had not been to church in a very long time, but even

he knew he shouldn't be thinking about sex in church. Politely focusing his attention on the preacher, he sat up and placed his hand on Amy's knee.

She dug her fingernails into a small piece of his skin and pinched.

He decided right there and then that a woman who did not give in easily had a lot to give.

"You are moving your beds in here?" Jacques asked in evident dismay after limping up the stairs to the loft apartment against Amy's wishes. "There are no rooms!" He swept his arm dramatically to indicate the dusty, box-cluttered studio.

"It's an adventure, like camping out." Amy stoically dropped her box of kitchen utensils on the tiny Formica counter. "I need to figure out how much I can leave boxed up and how much I absolutely have to have to get by until we find a new place."

Elise's teenaged nanny and her boyfriend entered with cartons of linens and towels, and Flint's middle-school boys carried up bed parts, showing off for Elise's gorgeous nine-year-old daughter. Amy directed the kids' beds to be placed in the corner where Jo's piano had once stood. She didn't want the children climbing the ladder into the loft.

Jacques stalked through the apartment growling at the lack of room and disparagingly wiping dust off fixtures. Good. Maybe once she saw him as the snobby rich boy he was supposed to be, she wouldn't tingle all over every time he looked at her. His kiss yesterday had turned her head so badly that she couldn't see the wolf in him any longer.

His behavior in church hadn't helped any. She hadn't

heard a word the preacher spoke with Jacques's muscular legs deliberately rubbing hers. She'd wanted to laugh and giggle like a teenager. And touch him back.

Keeping him distant from her children was the smart thing to do. They needed a man in their life too much. And apparently, she wasn't any less susceptible.

"I thought I was to be your bed-and-breakfast guest. How will you feed me if you are here?" he demanded, hitting his cane against the old wooden floor and glaring out the windows at the lovely mountain view.

Amy winced guiltily. "I promised the kids pizza and cupcakes tonight. I can't feed you that. I'll come up and heat one of the meals I froze for days like this. Just think, you'll have the whole house to yourself. You can wear your own underwear on your head if you like."

He snorted, but she didn't think it was with laughter.

"If I wished to eat by myself, I would have stayed at the motel. And breakfast? Do you leave me a box of cereal?"

He almost sounded hurt. She had *hurt* him? How was that possible? The whole world was his oyster, and she was just an irritating grain of sand.

"You have an entire entourage who will jump if you call. I have air mattresses that can be used for beds." She'd left the master bedroom furniture for Jacques and moved the smaller guest set down here for herself. "Tell Luigi to stay with you. I'll feed both of you and not charge extra. And if you don't want to eat at the café in the morning, I'll set the coffeepot on automatic and prepare breakfast sandwiches and muffins you can heat up. We'll work something out."

"Your house will not be sold for weeks! Surely I did not drive you from your lovely home with my presence?" He looked disturbed at the implication.

So much for seeing him as spoiled and demanding. He was *not* supposed to care if he'd driven her out of her own home.

If she was honest, she'd have to say he had. She hadn't slept a wink the night before, knowing he was under the same roof, so close, but so far away . . .

But that sounded too much as if she were running away, when she was actually running forward. This was her life now. If she quit thinking about the past, there was a certain amount of excitement in finding her own place.

To ease his conscience, she offered, "You will be here only until the bid decision is made on Tuesday. If you like, we can stay until then. I just thought you'd prefer to be alone."

"I am always alone," he said grumpily, opening the door of the small refrigerator. "I will call Luigi. You need not worry about us. We can feed ourselves."

Now she really did feel guilty. It was easier to feel guilt than acknowledge the twinge of pleasure from knowing he desired her company. "I will prepare your meals, don't be silly. We're not moving the family room, so you'll have the stereo and television. You can have your entire team up to work on whatever you work on all day. It's just more convenient for me to work and look after the kids if I stay here."

"Hey, Aunt Amy, where do you want this?" Johnnie held up a bed lamp, distracting her from the discussion.

By the time she'd sorted out the lamp and various other pieces of furniture she'd carried down in the pickup she'd traded for with Flint, Jacques had disappeared.

There were only so many hours in the day. She couldn't allow guilt to occupy them. She'd changed back into her white shorts after church, and later realized she was paying for her vanity in choosing her sexiest casual outfit when she discovered the dirt smeared across her rear.

When Jacques still hadn't returned by the time the beds were set up and boxes arranged against one wall, Amy went in search of him. She had to pick up the kids at Jo's, order a pizza, and run up to the house to fix his dinner. The Hummer was still parked in the street. He couldn't have gone far. Perhaps he'd been unwilling to climb those rickety stairs again with his stiff leg.

"Did you see which way Jacques went?" she asked the nanny as the girl climbed into Elise's Mercedes with Flint's boys.

"Zack?" the nanny repeated. "I saw him walk up Canary." She nodded toward the side street that wound up the hollow behind the town's business district.

Amy didn't think walking up hills was good exercise for torn ligaments, but she wasn't the man's keeper. Waving the kids off, she climbed into the pickup and drove around the corner to see if she could find him. He had his own transportation, but she didn't want to drive off after their brief disagreement. She knew she should hate a man who could destroy the town, but she wasn't any good at hating. If she wasn't so terrified about losing her home, she'd enjoy Jacques's playful humor and seductive flattery. She enjoyed his way with children far too much already.

Her heart sank when she found him in the yard of a familiar old house with a faded For Sale sign out front—the mill cottage.

He was prying loose the aluminum siding with his cane like a man on a mission.

As she climbed out of the truck, he looked up and grinned in delight. "I think it is an original Craftsman!"

She didn't think there was one man in this entire town who recognized the architectural significance of her secret gem—except this one. He was too damned perceptive and clever—

Giving him the power to steal still another of her dreams.

≼ FIFTEEN ≽

"It is not a Craftsman," Amy argued, wrapping her arms around her middle to prevent herself from flinging them around the solid porch posts and screaming—*Mine, mine, you can't have it!*

"Of course it is. Look at the huge bungalow porch, the posts that are wider on the bottom than the top, and under here . . ." Jacques jimmied up the tacky old aluminum. "Cedar shakes!"

"Bungalows don't have two stories, with an attic," she pointed out, then wanted to smack herself. Instead of pointing out all the obvious features, she ought to be wooing him away with promises of food. Why on earth was he looking at houses?

And if he won the mill and knew how valuable this house was, she'd never be able to buy it cheaply. Her heart sank down to one of her little toes. She'd *kissed* this man, thought the unthinkable even knowing he would be leaving soon. Someone really ought to just slap her.

"The previous owners popped up the top story, probably when they added the aluminum." Jacques tilted back his head so the blunt-cut hair at his nape fell over his collar. "Look, the chimney is stone. Halfway up, the color and size changes. They made it taller. I don't suppose the seller would let us see it tonight?"

"It's Sunday night. I don't suppose they would," she said as briskly as she could, while her heart bled. "I need to pick up the kids. Do you want me to fix your dinner now or after I get them?" *Now, now,* she prayed fervently. *Get away from my house.*

"Aren't you curious? Don't you want to see inside? Do you think they kept the built-in cabinetry?" Instead of answering her question about dinner, he climbed on the sloping porch to peer in the dirty windows for all the world like a boy who'd just discovered a secret cave.

Amy wanted to cry. She didn't think there was a single man in the entire *county* who recognized the gem behind the dilapidated exterior. Why did this frustrating, fascinating man have to be so smart? Even Evan hadn't known what this house was, and he'd run the mill that *owned* it.

She'd tried to persuade him to live here when they'd first moved back to town, but Evan had insisted on all new everything. She'd understood. He'd grown up in ticky-tacky housing as she had. She just admired the timeless quality of handmade, and he preferred the planned obsolescence of technology.

Opposites didn't attract. They just annoyed each other to death. The humor of that observation steadied her nerves enough to argue.

"I thought you didn't like old things," she said, remembering Jacques's comments on Europe being old and her kitchen being modern. And then she mentally kicked herself again. He worked with historic designs. *Duh.*

"I like modern conveniences, but they can be added anywhere. New houses do not have the quality of materials, the labor of love, the craftsmanship of old ones. The workers who built this were *proud* of their work. They weren't throwing up a piece of generic crap."

Right on every count, but she couldn't let him rhapsodize about it, or with his relentless zeal, Jacques would be knocking on the Realtor's door next, and then he would discover his company was already bidding on the gem.

She caught his muscled arm and leaned closer to distract him into listening to her. "Europe is full of monuments of craftsmanship that you can admire shortly. Would you like chicken marsala for dinner? Perhaps a small green bean salad to go with it?" She lured him away from the window, one step at a time.

Her position had Jacques looking down the cleavage exposed by her golf shirt. She had not used her femininity to distract in a long time, but apparently instinct kicked in quickly because she stuck her chest out a little more. Fine, she would sacrifice herself for a house. It certainly wouldn't hurt. His gaze had all her juices flowing. She'd forgotten she had breasts until Jacques touched them. They swelled now, aching for a repeat of his caresses.

But despite his temporary distraction, his formidable focus remained on *her* house. "But can you not see?" he persisted, following her down the stairs. "This house is perfect for you. Your beautiful antiques—the styles are Mission and Stickley, exactly what this house needs!"

For *her*? The madman wasn't distracted but looking at houses—for her? Stunned, she swung around to study his earnest gaze.

"I know." Amy bit her lip to prevent saying more. She had spent years refurbishing Arts and Crafts pieces that would fit the bungalow. "But I can't buy a house unless I have a job." She really didn't want to go down this path, not the way she was feeling right now. He'd have her feeling all warm and fuzzy and trusting, and then he'd lower the boom. She refused to be that easy to push over.

"You have a job," he protested. "Perhaps business is a little slow, but surely a place like this cannot cost much. I have just worked on land prices for the bids, and it costs nothing here compared to other places."

Amy relaxed slightly when he continued down the cracked sidewalk away from the cottage. "The café puts food on the table, nothing more." To keep him diverted, she opened up and offered a slice of herself. "Unless the mill reopens, we'll have to leave town so I can look for work elsewhere."

"That will never do!" He halted instead of opening the door of her truck, and stared at her in incredulity. "You are not meant to work in a filthy mill. You belong with your children."

With a look of annoyance, she opened the passenger door for him. "That's a sexist thing to say. I'll be fine at the mill. I have a degree in design. I'll finally put it to use."

Instead of climbing in, Jacques limped around to the driver's side to open the door for her, scowling as he did so.

"You're limping. You need to rest that leg," she scolded, taking her seat so he'd go back and sit down.

"I'll have the damned thing operated on," he said in a clipped tone unlike his usual cheerful one, then slammed the door after her.

There wasn't a lot she could say to that. This was an idiotic argument. They were both trying to take care of the other. How stupid was that? It wasn't any of her business what he did with his leg, or his arms, or any other body part. They were headed for a showdown, and in another day or so, after the explosion, they'd be off in opposite directions.

If she felt strangely bereft at the thought, it was only because Jacques and his friends had been such a welcome distraction in this unsettling time of her life. It had absolutely nothing to do with smoldering kisses and laughing charm and a man who actually understood about lovely old homes and Stickley antiques.

Her nose would grow three feet if she lied to herself any more.

Sitting in Amy's silent family room on Sunday night, Jacques slammed down a copy of the bid proposal Pascal had delivered to the judge. He'd just checked the lot number of the land in the bid against the realty company's Web site and matched it to the old house on Canary Street. The mill owned the house Amy wanted. "I hate this."

"Tell it to Pascal," Luigi growled from the recliner in front of the television. He had a beer and pretzels and was happy for the first time since their arrival. "I didn't have anything to do with it."

"I hate it that Amy isn't here. This is her home. Look at those rugs. Someone handloomed them. And the embroidered cushions on that rocker. These are not pieces of plastic bought at the local McWal-Mart."

He glared at the picture of a plastic family over the fireplace. That was not his stubborn, creative Amy sitting in a chair beneath the hand of a blond man wearing a satisfied smirk. The Amy he knew and appreciated was all natural, without the lipsticked smiling sophistication of the woman in the painting.

The woman in the painting looked like every other woman in his universe, primped, painted, and perfect. Could he be wrong about her? Impossible. That painting was the human equivalent of aluminum siding over Craftsman wood shakes.

"She'll be keeping her furniture. It isn't as if she sold that, too." Luigi turned up the sound on the car chase, clearly not *getting* it.

Jacques tightened his mouth in frustration. He couldn't just sit here and do nothing. Even if someone crossed the judge's palm with silver and Saint-Etienne Fabrications lost the bid, the mill could not last a year under the town's plan. He'd seen their plan. It was brave and bold and full of heart. It just wasn't feasible.

Which meant Amy would lose her house and move away from her family. It would break her heart.

If he won the bid, he would own the house that ought to be hers. He wasn't a fool. He'd seen the panic in her eyes. She desperately wanted that house.

And like a monumental idiot, he wanted her to have it. He ought to examine his motivation, but he preferred simple one-two-three logic. She wanted the house. She deserved the house. He wanted her to be happy. He wanted her, period. He had the ability to give her what she wanted. A house was far more practical than the bouquets and diamonds he usually showered on his women. Amy would prefer practical. Appealingly simple and logical.

He picked up the proposal again, finally comprehending the extent of power that this document wielded to shut down lives—lives that had touched his this past week.

Heaven only knew, he didn't have adequate judgment

to play God. He'd certainly displayed that flaw in glorious Technicolor. He knew business, computers, and historical design. He was appallingly deficient at personal relationships. Once upon a time he'd suffered from the idiocy of believing he could overcome his family propensity for emotional devastation, but he'd learned differently the hard way.

But if he could rent Amy's house for a few weeks, he could linger here a little, take a much needed vacation, and let his knee heal before he spent hours cramped on an airplane with no exercise to keep it limber.

A small side trip off his road to success wouldn't hurt anyone, would it?

"He wants to rent the house until closing!" Amy paced up and down the Stardust's wooden floor, clutching her elbows. It was Tuesday afternoon, the date for the court's decision on the mill.

Outside, heavy clouds had turned the day black, and a thunderstorm was dumping torrential rain on the mountain highway, creating waterfalls instead of puddles, forcing the sensible to stay home. The café's only customers were the mayor, Dave from the hardware store, and two town councilmen, all sipping coffee and talking desultorily while waiting for the judge's decision.

"Sounds like good money to me," Jo said sensibly. She scribbled in her rhyme notebook, then returned to spinning her stool and watching the rain come down. "What has your panties in a twist?"

"It means he knows he'll get the bid!" One ear aimed toward the baby monitor to listen for Louisa waking from her nap in Flint's office, the other waiting for the phone to ring, Amy tried not to split in two. "He's planning on staying to dispose of the mill assets."

"That's a pessimistic way to look at it. It could mean he was planning on helping with hiring and starting up the mill." Spinning to face the counter, Jo removed the last chocolate doughnut from the case.

Amy snatched the coffeepot from the burner and refilled the cups at the mayor's table. "I heard Mary Jean and Eddie took jobs over in Charlotte and are moving out," she called over her shoulder at Jo. "That will break up your band."

Jo shrugged. "Music seldom pays. It's all about sales these days."

"Eddie will be selling cars," Dave attested. "Young people like that need a future, and we just plain can't offer it. I heard Mary Jean found a place at the mall. My wife's going to miss her babysitting."

"We all are." Too keyed up to be polite, Amy returned the pot to the burner and continued pacing. "There won't be anyone left around here. We can board up the town and post a For Sale sign. Maybe some rich tourist will buy it."

Lightning flashed in the distance, followed by a low rumble of thunder.

"Any ducks swimming down the street yet?" Jo called, shutting out the discussion.

"Nope, but Myrtle might shortly." Amy checked the purple concrete pig at the corner of the café, but sturdy Myrtle didn't seem in any danger of floating off.

The phone rang, and everyone jumped. Despite the desultory conversation, nerves had stretched to their last raw edge waiting to hear the fate of the town.

"That'll be Flint. Hand it over." Jo stretched out her hand so that Amy could place the cordless in it.

Except for the roll of thunder and the pounding of rain, the café fell silent, its occupants hanging on every word. Flint had volunteered to wait at the courthouse in Asheville for the judge's decision and call as soon as he heard.

"Yeah, he said that?" Jo nibbled her pen tip. "Well, creditors rule, I guess. Yeah, yeah. You want to talk to Amy?"

Amy tensed. Jo's tone was not jubilant. She hovered close, just in case.

"Yeah, you're right about that. Love you, too. Check to see if I'm alive when you get here. Right." She hung up.

Every eye in the café was on Jo.

"It's all over but the death knell." Clicking off the phone, Jo heaved her mug at the stainless steel stove. The sturdy pottery crashed and bounced—the only sound in the room. Everyone knew what it meant when Jo flung dishes. "The judge sold the mill to the most cash, and that wasn't us."

In the gloomy silence following her announcement, the lights flickered, then went out, flooding the café in darkness.

"I didn't do that," Amy said automatically. But she might as well have, for all anyone listened. A burglar alarm screamed somewhere up the street, and every window on Main Street went dark.

≪ SIXTEEN ≫

"Why must you return to such a tedious place?" Cat protested as they rode in the Hummer from the courthouse to the resort. "Send someone to pack up the patterns and let us go home. You have what you want."

No, he didn't, but Jacques didn't bother responding to Cat's whine. Leaning his head against the front headrest, he tried to luxuriate in the usual adrenaline rush of winning.

The old ego boost wasn't there.

Amy and the town had fought so bravely. All he'd done was flash cash and impressive credentials. It had never been a contest at all.

"Champagne buffet at the spa?" Brigitte suggested from the seat behind him.

Jacques knew she had her BlackBerry out and was already hunting up the appropriate contacts to set up a celebratory dinner. She'd done it for him on numerous occasions. Bright lights, music, champagne—that's how he'd lived his life these last years—surrounding himself with illusions of happiness.

He had a wonderful life. He had accomplished everything he had ever set out to do. He was sitting on top of the world.

So why didn't he feel like celebrating? He'd just bought

a lost piece of history, a challenging project that would create a dream collection of design patterns he could sell to every museum and historic home in America, opening entirely new doors for his company.

Perhaps he was ill. He would have Amy take his temperature and fix him chicken soup. Just the thought of Amy leaning over to caress his brow made him feel better. Maybe she would wear a loose shirt and he could admire . . .

Amy was more likely to beat him with a raw chicken carcass than take his temperature. He'd stolen her future.

Not entirely, his inner voice reminded him. He'd told the judge he didn't want the cottage. Actually, he wanted it very much. It would make a wonderful mountain escape once he'd sent a crew in to bring it up to date. He'd love making design decisions for his own home. He could return here every summer, terrorize the turkey shoot, hang out at the café with Amy and friends, drop out of the fast lane for a few weeks a year.

He had a terrace apartment in London, a penthouse in Paris, and a villa in Italy. Who was he fooling? He'd never return here. He had no reason to.

"Arrange the buffet," he agreed, but it wasn't champagne that he wanted.

Perhaps he would feel better if he told Amy in person that the judge had accepted her bid on the cottage.

"I'll join you after a while," he said once the Hummer pulled up to the resort and everyone else had climbed out. Before Cat could complain, Jacques shut his door and signaled Luigi to drive on.

Without being told, his driver took the road to Northfork.

*　　*　　*

"What in bloody hell?" Sitting straight up, Jacques peered out the Hummer windshield as they drove around the bend and descended the hill into a lightless town of wet shadows. If he looked closely, he could see a flicker through a window here and there, but for all intents and purposes, the usually well-lit town blended into the darkness of the tree-studded hillside.

The thunderstorm had retreated to flashes on the far side of the mountain. The rain had stopped, but clouds still hid the stars.

Above the town, in the upper parking lot, flames leaped and blazed against the black sky, flickering pink and orange beneath the cloud banks.

"Bonfire?" Luigi suggested, slowing down to traverse an empty Main Street. Even the fake Victorian streetlights were out.

"There are no lights! Are we in the right place? I know they roll up the sidewalks after dark . . ."

Luigi slowed so the Hummer's headlights cut across dark storefronts and illuminated the street that wound up the mountain to the residential area. "Electricity must be out."

"Amy." Jacques slammed his head back against the headrest and winced. She had even him believing their silly superstition. He could imagine her furious enough at losing the mill to blow the electric grid across half the state.

Luigi chuckled as the headlights struck a line of trucks and cars pulled off the side of the road. Across the parking lot where the vehicles should have been was a banner stretched from one telephone pole to the next, framing the bonfire behind it. "This place sure knows how to throw a party," Luigi said in admiration.

Jacques read the banner in horror and disbelief. WEL-COME, ZACK, HONORARY CITIZEN. " 'Zack'? *Me?* For what?"

But already the athlete's hum of adrenaline lifted his spirits at the sight of the crowd rallying around the bon-fire. Competition was pointless without the recognition of accomplishment at the end. For the first time this day, triumph surged. They didn't hate him!

Or—did the town believe it was their victory, too? Did they think he meant to reopen the mill and put them to work?

Damn.

The tantalizing aromas of barbecuing food seeped through the Hummer's open window, and he realized he hadn't eaten since breakfast. He was suddenly starving.

Luigi maneuvered the massive vehicle off the road to the accompaniment of a sunburst of red and orange sparks igniting overhead. The traditional *oooohs* and *aaahs* followed, and then someone distinctly yelled, "Zack! He's here!" and a chorus of cheers rang over the noise of the exploding fireworks.

"If this is Northfork *losing* the mill bid," he muttered to his driver, "what would they do if they won?"

"Rode you around town on their shoulders, given you a ticker-tape parade, and the key to the city. Jeez Louise, they're setting those things off in the parking lot. They'll blow us all up."

Luigi's Brooklyn origins occasionally penetrated his European sophistication.

Jacques flung open the car door before his driver could decide fireworks were too dangerous for his health.

He craned his neck to watch red and blue rockets shoot across the clouds, leaving streamers of gold and orange that whistled and swirled in sparkles and smoke, and a thrill coursed through him. He'd always watched fireworks from penthouses from a distance. He'd never stood in the camaraderie of the mob directly beneath such a joyous display.

"Zack, Zack, Zack!" The crowd began chanting as he stupidly stood there, hands in pockets, watching the sky, feeling as if he were ten years old.

Startled by the shouts, he returned his attention to the throng filling the parking lot. Lawn chairs and blankets inhabited by young and old took the place of the vehicles that usually occupied the blacktop lot. A gazebo housing a few benches for tourists had been turned into a makeshift stage. A local band plucked on acoustic guitars while teenagers gathered in the shadows behind an enormous bonfire. Younger children dashed through the crowd, their elders occasionally hauling them from their feet when they became too rambunctious.

It looked like what he'd always imagined a Fourth of July picnic would be. All they needed was ice cream and hot dog stands. He'd never been a participant in community activities. He'd never belonged to any one community. How had he lived all his life without realizing that?

The mayor and some of his cronies shoved their way through to pound Jacques on the back.

"Welcome, son!" the avuncular mayor cried.

Jacques didn't think the mayor was any older than he was, but the politician was of no interest to him. His gaze had finally locked on Amy basting delicious-smelling delicacies on an enormous black grill shaped like a barrel. She didn't look his way, but he had no intention of letting her ignore him.

She knew what he meant to do with the mill. Why had

she not informed the rest of the town of his plans? If these people had so much as an inkling of his intentions, they'd take him apart with pickaxes.

What the hell was he doing here anyway? He could scarcely enjoy being the town hero when he was really the villain.

He shook hands, smiled politely over handshakes, endured slaps on the back, and never diverted his attention from the woman in a beige halter top and short shorts dousing chicken with barbecue sauce. She was wearing a red apron to protect her from the leaping flames, but her bare back was turned toward him. Brown, smooth, with a little mole on her right side, he noticed as he approached.

He wanted nothing more than to kiss that little mole. He would wrap his hands around her bare waist, lift her off the ground, and nuzzle until she squealed. And then they would see what happened next. He still had the keys to her house.

That she had every right to murder him there gave some pause for thought.

Someone shoved a plastic-coated paper cup into his hand. More fireworks exploded, accompanied by the shrieks of children burning marshmallows over the bonfire. He checked for but didn't see Josh and Louisa playing by the fire, thank goodness. They were much too young.

He located Amy's children playing near their grandmother near a line of smaller grills where their Uncle Flint was flipping hamburgers and his sons were shoveling the meat onto buns.

An amplifier sputtered into life, and a screech split the air.

"Got it hooked up to Dave's generator," the mayor said proudly. "Amy thought of everything."

Jacques recognized Jo's clear soprano breaking into a chorus of "For He's a Jolly Good Fellow." He thought maybe he ought to just crawl under a rock and stay there.

Amy turned and caught his eye then, and from the look of angelic innocence in her expression, Jacques knew he'd been set up. She damned well knew he meant to let the mill rot, and she was deliberately twisting a knife in his gullet.

He'd suffered a lifetime of manipulation, caught between his parents and their eternal battles. He'd learned how to walk away. Walking away might be one of his best Olympic sports. He ought to turn his back on the conniving, adorable little witch.

And still he kept striding toward the rebellious powder puff with pink cheeks and defiant green eyes across the lot. The mayor followed, slowing him down. Jacques pounded the mayor's shoulder, nearly knocking him over, and escaped while the other man stumbled.

He never turned down a challenge, and she had thrown down a bloody huge gauntlet.

Amy returned to basting shish kebabs but glanced over her shoulder the instant Jacques reached her. She was wearing those sexy hoops again, the ones that beckoned with their sway against the vulnerable curve of her throat. He would love to have Amy alone and wearing nothing but those provocative earrings.

The crowd had given up on the unfamiliar verses, and Jo's voice rang over the clearing. More fireworks exploded, leaving the damp air heavy with sulfur. He thought he might explode with them, but it wasn't sulfur that would ignite him.

"What is the meaning of this?" he demanded, gesturing at the cheering, celebrating throng.

"No electricity. So . . . we have to empty the freezers," she called cheerfully over the myriad pops of noisy firecrackers.

"And that explains the banner? And the fireworks?" He tried to work up a good tantrum to fight his terror of the decision she was forcing on him.

"Oh, that." She waved her spatula nonchalantly. "We're showing our support. The best man won, and we want to show we're not sore losers."

He'd bet even money that this highly intelligent—extremely devious—woman had incited the population into believing he would actually hire them.

He ought to be furious at her manipulation. Instead, he felt as if she'd hit him over the head with reality and left him spinning. *Amy wasn't devious.*

She was creating fantasies. She actually thought that if she showed him the importance of the mill to the town, he might develop an altruistic streak to match her own. She thought more of him than he did of himself.

He ought to turn around and march straight back to the Hummer, leave for London tomorrow, and let Pascal handle the sale of the equipment. He could be in his computerized office, scanning in the cards, and developing new designs before the end of the week.

But Jacques suddenly had no interest in London, offices, or designs. Why did he feel as if those things were the past, a world in which he no longer had any interest? And the brilliant green eyes challenging him and an entire town welcoming him offered a *real* future?

He'd lived everywhere and never felt the need to belong anywhere. So, why was he still standing here? Surely he didn't believe he could be the hero these people thought him? That was ridiculous. He was a businessman, not a hero. Amy seemed to think otherwise.

Did she really think that much of him? The possibility dazzled more than the fireworks.

"What happened to the electricity?" he asked, side-stepping the issue. He had to conquer his rampaging libido, drag his gaze away from her dancing hoops and the sexy mole, and seek good sense.

"Guess the town couldn't pay the bill," she said airily, shrugging and flipping a chicken breast. "Life goes on."

"Hog wallow," he said. "The transformer blew out."

"The correct term is *hogwash,* and it doesn't matter why the electricity is out. We still have to eat. Good thing it isn't winter yet. Most everyone uses electric space heaters for heat because fuel oil is too expensive."

"You are not making me feel guilty," he asserted firmly. "The mill has been defunct for over a year."

"We've lived in hope for a year." Still smiling, Amy used tongs to place a charcoaled chicken breast on a grilled wheat bun, then handed it to him. "Now, we either get back to work or close up the town and move on. Tomatoes and lettuce are over on the table. That's Jo's punch in the red cup, so I'd be wary of drinking it if I were you."

She turned her tanned and attractive back on him to put a hot dog on a bun for a teenager. She didn't raise her voice, argue, or go after him with a knife, and still, she gutted him.

If his finer qualities rated higher than mediocre on his best day, he did not want to know about it. She definitely saw more in him than was there.

Dave from the hardware store grabbed Jacques's elbow. "Speech!" he yelled over the crackle of a string of firecrackers someone had thrown into the bonfire. "It's not often this town attracts this kind of attention."

He pointed at a circle of men in rumpled white shirts gulping down free hot dogs and hamburgers while keeping an eye on the Hummer, Luigi, and Jacques. They were also holding plastic cups of Jo's fiery cocktail. Around them, television camera crews waited, leaning on their equipment and watching the circus.

Trying to disguise his inner panic, Jacques set the plastic cup aside and slathered Amy's relish on his bun. He'd learned to appreciate the salad dressing concoction she'd served him for lunch this past week. It beat ketchup, any day.

He studied the reporters waiting expectantly. What in hell would happen if he announced his true intentions? Would the crowd shoot him like a turkey? Beat him into the blacktop? He figured he and Luigi could double up a lot of soft bellies and maybe cut a swath to escape, but fighting his way out of town didn't appeal to his pride. He knew he'd been had. He glanced back at Amy, and she gave him a wink.

Five minutes ago he would have done handstands for that charming wink from the prim Miss Amy. Now, he saw he'd seriously underestimated the power of a woman. He glanced at the stage where Jo was finishing up her song. Flint leaned against the gazebo, arms crossed, watching his wife, but the instant Jo finished singing, they both turned expectantly in Jacques's direction.

"Speech, Zack," Jo called into the microphone.

The crowd picked up the cry. *Speech, speech!*

Hoss and Jimbo, the local rock-climbing expert, leaned against each other, sipping from red plastic cups and grinning. Even Marie Sanderson picked up little Louisa and let her wave at him.

It was a damned Mickey Rooney, Judy Garland presentation. Jacques's mother had all those corny films on tape and played them while she worked. His father called her art saccharine for good reason. She called her paintings an emotional tribute to hard work and sacrifice. They were both right. Jacques had just never expected to walk into a scene from one of his mother's sentimental paeans to the workingman.

He glanced at Luigi and the Hummer. He could escape. He didn't have to do this.

Josh tugged on his trouser leg, drawing his attention downward.

The child handed him a melting ice cream cone. "You can have a lick if you want," he said seriously.

A tidal wave of emotion buoyed Jacques and swept him out to sea, far beyond the safe waters he knew and into dangerous undertows.

"Thanks, Son," he muttered, pretending to lick and handing it back to the boy. "That's good stuff."

Josh nodded seriously. "Think Luigi would like some?"

"I think he would, if you go straight to him and come right back here."

The boy grinned. "Yeah, that's what Mommy always says."

The crowd continued shouting, "Speech, speech," and grew silent as Bill and Dave shoved Jacques toward the stage.

And he let himself be shoved.

≪ SEVENTEEN ≫

"You are one mean woman, Amaranth Jane," Jo murmured in admiration after abandoning the gazebo to Jacques and joining her sister at the grill. "How did you know he wouldn't go straight for the airport from the courthouse?"

"Because he hasn't packed his suitcase," Amy answered absently. Her heart had stopped beating, and she wasn't entirely certain her lungs still worked while she waited to hear his decision. The world stopped turning the instant Jacques stepped up to the microphone.

She was pretty certain he'd been furious with her when he realized how she'd put him on the spot. But she'd damn well take red-hot pokers to his hide before she'd let him turn his back on the town and walk away unscathed. Maybe people didn't listen to *her,* but a crowd like this was hard to ignore.

A teeny tiny frozen part of her prayed frantically that he was the strong, good man she saw beneath the designer clothing. Nothing in her life had ever led her to believe men were anything except pigeon droppings, and yet she still hoped for the best. Jo used to call her Calamity Jane. Pollyanna Jane was more like it. Despite all the dire warnings in her head, hope filled her heart. She'd thought Evan had beaten the optimism out of her.

Apparently, she was wrong. Her breath caught as Jacques stepped up onto the stage.

"Ladies and gentlemen," he said into the mike. He stood tall and confident on the bandstand, observing the crowd from beneath an unruly lock of hair. Even the fireworks silenced at his words. "Hoss and Jimbo," he added, quirking an eyebrow at the two big men who'd teased him mercilessly. The crowd laughed.

"He's good," Jo acknowledged reluctantly.

He'd have to be better than good, Amy figured, but she strained to hear what he had to say rather than talk over him.

"Every one of you is aware of the difficult economy," Jacques continued, scanning the silenced crowd like a politician. "Quality goods cannot compete on a scale with cheap foreign markets."

The crowd murmured agreement. Amy's fingernails bit into her palms, and she realized she was shivering in anticipation. He looked so comfortable up there, one hand in the pocket of his trousers, shoving back a nubby-textured raw silk sports coat that must have cost more than her wedding dress. He had that self-deprecating Hugh Grant smile happening, with just a hint of dimple. He appeared human and accessible and not like the robot of riches that he portrayed. Every particle of her that was female whimpered in lust.

And believed in him.

That realization almost took her down. How had he released the hope she'd locked away?

"I represent hundreds of stockholders," Jacques continued in a booming voice that carried through the night, "people like you, who expect me to make money on the savings they've entrusted to me."

Amy tightened her lips to keep from uttering an expletive. Jacques looked directly at her, and she figured this was where he cut off the limb she'd climbed on to get in his face. She could survive the fall. She simply didn't want all these anxious people going down with her.

She wished she could disappear in a puff of smoke rather than disappoint her friends and family, but she stood firm, meeting his gaze without wavering—although the raw strength of his direct midnight stare might give her a heart attack.

She wasn't backing down to any man ever again. Hands on hips, she glared back. Jacques grinned.

"But a conscientious Christian lady in this town has shown me that sometimes it's better to tend our fields and earn smaller profits now in order to reap greater rewards in the future."

Oh Lord. What was he saying? Amy grabbed her throat, and she really did stop breathing.

He held the crowd spellbound, although several people glanced her way. She wasn't used to being the object of anyone's attention, so she disregarded the stares, focused on Jacques, and prayed furiously.

If he did what he appeared to be doing, she'd gladly believe in Santa Claus.

"I'm not making any promises," he said, "but I want to try hiring a small—*very small*—skilled workforce to produce the historic designs for which this mill was once famous."

A cheer or two rang out, but battered by too many defeats, the town waited for the other shoe to fall. *Small* didn't encompass much.

A tear trailed down Amy's cheek, and she waited, torn by anxiety.

"If we make this production a success, your mill, and make no mistake—the mill is as much yours as mine—will have room to grow for years into the future. I'll begin hiring mechanical staff to repair and maintain the equipment starting Friday of this week." He shouted this last over the explosion of screams and cheers and firecrackers.

The remainder of the fireworks left over from their rained-out Fourth of July celebration exploded in a bouquet of sparks against the black clouds overhead. The local band—without Eddie—plugged into the generator and struck up a guitar-whining "Star-Spangled Banner" at the burst of an American flag in red, white, and blue stars across the sky.

Tears poured down Amy's cheeks, and sobs racked her. The crowd shouted, "Zack, Zack," and Jo leaned over to whisper, "Guess there should be a Union Jack up there, too, hmm?"

Laughing in relief, hugging herself to hold in her hysterics, Amy nodded. It wasn't everything she'd wanted, but it was a start. And Jacques had done it. He was opening the mill—they had a future!

Instead of meekly caving to Jacques's distracting charm, she'd pushed back, and he'd responded just as she'd hoped he would, proving he was the savvy man she thought she'd seen beneath the surface glamour. She was still too rattled to completely grasp what had just happened.

When she saw him heading their way carrying Louisa and followed by their mother, her remaining defenses shattered. She couldn't face him without her shield of anger. She couldn't trust herself not to fall into his arms and sob all over him. And she knew where that led.

Amy turned and ran for the protection of the darkened café.

Fighting his way through reporters, cameras, and microphones shoved in his face, Jacques watched the reward he'd worked to earn run away, and he froze in shock. What the devil had he done wrong?

He wasn't used to women running away, especially after he'd handed them what they wanted. He had expected . . . Hell, he'd expected her to act like the women in his set—flinging themselves in his arms and kissing him all over and pretending they were his for the asking.

He hadn't been thinking with his head at all. He'd just committed himself to the impossible in return for another chance to get his hopes crushed.

The little girl in his arms shouted, "Wheee!" and pounded his starched shirt with grimy hands at the sight and sound of rockets ringing through the air. He was still stunned by what he'd done, but Amy's reaction topped his performance in spades.

"Amaranth doesn't like people to see her cry," Marie said matter-of-factly, reaching for Louisa. "She's probably scrubbing pots."

Marie wandered off with her granddaughter, leaving Jacques to sort it out. Amy was angry? Why would she cry?

Men pounded his back again. Jimbo handed him another of Jo's plastic cups. He was called "Zack" so many times he forgot he'd ever been called anything else.

He tried to follow the path Amy had taken, but men with weathered faces and oil-stained hands approached him, asking questions about the jobs he'd offered. Women hung in the background, listening eagerly, their lined faces shining with hope.

He felt like a shit.

He offered so little, and they thanked him too much. He just wanted an excuse to stay and play a while longer. He really wasn't making that much of a difference. The business would probably lose so much money the first year that he'd still end up selling the place.

He hated losing money. He hated losing, period. The odds were totally against him.

But maybe it was time to start testing odds instead of taking on sure things?

Tightening his mouth in resolve, Jacques shook off his shock, pounded the backs of men twice his size until they staggered, and forced his way through the crowd in the direction he wanted to go.

Toward Amy—Amaranth Jane. Somehow, the outlandishly defiant name finally fit her.

He approached the Stardust from the side alley but didn't see any light in the upstairs loft she and the children had moved into. Striding around Myrtle the Pig on the corner, he saw a small light through the café's mullioned front window.

He leaned against the door and it opened. People seldom locked doors in Northfork, but the café was usually locked to indicate when it was closed.

Amy didn't look up at his entrance. In the light of a kerosene lamp, she carefully smoothed creamy icing over an array of cupcakes. Patiently, she pressed candies into them, then licked crumbs off her fingers before reaching for a towel.

"You ran away," he said accusingly.

She didn't answer but returned to pressing candies into icing.

He didn't know what he was doing here in this preposterously decorated room on the far side of the world from anywhere. He had probably just made the biggest mistake of his life.

He'd done it for her. And she had run away. Why?

A brown curl fell over Amy's nose, and she blew it away while she carefully placed a candy corn nostril on a pig snout.

In that moment, watching her gentle patience, something hard and brittle inside Jacques shattered. Emotions he did not dare examine broke free, and he acted on a flood of longing for something he could not name. He leaned over the counter, tucked the escaped curl behind her ear, and brushed his lips against hers, reveling in their surprise and the hungry clinging that declared her true desires.

Amy gasped and backed away, rubbing her icing-coated hands on her apron. Through the dim light of the lantern, he saw her eyes widen like big cat eyes. Bracing his hands on the counter, Jacques vaulted over it rather than waste time letting her escape around the barrier.

"You are a vixen, Amaranth Jane," he murmured, crowding her against the cold stove. "And I demand a reward for performing to your expectations."

"I didn't . . . I . . ."

He hushed her with a kiss. She twisted her fingers in his shirt as if to shove him away, but she forgot to shove. Her mouth was as hot and eager as his once he persuaded her to open for him. In triumph, he clasped his arms around her lovely bare waist and lifted her against him, savoring the crush of her ripe breasts against the hard wall of his chest while they drank of each other.

"Don't, please, we can't," she murmured when he moved his kisses to the corner of her mouth to give them both a chance to breathe. But her arms crept around his neck even as she protested.

He adored the feel of her sticky fingers in his hair and on his nape. She smelled of vanilla and fireworks, and if he were the Neanderthal type, he'd take her right here and now, assert his claim, and bellow in victory.

Unfortunately, he was too civilized to maul a woman in such a crude manner. He wanted her to remember their first lovemaking with sensual pleasure and not with bruises.

"We can," he murmured, snuggling her belly next to his crotch so she had no doubt of what she did to him. "Tell me we can. I will take you anywhere. Would you like to see Paris?"

She gave another of those sexy little gasps, and before she could argue or refuse, he licked sugary icing from the corner of her mouth and claimed her lips all over again. Her shudder of surrender was everything he'd hoped it would be. In a heated rush of desire and relief, he rocked her back and forth, stroking her smooth skin, murmuring practiced phrases between kisses.

She was putty in his arms, moaning and kissing as if he were a banquet and she was starving. He loved being her banquet. She could gobble him up any day.

Except, the more she took, the more he wanted to give, and he was in serious danger of drowning in this whirlpool of passion.

A door slammed open and sulfur-scented air rushed in. "Ames, we're outta . . . Oops, sorry, party on," a feminine voice sang.

Amy hastily released Zack's—Jacques's—neck and pushed against his chest with both hands. "Jo, wait. I have to go." She said this while wiggling free of his sinful grip, then gulped for air and tried to steady her trembling knees by grasping the counter.

"We've got the kids. You don't have to go anywhere," Jo called through the semidarkness. "The guys can buy soft drinks instead of my lemonade." She started to close the door, then hesitated. "You be good to my big sister or you'll have a town after you with butcher knives, y'hear?"

Amy considered melting through the floor in humiliation, but Jo charged out, slamming the door after her. More fireworks exploded. For all she knew, they'd never stopped. Her head was one explosion after another from Zack's kisses and solid male presence crowding her against her familiar counter.

Zack. The name sounded as if he belonged here. And he didn't. Fireworks wouldn't change that.

Her palms pressed against the thin cloth of his shirt. She could feel the tension in his hard muscles and the erratic pounding of his heart matching her own. She wanted to draw away, but she was afraid her knees would buckle. She didn't want to let him go for fear he was just a mirage.

"What just happened here?" she whispered, mostly to herself. She felt as if she were spinning in circles like a giant whirligig, and she couldn't believe any of this was happening, not to *her.* Handsome, sophisticated, European businessmen didn't romance lonely divorced mothers of two.

"We were carried away on the wings of desire?" he suggested with a grin in his voice. He placed his strong hands around her waist again. "Shall we do it again and analyze it this time?"

She shoved at his chest, but she might as well have tried

to move a refrigerator. Now that her feet were back on the ground, she could appreciate the strength of the man pinning her to the stove. She had a thing for strong men, ones who could lift her as if she were a bit of straw and make her feel safe. Ones who could blow her mind just by holding her. She did her very best to pretend she hadn't noticed the size of the erection rubbing against her belly. It had been so long . . .

She shook her head free of images of a naked Zack and felt her messy hair hit her cheek. "When does your flight leave?" she asked, forcing reality into the equation.

"I'm starting a new business in Northfork, remember?" he asked with just a hint of irony. "I can't leave."

Taking a deep breath, she found the willpower to slip sideways between him and the stove. Her breast brushed against his arm and sent an entire new surge of need pounding through her. "I can't believe you agreed to that," she said hastily, trying to bring her head back where it belonged. "You have no comprehension of how much it means to the town to keep the mill running."

"I'm beginning to understand," he said drily, letting her escape. "That was quite a performance you orchestrated out there."

She suspected anger simmered not too far below his surface pleasantry. He wouldn't be the type who would appreciate having his hand forced.

Conflict terrified her. Her normal response was to placate or run away. She couldn't do either this time. Too much rode upon his staying and helping to reestablish the mill.

"Thank you," she whispered, not for the compliment, but for staying. She didn't persuade her tongue to explain the difference.

"Thank you for believing in the impossible," he said softly, seeming to understand. He brushed his hand against her cheek, and her knees threatened to buckle again. "It is a challenge, right?" He lifted her chin so she had to meet his eyes.

In the lantern light, she could see the fear behind his unusually flinty gaze, and she nodded agreement. "A challenge, yes," she whispered, grasping that there were many layers of meaning left unspoken.

The overhead lights flickered and flashed on.

Outside, a cheer rang into the overcast night, and bottle rockets exploded, rendering further conversation unfeasible. For now.

⚜ EIGHTEEN ⚜

"I don't know what I'm doing," Amy muttered, sipping her coffee and adjusting a pan of muffins in the Stardust's oven.

"You're applying for the position of executive manager," Jo told her firmly, nudging her away from the oven with her hip while tying on an apron. "The town's counting on you. Get out there and fight."

"Fight?" Amy gave her sister an incredulous look. "Did it look like I was capable of fighting last night?"

Jo chortled. "Oh, yeah. You had the man flattened. Go exercise those Sanderson wiles, Sis. Nail him before he knows what hit him."

"I'm the one likely to get nailed." Amy tried not to shiver too obviously at the image rising in her head of Zack naked and on top of her, nailing her in the only manner her present fantasy could conjure.

"Try it, you'll like it." Jo poked her with a sharp elbow.

That was the problem. She might come to like it too well. And she wasn't allowing men in anymore. Certainly not suave Europeans who would love her and leave her for a larger world. She was standing on her own these days, in the secure world she'd chosen.

She had her kids to think about. A shattered mother would be very bad for their emotional upbringing.

"I think I'd rather move to Asheville and work at Belk's." Amy set down her mug and watched the shadows on Main Street dissipate with the first rays of dawn. "I don't need a nabob who will be here today and gone tomorrow, or an entire town depending on my rusty skills."

"A 'nabob'?" Jo hooted and removed the muffins from the oven as their first customer walked in and took a booth. "Is that like a French film star? Zack's *hot,* babe. Cut your teeth on him, and you can have any man you like after that." To the customer, she called, "Be with you in a minute. The muffins just came out of the oven."

Their customer waved agreement and shook out his paper.

"Get real. *Zack* will wring me out and leave me dry. I just can't do that again, Jo. I *can't.* I'm the settling-down kind, and he travels Europe. I don't even know what he sees in me except availability."

"He has the lioness for availability. Did he go back to her last night?"

"No, he went back to the house. He called to ask me how to make the microwave quit blinking." Amy popped muffins out of the pan and onto a platter.

Jo chuckled. "He's all yours then. He's a type A competitor who needs a challenge, and you're it. Enjoy it while it lasts." Picking up the coffeepot, she wandered to the booth to take an order while more of their regulars entered in pursuit of their morning caffeine fix.

A challenge. Amy stared gloomily out the café's mullioned window. She didn't need any more challenges in her life. She had more than she could handle already.

But she'd had security, and look how well that had worked out.

She picked up a second coffeepot to begin filling cups when the Hummer roared to a halt in front of the café and Jacques climbed out. He was wearing stiff dark wash jeans and a Lauren work shirt, probably straight off the rack at Belk's. Over the casual attire he wore a tailored brown tweed jacket that likely cost twenty times the jeans.

Amy let her lips curve upward at the sight. Jacques— Zack—was doing his darndest to fit in, and he still looked as if he'd stepped fresh from prep school. It wasn't just the clothes or his stylishly tousled hair, but the self-assured way he carried his lean length and glanced around as if the day was his and the world acknowledged his wishes. She must have imagined the fear she'd seen in his eyes last night. Men who owned the world knew no fear.

Her heart did somersaults just from watching him. She'd trusted that he would do the right thing last night. Now she had to figure out what the right thing was for her. And act on it.

The Hummer drove off, and Zack shoved open the Stardust's door. "Ready for work?" he called jovially.

Amy poured boiling water over tea leaves, then pushed a cup and saucer toward him on the counter. "I left fresh bagels and muffins at the house. Didn't you like them?"

"The muffins are not so sweet without you to serve them. And we need to get down to business immediately."

Amy couldn't decide whether to laugh at his perversity or hit him over the head with the cinnamon Fiestaware cup. The laughter in his eyes and the dent forming in his square jaw prevented either. He knew darned well what he was doing to her. He wasn't a stupid man. He had said this would be a challenge, and he was proving his point. They might kill each other before this was over.

The mill would work. She knew it would. Amy straightened her shoulders, slapped the teapot onto the counter in front of him, and flung off her apron. She'd think of him as *Zack,* the mill's new owner. "Where do we begin?" Behind her, Jo snorted to cover a laugh.

Zack pointed at the stool beside him. When Jo provided another cup, he poured tea for Amy and himself. "I've called Brigitte to join us. She'll take notes. For now, we will eat and be charming to each other."

Had he been an American aggressive type-A telling her to sit down, shut up, and wait for his secretary, she would have balked. Instead, Zack had learned to smile and be charming to get what he wanted. It worked, too.

Falling easily into her old role of waitress, not country music diva, Jo poured tea and set out plates of scrambled eggs and carrot muffins decorated with Louisa's infamous pig *snoses* while Amy settled on the stool indicated and tried to think like mill management.

"Where are the little ones?" he asked, shattering her image of detached executive.

"Josh is riding to school with Flint and the boys. Louisa is watching cartoons in the office. Can't you hear the monitor?"

He tilted his head and listened. "Ah, yes, the Siamese cat, what is her name? The little one is singing—to her dolls, maybe?"

"How did you know?" Amy sipped her Keemun, doing her best to pretend this was just a business meeting and that she wasn't bowled over and cross-eyed over a man who knew about Sagwa and a three-year-old's dolls.

He waved his hand. "No matter. How will you care for Louisa while we work? We cannot set up a day care in the mill until we are up and running. I am risking enough of my investors' money as it is."

"Are you saying I'm hired? Just like that? You have all those people down in Asheville who probably know more about mills than I ever will. I don't want you wasting money just because . . ." She'd been about to say *just because you want to nail me.* She'd dug her hole a little too deep, and she hastily attempted to backtrack.

Zack laughed, and the corners of his eyes turned up mischievously. "Just because I want in your bed?" he inquired, as if the whole café weren't straining to hear his every word. "It is because of what you asked—you are more concerned with the mill's existence than yourself. You're the kind of employee I must have. It is *people* who make a profit, not the machinery or the management techniques or the fancy accounting."

"Wow," Jo whispered. "If I weren't already taken, I'd be all over a man who *gets* it. Ames, grab him."

Not in the least embarrassed by Jo's crass comments, Zack gave Amy a slow, seductive smile. "Yes, please snatch me."

She would have slid under the counter in embarrassment except he returned to the topic in the blink of an eye. "My company is small and very dependent on the expertise of my employees. I have had to learn how to make the most of the best. There is no room for slackers in small business." He pointed his muffin at Amy. "Day care?"

"Salary?" she spurted out before she could get cold feet. Her entire life balanced on money right now.

Zack smacked his forehead. "I forgot! How could I forget? You who make my head go 'round." He pulled a packet of papers from the inside pocket of his tailored sports coat. "Here, these are for you. The judge says you must sign and provide a deposit, and you have thirty days to complete the transaction."

Gingerly, Amy lifted the official-looking documents. Her gaze instantly located the address on Canary Street, and her stomach clenched. She scanned the rest of the paper, then started at the beginning and read more slowly, not believing she'd done it.

She'd bought the cottage. All by herself. With the help of her friendly mortgage lender, of course.

"It's mine?" she asked in disbelief. Then as she realized to whom she was talking, her head jerked up, and she glared at him. "You didn't do this? It's just me, right? He's accepting *my* offer?"

"Yes, of course." He gestured airily with his half-eaten muffin. "I have no use for a run-down cottage, so the judge took the only other offer—yours. I cannot imagine how you will have time to fix it up, either, but that's your problem."

Amy suspected he'd had something to do with it. The judge would have gladly sold the entire lot to the highest bidder without any consideration to her little offer. But she wouldn't argue with the results. If she hadn't had the nerve to make the offer in the first place, the judge couldn't have accepted it. Clutching the precious document to her chest, she asked again, "Salary?"

He sighed. "It cannot be great. The expense of purchasing the mill has drained our cash. I had hoped to sell the equipment to cover the costs until the designs are ready. Brigitte will look up government grants. You will be on my company's health plan, of course, as soon as we establish one here. As will everyone else."

Then he named a figure that would easily cover payments on the cottage's small mortgage. Amy closed her eyes and sent a prayer of gratitude winging heavenward.

"Amy?" Zack asked cautiously. "Will that suffice?"

Her eyes flew open, and she felt as light as a helium balloon floating heavenward. "Yes, that will suffice nicely, thank you. Some of my friends are talking of setting up a day care for the people you hire. They're experienced and won't have any difficulty getting a license. See, you've already generated another business!"

He looked astounded. "I did that?"

"You will, if you hire enough workers. It won't take many to fill a day care with kids. Once we have enough employees, you can let Manny bring his hot dog cart to the plant at lunchtime, and he'll have an income to supplement his social security again. His wife's medicine costs so much they've been talking of selling their house."

Fielding customers as they dropped in, Jo stopped a moment to add, "If you're really going to buy that shack, Ames, you can put Harry to work. He's not much good at climbing ladders since he broke his knee, but he still knows his way around a saw."

"And if we do not make money?" Zack asked worriedly, keeping his voice low as the stools on either side of them filled with the morning regulars.

Amy patted his hand. "We'll be no worse off than we were before."

Which was a lie, but she didn't have the heart to tell him. She'd be saddled with a mortgage and no job. Without the mill, the housing market would collapse and poor

Manny wouldn't be able to sell his home to pay his bills. Her friends would borrow money to start the day care and go broke. Zack would work all that out by himself should he ever take time to think about it.

Her duty wasn't to worry what would happen if they failed. Her duty was to see that the mill didn't fail.

And to remember that Zack was now her boss and there was a conflict of interest in carrying on a useless flirtation.

⫷ NINETEEN ⫸

On Friday, Jacques—who had to start thinking of himself as *Zack* if he meant to stay here for long—walked around the immense looms he'd fully intended to sell, listening to the mechanics he'd hired mutter among themselves. Amy had been right. The looms were new and in excellent condition. He'd bought a bargain.

"We'll need to order computers." Thinking aloud, he waited for Brigitte to make notes in her BlackBerry. "Do we have anyone available locally with computer skills?" he asked Amy.

She was taking notes in some incomprehensible shorthand in a steno notebook. He had to bite back a smile every time he watched her studiously bent over the pad, nibbling on her pencil eraser. His new executive had tremendous people skills and creativity, but she lacked organization and business knowledge. He had Brigitte for that, but Amy looked so studious keeping her lists that he did not point out there was no need for her to do so.

At his question, she looked up with a hint of panic in her eyes. "Computer skills? You're installing computers before we're even up and running?"

"That's my business, luv," he reminded her. He was trying to woo her slowly, but she surrounded herself with family as defensively as he surrounded himself with friends. He fully believed anything worth having was worth working for, but they might as well be Montagues and Capulets for all the progress he'd been making. "We need computers to translate those design cards."

"I'll call my professors," she agreed after a moment's thought. "They probably know people from the closed mills in Kannapolis and elsewhere."

He could see she desperately wanted to hire her friends. Thankfully, she had the good sense to admit when she couldn't. Such honesty in a world of greed and deceit appealed to his inner nature, although his business head told him that her easy capitulation was no way to get ahead.

"Jacques, *mon amour*," an operatic soprano called from across the echoing length of the enormous building. A mixture of Italian and French followed, and Zack sighed. He'd known this scene was coming. Instead of hiding up here in the mountains, where everyone blanketed him in the excitement of questions about the mill, he should have gone back to the resort and soothed fraying tempers.

Cat wiggled her miniskirted hips across the planked floor, trailing a lace shawl down her back. Her spiked heels left dents in the soft pine planks. She wore her cascade of silver-blond curls down today—a Britney Spears look she was really too old to carry off. He couldn't remember why she was in his life. Rome. He'd picked her up in Rome because of her designer connections. She liked having an escort to the best parties. That seemed a lifetime ago.

"*Chérie,*" he called cheerfully, feeling Amy stiffen and edge away. "Have you come to help me choose our décor?"

He was exceedingly grateful their audience couldn't translate Cat's histrionic response. While she rattled on, Zack raised questioning eyebrows at Pascal, who had been blatantly unavailable these past few days. Unlike Cat, Pascal worked with *him*. Zack relied on his financial expertise and investment money.

It looked as if he would have to find a new investor. When Zack didn't reply with placating apologies, Cat flung her long, lithe curves into Pascal's arms to weep torrentially. Pascal didn't flinch but held her as one would a lover. Why had he ever thought life was amusing with a drama queen like Cat around?

If he carried that thought too far, he would squirm in discomfort. With just her steady presence, Amy sheered off another layer of his shallow life to reveal the nothingness beneath.

Instead of looking at him with the disgust he deserved, Amy sidled back to his side to whisper, "I don't suppose she just called you a horse's ass, did she?"

Zack laughed aloud, startling his already stunned audience. Amy's refreshing bluntness righted the kaleidoscope world he occupied. "She called me a despoiler of dreams, a man who cannot see beyond the nose on his face, a cad who expects the world to turn around him, among other things. Your translation is much more succinct."

She nodded knowingly. "Women don't like being dumped."

"Especially for a mill," he agreed. He'd had no idea how refreshing it was to have a woman who talked sense instead of hysterics. In his foolish youth, it had made him feel strong and masculine to console weeping women. Now, age and experience just made him impatient.

"But it is her own illusions that are shattered and they're none I have created," he reassured her.

Zack crossed his arms and glared at Pascal. "And you, old friend? Have I shattered your illusions as well?"

Still clad all in black, Pascal shrugged and continued patting Cat. "We thought we were here for a short visit. We do not mean to live here, where we don't belong. Where *you* don't belong," he added meaningfully.

Zack went cold. Pascal was right. He glanced around at the production designers and entourage Cat had dragged in with her. As if they were spectators in a zoo, her companions studied their primitive surroundings and the jeans-clad and T-shirted mechanics. The gap between rich and poor, rural and city, was enormous enough without throwing in the differences of language and culture.

What the devil was he thinking? That he could belong here, where just his choice of vehicle raised eyebrows? Where he couldn't speak without causing heads to turn?

"Is this where we all sing, 'It's a small world after all'?" Amy murmured with laughter in her voice, apparently unaware of his frozen shock. She was a little angel sitting on his shoulder, flapping her wings to swat him in the right direction.

The ice forming around his heart melted in a hot rush of desire, and Zack grinned, recovering from his momentary paralysis. "Pascal, old friend, you are a bigot, albeit a brilliant one. Go home. Take Cat." He glanced at Brigitte, who had lowered her head and huddled her arms around herself. Bad body language if he'd ever seen it. "Brigitte, my right hand, would you leave me, too?"

She cast him a frowning glance and nodded curtly, once.

He winced. She had been at his side for years. It wasn't as if he meant to live here forever . . .

He looked over everyone's heads to the entrance, where Luigi leaned his bulk against a door frame and studied the situation with a stoic expression. Luigi was more friend and father figure than employee. He would hate to lose him. At Zack's glance, Luigi offered a crooked grimace and shook his head. Zack sighed in relief. Luigi had known him long before he had entered Cat's glittery world. He was loyal to the man, not the money.

"You can run this operation from home," Pascal insisted. "You have other interests that need your attention. There is the Galway project waiting."

The castle, the magnificent Irish castle. He loved Ireland, the lyrical voices, the outrageous tales, the music. Ireland was close to home and all his friends. He could fly to London in a heartbeat, party all night, and be back at work in the morning. He and Gabrielle had celebrated their first anniversary in Dublin . . .

He'd lost himself in partying to eradicate those memories.

He didn't need to lose himself in partying here, and Zack recognized his immense relief at that knowledge. Since arriving, he'd lived a *real* life of sorts. None of the people in Northfork reminded him of Gabrielle. He did not see Danielle playing in the corners of the dirty mill, or hear his wife's voice calling from the woods she would never have entered. He could be himself here, his current and future self, and not the old self that had died with his small family. He felt as if he was moving forward, at last.

He could not expect his staff to feel the same.

"Brigitte, you can research the Galway tapestries as well as I. You do not need me to research rushes for the floor. We have done castles before. Go. I will not keep you. But I am needed here, for now."

Needed, literally. It had been a long, long time since anyone had actually relied on him for more than his opinion on wallpaper and the latest software.

It had been a long time since he'd felt strong enough to be relied on.

Brigitte solemnly handed Zack her PDA of notes and addresses. Cat wept hysterically and tried to throw herself at him, but Pascal held her back. Cat didn't try very hard, Zack noted cynically.

"Let us know when you return," Pascal said, letting Cat cry on his shoulder. "How long do you think it will be before we can start referring offers to you again? A week?"

He felt Amy tense beside him, but he did not dare look her in the eye. He had no idea where he'd be a week from now. A week *alone* in these mountains, without most of his friends and staff—it seemed an eternity just then.

"We'll keep in touch," he answered noncommittally.

Watching his traveling companions—the only life he had these days—file out, leaving him behind, Zack wanted a stiff drink. No one in Northfork sold alcohol.

What in hell had he got himself into? These weren't the civilized environs he knew. He couldn't even have a *martini* unless he made it himself, after driving an hour to obtain the ingredients. He was seriously tempted to run after his friends.

"We can do it ourselves," Amy said stiffly, apparently reading his body language as well as he'd read Brigitte's. "We have the skills and knowledge. Take your design cards and go."

He glanced down at her shiny brown mane. "You would like that, would you not? You'd have everything you wanted, at my expense."

Propping her hands on her oh-so-businesslike skirt, Amy glared back at him. "You're the computer expert, not me. What do you think?"

"That you can't do it without me," he retorted without hesitation, only recognizing the truth of his response after he'd said it.

"You've got that right," she said, to his surprise. "So, Mr. Know-it-all, where do we find the computers and who applies for the government grant if Brigitte is gone?"

"You?" he suggested, arching an eyebrow with interest.

She swiped the PDA from him. "Damned right, just as soon as someone transcribes the contents of this gadget to paper."

Zack winced as the expensive *gadget* emitted the machine equivalent of a squeal of terror. To his relief, Luigi rescued the whimpering BlackBerry and stashed it in one of his capacious pockets.

"Consider it transcribed." Shedding his doubts in favor of his confident façade, Zack took Amy's elbow and steered her toward the exit. "Gentlemen," he called to the mechanics, "you will start Monday. I expect to have the plant fully operational by month's end."

Mainly, because his company's cash flow couldn't pay salaries much longer than that without some influx of revenue. Pascal's fascination with Zack's European contacts had made him one of his main investors. Zack had a feeling that source of cash had just dried up.

"Technically, you can't do anything to this place until you sign the closing papers." Stepping gingerly down a mossy brick path, Elise followed Amy around the cottage. It had been over a week since Zack's friends had departed. The mill machinery was operational. Computers were arriving daily.

Now all they needed were the designs, and Zack and the new computer person had been working night and day, feeding the cards into the machines, performing their magic.

She knew the mill was bleeding cash with no immediate hope of return.

"You have another week before you can close on your place and complete the purchase on this one," Elise reminded her.

"Look, there's a rhododendron under the honeysuckle!" Amy exclaimed, pulling the tenacious vine off a hedge of shrubbery in the cottage's backyard. She couldn't stand waiting any longer. She had to *do* something, despite Elise's logic. "Can you imagine how gorgeous this could be in spring? I could put a little brick patio over by the back door . . ." She swung around to fix the yard's dimensions in her mind. An ornamental cherry in that back corner perhaps . . .

"Amaranth Jane, are you paying any attention to me at all?" Elise asked in exasperation.

"Nope," she replied. "I've worked myself half to death all week and I want some reward. It's not as if I'm breaking and entering. The yard needs work right away. I can't do it in snow. And the labor will be cheap," she finished wryly, referring to herself.

"Didn't you get paid yet?" Elise demanded. "Is he working you to death for nothing?"

Amy thought she'd best not tell her lawyer she'd work for Zack for free just to hear his outrageous compliments and enjoy those few brief interludes when he'd take her hand and send her thoughts spinning off their tracks.

Knowing Elise, she'd be filing charges for sexual harassment.

Insanely, she wanted to be harassed. She hadn't felt so alive in years. Maybe in her whole life. And even though she knew she was mad to feel this way, it seemed safe enough when surrounded by friends and family. It wasn't as if she were going out alone on a date. She had to be wary with her heart, but that didn't stop her from admiring her new boss more with each passing day. He knew everything involved with creating fabric from the inside out. He tackled his projects with refreshing enthusiasm, and actually *listened* when she spoke. She was in desperate danger of losing her wary heart to a man who could be gone next week.

"I've been writing for government grants. I don't have the payroll system set up yet." Amy ripped out vines by the roots, uncovering the skeleton of an enormous rhododendron and a few small azaleas. "Evan's old secretary is giving notice at her job in Asheville. Emily said she'd help me set up the bookkeeping next week. We're a very small operation at the moment."

"And you're confident he has the cash to make this work?" Elise asked suspiciously.

"He had the means to convince the court. That's enough for me. I've given up fretting over what I can't control. Now, this yard, *that* I can control." Happily, she dug through layers of old leaves and pine needles to discover autumn cyclamen peering up from the rich soil. Slug-eaten hostas promised a gorgeous ground cover under the trees in summer, once she set out some beer bait.

"I need to look into his background," Elise decided, poking at the leaf debris with the sharp toe of her shoe.

"Rich men don't let their staff desert them like that. It's highly suspicious."

"You're highly suspicious." Amy laughed. "Investigate away and let me know what you find. All I know is that he's hired the personnel I recommended, and he's feeding info into computers around the clock. I'd be more suspicious if he was flashing cash and doing nothing, but he's practically living at the mill. If I didn't take him meals, he'd starve."

Changing the subject, Elise examined the back of the run-down cottage. "Have you had an exterminator check for rats and roaches in this place?"

"Oh, I've already set out traps. The Realtor is a friend of mine and he gave me the keys. He said I ought to bill the court for extermination."

"There are times I almost envy you." Elise studied the cottage's mildewed siding. "This isn't one of them."

Amy grinned. "Well, I have the imagination you lack." Normally, she admired Elise's practicality and can-do as-sertiveness, but right now, she felt sorry for a friend who couldn't see beyond the obvious. "This place will be grand in a few years. It's the home I've always dreamed of. I'll have roses growing up a screened porch by next year. A fountain and a patio in year or two. Benches tucked in among the shrubbery so guests can slip away for privacy when they want. Louisa and Josh will have an at-tic playroom for winter and an outdoor one in summer. I could even walk to the mill if I like. It's just over the hill."

Amy straightened her shoulders uncomfortably under Elise's gimlet gaze. "What?"

"You know that man of yours will be returning to Eu-rope and his fancy cars and houses one of these days, don't you?"

She did, but she didn't want to hear it. "He's not any man of mine," she protested.

Elise snorted. "Who's been feeding him all week? It's a good thing he has that driver to run his laundry to the dry cleaner, or I'd bet you'd be doing that, too."

"He's paying me a fortune to stay in my house!" Amy argued. "Fixing his meals is the very least I can do. Besides, the kids adore him. When he's not at the mill, he sits down on the floor and plays with them while I cook." She fought a shiver of fear when she realized just how much her children adored a man who paid attention to them. She might live through another heartbreak, but she didn't want her kids thinking all men packed up and left like their father had.

"And who does he play with after they go to bed?" Elise asked, arching her eyebrows.

"I take them back to the loft," Amy said indignantly. "He's my boss. We're just good friends." Except for those stolen kisses. And the way Zack looked at her that made her go up in flames and had her tossing in her bed at night. And the way he made time in his busy day for her. She wasn't so blind that she didn't notice she was the only one who could make him look up from his fascination with his computers. Yesterday, she'd done it because she was tired and discouraged and needed the thrill his heated gaze gave her. Evan had never given her a second glance when he was working. She was giddy with feminine power these days, and she was letting the fantasy go to her head.

But Zack was her boss, and he wouldn't be staying, and they were both grown-ups who knew the rules. Sometimes, she wished she could be just a little less grown-up.

Car tires crunched in the gravel drive, and an old-fashioned car horn ah-oogahed. Zack had let Luigi take the Hummer back to the rental dealer in Charlotte after he'd discovered an antique Bentley for sale in the newspaper.

Amy felt a blush creep into her cheeks even before Zack's cheerful voice called out.

"I've done it, I've done it! Amy, come see!"

"He won't be staying," Elise reminded her, keeping her voice low as Zack circled the house and approached them. "Have fun if you like, but remember fun is all you are to him."

Amy knew she was right. Zack had never made any pretense otherwise. He simply waited for her to accept him on his terms, and so far, she couldn't.

Watching the excitement dancing in her employer's square-cut features, she didn't know how much longer she could resist.

❈ TWENTY ❈

"A bit touchy, isn't she?" Zack asked, watching Elise swing down the drive, blessedly leaving them alone.

"Elise? Elise is a mystery. She has this fabulous city life on the other side of the mountain, yet she spends half her time out here in the country these days. I think something is tearing her in two."

"And what do your wise eyes see in me?" he asked.

He almost held his breath when she turned her wicked green gaze in his direction, but he managed a jaunty smile and a wink at her solemn expression.

She snatched the papers from his hand. "I see a wealthy businessman with a brilliant mind and too little to occupy it."

She was too damned close to the truth for comfort. As she examined the computer-generated designs, he bounced impatiently on his heels, waiting for her reaction. He had expected shouts of jubilation and praise, not this narrow-eyed study of every detail.

"These colors will never sell," she said, plunging his heart to the dirt and walking all over it. "But the designs . . ." She flashed him a look of awe and delight that let him breathe again. "They're more than I *imagined*," she said in excitement. "I cannot believe . . . They're even

better than the French *toile*. Is it possible . . . I know it's
not historic, but . . ."

Zack frowned. "It must be historic. That is the *point.*"

"Maybe. Yes." She shuffled the design pages until she
uncovered one depicting a scrolled tapestry of feathers
and leaves. "Who is to say this had to be done in mus-
tards or olives just because they were fashionable in
1780?"

"But look . . ." He pulled another page from the stack.
"The *toile* and the brocade were made to go together."
He glanced around. "Is there a place to lay these out?"

"Inside." She produced a key from her jeans pocket
and climbed up the rickety back porch steps.

Watching the enchanting globes of her denim-clad pos-
terior swinging up the steps immediately distracted him
from the job at hand. He'd been the perfect gentleman
for a week while she drowned him in the soft scents of
vanilla and jasmine bath powder. He'd resisted kissing
her every time she turned her big eyes questioningly to
him, or her pouty lips parted to chew on a pencil eraser.
He felt as if he'd spent forty days and nights in the desert
without food and water, and Amy was an oasis forever
out of his reach.

And she was letting him into her house, alone, just the
two of them.

What would she do if he reached for her once they
were out of sight?

Entering the dilapidated kitchen, Zack scratched any
thought of lovemaking. He wouldn't take any woman on
that cracked and filthy linoleum or even on the aging
Formica counter. He should have insisted that she come
back to her real house with him, where there were beds.

And Luigi.

Sighing, Zack set aside the fabric designs for the moment and turned his professional interest to the architecture of the Craftsman cottage. "The original built-in china cabinet is still here," he said with approval, running his hand over the painted corner cabinet in the large kitchen. "I wonder what wood is under here?"

"You want the grand tour? It takes a lot of imagination to see beyond the deterioration," she said tentatively, as if she'd been laughed at before for the suggestion.

He hesitated. Once upon a time, he and Gabrielle had bought an old flat. He'd loved stripping off the paint to find the majestic mahogany beneath. They'd breathed paint stripper and stain and sealers for a year. He'd been young and foolish and deeply in love—

Love was an irrational emotion. He wasn't going there these days. Oddly, the thought saddened him.

"I know, it's a dump." With a shrug, Amy began laying out the designs across the Formica.

He could hear the excitement leach out of her voice at his lack of enthusiasm. She was much too perceptive, this fascinating partner he'd acquired. Catching her arm, Zack steered her toward the next room.

"It will take much work," he suggested, gazing upward at the sagging false ceiling, speculating about the antique crown molding that might be hidden behind it.

He tried not to think too hard on how Amy fit next to him, as if she were an extension of himself that he could draw closer anytime he wished. What he wanted was sex. Perhaps he could steal a little kiss. . . .

As if she read his mind, or suffered the same frustrated tension throbbing in him, she pulled free to grab a discarded two-by-four off the floor. He admired the way her jean shorts shaped to her rounded bottom, then ducked as she whacked the lumber against the sagging ceiling.

"I've been itching to do this," she said with satisfaction, pounding until it shredded and fell, filling the air with dust.

"You are mad! You will kill both of us!" He grabbed her elbow again and dragged her toward the clearer air of the kitchen. "You must hire professionals to do this sort of thing."

"I can't afford professionals. I'll buy a mask and cover the ceiling with plastic before I tear up any more, I promise. I just wanted to see what was under there."

She tried to shake free and return to the front room, but this time, Zack didn't let go. If she meant to be reckless, so would he. Instead of pampering her like a precious princess, he pulled her tempting curves up against him, catching both arms so she couldn't wallop him with her timber.

"You will have to wait for the dust to settle before looking," he murmured, gazing into her eyes as they widened. Was that interest or fear he saw there? Only a taste would tell.

He lowered his mouth to hers and licked lightly at her lips. She gasped but did not retreat.

Her weapon fell to the floor as he deepened the kiss. He hummed with gratification when she wrapped her arms around his neck and caressed his nape. Her mouth and tongue were as hungry as his. All week, they had been resisting this. Released from the torment, at last, he could not get enough of her. Why had he thought he must protect her from what was so natural?

He raised her to her toes and crushed her against his chest, needing to have all of her in his arms. She didn't hesitate. Her hips moved against his, inspiring more than hope with the rush of his blood southward.

This was neither the time nor the place, but there might never be another opportunity. Zack slid his hand between them to cup the fullness of her breast, and nearly went up in flames at her moan of pleasure. That he had the power to make this willful, wonderful woman desire him accelerated his demands.

He knew all the practiced moves to seduce a woman, but none of them applied here. That this woman whose intelligence he respected returned his desires fanned the fire of need burning within him. Amy wasn't a cunning seductress out to get what she could. Her hungry whimpers filled him with a sense of satisfaction he hadn't experienced in years. He would be the lover she'd never had, the teacher she needed to free herself, and she could teach him to be himself again. They were perfect for each other.

He claimed her mouth with his tongue, and she dug her fingernails into the fabric of his shirt. He wanted to take her slowly, enjoying every minute of her surrender, but in these surroundings, he could do no more than kiss her and wish a bed would fall through the ceiling.

He lifted her to the kitchen counter so he could open her shirt buttons. She instantly took advantage to run her hands beneath his polo shirt. Pure pleasure flowed everywhere her fingertips slid over his skin. He almost dropped her at his body's sharp, ecstatic reaction when she tweaked his nipples.

Unfastening her front bra clasp, he returned the favor, inciting the aroused buds of her breasts. She cried out with an eagerness that told him better than words how long it had been since a man had touched her in such a way.

"Amy," he murmured, kissing her cheek, her hair, then working his way down her throat to his heart's desire. "I have been wanting this for so long. Tell me you are ready."

She dug her hands into his hair and arched into him, speaking without words.

Just as Zack closed his mouth upon her breast, a pounding on the front door jarred them back to reality.

Willing the intruders to go away, he suckled, drawing her sweet-scented flesh deeply into his mouth until she cried out with the pleasure of it.

"Ames! Don't make me walk through that grass in these heels!" came a shout from the front porch, accompanied by more pounding.

"Mommy! We got creams!" a childish voice added.

Amy groaned and pushed Zack away. Her breast was still wet from his mouth as she hastily fumbled with her bra. Panting, Zack returned her to the floor and rested his forehead against hers while he brushed her hands away, fastening the clasp with tenderness, then caressing the skin exposed at the top with gentle fingers, sending further shivers of desire down her spine.

"Tonight," he said roughly. "We will go out. You are permitted dates, are you not?"

Amy was too terrified by what they'd done to answer. The reasons she should say no were pounding at the door. The children didn't need to have their security torn in two when Zack left. *She* didn't need her heart torn again. But despite all logic and common sense, she wanted to say yes, *yes*, please.

She tried to button her shirt, but her hands still felt the heat of Zack's hard chest, and her fingers wanted to curl into the soft nest of hair she'd discovered there. He was all hard angles and wide, muscular planes, and she desperately longed to explore a man who could lift her off the floor without effort.

She ached in places she'd forgotten existed for so long that she couldn't remember the last time they'd been satisfied. She wanted Zack with every ounce of hormones in her, and they were multiplying rapidly.

"We will do this, Amy," he said decisively for her. "It is just a matter of time. It might as well be tonight."

"I can't. I'm watching Flint's boys tonight," she said with genuine regret as he pushed aside her shaking fingers and buttoned her shirt. Before he could pose any further objections, she shoved away and raced for the front door. She prayed the mess in the front room accounted for her rumpled state.

She finally figured out the front lock and opened the door while Zack wisely remained out of sight. "Ice cream!" she cried, sweeping Louisa up in her arms and stealing a lick of her cone before Jo could say a word.

"Did you decide to destroy the place before you moved in?" Jo asked, swinging into the room in heels and shiny capris topped by a fringed halter. She gazed up at the hole in the ceiling, apparently not noticing Amy's frazzled state.

"I wanted to see if there was crown molding on the ceiling. Am I late? Elise just left, and I thought I had time to look around."

"Elise? Isn't that Zack's Bentley out there?"

Ha, as she'd suspected, Jo wasn't completely innocent. Amy frowned at her sister, but Jo wasn't paying the least attention. She was picking past the debris to the Art Deco staircase.

"He stopped by with the new designs." She'd forgotten all about them. How could she have forgotten the town's entire future? He had her head so turned around she didn't know up from down. "We were spreading them out on the kitchen counter. You want to see?"

"Is he decent?" Jo asked, arching an eyebrow expressively. "If he is, he's not the man I thought he was."

Amy heard a cough from the kitchen and could envision Zack choking on laughter. The rat. She hid her blush behind Louisa's curls. "Your aunt Jo is a naughty, naughty girl."

Louisa nodded eagerly. "Bad girl," she cried gleefully. "Go to your room."

"You're raising a parrot, you know that, don't you?" Grinning, Jo stepped over fallen plaster, diverted from the stairs by the cough in the kitchen. "You decent in there? Coming through!"

If Amy hadn't already spent a lifetime enduring her extroverted sister's embarrassing behavior, she would have sunk through the floor right now. Instead, she followed resolutely behind, wondering what she could possibly have been thinking to let one little kiss get so far out of hand. She ought to be steering a wide berth around her boss instead of inviting him inside an empty house, out of sight of the world.

Amy Warren, you did that on purpose, she scolded herself. She wasn't a teenager anymore.

But some small part of her reveled in discovering her new rebellious streak. She'd been the Good Girl for far too long.

"You'll have to drive a Ford truck if you want to sneak

around with my sister," Jo said jovially upon locating Zack in the kitchen.

He leaned against the counter, arms crossed over his broad chest, looking as if he wore plaster dust in his hair every day. "I do not need to sneak," he countered. "If I wish to have a business conference with my executive manager, I have every right to do so without being accused of sneaking."

He was *protecting* her, Amy realized in admiration. Of course, he was probably accustomed to cheating wives and that sort of thing, but still, it was sweet.

"See there," she said in satisfaction, setting Louisa down on the counter, "I'm a fancified business executive and get to make decisions. You'll have to quit treating me like your waitress."

Jo laughed. "You are talking to the Queen of Wrong Choices, folks. Don't give me that guff. I'll take the kids to church tomorrow. Lightning won't strike if you two don't show up."

Amy wondered if it would be counted as first-degree murder if she took the two-by-four to her sister's extravagant blond hair and dented her scalp a time or two.

Zack grinned in appreciation. "Wrong choices?" he inquired, deftly avoiding all the verbal pitfalls Jo opened to go after the safe one. The man was a first-class conversation manipulator.

"You and Amy can have a long talk about all my faults tomorrow. For now, I have to drag her out of this house to feed our starving kids while Flint and I play hooky for a while." She glanced at the display of fabric designs with disinterest. "These will return the mill to operation? Ugly."

"We'll make them red and add sequins for you, Jo." Amy carefully stacked the sheets of valuable historical designs, some of which hadn't seen the light of day in a century or more. She wanted to study them when she had a chance. "You're welcome to join us for supper, Zack. Where's Luigi? I can feed him, too. I'm just firing up Flint's grill."

Since they'd closed the café's dinner business, she'd been fixing meals up at the house. She had to break that habit by next week, when strangers moved in. Where would Zack live then? Or would he be gone now that he'd accomplished what he set out to do?

He accepted her invitation to the cookout with a devastating grin.

Amy didn't know whether to be relieved or afraid. After what had just happened here today, perhaps he ought to go down to Asheville and seek his own kind.

From the heated look in his eyes, Zack had marked her as the kind he sought. She didn't know how she should feel about that. She was a one-man woman, wasn't she?

Remembering how he'd made her feel, she briefly closed her eyes and admitted the truth. She would take Zack any way she could have him.

She, Amy the Proper and Emotionally Suppressed, was ready to embark on an *affair*.

≈ TWENTY-ONE ≈

"Mommy, doorbell!" Josh chimed in company with Jo's doorbell, running to join Amy and Louisa in the kitchen. He'd been playing upstairs with Flint's boys but must have decided to check on the progress of supper.

Amy nervously brushed her hands off on a towel. "Why don't you take Louisa outside on the swings? I'll be right out in a minute." She headed down the open hall of the cabin's cathedral-ceilinged front room. Flint and Jo needed wide open spaces for the boys and their music, or their house would probably bust at the seams, she reflected.

If she concentrated on the familiar, she wouldn't have to worry about seeing the man with whom she had become much too intimate this afternoon. She blushed just thinking about what they had done, and how they could have been caught doing it. But her breasts burned to do it again, and she was wishing she owned sexier underwear. She brushed a wayward lock of hair back from her heated cheek.

"Aunt Amy, can we put the hamburgers on? We're starved!" Johnnie called from the loft balcony, where a stereo boomed.

"Start carrying the salads out to the picnic table, and

I'll put the burgers on in a minute," she called back. "Keep an eye on Louisa and Josh until I get there."

The pounding of teenage shoes on the back staircase spoke of hunger and not eagerness to obey her command, but she'd counted on that. She preferred to have all the kids out of the house when Zack came in. She wanted at least a minute alone with him to steady her bouncing nerves. Her pulse pounded like a love-struck adolescent's.

She bit her lip to add color before she opened the door—and almost fell backward as Evan stormed in.

"Who is that guy and why is he staying in our house?" her ex demanded, stalking into the big front room as if he owned it.

Evan's size used to reassure her. She'd loved him for being her bulwark against the world's storms. Now she saw how he used his bulk to intimidate, and she refused to be intimidated. Hands on hips, she remained at the open door, studying the situation rather than bothering to respond similarly to his angry outburst. Evan had obviously gone to their house first—without calling. Tracking her to Jo's had no doubt strained his sociability.

"I didn't expect you this weekend," she replied mildly, casting a glance to the gravel drive, where a Bentley rolled to a halt next to the Beamer Evan had kept in the divorce. She thought she was seeing the scenario now, and she couldn't resist smiling, wishing she'd seen how that battle had gone down. "And the house is mine, not yours, if you'll remember correctly. I can do with it what I will."

Wearing tan tailored trousers and a black knit golf shirt that molded to his athletic shoulders and six-pack abs, Zack strolled up to the porch, not a feather ruffled by the obviously irate earlier encounter with Evan at the other house.

"Are you *living* with that creep?" Evan shouted. "I'll not have my kids in the same house with—"

"A foreigner with too many teeth and headlights you will punch out?" Zack finished for him in his clipped British accent. Carrying a bottle of wine, he winked at Amy, draped his free arm across her shoulders, and raised his eyebrows at her furious ex. "He is like a bull in a . . ."—he glanced around at the cabin's huge paneled living room—"in a barn?"

Amy tried not to giggle. She had a house full of kids and a grill that would burn out if she didn't get food on it soon. She'd grown up admiring the testosterone wars fought over Jo, but she was too busy to appreciate male idiocy now. "The kids are out on the swings, Evan, but they're not expecting you. I can add a hamburger to the grill, if you want one. I assume you've met Zack?"

"You haven't explained what he's doing in our house, Ames!" Evan shouted.

She disentangled herself from Zack's much too masculine and proprietary hold to return to the kitchen. His spicy aftershave had her stomach rumbling. Or other parts lower. She needed to remember that Evan likely had fifty pounds and four inches over Zack, but Zack packed an athlete's power and muscle. A war would not be pretty.

"Sleeping there, as far as I know," she called back. "But ask Zack. It's not any of my concern."

"What do you mean it's not your concern?" Evan demanded, following her.

"She means I have paid for the privilege of having the

house to myself, and I can walk the ceilings if I like, as long as I do not harm the premises." Unperturbed, apparently indulging in masculine amusement at Evan's bluster, Zack set his wine bottle on the counter and sampled an olive from the Greek salad.

Amy was excruciatingly aware that Zack was following her every move. Knowing his competitive instincts, she could tell he was assessing Evan, the situation, and her reaction, processing everything through that high-caliber brain of his, and probably making mincemeat of it.

She had this kind of argument with Evan all the time now. It was meaningless. Evan just liked to have his way, and now she finally had the freedom—and gumption—to defy him. She'd bitten her tongue one too many times when they'd been married not to enjoy upsetting his applecart now.

"We close on the house on Friday," she reminded Zack, ignoring Evan. "I'll have to remove the rest of the furniture by Thursday night. Do you have a place to go yet?"

"You will own the cottage Friday, will you not?" he asked with carelessness, moving on to sample the bruschetta.

Adam burst in to grab a platter, glance at the adults, and rush back out again without asking about the hamburgers. Smart kid, Amy figured. She knew from Jo's explanations that Flint's boys had endured a lot of confrontations between their parents in their growing up years. She had no desire to remind them of that unhappy time.

"I'll sign the deed Friday, but the cottage won't be fit to move into. We'll have to stay at the apartment for a while longer." She elbowed her ex from blocking the refrigerator. "Go visit with your children, Evan. They haven't seen you in a month."

"I want to know what the hell's going on here first. Where are you moving my kids that isn't fit for living in? What apartment?"

"Oh, did I forget to tell you?" Reaching for the ketchup, Amy turned to bat her eyelashes and plaster on a fake smile. "I bought a house." She didn't add, *and I did it without you*. She was still pretty amazed herself.

"How can you buy a house? You don't even have a decent job." Evan scowled, crossing his arms, making it obvious he had no intention of leaving while Zack was there.

Opening drawers until he located a corkscrew, Zack wasn't in any hurry to get out from under foot either. He tutted disapprovingly at Evan's comment. "You doubt that the inimitable Amaranth can look after herself? No wonder you have communication problems."

"The only thing *inimitable* about *Amaranth* is her ability to run up credit cards!"

Lifting the tray of prepared hamburger patties, Amy escaped the war zone for the more pleasant company in the backyard. It might be amusing to be spoken about in the third person, but she had hungry kids to feed and not a lot of patience for male posturing these days.

She'd be a little more pleased that Zack thought her *inimitable* if she didn't believe he was just figuratively punching Evan's lights out. Zack's civilized exterior didn't fool her for an instant. Beneath the smooth tailoring and behind the charming smile was a man who had a mind with wicked teeth and the conscience of a wolf.

"Mommy, my tummy hurts." Louisa wrapped her chubby arms around Amy's knee, immobilizing her.

"You didn't eat those green apples, did you? I told you they'd make you sick." She looked around for help. "Johnnie, would you take this tray for me? Carry it over to the grill."

Wearing his hair buzzed short these days, still sporting a gold earring and the first signs of adolescent acne, Flint's twelve-year-old loped over to take the tray. "Are you sure there are enough?" he asked, eyeing five pounds of hamburger with disappointment. "I could eat a horse."

"I don't recommend it or your tummy will hurt, too. There are bratwursts in the refrigerator if those aren't enough. Try some of the salads." Amy reached down to lift Louisa from her leg.

"I don't like onions," he replied, galloping off with the burgers.

"I like onions," Zack murmured near her ear, deftly handing her a glass of wine while taking Louisa from her arms. "They have many layers and taste spicy."

Just the rumble of his voice could shiver her spine into a puddle of lust. Amy sipped the wine to steady herself, then glanced at the glass in surprise. It was the most delicious wine she'd ever tasted, and probably cost ten fortunes. "I cannot deal with this," she muttered, fortified enough by the adult beverage to admit her tension. "I cannot. Back off, Zack, or I'm likely to hurl."

"Hurl what?" he asked with interest, backing off with Louisa in his arms.

"You don't want to know." Amy eyed Louisa contentedly curled against Zack's neck, touched her little girl's forehead to test for fever, and frowned in concern, forgetting both wine and argument. "Maybe you better set her on the porch swing and let her rest a bit. She feels kind of warm."

"Give her here. I'll take care of her." Marching down the back steps, Evan reached for his daughter.

"Daddy!" Josh cried joyfully, jumping from the swings to race across the yard.

Louisa grinned and held her arms out for her father, too.

With reluctance, Zack let the little girl go. She'd felt so right breathing her baby breath on his neck that his heart had almost broken to give her up. How could he ever forget the feel of wiggly weight in his arms, the baby-powder scents, the childish giggles? Better that she go to her father, where she belonged.

And that he stay and admire the children's mother. Amy had changed into a gauzy peach-and-lemon shirt over a lemon tank top and matching shorts. He loved the free-flowing lines and soft colors on her. They suited her much more than the dull, tailored outfits she wore to work.

"Hey, Son." Evan rubbed Josh's hair while bouncing Louisa on his arm. "Want to go home with me tonight?"

"Johnnie's gonna teach me to climb the apple tree." Intent on his own program, Josh ignored the question. "Mommy, when are we gonna eat? We're starving."

He imitated his older cousins so well that Zack laughed. Aware that the other man threw him a look of annoyance, he tried not to make the evening any harder on his hostess by explaining his laughter. "I will help your lovely mama make burgers so you will not starve, all right?"

"Yeah!" Josh pumped his fist in the air. "I want mustard and pickles."

"And salad," Amy reminded him. "Eat some of the

tomato bread and I'll fix you a plate of macaroni in a minute."

Zack watched the older boys scarfing down bruschetta as if it were peanuts and decided that must be the *tomato bread*. Josh ran off to join them, leaving his father without a backward glance. Zack could almost sympathize, except Evan seemed more intent on antagonizing Amy than paying attention to his marvelous son.

"Where are you taking my kids?" Evan demanded, following Amy and Zack across the yard to the grill rather than putting Louisa on the porch. "I have a right to know where they'll be living."

"If you had bothered to come and pick them up when you were supposed to, or even taken some of your precious time to call, you'd know by now."

Zack thought perhaps he ought to disassociate himself from the family argument, but he hated to see the little girl caught up in it, and he disliked deserting Amy if she needed his help. He knew nothing of grilling hamburgers, but he had a lively interest in walking all over brutes who growled and made others miserable, especially at a party.

"If the little one is feeling poorly, perhaps I could take her to the porch?" he suggested. He wanted to add that Louisa shouldn't have to hear her parents argue, but he thought Amy understood that. He'd suffered enough family fights to know children didn't need to hear them.

She gave him a look of relief that confirmed his opinion. "Would you, please? Sometimes she just gets too excited."

"She's not too excited," Evan argued, refusing to release the toddler. "I can take care of her just fine."

Amy slapped meat patties onto the grill. "Excellent. Then go sit with her on the porch swing until she's feeling better. I need to get these cooked before the kids start chewing my ankles."

"Daddy! Come see me swing," Josh yelled from the swing set.

"He's been asking for you for weeks," Amy said in a heated undertone. "Give him some attention."

Zack felt the other man's glare and realized he was an obstacle to Amy's wishes. Grinning, he saluted Evan and strolled away to see what the older boys were doing. He did not need to make Amy's life miserable. If it were within his power, he would sweep her away from all this. But she had responsibilities that tied her down, and he had no right to interfere, so he left the field. For now.

He might seriously reconsider his strategic retreat if Amy's ex continued to make an ass of himself in front of the children.

"Where's Luigi?" Adam asked as Zack helped himself to more of the excellent bruschetta before it disappeared. The fresh tomatoes and basil no doubt came from the garden in the back corner. The vines were almost spent, but he could see a glint of red here and there. Bruschetta should be made only with the freshest of ingredients. These might be the last of the season, and he savored the spicy sweet blend of flavors.

The picnic table was covered with an assortment of plastic-wrapped salad bowls. Picking up a heavy paper plate with one hand, Zack unpeeled a bowl with the other. "Luigi went to see a movie in Asheville." More likely, he went to find a woman. With no corporate spies to terrorize and no gyms to work out in, Luigi was bored.

"You should ask him to teach you sharpshooting. He is an expert."

"Would he? Teach us?" Johnnie asked in awe.

Zack shrugged. "Sure. He taught me."

From the corner of his eye, he watched Evan reluctantly leave Amy to see what his son was doing. The man had no clue how to play with his children, it was evident. He held a sickly Louisa like a bag of feed and stood at a distance from his little boy, watching Josh pump his legs to set the swing in motion but making no effort to help him swing high, as the boy so obviously wished to do.

To interfere, or not to interfere. That was the question. Whether 'twas nobler to suffer the slings and arrows . . .

Oh, hell, it was just more fun to interfere. Bullies needed to be pulled up short and taught to mind their manners.

"Try some of this green salad." Zack pointed at a delicious layering of peas and onions and other tasty tidbits. "I think it has peanut butter and octopus tentacles in it."

"*Ooo*, gross!" both boys exclaimed, reaching for the bowl.

Smiling, he strolled away. He'd been a boy once. Octopus tentacles were quite an attraction.

He checked on Amy. She was flipping hamburgers and pretending not to notice what was happening with her ex and their children. Mothers had eyes in the backs of their heads, though. She knew precisely what was happening. All the better for him.

The children were not his responsibility, but removing the competition from the playing ground was always a source of pleasure. Zack stopped behind Josh's swing. "Want a push? I bet you could see the stars if you went higher."

"Higher," Josh yelled with delight.

Catching the swing, Zack shoved him harder, and Josh squealed, "Higher!" Zack obliged.

Not unexpectedly, Evan stalked around the swing set and shoved Louisa at him. "I can do that."

"I am sure you can," Zack murmured, taking the bundle of dirty pink topped by blond curls from Evan's hands. Louisa didn't complain about the transfer. Sucking on her thumb, she curled into Zack's arms.

She was a heartbreaker, this one. But he was intent on bigger game, so he needn't worry about broken hearts. Taking the second swing, he rocked her gently, smoothing his hand over her back, while watching Evan push his son toward the sky. Zack figured the new shirt he'd worn just for Amy's admiration would suffer dirt stains from Louisa's knees, but the pleasure of the child's trusting hold was worth the price.

"Not that way, Daddy," Josh cried when his father almost pushed him from the seat with his big hand at his back. The swing twisted awkwardly and the boy nearly fell.

"Don't do this often, do you?" Zack asked cheerfully.

"And you do?" Catching the chains, Evan attempted to shove the swing from above Josh's head.

"I climb ropes, swing swings, anything to keep in shape," Zack agreed with perfect honesty. "One does not need to be a child to play."

"Men work. Children play."

The swing careened sideways, and Zack had to abandon his seat for fear of a crash. Josh looked a little dazed but happy, so Zack refrained from commenting. Louisa snuggled her nose into his shoulder. "My tummy still hurts," she complained.

"Then let us take you back to your mama," he suggested. "I will learn how to flip burgers just for you, *n'est-ce pas?*"

"Nessy pa," she agreed, happily parroting new words.

"I'll take her. I can flip burgers." Having given Josh another push, Evan grabbed his daughter from Zack's arms.

Twisting to watch his father, Josh lost his hold on the chains after the rough push and, with a cry of terror, flew off the seat and slammed onto the ground, knees first.

With her brother's first wails, Louisa puckered up and, lifting her golden curls from Evan's shoulders, hurled green apples and ice cream down her father's shirt collar.

⋘ TWENTY-TWO ⋙

"Honestly, Evan, you won't die of a little upchuck. Josh is the one who's bleeding, not you, and he's making less noise."

Barely keeping a lid on her boiling temper, Amy held out a hot washcloth to her ex while cradling a sobbing—smelly—Louisa to her shoulder. "Just wash off his knee and put a Band-Aid on it, or hold Louisa so I can do it."

She didn't even bother turning to Zack for help. The great Olympic champion looked green and was pouring a second glass of wine at the far end of the kitchen. He'd been doing amazingly well earlier, until the kids reached the crying, bleeding, throwing-up part that was the downside of parenthood. She could excuse him for not joining in. She assumed he'd had little experience in dealing with crying children, and these weren't his kids.

But Evan ought to be smacked upside the head with a wet flounder for caring more about his clothes than his weeping children.

At the moment, Evan was too busy stripping off his ruined shirt to find bandages. "This is a Joseph Abboud, dammit! I just bought it. Why the hell are you having a party when she's sick? She ought to be home in bed."

"Just put the damned shirt in the wash. At least finish

the hamburgers so the boys don't start gnawing on their knuckles."

Balancing Louisa in one arm, she rubbed the soapy washcloth on Josh's knee and ignored Evan as he strode half naked through the kitchen to deposit his precious designer shirt in the laundry room. She'd grown up doing without luxuries just as he had, but she still knew people were more important than material things. Maybe men should nurse children so they could get in touch with their inner nature. Providing men had any inner nature other than a need to succeed.

Zack remained frozen and pale near the back door, intelligently staying out of her way. She didn't expect him to step up to the plate when it came to crying children. It wasn't his responsibility. It was Evan's.

When she lifted her head to glare angrily at Mr. Stupid for ignoring her second request, she noticed Zack's handsome mouth tightening. Not only was he looking a little green, but his usually laughing eyes looked unhappy and stared at some point beyond her shoulder, as if not seeing the room at all.

If she needed any reminder of their differences, the kids had offered the perfect opportunity. Any sexual fantasies she may have entertained fled in this crash with reality. This was simply a mundane family scene of the sort she handled every day. It infuriated her that Evan refused to deal with it, but Zack's reaction was not only useless, but puzzling. First, he had looked terrified, and now he didn't seem to be present at all.

She was amazed he wasn't spinning the Bentley's wheels in escape. "Will someone please rescue the hamburgers?" she shouted.

Abruptly drawing back to the chaos in the kitchen, Zack finally met her gaze and set aside his glass. Looking relieved at finding an excuse to escape, he nodded and slipped out the door to see that Adam and Johnnie were fed and reassured.

She sighed in relief at this lifting of one small burden. He might not handle crying children, but he did what he could, more than she could rightfully expect.

Murmuring comforting words to her sobbing children, Amy began the process of restoring their fragile world to normal. The men were adults. They could damned well take care of themselves.

He was a coward.

Utterly amazed at that discovery, Zack had spent a lonely night roaming mountain roads, unable to tolerate the haunting emptiness of Amy's once beautiful home. Luigi hadn't returned from the city. And Amy had refused to bring the children back to the house, insisting home was where their beds were—in that tiny little apartment. Where he couldn't go.

And he'd been relieved.

How the hell had that happened? He'd always nursed Danielle's bruises. He was an expert at bruises, after all. Pentathlons did not happen without pain. He'd always been the one to get up with her when she was ill. He hadn't been squeamish—as Gabrielle had been—until the night they'd died, and then he'd started seeing Danielle in his nightmares, with blood streaming down her head, crying for him, and his heart had cracked irreparably. He hadn't been there for her that night. He'd arrived too late.

Crying children had sliced his cracked heart into sushi ever since.

After ten years, the nightmares were gone, but at the moment, his head was spinning so hard that past, present, and future were all jumbled inside him. That had not been little Danielle getting sick last night. He'd had nothing to do with Josh's bleeding knee. None of it was his fault, no more than Gabrielle's accident had been his fault. That was guilt by association, as the therapist said. Irrelevant.

He'd run from the painful recollection of his nightmares.

It had taken him the entire night to work that through his head, and he'd only examined his actions because it had felt *wrong* to leave Amy. He'd always been able to blithely extricate himself from personal responsibility, but this time, he'd felt like a bloody heel.

Amy had been in grave distress last night, and like her poor excuse of an ex-husband, Zack had *wimped out*. He was pretty certain that was the expression the teenagers used. He'd flipped hamburgers, talked music with Flint's sons, and left Amy to deal with bloody knees and sobbing angels.

He had always prided himself on his courage, but a child's tears had left him helpless. At least he'd stayed until Flint and Joella had returned. Evan had stormed out after a loud and furious argument they could hear from the backyard.

Having parked the Bentley in the upper lot, empty stomach churning, Zack walked down early-Sunday-morning Main Street with his arms loaded with grocery bags. The sun was just a pale orange promise on the horizon, but he knew the path through the shadows. Even the café lights weren't on yet.

He'd dug out his oldest shirt, the one with the frayed collar and cuffs he couldn't bear to throw out because he'd worn it the day he'd won the bid for his first job. It was his lucky shirt. He'd meant to wear it the day he'd won the mill bid, but he'd had Amy on his mind and had forgotten. And he'd still won. So maybe the shirt didn't have much to do with his success.

He had Amy on his mind a lot these days. He hoped it was just because he was in desperate need of sex, because their lifestyles would never suit them for anything else. In any other circumstances, he would have backed off to regroup with a partying woman, away from the marrying kind.

But today, he felt the need to prove that he wasn't a coward. It mattered that Amy didn't think of him as one.

He almost tripped over his feet. *Amy mattered.* How in hell had that happened?

If he had any sense at all, he'd run the other way before he'd committed himself to more than the mill. What else was he liable to commit to while under the influence of Amy?

More than he could handle.

Never. He never backed down.

He'd been small as a boy and had learned martial arts to prove to the bullies in boarding school that size didn't matter against courage. As their pampered only child, he hadn't been allowed by his parents to compete in the rougher contact sports like soccer. In retaliation, he had excelled at fencing, artillery, and equestrian athletics.

He had a history of standing up to naysayers, of tackling impossible projects and overcoming overwhelming odds.

He'd spent these last ten years rebuilding his shattered life to an image of his own choosing. He'd even dared to let Amy's charming children get close to him, without sliding into a blue funk. He hadn't fallen into an abyss of despair or terror after the Porsche accident.

But he'd run away because of a bloody knee and a little vomit? No way. If his nightmares returned, they were one more fear he must conquer.

He climbed the loft stairs and heard the cries of "Mommy!" that indicated the household was awake. Light streamed from the apartment's second-story window overlooking the mountain. He assumed Amy had been up for a while, maybe longer, if he correctly remembered nights with a sick child.

He'd had grand plans for this day, but he understood that Amy would never leave an unwell Louisa to come out and play with him. He had an immense amount of work he could be doing instead of coming here. He usually used this time of day to review e-mails and return phone calls to his European projects.

But this was Sunday. He was entitled to a day off.

Balancing the plastic bags on both arms and in his hands, he rapped on the door. A tousle-haired Josh, still in his pajamas, opened it.

"Good morning, Josh. How's that knee today?" Not waiting for an invitation, Zack shouldered the door wider and strode past the wide-eyed little boy. "Good morning, Amy," he called over the sound of rushing water from the apartment's small bathroom.

He smiled broadly at a chirp of surprise. The water

suddenly shut off while he placed his bags on the galley kitchen counter.

He lifted Josh to the counter so the boy could show him his colorful bandage. Zack's heart stuttered painfully at the towhead's eagerness to display his hurt and declare himself too big to cry.

Zack nodded gravely as he emptied a bag. "How would you like to try my favorite breakfast, Sir Josh of the Brave Knee?"

"I like Cocoa Puffs," Josh declared.

"You can have Cocoa Puffs anytime," Zack scoffed. "Only today can you have Zack's Amazing Raspberry Scrumptious Cheese Crepes."

Sensing Amy's presence, Zack took a deep breath to steady his nerves before he turned around.

"Crepes?" she asked. Layered curls falling over her forehead, she expressed suspicion and surprise in a deliciously sleepy combination.

Her unfettered curves looked wondrously sexy even in striped seersucker boxer pajamas, and he had to rein in his sudden rush of lust with concern.

"Coffee first," Zack affirmed, examining the dark circles beneath her eyes. "Do you prefer Hawaiian or Peruvian?" He produced both kinds to show her.

Holding a pale cherub against her shoulder, she rubbed her eyes and stared as if he were a mirage. "I prefer tea, I think. What are you doing here?" A puzzled frown marred her brow.

"Did we not have a date for today?" Wiggling his eyebrows mockingly, he returned to rummaging in the sacks, producing several cellophane-wrapped boxes. "I could find only a supermarket open last night. Their tea choices leave much to be desired. Do any of these appeal?"

She stared back and forth from the stack of tea boxes to him until he feared she was about to heave him out upon his presumptuous ass. He breathed a sigh of relief when she finally replied.

"Are you a hallucination? Or have you been up drinking all night and your fuddled mind thought this would be fun?"

"You wound me, Amy. You forgot we had a date." He found her teakettle and filled it at the faucet, and then began looking for a mixing bowl and spoon. "Sir Josh, if you will look in that bag beside you, you will find plates with which to set the table. Can you do that?"

Josh tilted the Wal-Mart bag and removed the child-sized plastic plates. "Oh, boy, X-Men!" Generously, he held up a second plate for his sister to inspect. "Look, Lou, Dora!"

Louisa brightened and held out a chubby hand for the pink plate. "Dora!" she confirmed.

"They have to be washed first," Amy warned, setting her daughter down, then lifting Josh from the counter.

Zack tried very hard not to watch as the child's weight dragged the pajama top down her breasts, but he was a man, and she was very much a woman, and her lovely curves made him sigh in gratitude.

"I like your hair that way," he murmured once the children grabbed their prizes and ran off—apparently to wash them in the tub. "It is all sexy and curly, as if you just rose from your pillow."

She ran her fingers through the rumpled layers, and from her expression, he assumed she was deciding whether to bark, bite, or bait him. Holding the discovered bowl and spoon, he leaned over to kiss her nose before she could do any of them.

"I have not done this in a long time," he whispered. "Let me see if I remember how."

She blinked in surprise and warily stepped out of reach. "Why are you doing this now? And what exactly is it that you are doing?"

"Always the practical American." He waved his spoon in despair, then added flour to his bowl. "A European woman, now, would smile mysteriously, kiss my cheek, and wiggle sexily toward the bedroom, where she would change into something both frothy and erotic before returning with an ice-cold bottle of champagne for us to share."

A broad smile reluctantly transformed her face. "European women keep chilled champagne in their bedrooms?"

When he reached into the apparently bottomless grocery bag to produce the champagne, she burst into laughter. "You are *insane!* I am employed by a madman. Perfect, absolutely perfect. I think I'll go find something 'frothy' to put on. That way, when Louisa throws up again, I will be dressed for it."

Trailing gales of laughter—or hysteria, depending on how sleep-deprived she was—Amy ran up the stairs to her loft bedroom.

Zack straightened his shoulders and attacked the crepe batter. He thought that had gone rather well. She hadn't thrown him out, and he hadn't run in panic at the heart-wrenching sight of mother and children in Sunday morning dishabille.

*   *   *

"I promised to come get them," Jo reminded Amy over the phone line. "If Louisa isn't running a fever, she should be fine. You're entitled to some time off, and it sounds like Zack is working hard for his reward."

Amy could hear her sister's grin. Instead of laughing, though, Amy was freaking out.

She wasn't used to having a man in her *kitchen*—much less one who could produce devastatingly delicious raspberry cheese crepes, then cleaned up after himself.

She wasn't used to a man who had a gleam in his eye when he looked at her, to match the glitter in his earring when he tilted his head to listen to a child's prattle. Zack was wearing an old frayed dress shirt and jeans, and he still looked like a modern pirate. His looks stole her breath, but his gentleness with her children was in danger of stealing her heart, and she simply couldn't afford the loss.

She'd had a brief moment of hope when Louisa had turned pale over breakfast and declared she was about to throw up again. Zack had turned equally pale and froze in the middle of a silly song involving geese and unfriendly ducklings. She'd thought he'd excuse himself and flee when she hastily hauled Louisa to the commode.

Instead, he'd arrived minutes later carrying a warm washcloth and had taken Louisa into his strong arms, relieving Amy's aching ones.

She'd wanted to cry with the realization that real men were amazingly masculine when they did gentle things with their big competent hands. Real men didn't have to bully and intimidate to be macho. That's when panic had set in.

"Another time, Jo," she told her sister. "I don't want you exposing the boys if she has a bug, and you have to

guard your voice if you're going to Nashville next weekend."

After finally talking Jo out of babysitting, Amy hung
up the phone to find Zack holding Louisa and watching
Amy curiously.

"Did you wish to take them to church this morning?"
he asked without inflection. "She really didn't throw up.
She's just frightened she will."

Amy didn't hear condemnation in his voice for her
having turned down this opportunity she'd given him
every right to expect, and after he'd been so wonderful
and understanding, too.

She'd made no promises. She didn't have to apologize
or explain. She knew that if she went to bed with this
man, he'd have her heart in his hands. She simply wasn't
modern enough to have sex without a relationship, so she
might as well establish the parameters now. She had to
think of her children first.

Elise had reminded her that no man was ever this wonderful once he had what he wanted. Yet the longer she
knew Zack, the more she wanted to be with him—at the
mill, at home . . . in bed. She was on rocky ground here.

For the sake of the children, she had to resist Zack's
appeal. It wasn't as if he'd made any pretense that he intended to hang around for the long term, and not only
did the kids not deserve that kind of heartbreak again,
they didn't need to see their mother fall apart at the
seams just when she was getting her act together.

She shook her head regretfully. "No, I think Louisa
needs to stay home and be quiet for a while," she murmured. He really was the kind of man she'd love to love,
had there been any chance that he wanted what she did.

But he didn't. "You can go, if you like. I really appreciate breakfast. I was exhausted."

He nodded as if he understood. "It is harder to see them ill than it is to go without sleep. It is not something I am eager to repeat soon. You are a very brave, strong woman."

Repeat? Amy brushed her hair out of her eyes and shook her head at this over-the-top flattery. At least he was honest about not wanting to be around sick children, although she had to wonder where he'd gained his experience. He'd said he wasn't married, and he'd mentioned no children—but something in his regretful look said otherwise.

That was what dating was about—getting to know each other. Except she knew in her bones that getting to know this man would be a dangerous step in the wrong direction.

"She ate too many green apples," she said, giving him time to offer answers before she had to ask the questions popping to mind. "It was hardly a life-threatening situation. Parents get used to it."

"Not all parents," he murmured, returning Louisa to her. "And you can never know for certain that it is just green apples. We would have lost Danielle to meningitis if the doctor had not finally realized it was more than a cold bug. Any illness can be life-threatening at that age."

Danielle? The name opened a door to an intimacy that she'd tried to avoid, shattering her shield of denial. Zack fit the image of carefree bachelor so easily. Only—except for his reaction last night—he had acted like a parent from the moment he'd seen Louisa. Amy's soft heart responded instantly, wondering if he'd suffered a disastrous divorce, if he missed his daughter, or worse yet . . .

She hugged a sleepy Louisa tighter and studied the pain in his dark eyes and knew at once that he'd lost a child. Had that been why he'd withdrawn last night? It broke her heart just imagining a father's anguish at losing a child. Had his wife taken their daughter away?

"But she survived the illness, didn't she?" she asked, dropping all her sorry defenses in a need to reach out to him.

Zack's smile disappeared and his eyes wrinkled in weariness. "Yes, with proper treatment, I got to keep her for another year."

She knew she shouldn't ask. She knew exchanging private thoughts would break down any barrier remaining. Zack obviously wasn't one to talk of losses, but that kind of pain shouldn't be pent up and buried beneath a layer so fragile as smiles and charm. Like a festering boil, it needed to be lanced and drained if he was to heal. It wasn't her duty to heal him, but she couldn't bear to watch him suffer. "What happened?" she whispered.

He shrugged carelessly. "I married too young. Gabrielle was even less mature, and I indulged her too much. And then, when it was not expedient to indulge her, I expected her to grow up. That was very stupid and arrogant of me." His voice broke, and a corner of his mouth slanted upward in a self-deprecating smile.

That explained nothing. She wanted to smack him for his evasiveness, but men despised letting people see their pain.

Just knowing he'd been married before, knowing his wife's name, was difficult. She should back off now, let him throw up the charming barrier he used to prevent anyone from getting close. If she started removing the barrier, brick by brick . . . She hesitated, knowing she teetered on a dangerous brink.

Elise would tell her to back off, not to get mixed up in his problems, but she wasn't Elise. She needed to see the man behind the charm. She abruptly realized this was why she couldn't relate intimately with this fascinating man—he was holding her at the same distance as she held him.

If she pushed for more now, it would be admitting that she wanted the distance eliminated.

"How old were you?" she asked, throwing him an easy question that didn't commit either of them. Yet.

She thought he wouldn't reply. He strolled into her crowded living room and gazed out the enormous windows to the street below.

But instead of retreating behind his usual cheerfulness, he stuffed his hands into his back pockets and, not looking at her, began to speak. "I was old enough, but I should have given Gabrielle more time to experience life. One does not consider these things when a woman carries your child. We married in college and were deliriously happy. Danielle was the love of our lives."

She could hear the adoration behind the pain. Tears lined her eyes. She had known this man hid layers of depth she'd barely glimpsed. She could hear the passion and devotion crying out from the bottom of a deep well where he'd buried them. He must have suffered horribly to bury a character as strong as his. And she could no longer resist removing the next brick in the wall.

"Children change us," she whispered in agreement.

He nodded and finally turned to look at her. Grief carved lines beside his eyes, but his chiseled lips tilted in self-mockery as he studied Louisa's golden curls on her shoulder.

"Our daughter did not change me enough. I have always been too ambitious, too centered on my own concerns. It was our anniversary. We were to have a lovely vacation in the Italian Alps. We were in Florence, an amazing city. You must see it sometime."

Amy would give half her teeth to see Italy. She merely nodded agreement.

"I was just starting my software business. I had an important prospect who was running late. He asked me to wait until the next day to meet with him. Gabrielle had spent the day packing and was all excited. She loved the Alps. Danielle looked adorable in her new ski suit."

His anguish revealed the ghost of a man whose life had been destroyed. Amy suspected he never let anyone see this man who knew what it was to lose everything. She wanted to take him in her arms and tell him . . . What? There was nothing she could say that he hadn't already heard. Her heart ached for him.

He managed a short careless shrug that no longer rang true. She understood better now that he wasn't a careless man, nor a thoughtless one.

"We argued. Gabrielle wished us to leave right then. We had a babysitter waiting and a romantic dinner planned. I told her business was more important. That was no doubt the stupidest thing I have ever said."

Amy leaned her head against Louisa's. "No, it isn't," she murmured. Louisa had fallen back to sleep. "You were planning their futures, and that was very important to you."

That was the excuse she had given for Evan's behavior

for years. In Zack's case, it might actually be true. Still, it was another bad sign.

Zack smiled briefly as he approached to cup Louisa's head, perhaps looking for an anchor against what he had to say next. "You're too kind. Gabrielle's feelings were hurt, and she could be quite stubborn. It was convenient for me to overlook that. Any other time, I would have found some pleasant entertainment to distract her from the disappointment and promised her the moon if she waited. But I was too *busy*." He said the last in a tone of self-disgust.

Amy touched his bare arm, aware of the crackles of electricity between them. His words had to be said before they could proceed further. She waited silently, expectantly.

He dipped his head in acknowledgment. Pain tightened the muscles of his jaw. "When I returned to work, she took our car and our daughter and headed for the Alps on her own. The weather turned poor. The car was not designed for icy conditions. Perhaps the angels deserted them, I do not know. A moment was all it took. I should have been with them."

Tears streamed down Amy's cheeks. She heard his resignation, knew he thought the angels had deserted him as well. And he'd spent these last years going to hell to prove it. She shook her head, but words could not come. There were no words for such devastation. It was obvious he'd loved them both deeply. The way he stared down at Louisa proved he still had the capacity to care, though he worked hard to hide the fact. His deliberate nonchalance wouldn't wash with her ever again.

His revelation had destroyed her shield of wariness as

well as his own. "I'm sorry," was all she knew to say. Arms full of sleeping child, she rubbed her cheek against his bare arm in a gesture meant to comfort.

Zack stiffened at the contact, but she didn't step back or offer the pity he feared. "The hurt never really goes away, does it?" she asked. "Or the guilt."

His eyes darkened with anguish, and he cupped Louisa's curls. "No, it never does. I have tried burying it, but you . . ." He traced his finger down Amy's cheek. "I would not hide from you. I suppose, sometimes . . . a burden shared becomes lighter."

Amy couldn't speak, couldn't do anything except meet his gaze above Louisa's head. Panicking, she thought she would have been better off not knowing that she might be the first person he'd shared his sorrow with in a long time. The warmth building between them terrified her. This wasn't just sex.

Still, she didn't regret knowing that he was a man who felt deeply. No one could doubt the humanity of a man who had done what was right and opened the mill to operations, risking his business in the process. She'd been drawn to him from their first conversation, with its lack of awkward or strained silences. The connection of sharing felt too right.

Everything about him seemed right. It was their situation that was impossible.

Saving her from sailing around the bend and out of sight, Zack smiled impishly again and kissed Amy's nose. "I never had that tour of your lovely new home. Shall we see how it looks in morning light?"

≪ TWENTY-THREE ≫

"I wager there is golden oak beneath this hideous paint." Zack smoothed a loving hand over the cottage's Art Deco stair rail as if he'd not torn open his chest earlier that morning and revealed the gaping emptiness inside.

Having this house to examine gave his head and heart a more practical direction while he tried to figure out who he was now. And who he wanted to be.

Amy had asked him for his suggestions on how best to tackle restoring the cottage, as if she'd known he needed something concrete to accomplish. She had an unerring instinct for diverting minds from unhappy paths.

"But stripping it would take forever or cost a fortune." Amy proceeded up the worn stairs to the upper story. "These small bedrooms will suffice for now, but I'd love to see some of them turned into bathrooms."

Keeping an eye on Louisa working her way up the long flight, Zack lingered behind as Amy swept through the upstairs hallway, opening doors. She'd come closer to him than any woman he'd known since Gabrielle, and they hadn't even had sex yet. Perhaps *because* they hadn't had sex. Instead of indulging in physical satisfaction and moving on, he was dangerously on the verge of old-fashioned courting.

"The house is more spacious than I assumed." He admired the high ceilings while surreptitiously admiring feminine curves. This was comfortable ground—lusting after a woman who sent him smoldering looks from beneath delightful long lashes when she thought he wasn't looking. He was always looking. Today, she wore simple jean shorts, but her copper-colored tank top had little flowers adorning the neckline, drawing his eye to creamy shoulders and lovely arms.

"The house has been added on to more than once," Amy agreed, checking a hall closet. "I assume the mill's CEOs lived here well into the fifties or sixties."

"Still, it has much charm." Having followed Louisa up the stairs, he peered into a bedroom overlooking the big backyard. His career had been made by his ability to look at old houses and see how they should be, but this one struck him very personally. His vision of the renovations had little to do with the historic and a lot to do with the comfort of Amy and her small family. "The sleeping porch could be turned into a lovely glass parlor for the master bedroom."

"Josh, keep Louisa away from the windows." Amy kept one eye on the children. "I'm afraid it isn't safe." She came to stand beside him at the French doors. "I don't think we can move in until that ceiling is pulled down, and all the lead paint has been removed."

"How long will that take?" he asked, doing his best to keep his mind on the task and not the woman standing so close he could clasp her hand if he wished. She hadn't shied away from him when he'd revealed the depth of his shame and grief over losing his family, but she was as nervous as a newlywed now. He found that very interesting.

"As long as it takes. The kids don't mind the apartment, and Jo is letting us have it for free."

Zack opened the French doors and stepped onto the sagging porch. Amy prevented Josh from following.

"The mill is just over those trees?" he asked.

"There used to be a path leading down to it, but it's overgrown and washed out."

For the first time in a long time, genuine excitement surged through him. Zack eagerly swung around and grinned at his practical Amy. He hadn't used his cane since he'd settled in with his computers, and bouncing in excitement, he didn't notice his knee now. "Let me stay here and start working on this," he said, completely catching her—and himself—off guard.

"Here?" she squeaked. "It's filthy. I might be able to clean out the tub, but the shower has to be rebuilt. I have a few rugs for the floors, but I can't afford to start on the kitchen—"

"It has a stove and a refrigerator, does it not?" As the idea gripped him, he strode through the bedroom to sling open doors just as Amy had done earlier.

"The stove is an ancient electric and the refrigerator is tiny." Amy had spent many nights listing the house's problems, but she'd still been unable to talk herself out of it. She adored the high ceilings, the built-in cabinetry, the gorgeous sunporch, the huge backyard . . .

"They're fine for me," he said with a dismissive wave. "I always work close to my projects. In rehabilitating old castles, I have lived with a hot plate and a cooler. Here, there should be running water at least."

Amy stared after him in shock, letting the kids run happily in his path. After his tale of Italy and the Alps, she'd thought for certain he'd wallowed in wealth all his life. But after he'd exposed his deep-seated grief, she wasn't in any state to deny Zack something that caused him excitement. She thought she was seeing for the first time the melding of the charming man with the grieving one, into the whole he ought to be.

He'd been wary of personal involvement of any sort when he'd first arrived. Now he was taking on both the mill and her house? She'd have a hard time concealing her hungry need for a man willing to dive headfirst into such hard work.

"It will be an adventure," he continued when she didn't reply. "May I borrow one of your beds or should I buy my own?"

"I was planning on hiring a van, moving the rest of our things into the dining room, and covering them in plastic until the work is done." There wasn't any way she could store all her antiques in the apartment, and Evan had expressed no interest in them, thank heavens.

"Excellent!" he crowed. "I will hire someone to clean up this suite for my use and borrow your comfortable bed and move in here. In return for the use of your property, I will offer you my expertise in restoration. The ceiling will go first, I think."

Without waiting for her agreement, he clattered back down the stairs to inspect the damaged false ceiling in the front room.

Shaken, overwhelmed, Amy remained in the upper hall, watching Josh and Louisa race from room to room of their new home, while she tried to figure out what had just happened here. And how she felt about it.

She couldn't get past the image of cosmopolitan Jacques Saint-Etienne sleeping in her bed, in the lovely high-ceilinged chamber she'd pictured as hers. Did he sleep naked? The thought hadn't bothered her in the other house. Why should it bother her now?

Because one house was the past and the other her future?

As long as she remembered it was the house that was her future, and not Zack, she might survive this new encounter with Zack's whirlwind energy without being swept away.

On the last Friday of the month, Zack watched as Amy crept quietly back to her desk in the office across from his at the mill. He'd known she'd left to close the deals on both her houses. He'd expected her to return jubilant.

She just looked exhausted and worried.

He should have gone with her. He should have sent lawyers with her.

He should stuff his protective instincts into a drawer and forget about them. Amy was a strong, independent American woman who didn't require his help. He was counting on that. After he'd exposed his insides so painfully, he didn't dare get closer to her until he'd had time to glue his shattered walls together again.

He'd spent this last week drumming up orders for the first fabrics off their looms. He'd learned about a major show in October, taking place just a few hours down the road, where he could display their goods to furniture manufacturers and decorators.

But watching Amy's slumping shoulders, he decided they both needed a weekend away from work. It was time to play.

Giving Amy time to answer her messages, Zack made a

few phone calls. He'd hired a truck to hold Amy's furniture until she could move it into her new cottage this weekend, but the house was by no means ready for human habitation. He could stay at the dilapidated cottage tonight, or at the motel again, but he had a better idea.

Plans laid to his satisfaction, Zack wandered across the corridor to Amy's office, propped his shoulder against the door frame, and crossed his arms until she noticed him.

She refused to look up from busily entering numbers into an old-fashioned bookkeeping journal. It was a good thing they were still a small operation. The new computer he'd bought for her sat unused.

"The computer will not blow up if you use it," he informed her.

"Promise?" She glanced at him skeptically, then returned to work as if he weren't there.

Zack almost laughed out loud. He wasn't accustomed to being ignored. Leave it to Amy to serve him up steady doses of humility. But he wasn't about to be denied on this. "As long as the work gets done, I won't argue with your methods. Come along. The first yardage should be rolling off the machine now."

Anticipation lit her eyes when she looked up, but then she saw him standing there—with an obviously amorous gleam in his eye—and she ducked down to her journal again. "I have to finish the payroll entries. Some of us need checks, you know."

With a sigh of exasperation, Zack strode into the small office, grasped her elbow, and hauled her from the chair. "You are not an ostrich to hide your head and pretend I do not exist. I will hire an agency to handle payroll. The checks for this week are already cut. You will not go bankrupt just because you are now a proud homeowner with a mortgage that keeps you awake at night. All that will be there when you come back. The first bolt can be experienced only once."

He steered her down the hall. A copier beeped and spit blank paper as they passed.

Grinning at this sign that Amy's resistance to change caused her nervousness, he gestured for his other office help to join them. He had a nice parade by the time he crossed the parking lot under cloudy skies to Building Three.

The entire workforce had gathered around the machine producing the complex textured design he'd chosen for their first sample. As the fabric rolled off the loom, all chattering hushed expectantly.

The apple green brocade revolved through the spool and passed the computerized optical scanners with flying colors. Everyone held their breath while hands-on experts checked for defects and passed on the yardage to Zack. He gave Amy one corner and he took the other, opening the fabric full width so they could examine the woven design for themselves.

"It is perfect," he said with reverence, thrilling as he always did at the intricacy of the work produced by man and machine. Raised feathers, scrolls, and delicate curves formed a cascade of embossed design. He knew precisely what kind of furniture this belonged on.

"The detail is exquisite," Amy murmured, running her fingers over front and back. "The fabric feels like silk." She looked up at all the people who had helped produce this rare material. "I think we've done it," she announced with a hint of wonder.

Cheers and rebel yells filled the building. Zack waved

for catering to set out the prepared buffet and drinks, and as the loom continued processing the cloth, the celebration began.

"Now we can leave." Zack caught Amy's hand again and led her toward the exit.

"Leave?" She glanced longingly at her friends. She'd made the hors d'oeuvres herself. She wanted to share in the food and excitement. She wanted to inspect every inch of the fabric, watch it come out of the wash and go into the processor. She couldn't believe they'd done it—she and Zack. They'd returned the mill to production! It was a time for celebrating.

But she was an *executive*. Maybe executives didn't celebrate. It wasn't as if they'd sold anything yet. Reluctantly, she followed Zack into a drizzling rain.

"Today is for celebrations," he said with excitement, swinging her hand. "You own a new home! We must find a housewarming gift."

Amy's mental gears shifted slowly. "Housewarming gift? For me? Right now, I just want some of that fabric—a pillow for my rocker, maybe."

Zack looked at her with fond amusement. Instead of heading for the office entrance, he steered her toward the Bentley. "You think too small, my Amy. Come on, we'll start with paint."

"Paint?" Still off-balance, she sank into the Bentley's buttery leather seat.

"I have spoken with your contractor. He will have the ceiling down this weekend."

"My contractor?" She was beginning to sound like the parrot Jo claimed Louisa was.

The car purred into motion. She could swear Zack purred with it.

"Yes, the one who wants to work on the mill offices. He wishes to show how good he is. I cannot stay in your charming cottage until he removes the old ceiling."

Amy started to panic as the car turned down the road toward Asheville and away from town. Zack had blessedly kept his distance all week, but his moods were mercurial. "Josh and Louisa expect me to pick them up at five."

"They will be happy to see your sister and mama, no?"

"Jo? Of course, but . . ." Finally recognizing the satisfied gleam in his eyes, she crossed her arms and glared. "What have you done now?"

He shrugged. "Only provided an evening of shopping. That is not so unpleasant, is it? We go to the home improvement store, look at some paint chips, have a nice dinner . . ."

His accent had become very French, and Amy's wolf alert shrilled.

But she knew how to handle Zack. And she was dying to look at paint chips.

Sitting back in the comfortable seat, she dreamed of an evening discussing cobalt tile and nickel-plated fixtures with a man who actually knew what she was talking about. She had set aside a few dollars from the sale of her house for the most pressing repairs.

She would simply have to think of Josh and Louisa when Zack flashed his thousand-kilowatt smile and chuckled in that knowing way of his. And she wouldn't notice how his tailored coat clung to his muscled shoulders. Or how his long fingers felt cupped around her bare elbow.

Paint chips, she told herself firmly. This was all about paint chips.

≪ TWENTY-FOUR ≫

"No, no, with the golden oak, you want the softer colors the blue-greens, the pale yellows, not the jewel tones." Zack snatched the cobalt chip from Amy's hand and deposited it in his coat pocket.

Even disagreeing about color with Zack was exciting. His passion for her home and the creative light burning in his eyes was sexier than the deliberately seductive smiles he'd used before. The more caught up he became in the process, the more his hands brushed hers, and the closer he slid to her in the leather booth of the restaurant, rearranging the chips and samples. When he became exasperated with her, he'd flick her earrings, and the reminder of shared kisses flared between them.

It was quite possible she was disagreeing with him just to prolong the exchange, to feel his thigh pressing against hers as he reached for a piece she moved out of his way. She was officially out of her mind and loving every minute of it.

"With the right shade of blue-green, I can still use cobalt accents. Give me back that swatch." Amy leaned across him, reaching for his jacket pocket.

Zack grabbed her waist and nibbled on her ear until she thought she'd have to slide under the table. She retaliated by blowing on the strong neck rising from the open collar of his shirt. He laughed and returned her to her seat. She waved the confiscated swatch in his face.

Away from work, away from the duties of parenthood, away from any responsibility at all, she felt as if the weight of the world was off her shoulders and she could open up to the fun she'd denied herself for so long. She adored playing with colors and fabrics, and Zack had swirled her through acres of them in a few short hours. No man she knew could endure that much nesting.

"Shiny cobalt tile," he said sternly. "Now, finish your wine or I will not show you my next surprise."

"Next surprise?" She sipped the extravagant chardonnay he'd ordered with their dinner. She'd never learned to be much of a wine drinker, but she could come to appreciate it in surroundings like these. Jo had told her about the restaurant with the fish murals on the ceiling and the leather booths, with real linen and real silver on the tables, but she hadn't thought she'd ever have the opportunity to eat here. Evan had always preferred to entertain at home, where she did the cooking.

She swirled the wine in the glass, relaxed on the comfortable bench seat, and absorbed the giddy ambience of fine food and an attentive, attractive man. For the first time since the divorce, it felt exciting to be single and carefree. "I don't need any surprises," she decided. "I just want to sit here and pretend this will last forever."

"No, you will miss tucking in little Louisa and teasing Josh and the patter of little footsteps in the morning," he corrected. "But it is necessary to take these breaks to appreciate what you have."

Amy looked at him in amazement. He was not only right, but dead serious, and she knew he was speaking from experience. He still missed his daughter. Her eyes misted in sympathy, and she reached over to pat his hand.

"Thank you," she murmured. "I needed this. You're a very wise man."

"No," he stoutly denied, "I'm a loose cannon, but that's neither here nor there. Would you like dessert, or shall we go on?"

She had thought he would take advantage of her sentimentality to make practiced love to her. She'd almost been hoping for it. After that explosive kiss and his revelations last weekend, she knew she was asking for trouble by being anywhere near him.

But tonight . . . Tonight she was having second thoughts. Unfortunately, apparently, so was he.

"I can't eat another bite," she admitted, smothering her disappointment. Give her an inch, and she wanted it all. She knew better. She would try to just enjoy whatever else he proposed for the evening without setting her future-planning meter into operation.

Smash that planner. Relax, she reminded herself.

Leaving cash on the table, Zack stood and held out his hand. "Come along, you will enjoy this."

She could play a little while longer, but if he meant to take her to one of those noisy bars Jo used to frequent, she wouldn't do much relaxing. She had two left feet and no interest in country music. But he'd been so patient with her, she could easily agree to follow him anywhere.

"Jo and Mama don't mind putting the kids to bed?" she asked, wishing she still had a cell phone to check on them.

As if reading her mind, Zack handed her his. "They assured me everyone will be fine, but call and see, just in case."

With his hand heating the small of her back, Amy punched in Jo's number and slid into the Bentley.

By the time she had said good night to Josh and was re-assured her small world was well, Zack had pulled the car up to a valet stand. She hadn't been paying attention to their route, but the stones of the elegant old lodge were unmistakable.

"The Grove Park?" she asked dubiously. She'd set up Evan's VIP guests at the inn, but she'd never even seen the spa. She'd always found better things to do with her time and money—most of them involving her family.

"A surprise party for two," he said firmly, steering her toward the spa entrance. "It is time you remember that you are a person, too, and you deserve occasional pam-pering."

Passing by the salon, a hundred thoughts raced franti-cally through her head, but she didn't have the presence of mind to utter one of them. The elegance overwhelmed her. As if he expected her to protest, Zack had an atten-dant waiting at the entrance.

"She is already beautiful," he told the smiling hostess. "You will make her *feel* that way."

"Of course, Mr. Saint-Etienne. All is as you requested."

He'd requested the spa? When?

In a state of shock, Amy watched Zack stroll away in the company of a male attendant. Obediently, she fol-lowed her hostess, unable to think of a diplomatic man-ner of extricating herself, especially when her curiosity about the spa screamed to be satisfied.

"That is so romantic," the tall, blond, and gorgeous at-tendant murmured. "No one has ever said anything like that to me."

Amy tried to remember the last time anyone had called

her beautiful. Evan had occasionally nodded approvingly when she frosted her hair and wore a designer suit, but she hadn't looked like herself then.

Zack liked her natural looks, unstyled hair and all? The possibility made her feel more feminine than she had in ages, and she looked eagerly around her. Everyone should experience everything at least once, right?

Knowing how many beautiful women must come through these doors, Amy was self-conscious as she undressed and donned robe and slippers. Her hair looked as if she'd barbered it herself. Which she had. She'd snipped the ragged ends when she didn't have time to make an appointment. And her fingernails! She clenched her fingers into fists to hide them. Evan was right. She really had let herself go this past year.

The gracious attendant didn't seem to notice as she led Amy past inviting rooms sparsely occupied at this hour to a private room with an enormous whirlpool bath and a massage table.

"Helga will take you from here. Enjoy!"

By the time Helga had questioned her enough to design the perfect regimen for her obviously mistreated body, Amy figured the masseuse knew more about her than she did herself.

Soaked in rose-scented waters, pounded with aromatic oils, detoxified, and relaxed with soothing lighting and the gentle hush of a waterfall, Amy fell asleep on the comfortable cot.

Hot towels laid over her back woke her gently. Eyes drifting open, her gaze fell on a basket containing a bottle of champagne and chocolates and a vase of roses that scented the air with a hint of cinnamon.

"Surprise," a male voice murmured from the direction of the whirlpool.

She jerked her head up, and for a moment, she had an out-of-body experience, jolted out of her old self into some giddy new stratosphere she'd never imagined.

Zack lay relaxed against the walls of the bath, his muscular arms resting on the rim, his eyes half-closed, his overlong hair wet and clinging in slight curls to his sun-darkened throat. His naked chest, covered in wet whorls of hair, filled the space above the water.

Amy wasn't fooled for a minute by his sleepy-eyed look. His gaze was directed at her bare breasts, and he was smiling. She grabbed a towel from her back and tried to wind it around in front of her. She frantically looked around to see who was watching.

"Come in. The water is delightful," he murmured. "The attendants are paid to leave us alone, and the champagne is well chilled."

It was on the tip of her tongue to tell him what he could do with his tools of seduction—when her driving need for new experiences kicked in. This was what she'd wanted, wasn't it? Seduction, raw sex, no-strings-attached love-making . . . Right?

Absolutely! The new Amy was a woman of the world who wouldn't fall in love just because she shared physical pleasure with a man. She was a grown-up now.

She didn't think she could release the towel.

"I will close my eyes," he suggested immediately, reading her mind for the second time that night. "The water is beautiful."

She didn't think his closed eyes would help, but the promise got her off the table and to the pool's edge, where she stepped in with the towel still around her. He was right. The warm, jetting, bubbling water was heavenly. She slipped into the far end of the tub and nearly melted, remembering to throw the towel to the tiles only at the last minute.

His toes slid along her legs, and she nearly shot right back out of the water.

"Relax," he murmured again.

"That's easy for you to say," she muttered, taking the glass of champagne he nudged in her direction. She closed her eyes to the sight of Zack's lightly furred chest and was grateful for the cover of bubbles on the water's surface as she sipped the chilled wine. Champagne went up her nose and she coughed.

"Sip, don't slurp," he said with a chuckle. "It is heady stuff, this vintage. I ordered it just for this occasion. If you will come here, I will feed you strawberries. I have been assured this is the very best chocolate coating."

Amy's cheeks heated, and the delicate bubbles she'd been drinking raced straight to her head. But parts of her that hadn't been alive in a long, long time were stirring with interest, and she couldn't sit here with her eyes closed forever.

When she opened them, she discovered Zack had slid around the circular tub to sit beside her. A chocolate-covered strawberry dangled temptingly near her lips.

"Open wide," he whispered.

And she did. With just his wicked suggestion, her legs parted to the excitement of jetting bubbles on vulnerable parts while she opened her mouth to accept his offering. In doing so, she leaned back against Zack's arm. He shifted her to his shoulder, and they were side to side, naked as the day they were born.

And she didn't flee.

Far from fleeing, she wanted to climb into his lap and have her way with him. She was so hot she thought she might internally combust if he didn't touch her in a vital spot soon.

He was all male muscle scented with some exotic spice the masseuse must have applied, and that Amy wanted to lick right off of him. The leg pressed along hers was all hard sinew and strength. His shoulder and arm cradled her as if she were no more than a small doll. She loved being held by this man, loved feeling alive and desirable like a woman instead of a machine.

She sucked the rest of the chocolate strawberry from its stem and let the flavors melt in her mouth, mixing with the champagne. She moaned a little with the pleasure of it, and he chuckled softly.

"You were meant for sensual pleasures, my Amy." His long finger reached to caress the tip of her breast where his arm cradled her. "You should not deny what you are."

His mouth closed over hers, soft and more intoxicating than the champagne. His tongue tasted of decadently delicious chocolate. His hand caressing her breast completed the task of arousing her from the stupor she'd lived in for so many years. Every nerve ending awakened and sizzled with spikes of electricity.

Amy ignored the flashing alarm signs and warning bells in her head. She was beyond being careful any longer. Tonight was hers. This fascinating man wanted her, and she wasn't losing the opportunity.

She tilted her champagne glass over Zack's chest and licked the spilled wine from his nipple.

⫷ TWENTY-FIVE ⫸

Had he not been sitting down, the tentative touch of Amy's tongue on his chest would have brought Zack to his knees.

He'd had champagne licked off him before. He'd had Jacuzzi baths and chocolate-covered strawberries and more.

He'd never had any woman like Amy to share them with.

It wasn't just that she was lush instead of willowy, wholesome instead of jaded, or shy instead of bold, although all these elements excited him with their newness and elicited conflicting needs to cuddle and ravish her at the same time. No, it was the inner strength of the woman emerging from her shell that fascinated and aroused him.

He tried to concentrate on the physical awareness of her ripe breasts brushing the hairs on his chest as she leaned over him. But it was the daring dart of her tongue across his skin that made him so hard he could barely restrain his urge to pull her over him right then. She was doing her best to seduce *him*. He'd stake his fortune and his reputation that she'd never seduced another man in her life—and the knowledge both humbled and excited him.

He caught her face between his hands and lifted her chin so he could kiss soft chocolate-coated lips. She sent his head spinning when she licked the juice from his mouth first.

Her tongue tasted sweeter than berries. He tried to reclaim control of this seduction, but her kisses were as hungry as his, and they nearly slid under the water trying to gulp each other down.

Coming up for air, he could no longer resist the soft press of her breasts against his side. He slid his hands to cup their generous fullness, lifting them to his lips so he could taste even more luscious berries. He thrilled at her cry of pleasure and crushed her closer when she grabbed his hair and held him there to taste as freely as he wished.

She was all women in one, lush goddess, nurturing mother, intelligent partner, and he was about to explode with his need to claim her. But he wanted this first time to be perfect.

Pleasuring her breast, he slid his arm beneath her rounded buttocks, lifting her so his fingers could slide along her sex. Amy's quick inhalation and widened eyes said all he needed to know. Her fingers bit into his shoulders as he tugged her across his lap. She didn't resist repositioning but kneeled over him, tentatively surrounding his sex with her palms so he thought he might expire of need right then.

"I have waited too long for this, my Amy," he murmured, stroking her until she closed her eyes and hummed with pleasure. "We have all night, but I need this *now*."

She spread her legs and came down on him without question or quarrel, smothering him in ecstasy, leaving him gasping for air. His senses reeled with the touch, taste, and scent of warm woman in his arms, pressed into his chest. His erection had grown so large, he feared he'd stretch her to breaking.

He lifted her from his lap to suckle at her breasts again, then lowered her more slowly this time, so slowly he thought he'd lose control before she closed over him completely. He fought for restraint so he could move within her, producing excited gasps. She moaned louder as his lips teased her breasts and his hands guided her hips in a slow circle.

He wanted to do this all night, yet his body countered with building urgency.

She pushed upward, almost relinquishing him, and before he could protest, she caught his head between her hands, closed her mouth over his, and plunged down again—while stunning him with a kiss full of passion . . . and demand.

"Now, Zack," she whispered, wrapping her legs around him in a way he could not refuse.

Relieved of all restraint by her request, he cupped her buttocks and pushed into her until she cried out with delight. Then he guided her into the driving rhythm he wanted, needed, and couldn't live without.

Once she grasped his needs and took charge of the passion incinerating them, he hungrily leaned over to suckle her breasts. His hands cupped her rounded hips, and he delighted in their supple movement as they moved together farther, faster. When he knew he couldn't restrain himself much longer, he slid his hand between them, found the nub of her sex, and pushed her over the edge.

Rather than cry out, she bit his shoulder. Triggered by that erotic charge, with her climax pulsing around him, Zack simply let go, giving himself up to the moment as if he were still a teenager in the first throes of blind love. He thrust hard and exploded in spasm after spasm, finally attaining the release he craved, while she clung to his neck and the warm water bubbled around them.

"I think I'll just slide under and drown happy," he managed to murmur as he wrapped her in his arms. After weeks of deprivation, he knew all her soft curves pressed into his hardness would have him aroused and aching again within minutes, if not seconds, but he couldn't let her go if his life depended on it.

"Take me with you," she replied sleepily, brushing her mouth against his before resting her head on his shoulder.

It wasn't until he'd nestled her tenderly against his chest that he realized what he'd done. By throwing away all his practiced maneuvers, he'd forgotten protection. He *never* did that.

The memory lapse was too Freudian to consider. He couldn't marry and have children with a woman like Amy. The match would be worse than the one between his mother and father. They would have to live on different continents and kill each other by phone.

He didn't want to argue with Amy. He wanted to play the role of gallant protector while enjoying her laughter, admiring her creativity, and exploring all the facets she hid from the world. And the only way he could do that was if they had no ties. He'd learned that lesson the hard way.

"We have two choices," he said into her ear, cupping his hands around her breasts and playing with their aroused nipples. "We can put on the bathing suits waiting for us and enjoy the romantic grotto, or we can slip on our robes and go up to my suite." He nibbled on her ear to encourage the latter choice.

"We can't just stay here?" she replied, scorching his chest with soft kisses. "We haven't finished the strawberries or champagne."

"I'll have them sent up to us." Not waiting for her decision, he rose from the water with Amy wrapped around him. If he didn't get out right then, he wouldn't be able to walk.

Walking didn't matter after all. She fastened her mouth to his, wrapped her legs around his hips, and within minutes, he had her beneath him on the cot.

With the cinnamon scent of roses filling their heads and the steam from the bath enveloping them, they sated the frustrations of the past weeks, oblivious of all but sensation.

Sheets like silk slid along Zack's skin as he turned to reach for the warmth he'd cuddled all night.

She wasn't there. He groaned into his pillow.

He could feel the glare of sunlight against his eyelids, but he left them closed, preferring to listen for telltale sounds that would give him an indication of what to expect. He was accustomed to waking alone, but he was abnormally disappointed to do so this morning.

One little night should not be so dangerous.

Perhaps Amy was the wiser of the two of them. They should not let themselves get used to cuddling or expecting romance.

A door clicked, and he lifted one eyelid to peer toward the bathroom, praying that its door was the one he heard and not the one to the suite. The bathroom door was wide open, and Amy wasn't in sight.

Panic rising, he flipped over to observe the other side of the room.

Looking adorable in the short-waisted jacket and draped skirt she'd worn to work yesterday, Amy stood beside a table tray containing hot dishes, teapots, and a pitcher of juice. At his movement, she poured a glass of juice and brought it to the bed.

"I have only the weekend to work on the house. Hurry up, sleepyhead; it's time to get moving."

"*Incredible!*" he muttered to himself as he threw off the bedcovers and ignored her offering of juice. Stark naked and still half aroused, Zack stalked across the carpet to snatch a pastry from the tray. It wasn't a substitute for the sweetness of woman that he preferred. "You are the least romantic woman in the world!"

Even as he bit into the pastry, he was startled to realize he didn't mind that she wasn't romantic. This was pure Amy smiling back at him in the mirror, undeterred by his reaction. Here stood the practical woman who disguised the seductress underneath—the seductress only *he* knew.

With Amy, he didn't have to be charming. In return, she didn't have to play at being what she wasn't to entice him. He loved just watching happiness radiate from her.

"Said the grasshopper to the ant," she replied tartly, as only Amy could do and not give off rancor. "It was your idea to shop."

"Not at the crack of dawn." His body ached for more lovemaking before returning to the grim realities of her world, and he wasn't ready to let her win this argument. "There is a reason for weekends."

"Of course! Weekends are for doing everything a working mother can't get done during the week," she replied as if he were simpleminded.

Zack swung around and caught her openly admiring his physique, and he had to slam his libido to a halt and rethink. She obviously wanted him, just as much as he wanted her, but did a hint of wariness linger behind her admiration? That she still doubted him hurt, and it shouldn't. He knew she was the settling-down kind and needed to be wary.

Why was he the one resenting that Amy was headed back to her life as if this were a casual affair? As he usually did.

"I work hard and I play hard. That does not make me a grasshopper," he said gruffly, grappling with his odd resentment.

"So do I," she replied. "But my idea of playing is with my new house. And since that was the purported reason for my coming here, you shouldn't be surprised if that's what I want to do."

He wanted to stage a scene where they either both walked off in a huff or ended up in bed again. That was normal in the world he'd occupied these last years.

He was tired of the scenes, he realized. He was tired of waking up in strange beds to women he didn't even like.

He liked Amy, in his bed and out of it, even when she was at her most exasperating, as she was now. She was running from him because she was scared and testing his staying power.

He didn't entirely know what to do about it. Not yet. He needed to go home and set his head straight. Was that how Amy felt, too? No wonder she was keeping her distance.

Thunderstruck by the realization that he could have a woman he enjoyed beyond sex, he almost dropped into a nearby chair.

It would appear that they might be on the verge of a real relationship—whatever that might be. He didn't

know what to do about it. Only one thing was certain—
he had just gone beyond fighting it.

Was that how Amy felt? As if she'd been smacked on
the head by a two-by-four and knocked under a steam-
roller? He would have to sort through the maze of that
possibility as soon as he picked his rolling head up off the
floor and set it on straight. He knew what "relationship"
meant to Amy.

He was only mildly terrified and not quite shaking in
his boots. Yet.

For the moment, he must deal with the impossible female waiting for his response. She was tapping her foot
and starting to frown.

Zack miraculously discovered a desire to knock down
ceilings and paint walls.

"Sit. Eat," he commanded. "I will shower. You will not
run away." Smiling broadly, he planted a kiss on her
cheek—anything more and he'd have her undressed in
seconds—and strode off to the shower whistling.

Amy held a hand to her cheek like an infatuated
teenager and tried not to melt through the floor as Zack's
beautifully muscular ass disappeared into the bathroom.

She'd been doing fine until that confident gleam had returned to his eye, and he'd started giving orders. She'd
felt very woman-of-the-world climbing out of bed, washing, and dressing while a handsome man slept sprawled
across the bed they'd made love in. She'd thought ordering room service on her own a brilliant idea to establish
her independence and the casualness of their relationship.

It was one thing to look to Zack for a job. That was
business. But depending on him to feed her and plan her
time off, that was scarily intimate and spawned thoughts
of planning days around him . . .

And mornings.

She'd faltered there for a minute when he'd actually sounded hurt and uncertain. He was the experienced one, wasn't he? She was the one who should expect more of an affair, right? Which was why she had to prove she didn't expect anything.

Now she was just plain confused. This was the reason she had resisted the idea of an affair for so long. She couldn't separate sex from commitment. And commitment with jet-setting Zack was out of the question.

She finished her glass of orange juice and poured tea. The kitchen apparently already knew Zack's requirements, because they'd sent up a real teapot and real tea leaves instead of hot water and herbal tea bags. She nibbled pastry and listened to him shower and was relieved she was dressed so she wasn't tempted to join him for a repeat of last night.

Last night had been . . . She couldn't think of words to describe how she'd felt or she'd cry knowing she'd never have another night like that again. Zack was ruining her for any other man.

Well, fine. She didn't want any more men.

She flipped on the television and half listened to a weather report about another hurricane barreling into the Gulf Coast. She flicked it off when Zack emerged smelling of sandalwood, wearing blue jeans and a worn work shirt, with his hair still wet and curling from the shower. Before she could say a word, he gathered her into his arms and drowned her in a kiss so hungry that he jump-started her stuttering heart and left her gasping.

"We are good together, yes?" he demanded, releasing her to press her into a chair at the table.

All she could do was nod. It was the truth, after all.

"Regrets, Amy?" he asked softly.

Her heart stumbled at the gentleness of his voice, and that he even considered how she felt. "No," she replied in a whisper.

"Then we will enjoy the day as we choose colors for your new home." Apparently satisfied with his decision for her house, he uncovered the hot plates and ravenously consumed the breakfast she'd ordered for him.

How did one pound a whirlwind over the head?

One didn't. One went to ground and didn't come out until the tornado had spun past.

⨾⟨ TWENTY-SIX ⟩⨾

"You need a nanny to keep up with this one," Zack declared the Monday evening after their brief sojourn in heaven. He captured Louisa and pulled her down from the furniture the movers had stacked in the dining room of Amy's cottage.

The contractor had ripped out the living room ceiling over the weekend, revealing deteriorating plaster and oak crown molding. Tired of the Motel 6 and eager to explore the possibilities of the Craftsman cottage, Zack had decided to move in.

"I need a million dollars and a yacht, too," Amy replied through a mouthful of pins. She tugged fabric more tightly over a rod and pinned it in place to provide privacy for the windows.

"No, I mean it, seriously," he insisted.

He'd known the day she'd stripped him down to his grief that she was more than the women in his past. He'd proved to himself that he could deal with children again. He'd tried the usual path of seduction, and she'd stood him on his head and bowled him over with her passion and joy. She was one woman in a million, the one with the power to return him to reality. The one with the potential to cause serious pain.

He'd been thinking hard for days, trying to find some

way of having this woman he wanted, despite all the obstacles bobbing ugly heads in their path. The question of
what to do about the children was one of many, many arguments they must overcome if he had any hope of building a relationship. He knew she didn't like to leave the
children, but his business involved travel, and he didn't
like to do it alone. They must find a compromise.

He'd had lots of experience in argument and didn't
want more. He had a feeling he had only one chance for
happiness and it had Amy's name on it. "She is too young
for day care. She needs personal attention."

"Uh-huh, as soon as I have that million dollars," she
agreed, jabbing another pin into the material.

"So, you do not mind nannies?" he verified with delight.

"Nope. When I have a million dollars, I'll stay home
and won't need one. Or maybe we'll all go sailing on that
yacht."

"You are not being serious," he protested. "You cannot
take children with you everywhere without help. Traveling is difficult for little ones."

Standing on a crate, she eyed him warily while jabbing
the last pin into the end of the makeshift curtain.
"Maybe I should have the house tested for mold. It can
have the same effect as drugs. Unless you're on drugs,"
she suggested, helpfully. "I'm not going anywhere anytime soon, so nannies are not a concern."

"But what about the sample shows? Do you not want
to see how people like the fruits of our labor? There are
shows everywhere. We could go to Paris, to Hong
Kong . . ."

"You are definitely on drugs." She climbed down from
the crate. "There are plenty of more qualified people for

the shows. Did you ever find out what's holding up the silk thread for the floral tapestry? That fabric is the key piece for the show."

The children were in the room. Zack couldn't grab Amy and kiss her and make her see what he saw. There were still too many questions to be settled before he could tell her his plans. He had to rein in his impatience before planning their future.

Their future. He was thinking in terms of a *future,* with building excitement and too many terrified questions. Most of the questions were his, he could admit. Was he capable of making a woman happy for longer than two nights? Could he handle children who got sick and injured on a regular basis? Was he too old to settle down? The last thing on earth he wanted to do was hurt Amy.

The next to last thing he wanted to do was lose her. Sometime this past weekend, he'd realized he had to think about tackling the largest challenge of his lifetime—marriage. Amy would settle for nothing less.

He'd already failed the challenge once.

So he tested the waters as he had not the first time around. This time, they were both settled into certain lifestyles, and the obstacles were larger than if they'd been young and unburdened. His goal was to encounter, explore, and remove the impediments one by one—

Not he—*they.* He'd lived on his own too long. Amy was accustomed to being part of a unit. He was not. He needed to start thinking in terms of both of them.

"The silk manufacturer's production is running behind," he said in answer to her question, trying not to think of failure of any sort. At least in business matters— he and Amy were of like mind. "We'll have to do without the tapestry for the show."

"Perhaps we could substitute the cotton prints?" she suggested. "Those are simple."

His cell phone rang, and he automatically carried it to the window for better reception while Amy checked the hem of her makeshift curtains.

"No, no," he shouted into the mobile clamshell. "Where are the mechanics? We cannot afford to waste the thread."

Amy winced and tried not to listen. The one machine had been jamming all day. They had precisely two weeks to get the samples ready for the High Point market.

Government grants took months. They needed cash now, and the market would generate it . . . if all went well.

She'd almost rather dream of traveling to shows in Paris and L.A. than think about broken machinery. What on earth had sent Zack off on that tangent?

He bit off a curse and snapped his cell shut, then paced the floor of the dining room. "The loom needs a new part," he growled. "We cannot make more of the brocade until it is fixed."

They needed variety to impress the buyers at the show. Their booth wouldn't be noticed among the thousands of other booths unless they had something exciting to catch the attention of jaded buyers. "How long will it take to fix the machine?"

"Maybe a week," he said with irritation.

"Then we need to start on the prints and the jacquard," she suggested. "The cotton isn't as rich, but the design is exquisite. We'll need flyers, brochures, maybe a direct-mail campaign to get out the word about the rarity of the historical design. If you would quit being so bullheaded and use more contemporary colors—"

"*Bullheaded?* You think I am bullheaded? You are the one refusing to go to the show, the one with the brilliant mind who would bury herself in this place and never venture beyond—" He shut up abruptly.

Amy glanced over her shoulder to see both Louisa and Josh watching him with dread in their eyes. They had heard her arguments with Evan too many times. And Zack had been observant enough to understand that. She breathed a sigh of relief at his wisdom.

In recompense, she offered what she could. "If you need me in High Point, I will go. I'm not afraid of travel, but I can't leave the children for long."

Zack ran his hand through his hair, gazed at the children with doubt in his eyes, then nodded. "We will discuss business at work. Tonight is for the little ones. You need a room you can play in while we work, do you not?" he asked them.

Josh shouted his agreement and Louisa imitated his shouts.

Amy could have kissed him. But kissing was way too dangerous. She'd avoided it ever since Saturday. It was bad enough hiding how she felt about Zack from the kids, but pretending to be no more than a corporate drone at work all day today was excruciating.

"The upstairs room?" Zack suggested. "We can set up Josh's train tracks there."

Accompanied by Josh's cheers, they hunted through the stacks of furniture and cartons for the toy boxes.

"You have so many beautiful pieces, it is a shame to bury them like this." Zack lifted an elegantly curved Mission rocker from the stack to uncover a box Amy thought might contain the train set.

"That's the rocker I'd love to use the brocade on." She

gestured at the wide oak seat. "A lovely thick pillow for the seat and a few loose pillows for the back, maybe in the floral silk. We ought to use a few of my pieces at the show as design ideas."

She'd just cast out the idea as a stray thought, but she sensed Zack's alertness instantly. He tensed, and began examining the stack of furniture with renewed interest.

"It is the wrong period," he murmured.

"People save what is good and use it in different generations," she suggested. "What are you thinking?"

She located the train box and Louisa's doll box while he frowned and poked through her antiques.

"I am thinking you are brilliant." He untangled a walnut settle with the slender back slats and arms of the early colonial period. "I am thinking we will need two booths at the show and some seamstresses. Do you know what shape the sewing machines are in?"

"In her day, my mother could take the machines apart and put them together faster than the mechanics. Do you mean this? I don't want to raise hopes, but Mom ran the samples department for years."

She tried to breathe normally, pretend this was just an impersonal business discussion, but she thought she would burst while she watched Zack pull out furniture and rub his jaw thoughtfully.

Jobs, even temporary ones, would add much needed cash to pockets throughout town. With Christmas coming up . . .

"Call her," Zack said decisively. "Ask her to come in tomorrow to see if the machines can be made to operate immediately and how long it will take to produce pillows. I think we need at least one bed to display a jacquard coverlet."

He paced up and down, thinking aloud, pulling out more furniture when his gaze fell upon other useful pieces. Amy was willing to sacrifice everything she owned to make this work. She grabbed his cell and dialed her mother.

"Mom, don't say anything to anyone yet," she said as soon as Marie answered, "but we need you at the mill first thing in the morning. We have questions."

Ending the call after arranging transportation, Amy hugged Zack's neck as if doing so were the most normal thing in the world. "It's going to work. I know it is!"

He wrapped both arms around her, hugged her close, and kissed her hungrily, as though he'd been starving since last they'd touched. Her heart soared with her hopes, and it was a giddy few minutes before she could extricate herself. Josh attempting to tug his train box to the stairs was sufficient warning that they couldn't mess around in front of the kids.

"I'll provide a nanny for them while we go to High Point," he said sternly when she pulled away.

She could see the heat of desire in his eyes, but also his concern. She couldn't trust the lust, but she'd learned his concern for her children was as reliable as her own. She nodded. "Or Jo, if she's in that week. I'll ask."

"I knew you would be an asset to the company," he said with pride. "Don't ever underestimate yourself again. If we succeed, you'll be the reason."

Astounded, Amy watched Zack lift Josh's box and walk out.

She was an asset? She couldn't even operate a computer. She couldn't fix machinery. All she had done was offer her furniture. And make a few phone calls. She wasn't doing anything more than she had done for Evan, except he'd never paid her for her ideas—not in money or gratitude.

Important people got things done, made things work. All she'd done was call her mother.

But she liked that Zack thought she was important. Maybe that meant he was suffering the same throes of lust and hero worship she was suffering right now. Her dreams these last nights had been filled with Zack, not just of sex, but of waking up with him, of talking over problems with him . . .

Juggling hope and caution was a balancing act she hadn't quite perfected yet, but if Zack stayed around long enough, she just might manage it. Listening to him singing the quacking-duck song as he hauled toys to the attic, she relaxed and decided to enjoy the moment.

Tomorrow always came too soon.

≪ TWENTY-SEVEN ≫

"No, no, Pascal." Holding his cell to his ear and shaking his head, Zack stood on the balcony overlooking the interior of Building Three, keeping an eye on production. "The show is next week. We're working around the clock. I absolutely can go nowhere until it is done."

The smaller loom chattered and clanged and, inch by inch, produced the marvelous jacquard in a goldenrod motif to complement the apple green brocade. The colors suited his demand for historical accuracy while meeting Amy's demand for marketability.

There were way too many variables in this venture. It required promotion and salesmanship he'd never needed for his former limited ventures. He'd never designed textiles for mass production before.

Pascal was offering a terrific special project, in Paris.

"Yes. In November." Zack didn't think he could accept the job even then. He was taking each day as it came, praying that all would work out. "Yes, it is an honor, but I am committed here."

He grinned at how easily the word flowed off his tongue after years of denying it existed. It was liberating to drop the continual struggle against his natural inclinations.

But the conflicts he and Amy faced were still valid. He

had to do this right this time, not just for his and Amy's sake, but because children were involved.

Ringing off with Pascal, he sought calm by watching Amy chat with their temporary sewing machine operators, examining the display pieces they'd created out of little or nothing, practically overnight. It would have taken weeks to order anything similar from China. These women could produce miracles in less time than he could place an order.

The mill and the show presented one headache after another, but those were material things, the things his life had been made of these last years. He did not fear them. It was Amy who had him pacing the balcony.

She belonged here. Even he, in all his selfishness, could see that. She knew the people, she knew the product, she knew the market. This was her world.

Europe was his.

His cell rang again. This was his personal phone, and everyone in Europe was at home at this hour with nothing better to do than check on him. It didn't matter that he was still in the middle of his workday.

He clicked on the phone just to shut it up.

"Jacques, I just talked to Pascal, he says you won't be home for Christmas!"

Zack contemplated accidentally dropping the phone to the floor below the loft.

If he did, he'd probably hit someone on the head, and they'd pick up the phone and have to deal with his mother. Not a bad idea, except he really didn't want anyone feeling sorry for him.

"Mother," he said politely.

"You sound just like your father when you do that enigmatic distant thing," she replied crossly. "And he doesn't mean it any more than you do. Shout, if that's what you want to do."

"I'm at work. Shouting would cause a certain degree of agitation." Zack headed for the stairwell in hopes that the inevitable disagreement that would result from this conversation wouldn't travel quite as far as in the warehouse.

"Agitation would be better than your usual ennui," his mother said. "Did Pascal lie about your being involved with a woman? Is it Brigitte? She's not your style, really, Jacques. Whoever it is, bring her home with you. You know I can't do Christmas without you."

"I'll be home for Christmas, Mother. Pascal simply wants me home sooner." Pascal wanted the prestige of working with Versailles, but Zack refrained from passing on that tidbit.

"He's your friend. He's concerned. Tell me you're not falling for some mountain girl. She won't fit in here. You know that. It's just a passing fancy because you're far from home."

Zack almost grinned. It was hard to take his mother seriously. She never thought before she spoke or she'd have bitten her tongue by now. "You're from the mountains, Mother. I don't see you having any difficulty fitting into London. When is your next gallery showing?"

"The first of December. You will be here, won't you? Your father won't come unless you call him, so you have to come. Is she pretty? Does she at least speak proper English?"

"Mother, I have three lines blinking and a secretary waiting," he prevaricated. It was far easier to lie than to argue. "I'll send you my flight schedule when I have it.

And you can call Father without my help. He always goes to your showings."

"No, I will not call the scoundrel! Do you know what he called my Fabergé design?"

"Sorry, Mother, I'll send you an e-mail. Have to go now." He clicked off the cell and stuffed it into his pocket just as he hit the exit door.

He stepped outside into the sunny mountain air and inhaled the scent of crisp autumn leaves.

"Bad news?" Coming from the main-floor exit, Amy followed him out and fell into step with him.

"Parental nagging. Is there some point at which we outgrow our parents?" He wanted to wrap his arm around her shoulders, but they were doing their best to behave properly during business hours.

But just Amy's presence reminded him of nonbusiness hours, when he could occasionally have her to himself. Still, it wasn't enough. He wanted to be in her bed all night, every night. He wanted to wake up with her tousled hair upon his shoulder. Stolen minutes and a hotel room weren't good enough for his Amy.

As one of Jo's songs said: "Lonely was a bad place to be." He hated spending his nights alone, thinking of Amy doing the same.

"If we're lucky, we might make friends of our parents, but even friends nag," Amy admitted. "My mother just finished telling me that we're wasting our money making expensive fabric, and we should be producing cheap towels that Wal-Mart can buy."

Zack laughed, letting the tension roll out of him. "So, mothers are not always right."

"Limited points of view," she agreed. "But they're

usually looking out for us. It's not bad having someone always on our side."

"Even if they don't agree with us? But enough of that. How are the samples coming?"

"The ladies are getting more creative by the day," she replied. "It's all I can do to hold them back and keep it simple. They've found an old love seat they want to upholster. I'm thinking we can set up tableaux of two rooms, with the cotton print as a tablecloth and the brocade as place mats for the dining room. We could serve cider and muffins and attract attention."

"Champagne," he said firmly. "These are elegant fabrics. We want a wealthy setting. Add silk tassels to the tablecloths and bouillon fringe to the draperies."

"Petits fours," she said excitedly. "We can decorate them and place them in gold boxes like Godiva chocolates. I'll find my wedding crystal. We can set the table with it, and use disposable cups for serving."

To heck with *professional*. Zack hugged Amy's shoulders and planted a kiss on the top of her head. "You are always a genius! People flock to food. Tell me what else they do at this show that we can do better."

As they entered her office, Zack crooked his finger at Emily, his secretary, and had her take notes while Amy rattled off the sales techniques she'd garnered over the years of Evan's attendance at the market.

"How did the mill fail with you to display the fabrics?" he asked, shaking his head in amazement as he made notes of his own.

"Me? I poked around and took care of the kids while Evan talked to the bigwigs." Using an electric kettle she'd brought from home, she poured boiling water over tea leaves. "I didn't have anything to do with the booths."

Amy waited for Zack's eyes to glaze over with disappointment.

Instead, he muttered something about Evan being one bolt shy of a pallet, his lips compressed into a tight line of disapproval.

"Unlike me, you're not cute when you get mad," she quipped. His always outraged reaction to Dr. Evil's idiocy was incredibly good for her ego, and she unashamedly enjoyed the sensation. She settled into the big leather office chair she'd brought from home, sipped her tea, and watched him pace.

Zack rubbed his hand over his face as if to erase his expression, then managed a crooked grin. "What am I, then?"

"Pretty much cross-eyed," she said decisively.

Behind her, Emily coughed on a laugh.

Zack's grin grew wider. Crossing his eyes, he looked down his nose. "Fine then. Emily, take note. Should Ms. Warren ever deprecate her abilities again, I want her marched to the computer room, where she is not to be allowed out until she produces the entire payroll report without reducing a single machine to rubble."

"Yes, sir. Permission to prepare requisition for new computers in advance, sir?"

Zack pointed to the door. "Out, Emily. And close the door behind you."

A shiver of anticipation tingled Amy's spine as the door closed. Whenever they were alone, Zack never failed to touch or hold her, as if he couldn't get enough. . . .

Now, there was an ego booster. Had she actually begun to hope he saw her as more than a brief affair? "In case you haven't noticed, I really don't have any experience at this business thing," she babbled, rattled by her realization. "But I think my ideas will help until I learn." Setting her cup down on the table beside her, she tried to keep her hand from shaking.

Firmly gripping both arms of her chair, Zack met her nose to nose. With his face directly in hers, Amy thought she'd stop breathing at his suddenly fierce expression.

"Your *ideas* are what got this mill running," he asserted. "Your *ideas* will keep the mill operating. What in *hell* do you think any other management does that you aren't already doing?"

She didn't know. It wasn't as if she could think with his face in hers like that. Instead, she wrapped her arms around his shoulders and nipped his neck.

"Ow. Vampire." Zack lifted her from the seat and stopped her cannibalization with a hard kiss.

She threw herself fiercely into the bracing strength of Zack's arms and kiss and adoration.

She wanted Zack. And her children. And muffins with pig snoses. And her cottage. She'd do what she had to do to keep them. But she really wanted Zack's respect and support as well.

As his mouth so expertly plied hers, Amy realized with mounting alarm that she really, really wanted Zack.

She just didn't know if he wanted to be kept.

In panic, she shoved herself from his arms, brushed her hair back to catch her breath, and picked up her notebook. She ignored the questions in his eyes as she headed for the door. "Um, I've found a photographer. We need to set up a shoot immediately if we want the brochures by next week."

She felt horrible walking away like that. That wasn't who she was.

She hadn't spent the last thirty-two years in total oblivion. No matter how Zack praised her, she knew precisely what she was. She was a caretaker, a nurturer, a creative who liked to dabble with ideas.

She wouldn't become what she was not, just to keep a man who might or might not come to town once or twice a year. Not anymore. She was willing to give her all—but she expected the same in return.

≪TWENTY-EIGHT≫

"Ah, that wallpaper design is from William Morris," Zack said with satisfaction, studying the Biltmore Estate's South Tower Room, renovated to duplicate the early 1900s style when the house had been built. They'd arrived in Asheville a day early to rest and plan for the trade show. Visiting Biltmore had seemed the ideal opportunity for both. "Excellent use of historic effect of a previous era."

Amy had been to the magnificently restored estate several times over the years, as a student and as a tour guide for Evan's guests. She'd never been through the mansion's elegant chambers with a man who so fully understood her awe and admiration for this historical legacy.

It was almost enough to distract her from the luxurious hotel room waiting for them down the road. Almost.

"They had twenty-one rooms for servants alone," she whispered so the other tourists wouldn't hear, "an entire floor for just the *help*. For what? Two people?"

Zack patted her back sympathetically. "My poor Amy, who would house the entire town here, if she could. Would it make you feel better to think of how many people they employed—the masons and plumbers and chimney sweeps . . ."

"Sixty-five fireplaces," she said, reading the brochure.

"Can you imagine cleaning sixty-five fireplaces? Two hundred fifty rooms?"

"And don't forget the swimming pool, and who waxed the bowling alley?" he reminded her with a twinkle in his eye. "Can you not picture yourself as a guest enjoying all this magnificence rather than as the maid who cleans it?"

"Wallowing in the lap of luxury while others work their hands to the bone? Nope, not me. Let's take another look at that hand-painted chintz. Is there any way we can duplicate that?" She took off at a brisk walk toward one of the other bedrooms, trying to convince herself that this conversation proved the distance between them. Zack was used to being the wealthy guest. She was more accustomed to being the maid. If she could just keep these differences in her mind, she wouldn't endanger her vulnerable heart.

But she couldn't, not when they laughed and worked together as equals. They were on the same wavelength, and that meant they were both thinking of that bed waiting for them, and a room with no children to interrupt, and . . .

"We must take a garden gnome home for you," he said abruptly as they came down from the tower rooms and passed the gift shop. "It will bring you good luck."

He was thinking of her garden? She blinked at him in disbelief, and he winked back, as if he knew perfectly well what was running through her head. Which he did. He knew her far too well, and she squirmed with discomfort. He'd stripped her of all her defenses. She simply didn't know how to do *affairs* and keep her distance. If they weren't so good together, if she didn't desperately long for their stolen moments together, she'd just bang her head through a wall and get the pain over with.

"Will he come to life at night and do my weeding?" she asked, hiding her delight that he knew whimsical would appeal to her. She stroked the red cap of a gnome who looked like Disney's love-struck Dopey.

"That poor fellow needs a home," Zack said decisively, picking up Dopey and taking him to the clerk. "He'll benefit from more nourishing surroundings than all this artificial light, don't you think?"

Amy laughed. She had a feeling he was talking about himself, and as much as she'd liked to envision him permanently in her garden, she wasn't foolish enough to believe it was going to happen. "How do you know he doesn't thrive on fluorescent?"

"Because I know. He will be much happier in your garden in your good care." He took the gift bag and her arm and steered her toward the exit. "I hope you have brought a fancy frock, as I told you. This will be the only night this week that we will share alone, you are forewarned. All is business once we reach High Point."

She had to be mad to have agreed to this. A romantic night of dinner and dancing and lovemaking with this sexy, fascinating man who made her feel like a woman again. . . . But she was determined to be strong, to show him she could be a woman of the world. Still, she had to admit her frailties. "I feel guilty leaving the kids to come here early."

"You have a life of your own," he said firmly. "You must live it while you can. The little ones are quite happy with their cousins." He helped her into the Bentley, then leaned over and kissed her forehead. "Are you regretting me, perhaps, hmm?" He raised a wicked eyebrow.

Oh, Lord, she had it so bad that his playful leer made her want to forget his promise of dinner in favor of the big bed he meant for them to share.

She wanted so much and could have so little. . . .

"Do I regret Dopey?" She produced the gnome and studied him. "Nope. He looks quite happy to be with me."

"Oh, he is; you may take my word for that." Whistling, Zack closed the door and returned to the driver's seat.

Amy traced the gnome's lips and glanced surreptitiously at Zack. He ran his tongue over his lips and made a smacking sound.

She burst out laughing and resolved to shut all misgivings in a closet for the evening. If she didn't know better than to lose her heart to a man who could be gone tomorrow, she might as well enjoy what they had together while it lasted.

"You are so *amazingly* brilliant." Amy laughed in delight as she stepped from the bedroom of their suite to the sound of a waltz flowing from hidden speakers and a handful of white-jacketed waiters setting an elegant table on the balcony.

"I thought you might prefer a place without crowds for this evening," Zack murmured, sweeping her into his arms and twirling her around the living room as if this were a Fred Astaire and Ginger Rogers film. While she'd showered and changed, he'd donned a trendy long black dinner jacket over a stiff, pleated white shirt with a mandarin collar. Gold cuff links glittered at his wrists and a small diamond served as collar button. He looked exactly as she imagined a European movie star would look gambling at the tables in Monaco. Her very own James Bond.

They waltzed as if they'd danced together forever. Feeling light-headed, she stroked the hair brushing his collar. He tugged her closer to nibble at her ear. The layers of green silk and chiffon that Jo had helped her pick out swung around Amy's legs, making her feel as graceful as the dancers on a movie screen. She had dreaded dancing in some loud nightclub or on a fancy dance floor where she would feel out of place. And Zack had *understood,* without asking.

"Thank you," she murmured. "This is so perfect I think I must be dreaming."

"You deserve to live your dreams, but I want to be the man who takes you there," he murmured back.

She laughed at the notion, but she floated across the carpet as if it were a magic cloud. Her, practical Amy, living a dream with a man who could make the stars fall with a snap of his fingers! For one moonstruck night, she could believe it.

When the waltz ended, Zack bowed elegantly, placed her hand on his arm, and led her outside to the balcony overlooking a stunning view of the tree-studded mountains, with the reds and golds and bronzes of the autumn foliage highlighted by the setting sun.

Amy gasped at the beauty of the idyllic scenery while waiters finished setting out china and silver on a linen-covered table. One popped the cork on a bottle of Cristal champagne and poured it into delicate flutes. Another pulled out a chair for Amy. After uncovering a deliciously browned roast duck, the waiters miraculously disappeared at a nod from Zack.

"It is a different view of your home, is it not?" He

moved his chair closer to hers and tipped his glass to hers. "To the wonders of home, be it ever so glorious."

She sipped and let the delicious bubbles tickle her tongue. How could she even begin to think in a setting like this, with a man like Zack beside her? She was aware of the closeness of his masculine thigh, the pressure of his foot against her sandal heels, the brush of his hand as he made the toast. This was the Zack she had imagined in his natural setting, the one who wined, dined, and danced with beautiful models in exotic surroundings.

And he was here, with her, making her humble home seem as wonderful and mysterious as his was to her.

Amy lost her last measure of self-consciousness and surrendered utterly to Zack's play. Wantonly, she sipped her champagne, nibbled the duck, and slipped off her sandal to run her toes along his foot. Zack laughed and shifted so she could stroke his leg, and she nearly ended up in his lap. He fed her oysters and apricot tarts while his eyes smoked with a desire she could feel deep inside her.

They talked about everything from favorite movies to space travel. Zack lowered his perpetual charm to argue vociferously in favor of exploring Mars until he realized she was simply baiting him by presenting the opposing argument. He leaned over and sipped champagne off her tongue, deepening their kiss until they had to either make love on the table or abandon it.

"Not yet, my Amy," he said, his voice a throaty purr as he pushed back from the table. "I want to dance with you and hold you close and make your dreams sweeter."

He swept her onto their own private dance floor again, and in Zack's arms, Amy finally fell madly, unalterably in love.

She hoped it was just the champagne and the giddiness of desire and the quiver of anticipation inspired by the heated look in Zack's dark eyes, but she wasn't examining or analyzing anything tonight. Tonight was for feeling, and she felt marvelous.

"I am brilliant, am I not?" he asked, raising a mocking eyebrow before pulling her closer.

The thin cloth of his slacks clung almost indecently to his narrow hips as he whirled her around the suite. Without giving it a second thought, Amy unfastened his collar to uncover soft curls against bronzed skin. He held her close enough that she could watch the fine hairs curl when she puffed on them.

"Ummm, enjoying this, are we?" he asked, returning the favor by blowing on her earrings.

He'd bought her delightful silver feathers that caught the slightest breeze and sparkled in the light. She'd spent way too much time admiring them in the mirror before she'd been brave enough to emerge from the bedroom. And from the heat of his gaze, she gathered Zack was enjoying them equally well.

But it was the sheer muscle of the man beneath the thin fabrics, the responsiveness of his body to her slightest touch, and the furnace blast of desire engulfing them as they moved as one around the room that she was enjoying most. Zack didn't push and pull and drag her across the floor but anticipated the music and the way they swayed together without need of any more than a gentle touch on her back or hip.

They were making love with clothing on.

The waiters returned to clear the room. The moment they closed the door after them, Zack smoothed his long-fingered hand down Amy's back, and her zipper whispered open. The strapless bodice fell with it.

She slid her fingers into the placket of his shirt and popped the studs, one by one.

He shrugged off his jacket and threw it across a sofa. She let her gown fall to her feet and stepped out of it as he swirled her in circles. His hand scorched her bare flesh when he pulled her back into his arms and danced her across the room again.

He lowered her into a dip and caressed the silk barely covering her hips. "Garters—for me?" he purred with delight.

She'd been unsure about wearing anything so blatantly sexy, but his pleasure in the discovery was worth hours of uncertainty. And this moment made them the perfect choice. She could never have imagined how effective they would be—as Zack's hungry gaze focused downward, caressing her breasts in the demi bra, fastening on the silky stockings and saucy green garters.

"I'll let you wear them, if you like," she teased, enjoying his pleasure by daringly pushing his shirt from his shoulders and planting a kiss at the base of his throat.

He chuckled and released her wired bra. Amy closed her eyes and breathed a deep sigh of relief and desire as his hands took hers and slid them around his neck, then cupped her unfettered breasts. She could feel his arousal against her belly, and the dance slowly came to a halt in front of the fireplace, where a small fire crackled.

Zack lowered his head to claim her mouth. Amy lifted hers to meet him.

"Tonight, you are mine," he whispered.

She didn't argue, because he was right. They were no

longer inexperienced in the way each other's bodies worked. She had learned he was sensitive to touch, and that she need only run her palms over his skin to feel his erection lengthen. He knew she responded to soft music and sweet tastes. She'd been seduced before he even laid her across the pillows on the floor.

"Stay with me, Amy," he murmured as the last of their clothing slipped away. "Let me show you the world."

And because he was showing her a world she'd never known, she let the words become part of the dream they were creating in the warmth of the flames, a dream she could never hope to attain, but one that opened her arms and heart and let her take him in.

For now. For the moment.

⫷ TWENTY-NINE ⫸

"Where are the brochures? They were supposed to be here by now." Amy dumped a cardboard box of supplies on an already cluttered table at noon, in High Point, after their heart-stoppingly blissful evening—and a fevered encore before breakfast.

Her insides were mush after Zack's fervent kisses, but as he'd warned, he was all business today. And she needed to be, too. The town and Zack and the mill all depended on them. Amy could feel a full-scale panic attack impending.

Their booth was on an upper floor of the multilevel furniture mart at the High Point furniture showcase. The aisles bustled with transport men in coveralls, business people in corporate attire, and a host of others in every state of dress imaginable, creating a state of organized anarchy.

That Zack and Emily and several of their other employees were standing there, waiting for her to pull the booth together, did not soothe her clamoring nerves.

"I need to find the receiving department. Where is receiving?" Trying not to dig her hands into the professional cut and style she'd had done yesterday so she wouldn't look like a heathen, she abandoned her search and shoved stacks of paper aside looking for the directory.

Zack caught her wrists and forced her to stand still. His strength was normally reassuring, his touch was always thrilling, but right now, she didn't have time for anything except a nervous breakdown.

"Emily will find the brochures," he said firmly. "That is her job. My job was to create these designs and now, to sell them. Yours is to display them. Now, put your magic to work. Where do you wish the table to go?"

He made it sound so easy. "The table? The table." She glanced around frantically, measuring with her eyes the size of the space they'd rented. "It will never fit. How did I ever think we would make this work?"

"The same way it will work in your cottage," Zack said patiently. "Think of this as your dining room. We have only one solid wall, so that is where the draperies go, correct?"

Drawing on his limitless patience, Amy took a deep breath. Zack had confidence in her. He wouldn't pitch a fit if she did this wrong. She knew how to decorate. One thing at a time.

She gazed at the blank white divider. "Yes, if this is the dining room tableau, we'll need the floral print and the wrought-iron rod across the back wall."

She turned to look for the drapery hanger, but Zack continued holding her while gesturing at one of the men he'd hired to move the furniture and samples in here.

"Management, remember," he murmured. "You do not have to do it all yourself."

Yes, she did. She'd always done it all herself. Chosen the fabrics, sewed the hems, hung the draperies . . .

Deep breath. She nodded, and after brushing a kiss against her cheek, Zack reluctantly released her.

"Now, I must make the contacts. That is what I do. You will be all right here with Emily and Luigi," he stated, as if there was no question.

Amazingly, his trust bred confidence that she could do this.

They would be spending the entire week together, a stressful week on which their entire futures relied, in more ways than one. She had to learn to stand on her own this week. She didn't know how Zack was feeling about his level of commitment, but she had to brace herself for whatever came when the trade show ended. He'd already exceeded his stay by far longer than even he expected.

"Yes, yes, I'll be fine," she said slowly. "If you do the talking and just leave me to do the decorating, this will be great."

Amy watched Zack stride off with the confidence of a man who knew his place in this chaotic crowd. He looked wealthy and aristocratic in one of his European designer suits tailored to his wide shoulders and lean hips. But he wore his high-collared silk shirt open with no tie, unlike most of the American businessmen around them, so even though he'd had his hair trimmed and removed his ear stud to look more professional, Zack stood out in the crowd.

People noticed him, which worked to his advantage.

Amy watched as he enthusiastically pumped someone's hand, grabbed him by the shoulder as if he were his best friend in the world, and produced a business card in one coordinated movement. She didn't doubt he'd judged the other man's samples, his status on the playing field, and the cash in his bank account at the same time.

This was only one tiny corner of the huge world Zack operated in. She'd only accompanied Evan here upon occasion, arranging private dinners with selected executives, acting as his secretary when necessary.

She turned to Luigi, who was leaning against a post, arms crossed, surveying the chaos with professional serenity. "Do you need to go with him?" she asked cautiously, knowing he preferred to guard Zack's back.

The driver snorted. "He's in his element here. You're the one who needs looking after. Just tell me what to do, and I'll find someone to do it for you."

Amy had to laugh at his way of phrasing it. "Fine. I need the table moved front and center. Snap your fingers, O Magic Genie."

She could learn to enjoy having someone else do the grunt work.

Returning from a page calling her downstairs to the reception lobby, Emily found Amy unwrapping the crystal glassware and whispered frantically, "The *Smithsonian* is here for their appointment with Zack."

The *Smithsonian*? Amy had hysterical images of the Victorian "Castle" of the institute trundling through the crowded aisles, its massive stones shoving booths aside and crushing the furnishings to splinters.

She'd been watching way too many cartoons with the kids.

"I can't reach him on his cell," Emily continued, glancing over her shoulder as if expecting monsters to leap from the crowd. "I left them at the reception desk. What do I do?"

Panic. Lie down and cry. Hide under the nearest bench. Why the devil hadn't Zack told her the Smithsonian was coming?

Because she'd have had a panic attack just thinking about it.

Gulping, Amy sat back on her heels and tried to think. "His cell wasn't working in the basement lunchroom." She glanced back at Luigi, who'd already lowered the carton he was carrying. "Would you go look for him there? And, Emily, keep trying to reach him."

She couldn't leave important people cooling their heels in this madhouse. An interview with the Smithsonian could bring in orders faster than the mill could produce them. She couldn't possibly give them the historical detail and production information that were second nature to Zack. She'd have to fake it until he got here.

"Escort them up here," she told Emily with resignation.

With Luigi hunting for Zack, and Emily off to the lobby, Amy checked the mirror in her compact to be certain she hadn't set her hair on end or smudged dirt on her face. She freshened her lipstick, applied mascara, and practiced the smile she'd learned for Evan's guests.

Left alone, she shook in her shoes and prayed she'd see Zack confidently sauntering through the crowd before the reporters arrived. She was an *executive* she tried to remind herself. A Very Important Person. She was not a housewife. She was a corporate officer with the lives of scores of families at her mercy.

How did people live with this responsibility every day?

"They're here, already? How unusually timely of them." Cheerfully, Zack shouldered the champagne crate his employee had lugged. "We'll need ice for this. There's a bucket in the truck, if you would be so good as to get it." As the worker hurried away, Zack glanced up to see Luigi shouldering his way through the crowd in his direction. "I am found," he called.

"Are you trying to lose the woman?" Luigi grumbled, taking the crate on his shoulder. "She looked like she'd pass out last I saw of her."

"These are intelligent scholars interested in the history of textiles and wishing to examine the valuable discovery we have made. Amy will handle them just fine," Zack said confidently, forging his way through the crowd.

"She's nervous," Luigi argued. "You're making a mistake if you think you can drag her around like you did the others, ignoring them and leaving them to their own devices."

For a moment, Zack worried. He had left Gabrielle to her own devices once, and look what had happened. Perhaps Luigi was right. Perhaps he should be more careful with Amy.

But he did not have time for alarm. Seeing the video camera ahead, he squared his shoulders and strode confidently through the crowd. He would rescue Amy and send her back to the hotel to relax.

As the aisle opened to allow Luigi to stride through with his heavy crate, Zack paused, stunned by the impact of their booths. He'd chosen a corner where they could be seen from two aisles. On this side was the living room tableau with the settle cushioned in blue silk jacquard. A hastily improvised quilt of their various red, cream, and navy printed designs hung casually over the back and arm, setting the colonial mood for his historic fabrics and tying together all the other colors in the tableau.

She'd created cream-and-gold trimmed swags for the navy velvet and framed the enlarged prints of other designs as if they were mullioned windows. The chaise longue was upholstered in the cream brocade and piled high with more pillows from their collection. A delicate-legged oak sideboard with a runner of cream silk decorated in their floral design added that touch of luxury he'd insisted upon.

She was brilliant and priceless.

Not seeing Amy or his guests in this space, he hurried around the corner to the dining room tableau, and again he paused for the sheer pleasure of it.

With her rich brown curls trimmed into neat layers that framed her oval face, Amy was a model of professional style. She chatted animatedly with a scholarly gentleman holding one of their brochures. Her eyes sparkled with interest, and her rosy cheeks nearly matched the lovely rose suit she'd chosen to wear. It was a matronly suit that deserved a Jackie Kennedy little pillbox hat and gloves, in his opinion, but somehow, Amy made it look as if she'd just stepped out of a Saks display.

The writer was drinking in her every word. Smiling with pride and fighting a decided twinge of jealousy toward the man holding Amy's attention, Zack shoved a hand into his pocket and strolled up as if he had nothing else in the world to do.

"Zack, I'm glad you're here," Amy said without a trace of hysteria. "I've been telling Mr. Minella how you discovered the lost designs and a little bit about the history of the mill. He's familiar with Ezekial Jekel's family history in New England."

Zack shook the journalist's hand, then nodded as he leaned close to whisper in Amy's ear. "I was going to send you back to the hotel to rest, but how can I do without you when you create such magic as this?"

Flustered but smiling radiantly, Amy stepped aside and gestured toward several corporate types examining their samples. "From local furniture manufacturers," she murmured. "I know them, so I thought I'd take them out for a quick bite before the reception. Luigi will bring you to join us when you're done here."

Before Zack could open his mouth to protest, his beautiful executive Amy took the arm of one of the suits and led the retinue toward the exit, leaving him alone with the reporter and photographers and a crate of champagne.

And he had worried about her . . . *why?*

"Look at the orders," Amy whispered as if fearful of waking jealous gods. It was the end of the High Point show week, and she flipped through sheaves of invoices they'd carried back to their hotel room.

It had been a long and exhausting week. Only having Amy to himself every night had kept Zack going. He'd once enjoyed feasting and partying at these industry gatherings, but he would much rather take Amy home and slip into something comfortable now, and not just their bed, although he would enjoy that as well. If nothing else convinced him that he and Amy belonged together, this week with her had done it. Waking up to her tossed curls, working closely in a high-pressure environment all day, listening to her intelligent insights over dinners filled with guests, making love to her in the moonlight . . . had shown him what he'd been missing for years. They'd scarcely had more than a few hours at night alone together, but she had been in this thoughts every minute of the day.

And still he couldn't get enough of her.

But he also missed the children. He missed his ugly desk in his even uglier office and the work they represented. He missed the people with whom they worked. And the challenge of the cottage.

He'd always liked watching his hard work create something new and strong, but this work was even more satisfying than filling his company's coffers. The sales Amy held in her hand would keep an entire town fed for another year.

"It was you who knew everyone and steered them our way. You didn't need me," he said proudly.

He wasn't complaining. Saint-Etienne Fabrications needed him. They wouldn't exist without his expertise. But with Amy in charge at the mill, he wouldn't have to feel guilty when he ran off to Paris to look after business. Amy could handle the mill with one hand tied behind her back. If only she would wake up and realize it.

Instead, her expression revealed fear . . . and maybe, sadness? Both tugged at his weakening heart.

"I didn't do anything but talk." She shrugged.

She was wearing the lovely rose silk knit shell and floral gauze skirt he'd bought for her this past week, and she looked exquisitely lovely. Looking at her, he was a well-satisfied man. If only he could persuade her that she would fit into his life in Paris or London just as easily as here.

But she grew mutinous and backed off every time he came near such a suggestion. He wouldn't give up his career. And it seemed she would not give up her home.

He had only to think of his parents to know how badly that worked.

"You have a way of talking that makes a man want to listen," he murmured, sliding his hand into her hair. He loved the silkiness of it. He loved more the knowledge that he had a right to touch her, and that she no longer turned away from his caresses.

Her eyes smiled when they met his. "You are so full of it, Saint Stevie," she said with laughter, easing the insult by meeting his kiss with the same hunger he felt.

It was amazingly terrifying how they fell into the familiarity of touching each other, kissing and holding hands as if they were mere adolescents. Zack slid his hands beneath Amy's silk shell and unfastened her bra, knowing as he did so that she would relax that stiff spine of hers and welcome his hands on her breasts with a sigh of appreciation and fervent kisses.

"After these past nights, I do not think I can bear to go back to sleeping alone." He drew off the shell and flung it with her bra onto the hotel dresser. "Perhaps we ought to buy that yacht you crave and sail around the world together."

She laughed into his mouth while her nimble fingers unfastened his shirt buttons. "A yacht big enough for a nanny and two children and a few schoolteachers?"

"If need be." He pushed down her gauzy skirt and let it fall to the floor with his shirt, lifting her to taste her breasts before carrying her to the bed and falling down beside her.

He wanted to ask her to marry him, but an industry meeting was neither the time nor the place. He wanted Paris and a diamond ring and sweet music to give her the special memory she deserved. He had it all planned out in his mind, once they had the market behind them. Once he was certain she would say yes. Which meant conquering her fears. He prayed that wouldn't take too long.

"This has been a lovely escape from reality," she murmured as they snuggled closer, naked chests touching and arousing. She nipped a corner of his mouth and ran her hands over his shoulders.

He didn't want this to be an escape. He wanted this to be the reality. He would work to make it so. "It has been all my pleasure, my love."

They kissed slowly, savoring what could be their last night together for a while. The scents of sandalwood and jasmine mingled with sweat and the metallic aroma of the rain that had slowed the final day of the market. Humidity curled their hair and moisturized their skin while they rolled amid the wrinkled sheets.

Amy moaned her ecstasy at Zack's expertise, and cried out in pleasure when his deep, hard thrusts brought them both to exquisite release.

He was a demanding lover, but one who took care of her in ways Amy had never experienced. She'd learned to eagerly anticipate their nights together, to share his joy or her frustration and release them in this joining of their bodies. She'd never known she could be seduced by a kiss on the back of her knees or reduced to molten jelly by a nibble at her nape or the caress of his toe on the bottom of her bare foot. She exhilarated in vibrant sensations that she'd thought lost long ago.

And when he'd worn out both of them, and they lay in each other's arms, mingling the perspiration on their skin, she could feel his heart beating with hers, feel his pleasure the same way she felt his breathing. And understood that they were sharing their days and their lives with this physical joining.

How would she survive when he returned home?

"This was such a huge mistake." She sighed and

snuggled closer, sliding her knee between Zack's thighs.

"Mmmm." He nuzzled her ear. "You are right. We should have ordered wine first. How can you ever forgive me?"

She wanted to giggle, but the future arrived tomorrow, and it oppressed the joy she'd learned at his hands. "I can see why you love this life, the wining, the dining, the lack of any duties other than being yourself. No dishes to wash, no beds to make. No responsibility except to get up in the morning and smile. It's an amazing life."

He laughed into her hair, and his hand did treacherous things to her breast. "It is all yours for the asking. Come with me to Europe. I will give you silk sheets and your own maid. We will find you beautiful clothes and a wee dog you can carry in your purse." He paused thoughtfully and nipped her earlobe. "The children will see all the sights of Europe."

She knew he'd been teasing at first, describing the glamorous shallow world where she didn't belong, but the serious note that had crept in when he mentioned the children opened the can of worms she'd been avoiding. She pushed him away and sat up. The patter of rain on the windows warned of impending thunderstorms, and she desperately needed to see that Josh and Louisa weren't afraid.

She desperately needed her feet on home ground to think through what was happening to her. "I need to go home tonight. You and Luigi can see to the packing up tomorrow just fine without me."

Zack caught the corner of the sheet she had wrapped around her and tugged her backward. "It is late. It is pouring hard and nasty out there. Listen to the wind. We have meetings tomorrow. After them, we will go."

"No, I need to go now." Instinct insisted, although she didn't think she could explain that to the satiated man sprawled naked across the sheets. There was no logic to this craving to see that her children were all right. "My truck is at the market. Could Luigi take me over there?" They'd used her pickup to haul boxes down. They'd need it to haul them back up again, but she didn't care. If she didn't get out now, this quicksand of luxury would pull her under, and she would never surface in her world again. She needed her children to keep her grounded.

"The children are fine." Zack sat up with the sheet over his knees. "Call, if you are worried, but they will be in bed."

She couldn't look at Zack sitting there all masculine amid the sheets, his hair tousled, his jaw stubbled, his sinewy arms ready to reach for her. Her womb clenched just thinking of how it would feel to climb back in with him. It was a damned good thing she used birth control, because they hadn't shared an ounce of sense between them.

The idea of creating babies together loomed too vividly in her mind. She had to get out before she started imagining a little boy with Zack's laughing eyes or a little girl with his mischievous mouth, and she fell into that hormonal trap all over again.

"I'll take the orders back to the mill and set up a production plan. I need to be home." Amy couldn't look at him as she escaped into the shower, but she mentally begged him to understand.

Zack followed her in, striding naked across the tiles, stepping into the pounding water to press her up against the wall, bringing his nose down to hers. "You are running away, Amaranth Jane. Why?"

"I am going home, Jacques Saint-Etienne, to where I

belong. Being with you is running away." Sidestepping
him, she reached for the soap.

"Being with *me* is running away? How? I will take you
home tonight, if that is your wish. I will take you with me
to Paris when I go next week. I want you to be home with
me."

Cold shock hit her with the same force as icy water,
and Amy stared at him with incredulity. "You are leaving
for *Paris*? *Next week*? When did you plan to tell me
that?"

Trying not to show how badly she was shaken by this
unanticipated announcement, she shut off the shower
and grabbed a towel. He was *leaving*. She'd known he
had to sometime. But the immediacy felt like abandonment to her, and she'd had enough of that for three lifetimes. Uprooting lives should take time. And planning.
And a better warning than this.

She had been determined to look on this as a brief affair, an escape from reality until she'd adjusted to her
new one. But she hadn't expected it to end so abruptly.

Accepting that she had to divorce Evan had come grad-
ually, after a long struggle. Accepting that she had to let
Zack go walloped her all at once. She was amazed she
hadn't hit the tiles and slid to the floor from the shock.

"I did not know if I could go until now. We have much
to do here." Zack grabbed another towel and began angrily rubbing his hair. "But you have done so wonderfully well that I thought it would not hurt to check on
another project. I have a *business* to run."

He was right, of course. He had a business, and it
wasn't hers. She knew that.

She would not cry. She refused to cry. She had cried for

months when Evan had left. She had no more tears left in her. She'd vowed never to need a man ever again.

He wasn't leaving her. She was leaving *him*.

Positive affirmations did not fill the hollow inside or avert the need to cry herself sick. She didn't want to think of being alone and vulnerable again. Amy stormed out of the bathroom, grabbed a shirt from the closet, and jerked it on, then rummaged in a dresser for panties before heaving all the rest of her clothes from the drawers into her open suitcase.

Zack watched her in frustration. "I need to do many things here, but my real work is over there. That is how I make my living. You *know* all this."

"I do know all this. It has nothing to do with my need to see my children *now*. My children come first. You *know* all that," she added, mimicking him.

"Why are we fighting?" he shouted. "I will take you home. You will see your children. We will make production plans. I will be back . . ."

He halted hesitantly, and she sent him a scathing look.

"Right. You'll be back. Sometime. Don't do me any favors. I am perfectly capable of making a production plan. We will find a plant manager because I sure as hell won't do it on my own. Unlike you, I have a life. Give us a call occasionally to remind us that you exist. But give us first option on the mill when you decide to sell."

She slammed her suitcase and jerked the zipper. It stuck. Of course it stuck. She didn't fix things. She broke them. It was a wonder she hadn't blown all the electricity in the hotel.

She hadn't blown any gadgets in weeks.

Shoving a loose sleeve into the bag, she tugged the zipper and got it closed.

"We cannot live on two continents," he said firmly. "What we have is special. We can't throw it away over a moment's disagreement."

"I don't want *special*!" she yelled in frustration and fury. "I want every day. I want boring. I want someone who hangs around long enough for meals and fights. *Special* is for holidays!"

"I'll take you home with me," he said with a shade of desperation. "I'll introduce your children to my parents. We'll share Christmas in London. Give me a chance!"

She did weep then. Tears started rolling down her cheeks and wouldn't stop. She didn't want him introducing her to his parents, pretending they had a chance. "I can't live in London." She hiccupped. "This is my home. London is where you belong. Let's not pretend anymore, all right? I've done what you've asked of me here. Just let me get my life back."

Wiping hastily at her cheeks, she retrieved a pair of slacks from the closet, pulled them on, then swept the rest of the hangers into her garment bag while Zack hastily dressed.

"I do not beg, Amy," he said through clenched teeth. "I offer you everything I have. I cannot do more."

"There is nothing you can offer me besides yourself, Zack," she said sorrowfully, rubbing her eyes dry. "I have a family and a home and a life of my own. I won't give them up for you."

He snatched the garment bag from her and opened the door. She didn't have the heart to look into his eyes and see anger there. Or even hurt. She knew he was capable of being hurt.

But if she left now, it wouldn't be as bad as it would be later, when they tore each other apart attempting to be what they could not because they were in each other's way. She knew that from cold, hard experience.

❊ THIRTY ❊

Amy insisted that Zack stay at the hotel. He insisted that Luigi drive her home in the Bentley. Since the rain was coming down in sheets, and she didn't look forward to the four-hour drive home in her current state of hysteria, she agreed. Her children needed a mother all in one piece.

When they arrived in Northfork after midnight, she apologized to Luigi. He seemed stoic about the whole episode, while still managing to emanate an air of disapproval. She swore she'd make up for the ungodly hour to him later, then stumbled upstairs to her empty apartment rather than wake Jo's household.

She crawled into her cold bed and shivered in the dampness generated by the torrential rain pounding on the roof, missing Zack's warm body radiating heat next to hers, yet knowing the longer she stayed and continued to dream, the harder it would be to say good-bye. She'd spent this last year sleeping alone. She'd learn to get used to it again. Somehow. In a million years or so.

Zack had wanted to take her and the kids to London. She'd thought he just wanted an affair. He wanted them to meet his parents. Was he insane? Or was she?

What he suggested was impossible. An international entrepreneur might be used to living on planes and in hotels. Change was nothing to him. He'd worked his way into the community, the mill—her life—in a few days, and could walk away just as easily.

She couldn't do that.

Assuming she could as easily fit into his life as he did into hers was a monstrous leap of faith even she couldn't make. It had taken her years to figure out what she wanted . . . and he wanted to turn everything she knew about herself inside out on a whim? Her children needed stability. Routine. Consistency.

He hadn't mentioned marriage.

What in hell was she thinking? She didn't want marriage, ever again.

She wept into her pillow, too exhausted to sort it all out.

The wind ripped at the roof over the apartment as Amy staggered from bed and wrapped herself in a robe the next morning. She'd left her electric kettle at the office, so she filled a saucepan with water for her tea and reached for the phone.

She hated wind. She watched the rain course down the huge windows, shielding the view of the mountain, and waited for Jo to answer the phone on her end.

"I got in late last night," she told her sister at her greeting. "I thought I'd take today off and putter around the cottage. What do you say I take the monsters off your hands? You've been a gem to take care of them. I owe you and Mom heaps and bunches."

"You got the mill running," Jo replied. "Mom thinks you walk on water. Of course, if you'll look out the window, you'll see that you might have to walk on water to get over here. The highway has turned into white-water rapids."

Amy carried the cordless to the front window and tried to see the street, but everything was a gray haze of wind and water. "That looks bad. Maybe I better go down to the café and start some coffeepots running."

She had an ugly thought. "Have you heard anything from the mill? Has the river started rising?"

Jo's usual effervescence went silent as she grasped the horrible implication. "Let me call someone to look. The SUV won't be safe out there. Or Flint could come up and get the pickup and drive over."

"Left the pickup in High Point. All I have is Luigi and the Bentley. I'll call Hoss. He has that old Land Rover. We might have to call off the shift today."

She hung up on Jo and flipped through her card file for Hoss's number. Punching it into the phone, she clicked on the television for a weather report.

She'd been living on such a high cloud this past week that she hadn't heard the news or weather or anything outside her own little bubble. This was what happened when grasshoppers convinced ants to play.

"I've just been down there," Hoss reported when she asked. "It's rising fast. The bridge ain't safe once the water goes over it. You'd better start calling and canceling. Guess that hurricane that hit the Gulf is finding its way up here."

Amy stared out the window in growing horror. "You remember what happened the last time a hurricane came inland from the Gulf?"

"Yeah, baby," Hoss said with regret. "That man of yours got a yacht to save us?"

Amy said a word that hadn't passed her lips in a decade, then started giving orders.

*   *   *

Zack found one of Amy's sweaters on the floor of the hotel closet. He picked it up, and the gentle aroma of jasmine wafted around him. His insides knotted at the memories produced by the scent.

He'd made colossal mistakes in his life. Letting Gabrielle drive to the Alps with Danielle had been one of them.

He didn't want to lose the woman and children he loved . . . again.

He couldn't help thinking that leaving Northfork now would be a mistake that would hurt a lot of people. But he didn't trust his own judgment. He wanted Amy, and he liked getting what he wanted. He was capable of justifying and rationalizing until he was convinced that going after her was the right thing to do.

Maybe she was right and they didn't belong together. His parents certainly had proved that love didn't make a marriage work. He thought his parents loved each other. They simply couldn't live together. Or even choose a country to live in. He and Amy had entire continents separating them. So maybe they needed time apart to think about it.

The only thing he knew absolutely was that he loved his work and he didn't want to return to the lonely way he'd lived these last ten years.

Crushing the silk knit in his fist, Zack punched Pascal's speed-dial number on his cell and waited for his financial adviser to answer. He watched the rain patter outside the hotel window and wondered if Amy had made it home safely last night.

Stupid thought. If she hadn't, Luigi would have called.

Amy hadn't called him this morning.

Absence might make the heart grown fonder, but

Zack's just plain hurt from her rejection. Contemplating strings of lonely mornings like this, he growled into the receiver when Pascal finally answered.

"Have Brigitte schedule my flight. I am almost done here. We have enough orders to operate for the next six months, at least. Set a date with the Versailles committee for next week. I am meeting with the Smithsonian next month, so I cannot linger over there. We will need to find a manager for the Versailles project."

He had spent ten years building his fame and reputation. It was time he rested on his laurels, picking and choosing his projects. He liked it in the States. He disliked Versailles. Easy choice. Those in the future might not be so easily decided.

He clicked on the local news to check the weather while he discussed arrangements for the project with Pascal. He muted the talking heads until the weather map appeared, then flicked the sound on in time to hear—

The hurricane hitting the North Carolina mountains has caused a landslide on the Blue Ridge Parkway, causing that road to be closed, according to the state police.

A choppy video of rushing brown waters and toppling trees followed. An SUV floated past the remains of a home crumbling into the river. A list of school and work cancellations scrolled across the bottom of the screen.

Zack didn't wait to see if the mill was listed. Cursing, he hung up on Pascal and hit the speed dial for Luigi's cell. And got no answer.

Now wasn't the time to panic. He'd do that later, after he found Amy and the children and saw them to safety.

If Amy didn't see the sense in leaving the mountains now, and coming to live with him, then his father would be right. American women were too stubborn and independent to live with.

Zack knew he was kidding no one, not even himself, but he needed a balm to soothe his rattled nerves, and Amy wasn't here.

The drive to the mountains would take hours. He prayed there were still roads left for him to drive on by the time he got there.

"The cell tower must be down." Luigi stoically clicked his useless clamshell closed and with Hoss's help, heaved a computer server onto a dolly.

"Leave, now," Amy ordered. "You and Hoss take the Rover and go. I'd appreciate it if you'd check on the kids at Jo's, but get the heck out of here while you can."

Hoss snorted. "Flint and Jo can take care of the kids. I'm not crossing that bridge now."

"And we're not leaving you anywhere near those computers," Luigi added ominously, pushing the dolly toward the lift to the second floor.

A gust of wind and rain swept water under the doors. It wasn't enough to cause alarm yet, but Amy didn't want to risk all of Zack's new equipment and their small inventory of cloth. She'd had Luigi drive her to the office so she could call every employee on their payroll and tell them to stay home, but some of their workers had insisted on coming in to help anyway.

The mill was their livelihood, and people up here knew how to fight for what was theirs. As long as the mill building itself held, they'd be fine. The heavy machinery couldn't be hauled to higher ground, but they were moving everything else that could be.

Hoss checked out the second-story windows and yelled down from the balcony, "Bridge is underwater. Hope y'all brought lots of good food."

Amy closed her eyes and prayed. She prayed for the safety of her children first. Flint's log cabin was sturdy enough, but if the mountain decided to slide, a cabin wouldn't stop it. At least they were away from the river. So was her mother. *She* was the fool down in the valley.

She wished she could sing like Jo. A good round of "Amazing Grace" would do wonders at a time like this.

The electricity flickered and went out.

"I didn't do it!" she shouted into the sudden darkness.

Nervous laughter rippled across the huge, echoing room. She'd counted a dozen employees hauling inventory up the stairs, most of them older workers without small children at home. The rain would stop soon, she tried to tell herself. All would be well.

Thunder rolled overhead, and the rain poured harder.

"Michael, row the boat ashore, hallelujah!" a voice sang out in the darkness.

Laughter followed, but more voices lifted in the old gospel song.

"Sister, help to trim the sail," Amy sang with the next verse. Tears rolled down her cheeks. She loved these people. She couldn't leave, no matter how much she loved Zack.

Thinking of him had the tears rolling faster. She loved his charm, his humor, and his intelligence. But most of all, she loved the man buried deep inside who so desperately craved the love of others. And before she could even consider all the permutations of that, she had to let him go.

"The river is deep and the river is wide," she sang with great feeling. The chorus had never held so much meaning as it did now, with the river slowly covering the floor of the old building.

Carrying a heavy bolt of tapestry toward the stairs, Amy splashed through an ankle-deep low spot. The mill had survived floods before, she told herself.

But cleaning the machinery would take months. They'd have to shut down production.

"Chills the body, but not the soul," rang to the rafters.

Amy wanted nothing more than to fling her chilly body into Zack's warm arms right now, apologize fervently, and promise she'd never leave again. She would never again force him into anything his sensible head said not to do, if only he would speak to her after this was over.

But she knew she lied.

She'd do it all over again in a heartbeat. She couldn't let her home die. So she'd simply have to find some way to save the mill by herself.

She guessed that was why bodies had souls. And hearts. Love and courage would keep them going when all else failed.

"There's benches over in the Music Barn," someone called from the floor. "Maybe we could prop some of these bigger pieces up on benches and hope the river don't rise much more."

Amy glanced out the window. Muddy water swirled across the parking lot and between the buildings. It wasn't deep yet, but it would rise swiftly as the river rushed down the mountain.

"Works for me," Hoss shouted, clattering down the stairs in his big boots.

Amy knew she didn't have the authority to stop him. She wished Zack was here to tell him they were fools, that machinery wasn't worth their lives.

She glanced up the hill where her cottage was hidden by trees. Without the mill, she'd lose her home.

"If anyone goes out there, I'm following," she shouted into the darkness below. "So you better think twice before you open that door, Hoss Whitcomb! That isn't white water out there, and you can't raft on it."

She could feel the fresh damp breeze and see the rectangle of light as he defiantly opened the door.

"It's just a little bitty creek, Ames," Hoss shouted back. "You just come right on out and wade in it if you like."

She smacked her hand into the wall as a line of people followed him out into the dangerously swirling waters.

"You can't stop people fighting for their lives," Luigi said from beside her. "Zack would have been down there, leading them on."

Which is why she didn't belong in his world. She belonged in her cozy kitchen, with her children at her feet, baking muffins with pig snoses.

But thanks to Zack, she'd learned she could do what she had to do. And do it damned well.

⚓THIRTY-ONE⚓

Zack steered the newly rented Hummer up the drive to Flint's cabin, the first stop on the way up the mountain. He wanted to carry Amy and her family out to safety, and renting another Hummer had seemed the best means.

The state police had tried to prevent him from driving in, but he'd circumnavigated their roadblocks. He'd driven over roads that were no better than creek beds. He'd ground fallen saplings and debris beneath the vehicle's huge tires. He should have turned back a dozen times, but he couldn't when his life, his future, was up the side of this treacherous mountain.

His knee ached from twisting it the wrong way. He'd worked it too hard and neglected it too long these last weeks.

Even admitting he was wrong wasn't sufficient to distract him from the mud pouring past the Hummer's wheels as they splattered up the gravel drive. He prayed Amy was here with her sister and the children. He knew he could get everyone out safely if they were quick.

He winced as he remembered Amy's mother had a home farther up the mountain, on the other side of town. They'd never leave without her.

One thing at a time. Find Amy and the children. If they weren't here, maybe they'd be at the apartment above the café. It was a little too close to the river for comfort, but it was on the main highway, unlike this mud trap of Flint's.

There were no vehicles in front of the cabin, and it didn't take a second glance to understand why.

The original owner of the land had stripped off the trees, and now the yard was a running waterfall of silt and rock. The house could wash off its foundation at any moment.

Don't panic, he told himself, attempting his cell again. Still no reception. The café next. Surely they were all at the café. Or maybe they'd taken the children over the mountain to safety. Maybe he was on a wild goose chase, imagining himself the white knight riding to their rescue when he was only making a dramatic European ass of himself. Everyone was probably drinking hot coffee and soup somewhere warm and dry right now, and they'd laugh themselves sick if they knew the silly Brit was having a nervous breakdown worrying about them out in this tempest.

At least the wind had died to a low roar, he tried to console himself as he steered the bulky vehicle down the river of mud to the road again. Flying debris had dented the Hummer's door earlier. It was mid-October, so most of the branches still had their foliage. Now he needed to fear only rain-laden trees toppling as their roots sucked from the mire. A slimy trail of fallen leaves added to the slipperiness of the water and sludge on the highway.

He used the Hummer's grill to gently push a young tree trunk from the road. He should have brought a chain saw in case he came across a larger obstacle. He'd packed fresh water and blankets and the kinds of things he'd been taught to have for emergencies, but fallen trees weren't a common obstacle in Europe.

He couldn't live in a country that would subject his family to hurricanes and tornadoes and earthquakes. England was far more civilized. He'd simply have to persuade Amy of that.

He knew he might as well talk to wallpaper.

Zack's knuckles were white by the time he arrived in Northfork. The day was rapidly sliding into night, but there wasn't more than a flicker of light in any window. The electricity had gone out again. Falling trees and limbs took the wires out, he'd learned.

He didn't bother parking in the lot on the far end of town but halted the Hummer on the sidewalk directly in front of the café and left the emergency lights flashing. The limited local traffic on the blockaded highway could pull around him.

Sliding across the front seats, he opened the passenger door and then hopped down, wincing as his bad knee almost gave way. The café door popped open before he reached it, and cheers rang from inside.

Word of the show's success had apparently traveled up here. He admired the strength of a people who could take this hurricane with such equanimity that they saw it as a passing disaster and cheered the promise he'd created of tomorrow. He ought to feel pride, but success wasn't as important as Amy. Or her children.

Anxiously, he scanned the room. He recognized the new waitress who'd taken Amy's place behind the counter and a number of people from the mill and church. He hadn't realized he knew so many people here.

But among all the apprehensive faces, he didn't see the ones he wanted, and his heart sank.

Jo hurried from the back, shoving long tendrils of blond hair from her face and looking worried. The effervescent Jo looking worried sent Zack over the edge.

"Where are they?" he shouted in what sounded like panic even to him.

"Flint took the kids up to Mama, where it should be safer, but then the phones went out, and we haven't heard anything since."

"Is Amy with them?" he demanded, already turning and heading back to the door.

Someone shoved a cup of coffee in his hand. Jo ran to follow him, grabbing a dripping slicker someone handed her. "She and your driver went to the mill early this morning. The bridge is out over the river, so they can't get back."

The memory of another night on a snow-slick Italian highway with flashing police and ambulance lights almost paralyzed him. Sick to his stomach, Zack left the coffee on a table and refused to open the front door for Jo. "You stay here, on the main road, where you'll receive communication faster than anywhere else."

"My husband and boys are out there somewhere," she stated flatly, hands on hips. "It isn't any safer here than out there."

"It is the way I'll be driving if I have to cross the river," he retorted. "I'll not have your life on my hands. You'll stay here and call if the tower starts working again. I'll check on the children first. Give me directions to your mother's."

He knew Joella was considered town royalty, but he'd reached the end of his patient nonchalance. Beneath his glare, even she backed down. She gave him a quick description of her mother's drive and bit her fingernail as he stalked out.

Amy was down at the mill, saving his wretched ass. He'd have to kill her for that, once he got his hands on her. Terror that he might never touch her again hollowed out his insides. He shot the Hummer into gear and proceeded up the mountain, deliberately not picturing rising rivers and flooding mills and buildings crashing into swirling water.

Children came first. Amy would want that. He didn't dare go after her without word of her children. He understood her well.

Trying to see through a windshield blanketed by torrents of rain, driving around boulders that had fallen from the bare cliff face, Zack prayed as he'd never prayed before. Facing the possibility that Amy and her children might be lost from this world, he lost his pride, his confidence, all those things that had kept him whole all these years. He was stripped down to raw nerves and a frantic desire to never again let them out of his sight—ever.

He'd sworn never to place his heart in the hands of another again, but he finally understood that before Amy and her children came along, he had been nothing. He'd built a shell of a man, and now all his carefully constructed camouflage was disintegrating, revealing the true man beneath—a man who needed a family.

He wanted to move forward. He wanted to be the man Amy thought he was. The husband and father who laughed with children and built communities, not the dilettante who played and pretended it was work.

He couldn't do it without her. That knowledge grew as he searched the side of the road for the decorative mailbox Jo had described as belonging to their mother.

Finding the landmark he sought, Zack turned the Hummer up another mountain of mud. If there was gravel on the drive, he couldn't tell for the rivers running down it. Was he fooling himself, or had the rain let up slightly?

He could see weak light flickering inside the humble home where Amy had grown up. It was little more than a clapboard cottage, with a sagging front porch and a sturdy rock chimney, but it had withstood the harsh elements over time.

He had to hope Amy was standing strong now, because looking at the dark shack, he realized he couldn't leave the children here without heat or water. The well would be on an electric pump. He knew all about old houses.

The hurricane-force winds had snapped a giant oak in half, missing the house by feet, emphasizing the danger. Zack offered up a prayer of thanksgiving and turned off the vehicle.

The graying front door opened, silhouetting Marie Sanderson's spare frame against a backdrop of lantern light. If anyone could keep the children safe, it would be this dragon lady Amy called Mother. Unable to summon the charm that had been his cover for so long, Zack limped out of the Hummer and up the porch stairs.

"The children?" he asked first.

She stepped back to let him in. Her cropped blond hair contained as much silver as gold, her face was lined with years of illness, but she gestured at a room full of active children as if she were his age.

"Rambunctious but all in one piece," she replied.

Louisa ran to leap into Zack's arms. He hugged her lithe body close and looked over her head to Josh, who was frowning with worry but easing toward him. Behind him were Flint's adolescent boys playing with some battery-operated game. Unfazed, they glanced up at him, then returned to virtually shooting each other.

The scene was so homelike and reassuring that Zack would have wept had he been a crying man. Instead, he crouched down and offered Josh a hug. "We were worried about you, big man. Thought you might have eaten everything in the pantry by now."

Josh's freckled nose wrinkled. "Nana has jars and jars of green beans. Where's Mommy?"

"She's still down at the mill. I have to go get her after I leave here." Zack figured that wasn't too much of a lie. He was getting Amy, one way or the other.

He glanced up at Marie. "There is room in the car to take all of you over the mountain to a hotel. It will get cold tonight."

She shrugged. "We have oil heat."

He didn't want to leave them here, not after what he'd seen. "I have to drive over the mountain until I find a place where my phone works. You will be safer out of this. The roads are bad and could get worse. You could be cut off for days."

He could see that concerned her. He pressed home his advantage. "I can persuade your daughters to join you more easily if we take their children out of here."

"They're all right?" Her eyes finally expressed the fear she had been hiding. She'd been up here all alone with these children through hurricane winds, toppling trees, and a deluge. Her spirit was tough, but the body was weak, and a mother's heart worried.

"They are being stubborn, so they must be fine," he agreed. "I have not seen Flint, though. Jo was concerned about him."

"He dropped off the boys and went to check on a friend for me. He's probably hauling people out of the hollow back there."

Flint could take care of himself. Zack had to look after the women and children. "Go pack their bags. I have heard of Gatlinburg. Perhaps the worst of the rain has not reached there."

"Dollywood," one of the boys suggested, proving he was listening for all his pose of blasé disinterest in the conversation. "They're still open."

Zack had no idea what Dollywood was, but if it was in Gatlinburg, then it was only an hour away. He prayed it was high and dry and had cell reception, because he already knew the road to Asheville was dangerous and didn't.

He prayed the river wouldn't rise any higher until he could rescue Amy from the valley.

The battery on their last flashlight was weakening. Luigi snapped it off, casting the second floor loft into darkness.

Below them, the water lapped against the walls of the old stone foundations and washed across the plank floors.

"I think the rain is letting up," Amy said with forced cheer, trying to ignore the emptiness of her belly.

"Don't mean the water's going down," Hoss replied laconically. "If you folks would keep more food in your desks, we'd be a sight more comfortable."

"A desk drawer ain't gonna hold enough food to fill you, Hoss," one of the workers responded. "We need to move the Stardust down here."

They'd run out of songs to sing when they'd run out of

fresh water and food. The toilet facilities were no longer working either. Everyone was soaked to the skin from kneeling in the rising water, unbolting the heavy machinery from the warping wooden floor.

"Maybe we ought to set up a dock on the river and keep sailboats for times like this," some other wit suggested.

Amy decided she could do without food and water, if she just knew that her babies were safe. She hoped Evan had come for them and taken them off the mountain. Maybe Jo and Flint had taken them down, if the road hadn't washed out.

She prayed Zack had had the sense to stay in High Point. The roads would be treacherous by now, and he wasn't accustomed to driving in hurricane conditions. She didn't want to have to worry about him on top of everything else. She wanted to think about Zack living his lovely, wealthy life in safety in the years to come.

Years that couldn't include her. She'd weep over the loss, but now she had to remain strong and fearless for the brave people around her. If Zack hadn't shown her how to be brave and stand up for herself, she would never have had the courage to do what she was doing now. She didn't know how she would go on without him.

People needed to come in pairs so that one could be strong where the other was weak. Life was much nicer having someone to rely on.

She would not cry.

"We can't see to do anything until morning," Luigi said matter-of-factly. "Might as well get some sleep."

"You planning on swimming out?" Hoss asked, propping his big feet on a bolt of velvet. He'd had to take his boots off after wading back and forth half the afternoon, hauling benches to prop up the machinery.

"Wrap up good in one of the heavier fabrics," Amy ordered, her maternal nature taking over. "We can't handle hypothermia under these conditions."

"Nicest covers I ever had," someone commented. "Have to get my wife something like this someday."

Amy distracted her thoughts from Zack and the rain and the lapping river and her empty belly by designing tapestry bedcovers in her head.

"Don't suppose anyone has a gun on them, do they?" Hoss called through the silent darkness. "I think I hear rats down there."

Shoot. Amy propped her arms on her knees and buried her face against them. She had a long night ahead in which to face her stupidity.

She was far better suited to a life without rats in it, a life that Zack had offered with all the best intentions. It was stubbornness and pride that had forced her to refuse him. And fear of another failure.

If she hadn't retreated to her usual fear of change, she could have asked Zack what his intentions were. That he wanted her to meet his parents had to mean he saw this as more than the affair she'd thought he wanted. She *knew* Zack. Underneath all that charisma, he wasn't the playboy type. Somehow, they might have made things work.

Stripped down to the raw essentials, she realized, all she had ever wanted was love and family. The community might appreciate what she could do for them, but they couldn't love her as her kids could.

Not as Zack could, if he would let himself. He'd wanted to take her and the kids with him to London, not leave her as her father had left her mother.

And she'd told him to go away.

≪ THIRTY-TWO ≫

With the first rays of dawn, the roaring *knock-knock* of a helicopter woke the weary, damp occupants of the mill.

Amy forgot the cold and her hunger and raced to a window.

Under a sky of thick gray clouds, the choppy river covered as far as the eye could see. The tops of trees indicated where the road had been. At least the rain had stopped. She couldn't locate her house from this viewpoint behind the roof of the main building.

"Don't see any boats out there," Hoss said, checking from a different angle. "Current is still pretty bad."

Someone else checked over the balcony to the floor below. "Ain't risen any. Foundation's holding."

That was a relief. They wouldn't be washing away. Yet.

The *flap-flap-flap* of helicopter rotors roared louder. Amy pushed at the window to pry it open, but years of paint sealed the casement.

"Over here," Luigi shouted, pointing at the ceiling. "Help me shove that desk over so I can climb on it."

Three men pushed the old wooden desk under the framed rectangle on the ceiling that gave access to the building's structural components. Luigi climbed up and shoved at the door, pounding until he'd loosened the paint and knocked the plywood into the attic.

"False ceiling," Luigi called back, his voice muffled from above. "Ductwork. Framing. Nothing sturdy to climb on unless you're into swinging on rafters."

The helicopter seemed to be hovering overhead.

Irrationally, hope rose in Amy's heart. She ran to another window, a wider one. When it wouldn't open, she picked up a metal folding chair and smashed it through the glass.

Hoss grabbed the chair from her and smashed out the mullions, knocking out glass shards with the chair legs before sticking his head out to look upward.

"Crazy bastard is climbing down a rope ladder!" he shouted in mixed dismay and excitement.

Crouching down to peer around him, Amy looked out and lost her breath.

Zack was dangling from a ladder, three stories above the flood, directing the helicopter with one hand while hanging on with the other. At sight of her, he waved and shouted something she couldn't hear.

"I think I'm going to throw up," she muttered, falling to her knees and clinging to the sill. "I'm closing my eyes now. Tell me when he falls."

Luigi arrived beside her, sized up the situation, and cursed mildly. Elbowing Hoss out of the way, he lifted Amy to one side, then sat on the sill to watch the helicopter maneuver.

"I am *so* not watching this," Amy muttered again. "Are you telling me he was an acrobat in the circus as well?"

She was so terrified her teeth chattered. Sitting down more firmly, she clutched her knees and hid her face against them rather than watch disaster strike. She would kill that idiot man the instant he appeared. If he survived.

At the same time, she started to shiver with joy and relief, and big fat tears slid down her cheeks.

"That's a damn big help. How is he figuring on getting us out that way?" Luigi growled as loud thumps hit the flat tar paper roof.

Or the side of the building. Amy couldn't tell. She wasn't looking.

They were quiet as they listened to footsteps overhead. Amy finally opened her eyes to study the desk the men had pushed under the attic entry. The others gathered around as Luigi climbed back onto it. Amy stayed crouched where she was, her heart pounding in terror.

"Look out below!" Zack's voice shouted from overhead.

Amy watched in disbelief as a rope ladder dropped through the opening and Zack clambered down. She could only shake in shock and stare at this wonderful, terrifying man who'd literally come through the roof for them.

"We didn't know if the structure was safe to land on," Zack was saying to Luigi, who'd caught the bottom of the rope and held it steady. "What have you been doing all night if you haven't found a way out?"

Amy stopped thinking about their plight and simply fell head over heels in love all over again at the sight of Zack stepping down from the desk, wearing a parachuter's coveralls. At least he had a helmet on, though that would do precious little for his knee. She would kill him once she caught her breath again.

Zack's smile flickered out as he located her huddled against the wall and crossed the loft to her. She'd have held out her hand for him to help her up, but she didn't think her knees would lock just yet. And her heart needed to stop thumping so hard.

"My babies?" she whispered.

"They're safe in Dollywood," he choked out quietly, as if keeping his voice under tight control. Before his words faded, he reached down and dragged her into his arms, holding her tightly. "You are the one who needs a nanny," he growled. "What possessed you to risk—" His voice cracked and broke off.

She felt his arms tremble in the same terror she'd shared, heard the quaver of relief in his voice before he stopped talking. Zack never stopped talking. She wanted to smile, but his strong arms tightening around her felt too good, and she couldn't lift her head. "You are officially insane," she murmured in wonder. "You could have been killed out there."

Zack had come back for her. For all of them. And no one seemed surprised except her. She let those realizations slowly sink in and warm her frozen blood.

She had no idea where they would go from here or how. She just knew Zack was with her, and the whole world was suddenly a miraculously brighter place. Even though the circumstances hadn't changed, she knew she was safe—because he was here.

"I didn't want Luigi and Hoss to engage in cannibalism while waiting for the water to recede," Zack said drily, leaning back just enough to cradle her face in one hand, to stroke her cheek as if to verify her existence. "You are all right?"

She nodded.

"You saved all the machinery and the fabric."

"Of course," she said with a slight shrug. "We all did."

"*Of course,*" he muttered, and pulled her close again to bury his face in her hair. "She saves all that is important to me and then she saves the mill for good measure, and she thinks it is as natural as breathing."

It took her a moment to absorb his words, and to laugh—*laugh*—in relief and sheer joy. She framed his face and kissed him softly in promise, then more deeply to show she would keep that promise. "While you risk my future climbing down that damned rope! You could have fallen!"

He pressed his forehead against hers, noses touching, their lips a breath apart. "Only if you offered to catch me. Come along, Miss Pessimism. I promised your children that I would bring you home safely, and I would not dare to disappoint."

"Do we sprout wings and fly?" she asked, unable to resist tucking a small kiss at the corner of his mouth.

"You climb the ladder to the helicopter," he said patiently.

Amy's knees suddenly melted to useless at the realization it was finally all over—the mill was safe and the town would survive and she would soon see her children again and *Zack had come back.* All the stress of the last weeks, the last years, drained out of her, and she collapsed against him, knowing that he would not let her fall. *Trusting* him not to let her down. She buried her face against his chest and tried to take deep breaths, but she kept hiccupping, and tears streamed down her face. She had no words for how she felt.

"I think that's how I feel, too," he murmured into her hair. "We will talk later, when this is all over."

She nodded into his shoulder. Borrowing from his strength, she locked her knees and stood straight. He reluctantly released her.

"How many does the helicopter hold?" she asked.

For the first time, Zack looked around him. He'd had eyes only for Amy. Now he saw a dozen employees anxiously shifting from foot to foot, trying not to stare. He glanced over the balcony railing to the flooded mill below and saw the muddy water swirling around his looms—or around the benches holding his looms out of the currents.

Stacks of fabric spilled across the balcony and into the second-floor offices. They'd saved everything.

"You are brilliant," he said in awe, understanding the heroism that had placed his investment over their lives.

"The mill closed the last time the inventory got wiped out," Amy explained. "We couldn't let it happen again. The town's existence was at stake."

No one disagreed with her.

"If I could give out medals for heroism, I would," he declared fervently. "I have never seen—" His voice broke over the enormity of explaining how he felt about near strangers having the courage and selflessness to risk their lives for him. For their town.

"I think the ladder's strong enough to hold us," Luigi called, interrupting Zack's sentimentality.

"If you climb up first, Luigi, you can help Amy out. When we're all on the roof, the crew will drop a hook to pull the ladder up." Zack counted heads. "But some of us will have to wait for a second trip. They can take only six people at a time. People with families first."

"Up you go, Miz Amy," Hoss hollered, dragging her toward the ladder.

She cast a terrified look back to Zack, but he remained determinedly smiling. He didn't want her going anywhere without him ever again, but the truth was, his life was worth far less than hers. Far less than these other men here with families at home. If a river of water came rushing downstream to wipe this building off its blocks, he'd prefer it took him and not the others who had so gallantly tried to save it.

All his knowledge and wealth were worth nothing next to the love of family. And if life was about making the world a better place and taking chances on love, then there was no greater challenge than living life to its fullest.

"Haul her out of here, Luigi," he called to his friend.

Zack glued on a smile as Amy disappeared into the attic. He let the other men decide who would climb up next. They had already proved capable of making their own choices. He'd once thought he could play God and change the lives of people, but it seemed they had changed his.

He didn't know them well, but he wanted to.

He was the last to climb out onto the roof. He unfastened the rope ladder from the knots he'd tied around a roof truss while Luigi caught the hook the helicopter lowered. The rushing wind of the rotors dropped the already chilly temperatures several degrees, but no one complained. They waited silently, their clothes flapping in the airstream, while the ladder was drawn back into the helicopter and fastened securely.

Zack held the ropes steady. He didn't dare reach for Amy again, or he might not let go. He nodded at her. Hoss pushed her from behind. She looked reluctant.

"For the children," Zack told her. "Go."

That did the trick, as he'd known it would. Hair blowing across her face, she scampered up the rungs. Unable to let a wisp of female outdo them, the rest of the selected group hurried to follow.

With a lump in his throat that he suspected was his heart, Zack waved them off. At least he knew she would be safe in the world somewhere.

As the helicopter swept away, he shoved his hands into his pockets and looked out over the swirling water far below. "How well can you swim, gentlemen? The dam upstream is in danger of breaking."

"He hired a helicopter," Amy said in incredulity, wrapping her hands around a mug of tea in the hotel room where Flint had taken her. She had no idea how Flint had learned where Zack had taken everyone, but the whole family was together now. "How does one hire a helicopter? Hand over a credit card?"

Picking at a guitar and trying to pretend she wasn't watching the TV, Jo shrugged. "The rich know these things."

Amy couldn't tear her gaze from the TV news. So far, the dam had held steady. If she'd known the damned dam was about to break . . .

She shook her head. She would have gone anyway. She couldn't have left her children motherless. But she might have insisted that Zack leave, too.

"Then he should have hired two helicopters," she replied, trying to keep the sob from her voice.

"I'm sure he would have if he could have," Flint said pragmatically from the bar of the suite they occupied. Pots of coffee and tea and bottles of soft drinks littered the counter. In the far room, the children shouted and tumbled on the beds, oblivious of the drama playing around them.

The national television news had finally picked up on

the thrill of six men stranded on the roof of a mill as the floodwaters threatened to wipe the town off the face of the map.

"The town ain't in any danger," Marie said with disgust at the newscast's hyperbole. "It's just the mill down in the valley. If they'd send their TV helicopters out there, they could pull them off the roof."

Amy wished her mother were right, but she knew better. "Those small 'copters only have two seats. The pilot can't let down a ladder."

"Well, if Zack hired them, why doesn't the crew go back out for him?" Jo demanded. "It just doesn't seem right to leave him there."

"He didn't know there were a dozen idiots out there." Sipping his coffee, Flint watched the news from behind Amy and Jo on the couch. "He only hired them for one trip. They had other jobs. And the National Guard can't be everywhere at once. They're safe for now. Others aren't."

"Then we ought to hire a helicopter, too." Amy pulled a pillow against her and hugged it, trying not to become hysterical. But talking about hiring a helicopter was pretty close to hysteria. Her credit was maxed out, and Flint and Jo were still living on the edge, paying off bills.

"I'm thinking you need to keep boats on that roof," Flint said. "Might come in handy occasionally."

"The water's not high enough. And they don't have a ladder to get down. Stairs should have been installed on the roof long ago." Amy prayed the day would come when they could add stairs. If the dam broke, there would be no building left to worry about.

She had rejected Zack's offer to meet his parents because of a crumbling old building that could soon be rubble? Was she that terrified of leaving her narrow world?

Evan had certainly done a number on her, if that was so. He'd made her afraid to move forward, to live and love again.

She clenched her jaw and corrected that thought. Evan hadn't made her do anything. She'd done it to herself by attempting to be the ideal wife, bending to his will instead of asserting herself and looking for compromises they could both live with.

If she'd understood that sooner and said yes, Zack wouldn't be out on that roof.

Facing Zack's world, leaving the safety of her own, couldn't be any scarier than what he was suffering. He deserved a woman who was as brave and strong as he was.

Be safe, please, she prayed. *I want to be like you.*

The realization of how deeply she'd fallen in love with Zack tore at her heart, and she hugged the pillow harder to hold back tears.

She'd have to trust Zack. She didn't need a psychiatrist to tell her she was afraid to trust again. But if she wanted love, she would have to learn. Zack was worth facing her fear of abandonment. He was the only man in her life who had come back for her.

❧ THIRTY-THREE ❧

Chilled to the bone and weary beyond belief, Zack could scarcely persuade his trick knee up the rope ladder when the National Guard finally sent in aid just before nightfall. He didn't curse the knee or the cold. He held all his emotions tightly wrapped in a neat little ball and would continue to until he saw Amy again. She held his life in her hands. Until he had her answer, he didn't know what to do next.

If she turned him down, he supposed he could return to Europe and let her run the mill here, seeing her once a year or so. He didn't know if he could tolerate such a situation for long.

He could go back to his old life, but he knew now that wasn't living.

Or he could put down roots and become so much a part of her life and her town that she could deny him nothing. It was how these people thought and lived. Family wasn't just blood relations. Every individual was a thread that held together the fabric of the community. He wanted to be a part of that.

Shivering, with an army blanket wrapped around him, he sat on the floor of the helicopter, stared down at the water, and waited.

At least the dam had held. They hadn't had to swim for

safety. The mill was still in one piece. They would need new floors, but the machinery might be salvageable. Those were all good things. If he wanted to plan a future, he could think about the orders they needed to fill. With sales like that, he could borrow money and hire more people. That should bring some relief to an area devastated by flooding.

The happiness of a town was not something he would have considered before Amy. He had much to learn from her. Maybe one step at a time was the way to go.

His knee was so stiff Luigi had to help him climb from the helicopter when it landed. Zack let the gears of his brain concentrate on how he would get from this strange airport to wherever Amy was staying.

Hoss opened the door to the low-lying building where they'd been herded. The other men stepped back respectfully to allow Zack to limp in first. He'd learned all their names and life stories over this past day. He wanted to make the mill a success so he could make all of them managers. He knew he was being irrational, but he was grateful for their support and for their courage. Medals weren't enough.

It took a moment for his frozen brain to process the screams of joy and blaring horns and colored confetti falling on his head. Not until familiar warm curves collided with him, nearly knocking him backward, did he wake up and smell the coffee. And Amy.

And Amy. Wrapping his arms tight around her, Zack whooped with joy and surprise and nearly wept in relief. Letting his spirits soar free again, he swung her in delighted circles, forgetting his knee, his weariness, and his shivering. She clung to his shoulders, buried his face in kisses, and even the roar of the band and Jo's soprano disappeared into the background.

Throwing out all his calculated plans for champagne and diamonds, he did his best to bend his trick knee so he could do one small part of this right, and ended up pulling Amy down with his attempt. "Marry me," he demanded fervently, holding tightly to her hands. "Marry me and we will work out all the rest."

She laughed and hugged him, kissing him with equal delirium, until his knee gave out and he staggered and fell on his rear. He sat down then to spread his legs out, nestling her in his lap and refusing to release her until he had kissed her into agreement.

But he had to come up for air sometime, and the moment he did, he insisted, "You must marry me. I will never find someone as perfect to love again. You are my night and day. My sun and moon. And I know I sound insane, but my brain is frozen, and all I know is that the perfect moment may never arrive and I cannot risk letting you go until you say yes."

Amy laughed softly and cuddled against his chest, where she belonged. He would never let her get away again, he vowed. Vaguely aware that the building was full of people milling around them while they wallowed on the floor, he didn't care. Not until he had his answer.

He tipped her chin. "I love you," he said. "That should count for something, shouldn't it?"

"Not always," she said softly, not tearing her gaze from his face. "But this time, it will, I swear it. I'm trusting you with my life and my children. I love you so much it hurts to think of never seeing you again." She sniffed and smiled through her tears. "Surely if we can make a mill work together, we should be able to make marriage work."

With joy, Zack saw that her eyes blazed with all the love and passion she applied to everything she did, and his heart filled to overflowing.

"Did I ever tell you that I would give half my teeth to see Europe with someone who knows it?" she asked. "I'm ready to go wherever you go."

Knowing Amy could do anything she put her mind to, Zack cheered and wrapped himself in her warmth. Only then did he recognize that the circus around them were her family and friends and half the town. The men who had been with him were surrounded in a sea of relatives hugging and pounding them on the back, so all the attention wasn't on him and Amy. He didn't see the children, but Jo and Flint were lining up a high school band for another chorus of some unrecognizable but celebratory tune. Balloons danced on the ceiling in the warm air. Even the national guardsmen received hugs.

Taking a deep breath, Zack returned his attention to his cautious Amy. "I love you. You love me. Say *yes,* and we will try together."

The smile he received in return was so breathtaking that he wished he could frame it.

Before she could say anything, a door opened, letting in a cold wind and a dramatic female cry of "Jacques! Where is my Jackie?"

Zack groaned and buried his face in Amy's sweet-smelling hair. "I do not believe this. Tell me a tall red-haired woman is not now bulldozing through this happy family gathering."

"No, she has gray hair with blue stripes, actually, and

that's the most dramatic caftan I think I've seen on a white woman. Oops, was that politically incorrect?"

Zack laughed softly. "That is my mother." He scrambled to his feet so he could pull Amy up beside him but refused to look toward the door. He preferred burying his face in her hair while she watched the drama over his shoulder. "Tell me you'll marry me, and I will help you escape."

"Oh, I think it's far too late for that," she mused, following the scene with much too much interest. "Jo has just blockaded her. Jo likes being the only attention-grabbing diva in the house. Does your father happen to wear a hairpiece?"

Zack groaned louder. "*Both* of them? In the same country? In the same *room*? Is there a back way out of here?"

"He's bowing over Mama's hand. He doesn't seem a bad sort. But I think your mother and Jo may enter into a hair-pulling contest if you don't intervene."

"She is my mother. I love her. But no one can deal with her." Zack kissed Amy's hair and straightened with a sigh of resignation. "You see why I cherish you? You can kill Porsches and make me laugh. You can save my mill and scare me to death. But you do not suck all the air out of the room just by existing. You have made me whole."

Amy looked astonished, then laughed so hard she almost fell over. "I fixed you?" she asked, gasping for breath between outbursts.

He nodded firmly. "I am repaired."

"Amazing!" she cried, before falling into another bout of laughter.

While she was so amused, Zack kept his arm firmly

around her waist so she did not flee in the face of Hurricane Virginia.

Zack's father saw him first. Smiling, he abandoned his wife to Jo and strode in their direction. Amy could see where Zack got his good looks and charm. Mr. Saint-Etienne bowed deeply over her hand.

"You are the heroine of the hour, am I correct?" he asked in a deep French accent.

"Amy Warren, my father, Aristide Saint-Etienne. And yes, she is the heroine of the hour," Zack proclaimed. "But we must return her to her children shortly. Not that I wish to hurry you away, but have you found a hotel room yet?"

Before his father could reply to his son's sardonic question, Zack's mother escaped Jo to fly across the room. With her arms outspread in the caftan, flying was precisely what she appeared to do. Amy stepped aside and watched in amazement as Zack submitted to his mother's smothering embrace, then expertly disentangled himself to return to Amy's side.

Understanding a man's family had a lot to do with understanding the man, Amy reflected. Zack had the patience of a saint for good reason.

"You are safe!" Virginia Adams Saint-Etienne cried. "You must come home with us immediately. Come along, let us leave before the mountains fall on us!"

Amy observed Zack and his father exchange wry glances. She waited to see how the drama played out. She wasn't certain of her place in Zack's world yet, didn't even dare think about it. But his parents were real people, not the exalted icons of her imagination. He had a real family, with quarrels and problems and intolerance, just like hers.

It might take time to braid the concepts of wealth and reality together, but Zack's down-to-earth common sense helped.

"The mountains will not fall, Mother, and I go nowhere until I have seen my investment safe. It is good to see you, though. May I introduce the woman I hope to make my wife?"

Amy tried to stand tall against the bulldozer personality of the famous Virginia Adams, but she thought she might sizzle beneath the laser beam of her blue eyes while Zack performed the introductions.

"*Hope* to make your wife?" his mother said icily. "It's not certain?"

"We have been a trifle busy," Zack said drily. "She has not yet had time to turn me down. I am hoping your arrival has not changed her mind."

He actually thought she'd run away from his mother? Amy laughed inwardly. She'd lived with Joella, the Walking Embarrassment, all her life. No, it was hating to disrupt the world of her children again and again that would influence her decision, not world-class drama queens.

She clung to Zack's arm, not yet ready to let the dream of him go. He could fly back to London and disappear forever if she didn't do this right. "Josh and Louisa are the only ones who might change my mind," she said quietly.

As if on cue, Josh's excited voice carried over the clatter of the high school band and media arrivals. "Zack, Zack! I saw you on TV!"

Spying Josh in the crowd, Zack crouched and held out his arms for the boy to run into. Amy's heartstrings tugged as her sleepy son ran straight to him. She glanced up to see Jo—mischievous gleam in her eye—set Louisa on the floor and turn her loose. The kids had fallen asleep in a back room while they'd waited for Zack's arrival. Jo had apparently thought it was an appropriate time to wake them.

"I wanta play, too," Louisa said jealously, rubbing her eyes and watching Zack and Josh.

"You have children!" Aristide Saint-Etienne exclaimed in delight, crouching down much as Zack had to hold out his hand to Louisa. "Will you say hello to me, young lady?"

"You have children!" Virginia said in approval. "And such beautiful ones! What a splendid family portrait they would make."

Amy experienced no regret at imagining two dark-haired parents standing over her fair-haired children— and maybe an infant in her arms with Zack's smile. She knew with complete confidence that Zack would become the father Evan never cared to be, and her insides performed a dizzy spin of happiness.

She smiled up at Zack's mother as Louisa happily fell into Aristide Saint-Etienne's arms. "Yes, I think Zack will look good standing in as their father," she agreed. "But persuading him to stand still is more difficult than persuading the children."

Ever observant, Zack jerked his head up at her agreement, but with Josh in his arms, he could do no more than watch while Amy stood her ground with the infamous Virginia Adams. Amy was grateful that he did not interfere.

Virginia nodded knowingly. "He has been running away for ten years. But I do not want him settling here. This is not his home."

"Home is where the heart is," Amy reminded her. "Zack has a big heart and many homes. We'll work it out."

And for the first time, she trusted Zack to let her do whatever it took to safeguard their happiness. She'd thought the security Evan had offered would provide contentment, but it hadn't worked that way. This time, it was up to *her* to know what she needed to be happy, and to stand up for herself if Zack started taking her acceptance for granted as Evan had.

And she wouldn't have to fear losing Zack even if she fought with him. They had argued, and he had still come for her.

Standing up, with Josh in his arms, Zack circled Amy's waist and boldly planted a kiss on her mouth. Amy tingled at the promise of his tongue, but he withdrew quickly so as not to embarrass her.

"The children need to be in bed," he told his parents. "I am staying here, for now. We will see you in London in December, as promised. I have a project in Paris next month, so perhaps we will meet before then. But right now, we all need rest. Shall I have Luigi take you to a hotel?"

Aristide handed Louisa to Amy. "If you would, please. We will see both of you in the morning?"

"Very definitely," Amy answered for both of them, as if they truly were a couple. "And if you're up to it, we can introduce you to the rest of my family. I believe you may have already met Joella."

"Ah, yes, the singer and her songwriter husband." Aristide glanced back, and Joella wiggled her fingers at them. "I think you and Jacques may have much in common with your families." He tilted his head obliquely in his wife's direction, then caught Virginia's elbow. "Come along, *ma chère*, it has been a long day." He steered her toward Luigi.

To Amy's amazement, Zack's mother complied, trailing a list of complaints, and with a last, lingering look to her son holding Josh.

"That went well, no?" Zack said with a heavy hint of irony.

"That went well, yes," Amy agreed.

Amy felt the intensity of Zack's gaze while she watched his parents head for the door. She breathed a sigh of relief as the Saint-Etiennes walked out in Luigi's care. Only then did she feel free to look up at Zack with the adoration she was feeling.

"Tell me I'm not crazy," she murmured for his ears alone.

He grinned from ear to ear. "As the song says, you're just a little impaired. But that is the only way to survive, *n'est-ce pas?*"

"Messy pa," Louisa echoed sleepily. "My messy pa." She reached over from Amy's arms to pat Zack's cheek.

Amy laughed until tears ran down her cheeks while Zack grinned proudly, waiting expectantly until she caught her breath.

She knew that look. It was the look of confidence he gave the world, but she understood the shadows underneath it now. His heart was in his eyes.

"Yes, Zack," she whispered. She smiled as his brows arched while he continued to wait with his head tilted toward her as if he couldn't quite hear her.

"*Yes,*" she shouted, "Yes, yes, yes, I'll marry you!"

The activity around them faded to nothing as the world shrank to the small cocoon they occupied, and Amy knew it would always be so, no matter how glamorous their surroundings.

❦ EPILOGUE ❧

"Astonishing!" Amy swirled happily in the newly re-furbished master bedroom of her dream cottage. "It's *ex-actly* as I envisioned it. The blue bouquets on the wallpaper are perfect! Can't you see vases of blue salvia and pink carnations and lavender in here?"

"My designers might." Zack chuckled, watching her dance around the house to which they'd just returned from their December journey to London. "But they have much to learn from your American experts if they are to put together the Smithsonian project this spring."

"With *our* fabrics," Amy sighed in delight, patting a cro-cheted pillow on the four-poster bed. "You are a genius."

"I know," he said immodestly. "The magazine article alone should enhance our reputation. The museum tableau will cap it. We will have work to last a long, long time."

Amy stopped her happy dance in front of him, wrap-ping her arms around his neck and lavishly covering his face with kisses. She adored being able to do this anytime she liked. She loved even better that this independent man did not push her away and tell her he was too busy for her expressions of affection. She loved that a man as strong as Zack needed her as much as she needed him. She had more blessings than she could count.

He held her closely against the wide chest she'd come

to know so intimately these past months. Zack's open emotions did not lessen his strength of character. She had watched him handle his termagant mother with amusement, set predatory old girlfriends straight, and handle delicate financial negotiations with assurance. She was the only one who could distract the arrogant prince into lingering caresses.

He kissed her nape and eased her toward the enormous bed. "It's you who makes it happen," he murmured. "I would not have thought to ask that our wedding gifts be donations to the victims of the flood."

"No, but you would have given away everything we received." She spun out of his arms to check the window overlooking the landscaping project down the hill. Zack had hired a company to repair the path so she could walk to the mill when she wished. In the morning, she would choose which shrubs and perennials she wished to plant.

Coming up behind her, Zack pulled his BlackBerry from his pocket. Sliding his arms around Amy's waist, he placed the machine in her hands. "Add the dates of all your family's birthdays, if you please, so I may see that they receive appropriate gifts when the time comes. They have contributed as much as my associates to that treasure trove downstairs."

Amy took the electronic menace he'd taught her to use and began poking in dates. Behind her, Zack chuckled and rocked her back and forth while she worked.

"I measure your contentment by the number of machines you do not blow up," he said. "I have not replaced a single bulb since we returned."

She elbowed him and continued with her typing.

"Add a week of holidays for our anniversary," he murmured, returning to kissing her nape. "We will have a honeymoon every year. You must show me this country. I have never seen the Rockies or the Mississippi or Texas."

"Business in Europe, play in America. Makes sense, although January isn't the time I'd be visiting the Rockies unless you ski." Amy handed him the BlackBerry, and it disappeared so swiftly she scarcely noticed the absence of his hand at her waist. "And you really think I can manage the mill when you go to Europe?"

"I know you can. We have good people in place. They will not even know we are gone on our honeymoon next week." His hand rose higher, encompassing her breast beneath the scanty designer chemise he'd bought for her in Paris. "You are certain we should not bring the little ones with us? They have been so very good. We could still take a cruise ship instead of a yacht, if you wish it."

"Josh needs to be in school, and Louisa has plenty of people to love her while we're gone. I'm thrilled to include them in our wedding, but I am *not* taking them on my honeymoon." Amy turned in his embrace and stood on her toes to press a kiss to his mouth. "It was lovely of you to think of it, though."

"I think I will soon grow tired of traveling without you," he murmured against her lips, maneuvering her up against the new wallpaper. "And then there will be babies. I will not wish to miss a minute of their changes."

Amy laughed as he held her captive with a hand on either side of her head, pressing kisses everywhere his mouth could reach. "You will miss the diaper changes," she told him, brushing her lips against his bristly cheek.

They had delighted each other when they'd discovered they both wanted more children. Zack loved children as much as he loved new challenges, and she loved him even more for knowing that.

"Possibly," he agreed, carrying his kisses down her throat to the tops of her breasts. "There will be nannies. You cannot do everything yourself."

"But this, I will always do myself," she murmured, burying her fingers in his hair and arching into him, thrilling to the sensation of his mouth on her breast through the silk. "You must agree to be a one-woman man or the deal is off."

Zack grinned down on her. "Do you think me a stupid man? I have found my treasure, and I mean to keep you." He sealed his vow with a fervent kiss.

"Promises are forever," she reminded him softly, removing his shirt.

"Into eternity," he agreed with a whisper of hope.

She read the passion and intensity of his gaze and understood that her fears were his, and they would overcome them together. "We'll celebrate one day at a time," she assured him, wrapping her legs around his hips and trusting him to take her weight as their lips and tongues came together.

And they celebrated the day joyously, with the winter sunshine pouring through the French doors and across the bedcovers woven on the looms of their mill, to their very own design.